SOMEBODY

Anita Anderson was born in Dallas, Texas and currently lives in a small mountain village in Wales. She's worked in television, written for newspapers, worked for an airline, cooked in a café, and managed an art gallery. She read Economics at Cornell University and Philosophy at Nottingham University. She has had short stories published in seven countries and humorous articles published in the national press. She is also a painter and has had one-woman exhibitions in England and in Wales. *Somebody* is her first novel.

ANITA ANDERSON

Somebody

HarperCollins*Publishers*

HarperCollins*Publishers*
77–85 Fulham Palace Road,
Hammersmith, London w6 8jb

www.**fire**and**water**.com

A Paperback Original
Published by HarperCollins*Publishers* 2002

7 9 8

This novel is entirely a work of fiction. The names,
characters and incidents portrayed in it are the work
of the author's imagination. Any resemblance to actual
persons, living or dead, events or localities
is entirely coincidental.

A catalogue record for this book
is available from the British Library

ISBN 0 00 711988 7

Set in New Baskerville by
Rowland Phototypesetting Ltd,
Bury St Edmunds, Suffolk

Printed and bound in Great Britain by
Clays Ltd, St Ives plc

To Huck Anderson

Acknowledgements

Special thanks to my brilliant editor, Susan Watt; to Katie Espiner, the copy editor with a gentle touch; and to all the other wonderful people at HarperCollins who have been so amazingly supportive and helpful.

A huge thank you to the RNA and their New Writers Scheme, for all the help, guidance, and friendship; especially Christina Jones who 'discovered' me in the NWS; to Katie Fforde for the RNA/Katie Fforde Most Promising Writer Award, which opened so many doors. Thanks also to Chairman Norma Curtis, and NWS Organisers Marina Oliver and Margaret James; and to all my other wonderful writer friends in the RNA.

Thank you to photographer Iain Coates; David Gleave for checking proofs, and David Price who now refers to his house as my 'London Office'. Thanks also to Miranda Lawrence, Jill Carpenter, and Elizabeth Gleave; and to all the Matrons at the University in Sewanee. And thanks to editor Jane Eastgate at RD and the entire RNA for the wonderful RNA/RD New Writers' Award.

1

'I'm sorry, there must be some mistake. Mr Bas Blackman doesn't have a wife.'

'You poor, naïve, little slut. Just give him the message that the tests are positive.'

I could hear a sort of chuckle before the woman rang off. I sat there in shock, blind to the restaurant around me, holding my mobile phone and staring at it as if it had just bitten me and would do so again if I moved. The most horrible thing was that I felt she was right. Well, not about my being a naïve slut, but that she was his wife, that Bas was married. Numerous things, tiny in themselves, seemed to add up. There were so many it was as if the curls on my head were rearranging themselves into the word stupid, branding me for life.

Instinctively I glanced around to see if everyone was looking at me and casually mashed down my curls. I'm a blonde and try for the sleek cool look. But when I get emotional, my hair twists as if steam is shooting out of my head. Well, it probably was. Ten minutes ago I'd been certain of my love for a gorgeous man, proud to be his partner in a company worth millions, into which I'd sunk four years of my life. With all the travel and the glamour of wealth added to our mutual attraction, our life together had been like a dream. But the problem with dreams is that you have to wake up.

I wanted so much to believe in Bas. I wracked my brain trying to reinterpret the phone call, but how can you explain away a wife? I thought back to when I first met Bas. He was living in a small but elegant service flat on Fifth Ave. It was as impersonal as a hotel, with no photos or personal ornaments. I'd thought the unlived-in look was just typical of bachelors, and not the mark of a married man.

I was sitting in a New York restaurant on a warm May evening waiting for Bas. He was already late, so his business meeting must not have ended on time. I quickly motioned to the waiter to replenish my drink. New York drinks are hefty, not the tiny little dirty-the-bottom-of-the-glass droplet one gets back home in London. 'Make that a double,' I added.

There are those stages you read about regarding grief and loss – first denial, then on to anger and whatever. I couldn't think straight. But without even stopping long enough for coffee in denial, I'd driven straight on to rage. I could have started the Great Fire of San Francisco with my thoughts. And the rage was fuelled with fear. I finally understood that the average person's fascination with the wealthy was not necessarily envy or admiration, but simply knowing that when the chips were down, they owned all the chips.

Before I could think things through further, Bas arrived. I just sat there as he leaned down to kiss me, although I did turn such that my head banged his nose. Rubbing his nose, he laughed and swung his lithe body down as the waiter showed up to bow and scrape and hand over menus, mine the sort that keeps the prices a secret. Bas ignored the menu and ordered lobster and then looked at me. When I said nothing, he told the waiter, 'Make that two. And champagne.'

Then he sat back and smiled. He really did exude warmth and had enough sex appeal to service a harem.

And when he was with you, he gave you his full attention, making you feel important, as if you were the luckiest person in the world. Almost everyone loved Bas, and I was thinking now that probably everybody had also slept with him. With my last vestige of hope that this wasn't happening I said, 'Your wife just rang, Bas. The office calls were switched to my mobile. She said to tell you the tests were positive.'

It was a moment or two before the words sank in and his smile began to resemble an egg cooked sunny side up that you've just poked with a fork.

'Now, Caron honey, I don't want you getting all upset. I know I should've told you. But why don't you think of it like this. Nothing's really changed except your perception of the situation. We'll still have the same good life and run the business together. I'll still be away travelling four days a week.

'I'm sorry she called you. My mobile battery ran out, which is why I couldn't ring you to say I'd be late. So that's why she rang the office. But I promise it won't happen again. And to be fair, it's only happened once in four years.' He reached over to take my hand and added, 'Honey, I love you and count on you and really don't want to lose you.'

I quickly shifted my hand out of reach. I'd rather have had a snail drool over it. At first I was speechless. I suppose I'd expected denials, maybe remorse, an apology, or maybe even bigger and better lies. Now it seemed like my only achievement was learning that Bas is probably just short for Bastard.

'Dammit, Bas, you sound like your brain's been fried with bananas. What do you mean nothing's changed? Everything's changed.'

He became very serious which always made his eyes

change to a darker blue. That deep ocean blue. Where sharks hide. 'You're just not thinking straight, Caron. We'll have exactly the same life. I'm exactly the same man I was an hour ago. And you know I love you to distraction. The only difference, and it's a little one, is how you're thinking about things. And that's abstract. The real life situation is really exactly the same.'

'That's only positive thinking getting its knickers in a twist, Bas. The real situation is that I've wasted four years with a lying, cheating creep. And what about those positive tests? Have you given me something?'

He smiled. 'Honey, not unless you're also pregnant.'

'I don't believe this! With all we've had together, you've actually been sleeping with your wife.'

'It goes with the job description, Caron. And before you ask, the next will be our fourth little baby. Well, that's kind of been the problem. My wife's always pregnant, you know, one kid after the other, and she loses interest.'

'Are you sure that's the reason? I'm not the least bit pregnant, and I've lost interest.' Had I ever been in love? Was real love something a person could fall out of, like rolling over the wrong way in bed and landing on the carpet? Like falling off a surfboard and drowning? Like growing out of an obsession with chicken noodle soup?

There was a silence while the champagne was poured and the wine waiter did his I Love Big Tippers tap dance around Bas. It gave me a chance to really look at Bas. Suddenly the man I loved, his good looks and charm and intelligence, seemed to melt away. It was as though he was completely hollow inside. No heart, no brain, no digestive tract. Probably the champagne would shoot

4

straight out like from those nude fountain statues in Rome. From pomp to penis in one squirt.

Bas' cool demeanour seemed slightly tarnished as he said, 'Now, Caron, I don't want you to even think about doing anything dramatic. This kind of situation happens all the time, everywhere. And everything works out fine.'

'Not always, Bas. There was that wife who cut off all the sleeves of her husband's designer suits. And another gave all his belongings to charity. One wife sold her husband's Porsche for twenty dollars. Maybe the most interesting case was when that woman cut off her husband's penis.'

Bas' face began to turn pink and little drops of moisture popped out on his forehead. 'That's not funny, Caron. And don't forget, I'm not your husband. I meant those cases, you know, outside of wedlock.'

My rage had settled a bit, into that comfortable stage where I could have stood up and screamed, the sound cracking the mirror behind the bar. 'Well, we might be outside of marriage, but what about business? I helped you build that business from scratch and I own part of it.' The actual arrangement had been that he'd put up all the capital and I'd run the business. Then after ten years I'd be a full partner and half owner.

He gave me his gentle smile and relaxed a bit. He did seem to think nothing would change. It was so bizarre I half expected him to pee out of his ears.

'Well, now, it's like this,' he said. 'Technically, you don't own a damn thing. So, honey, that's another reason for us to stay together.'

It was my turn to smile as I leaned across the table and said, 'Fuck you, Bas Blackman.'

He ignored me and carried on eating. I stabbed

through the shell of my lobster with my fork, which made a satisfying crunch, and left it there, thinking furiously. Probably as furiously as the lobster had. Our fates had been sealed during the same hour.

I'm certainly no saint, but this seemed a high price to pay for trusting, loving, believing. On the other hand, it was probably the standard rate for merely hoping. When the rust had shown through Bas' armour, I'd tended to ignore it. I'd written off the odd comment from his long-standing secretary to her old-fashioned ways. And I'd not given much thought as to why his four days a week away included Sunday. Not many places do business on the Sabbath. And at only thirty-nine Bas hardly needed to rest up after every flight. A man in love would rest up making love on Sunday nights. Well, now I knew that's exactly what he had been doing.

Bas dropped his napkin onto the table and motioned to the waiter. 'I've got to catch my flight. Sorry about that honey, but as you know, this contract's worth over a million.' He tried again to clasp my hand and my retreating wrist hit the fork still stuck in my lobster. It landed with a soft plop on his hand and cuff. Patiently wiping the area with his napkin, he said, 'Caron, honey, damn it to hell. We need to work this out and I haven't got a lot of time. Go on, call me names, cuss me out. Get it over with.'

'Oh, sure, Bas. How's this? "The next time you turn out to have a wife and four kids, it's all over!" Or, "Dammit, Bas, don't you ever go getting married on me again!" One reason there really isn't a way back is because you planted a little time bomb at the start of each year. And the second reason is that I do not knowingly date married men. I specifically asked you and you said you were single.'

'But Caron, you're a modern woman. You know that's what all men say. And, honey, it's because you didn't appear to be in a hurry to get married that I knew our partnership would work.'

I was at the end of my tether. 'I may have an aversion to marriage, Bas. But I also have an allergy for married men, and you've become the worst possible symptom. How could I ever believe another word you say?'

I'm not really averse to marriage, and I'd believed that Bas and I would get married one day. But to let him know that would be like a person who's been run over shouting, 'Come back, driver! You've only broken one of my legs!'

He took the bill that had been put onto a little silver salver, a reminder that a first class tip was the thing. When I didn't get up, he said, 'Look, honey, everybody tells lies sometime. It's practically de rigueur when you're afraid of losing someone you love. Think it over. You stay here, have a nice dessert and some coffee. You can pay with the credit card just like normal.'

I was doing my imitation of a fossil implanted in limestone, so he moved around the table and put his hand on my shoulder. 'I'm going to be back by noon tomorrow. In the meantime, I don't want you to do anything stupid.' He smiled as if he were on *Candid Camera* and the world was watching. Then he leaned down and added, 'You know I don't want to lose you, honey. But if you do leave, I'll make sure you don't get a penny. Or another job. As for damages, wrecking the place . . . well, enough said about unpleasant matters. You just think it over.'

Leaning even closer, he said, 'You know I don't like to go away worried. So how about a little kiss?'

Amazingly, in all our four years together, Bas and I

7

had never really been at cross-purposes, no more than say a heated discussion on a business strategy. And he really had treated me as an equal, been so attentive. I'd never seen a hint of this sugar-coated threatening aspect. Now I was finding out that the most seemingly perfect apple was harbouring two teaspoons of toxic waste. As he leaned closer, I said, 'Bas, I'd rather kiss a halitosis-ridden rattlesnake.'

I watched him walk to the entrance, wriggle into the coat being held for him, take the outstretched briefcase. I probably should have stood up and shouted, 'Stop thief!' Something to puncture his arrogance. He never even turned around before walking out.

But even then, I could think straight enough to realise I was lucky. He had behaved like such a thoroughbred bastard, such a total shit, that at least I would have no regrets. I wouldn't think of him on dark nights except to imagine him covered in honey and handcuffed to a beehive. Or trying to sail the Atlantic in an egg cup. Fried crisply in batter like a tiny shrimp. Thinking these thoughts made me feel better, until I felt almost human again. The first symptom was that I felt hungry.

I knew that if I left and went to a small café, they wouldn't take credit cards and now I needed to hang on to every penny I'd got. So I told the waiter to clear the table and start again, bringing me a couple of BLTs and a pot of coffee. The waiter said, 'We don't do bacon, lettuce and tomato sandwiches except at the bar.'

He would never have said that to Bas.

'And I don't pay bills when I'm still hungry.' I sort of picked up the bill and fluttered it about and stared him down. He gave me that frozen smile you sometimes see in films when someone's just been shot. Well, the bill I'd already got would be for several hundred bucks. And knowing posh restaurants absolutely hate single women daring to dawdle, I was determined to take my time.

I took a small pad from my Gucci handbag. I was also wearing an Armani suit. All these posh trappings were now making me feel like a second-rate actress fitted out by the wardrobe department. A sham, a fraud. Nothing to remain after the last curtain call. Well, I suppose all of life is a bit like that, except I was determined to crop up on another, better stage.

I began my lists. First, where should I go? That was simple. I'd move to London, the only other big city I really knew besides New York. I'd been happy in London, and it would be harder for Bas to scotch my job chances there.

Second, my assets. Of course my clothes were mine. Unfortunately, I'd never much liked jewellery – it made me feel like a living noticeboard. So any presents Bas had bought me tended to be things like paintings or other items for the flat, which might not now be considered mine. The penthouse apartment on Fifth Avenue was in the company name. And obviously the company was in Bas' name. I had previously made small noises about this, but Bas had insisted that for tax purposes it would be better to have the new company tied in with those he already owned. And as finance is my field, I didn't have a good argument. It would have amounted to a lack of trust.

One of the few things I learned by heart at school came back into my head: 'No lesson seems to be so deeply inculcated by the experience of life than that you never should trust experts. If you believe the doctors, nothing is wholesome. If you believe the theologians, nothing is innocent. If you believe the soldiers, nothing is safe.' Lord Salisbury was of course before Bas' time, or he might have added: And if you believe Bas Blackman, you need to clear out your brain with a vacuum cleaner.

We kept petty cash in the office, which was in our, sorry *his*, flat. I could get hold of that, but it reminded me I needed to be out before the secretary arrived for work in the morning. And I could use the credit cards. But there wasn't a lot vacant on those. My air ticket to London could go onto the tab at the travel agency.

I realised I had to be careful. Bas seemed to hold all the aces, and I didn't want to be done for theft. I'd been totally besotted with him and believed absolutely that the company was ours. So when he suggested we keep pouring all the profits back in, and only take out expenses, I had agreed. With the result that I'd had no actual salary to save or invest.

As for my contract, well I didn't have one. But I'd signed so much correspondence that it could definitely be proved that I was an employee. And all employees have rights of some kind. I could write cheques up to five thousand dollars without his added signature. So I decided to officially sack myself and pay myself that amount for having had my contract cut short. One computer transaction and the amount would be switched to my personal account.

After all my hard work and eighteen-hour days, it was a pretty pitiful amount. Several thousand pounds sterling and an air ticket, to begin all over from scratch. I'd be lucky to find a branch-share in a tree house in London. It might have seemed to me like riches four years ago, but compared to my deferred salary and share in the company it looked like a couple of salted peanuts. Having finished my sandwiches and coffee, I looked at the new bill that the waiter had brought. No silver tray, just the piece of paper by my plate. I signed the credit card chit without adding a tip. Then I took a taxi straight to my parents' home.

When I was in my late teens, we'd moved from London to New York where my dad was offered a tenured chair at a university. After graduating from University in business admin, I got a job in a stock brokerage firm, starting as a trainee trader. A woman could shatter the glass ceiling there with her first big deal. And then Bas, one of our best clients, poached me to start a new company. I'd been dating him for a bit already and it wasn't long before I moved in with him. My parents did their nut, 'All that money wasted on your education!' Basically they thought Bas was smooth and slippery, like melted vanilla ice cream. They were never going to like him, and now they'd been proved right.

When I reached the house, what I wanted most to do was to cry and moan and be hugged and pampered. But my family wasn't like that. My parents were old enough to be my grandparents. And my ivory-tower academic father used to call me their 'Happy Little Accident'. He meant this kindly and said it proudly, usually. My mum, possibly in reaction to Dad's being an out-to-lunch type, tended to make lunch her main priority. Her greatest passion was playing bridge.

Anyway, everybody's got a parent story, and no one's perfect. I had a happy childhood, and while often I hadn't any notion what Dad was talking about, I could always communicate with Mum so long as I stuck to bridge terminology. For example, when I had a date, I could say we're making up a foursome. Or when I screwed up, my defence was that someone had to play the dummy.

When I told them what had happened with Bas, there was a long silence. The strain of trying not to say, 'I told you so,' was actually making their ears turn red.

Then Dad said, 'This isn't good news, Caron.'

Mum said, 'There's always a bright side, dear. With your next game, I suggest you up your bid in life.' She was probably trying to boost my confidence and meant I should value myself more. Or she could have simply been consoling me for playing such a lousy hand with such a loser partner.

Dad did ask if I wanted him to write a cheque for anything. And Mum said if I wanted to take Bas to court there was a lawyer in her bridge club who was trumps. But there was no going back to being their little girl, even if I'd wanted to. The only time I'd seen my parents sadder than when I'd gone to live with Bas was when they were faced with the possibility of my return home.

They readily agreed for me to store stuff there until I got my own place. Mum rang our old neighbours in London and arranged for me to stay with them until I, as she put it, 'Got dealt a better hand.' Our whole meeting took less than twenty minutes. And I couldn't take umbrage with their relief that I was going to London, because I could remember my great delight when I'd moved out before.

There wasn't really anyone else to say goodbye to. I'd lost touch with my childhood mates, but hadn't moved to the USA in time to gel in high school. I still kept in touch with some university chums, but we'd all scattered after graduation. And once you're in a relationship it's easy to forget that in the garden of life, friends are the trees and evergreens. Lovers are more like annuals, nice and bright for a season, already dead when you admire them in the vase. I'm not usually so grumpy, but I'd really thought Bas was permanent – not just a bit of poison ivy that I'd mistaken for a sweet pea. I'd sort of wondered why he only had colleagues instead of friends, but of course it was obvious now that he had a whole other life. I'd just been convenient for the bed and boardroom.

When I arrived at the Upper East Side penthouse flat, I just stood inside the front door and looked. I suppose I'd thought I'd be sad to leave such a glorious place, but like everything else to do with Bas it now resembled a stage set. Well, a life built on lies is a fantasy, a fiction. Then I began to move like greased lightning, emptying wardrobes and drawers faster than a first-rate burglar. If I wasn't out before Bas returned, there would be all that talking again. And he'd probably arrive back with presents, having remembered how to act contrite. There's no telling how many people spend their lives in hell simply because it seems easier to stick around. Of course it's not really easier, because treading water all those extra years means you get too tired to outswim the piranhas.

First I packed everything I could take on the aeroplane. I could have gone first class, as the company was paying, and that would have had the advantage that they don't weigh luggage very carefully. But I'd booked economy. My most desperate feeling, near to panic, was the need for something real. To get off the cheap stage set and become alive again. And there's hardly anything more real than the back of an aeroplane.

Within the hour I had six boxes and all Bas' spare luggage packed and marked and in two taxis en route to my parents. Some would be shipped on when I had my own London address, and the rest could collect dust for a while. By rights, everything in the flat was half mine. But there weren't any obvious valuables such as diamond encrusted letter openers or solid gold vases that I could tuck into a case. Anyway, I had to be practical and take clothes so I could get a job. Already the stack for the airport included extra stuff I'd need to wear on the plane.

As Bas wouldn't provide a job reference, I'd packed disks of projects I'd done which would have to do as a CV. Because Bas was concerned about hackers, these weren't kept on the actual computer. I normally kept them in a long narrow music box that played 'Yankee Doodle Dandy'. It was one of my favourite things, painted in childish primary colours and adorably ridiculous. So I packed it, too.

It was three in the morning, and the taxi wasn't due for another ten minutes. It was really tempting to spend the time wasting the place. But it had so recently been half mine that it would have felt like spitting on your own plate. So I opened a bottle of champagne and poured a glass. I was looking around to make sure I hadn't forgotten anything when my eyes settled on the painting above the marble mantle. It was gorgeous. And small. Why not?

As the highly tipped but still reluctant driver loaded the taxi, I locked up, slid the keys under the door, and then settled in the back seat with my glass and the bottle of champers.

Speeding through the New York streets that aren't empty even in the middle of the night, the driver said, 'What's widda champagne? You celebrating or sometink?'

It was the first time I'd relaxed since that phone call from Chicago. Only nine hours between learning Bas had a wife and leaving the flat had left little time to think. And the time in between certainly hadn't felt like celebration. It had felt like panic and desperation and sadness, with a couple of helpings of fear and shame. Now I was feeling a combination of exhaustion and jubilation, where you feel total collapse while hovering a few feet off the ground.

Then another tag came flying into my head – either it was prompted by the champagne bubbles, or I have that kind of wiring in my brain. I think it was Christina Rossetti: 'Better by far that you should forget and smile than that you should remember and be sad.' I tried a smile and my face didn't shatter. I sipped champagne and smiled some more.

'Absolutely,' I said to the driver. 'I'm beginning a whole new life.' All I needed to remember was not to fall in love again. Well, it wasn't quite all. I nearly jumped out of my skin when I realised my mobile phone was ringing.

2

Bas was like a toothache you hoped would just go away. No sooner than you organise your own thoughts and become complacent, it suddenly feels like someone's in your mouth wielding a sword. I wanted to toss the mobile out of the taxi window. But with my current luck, a cop would pick it up and take the call.

'Caron honey, I know it's the middle of the night, but I was kind of worried about you. Were you asleep?'

Worried about himself, more likely. When he wanted to go to bed, he would say to me, 'You're looking tired, honey.' When he wanted to eat, he'd say, 'You look famished.'

I took a deep breath and said, 'No, Bas. I'm just sitting here drinking champagne.'

I could hear him sigh with relief. 'Thank God, honey. I was worried you might be doing something stupid.'

'I haven't wrecked anything. I haven't set the place on fire. Or were you thinking I might leave you? I mean, Bas, would I do a thing like that?'

He laughed so I laughed too. Soon the taxi driver was also laughing. Hilarity is almost as contagious as yawning. 'I've misbehaved real bad, Caron, and I want to make it up to you. What's that noise?'

'I'm just pouring a bit more champagne.'

'That's my Caron! I don't know why I was worried. I mean I should have remembered how sensible you are, that you'd just have a few drinks and write that whole episode off as ancient history.'

That meant he'd had lots to drink and was thinking that his being married was no more serious than getting a parking ticket. Just pay quickly and park where you like tomorrow. 'Are you in bed, Caron honey?'

'Not exactly, Bas.'

He laughed and asked jokingly, 'Well, are you alone?'

'Yes, except for one man.'

'What? Who?'

'I don't know his name. If you want to wait I can ask him.'

He laughed again. 'At least you haven't lost your sense of humour. See you about noon. I love you, honey.'

I had to say something but didn't want to say anything terribly rude until after nine o'clock when the bank would have transferred my severance pay. 'Bas, I'm holding my glass high for a toast. Here's to my new life!'

'Oh, that is such a positive statement, Caron! Here's to your new life! And I'm sure it's going to be a hell of a lot better than the old one.'

'I couldn't agree more, Bas.' I rang off and put the mobile back in my shoulder bag just as the taxi pulled into the airport.

Before I teamed up with Bas, I always travelled sardine class. Dressed to the hilt, I often managed an upgrade to first. But that wasn't going to happen now, unless they decided I was a Martian needing quarantine. Even using Bas' luggage as well as my own, I'd run out of space. So I was the only person in early summer wearing fake-fur lined boots and a matching ankle length lined coat, under which was a tweed Dior trouser suit, a white linen jacket, and a Burberry mac. I won't describe all the items sticking out of pockets. If I was subconsciously preventing male attention until my ego lost the bruises, I couldn't have done better unless I'd worn a badge saying Vice Squad.

There was a big fuss when I checked two extra bags, paying the difference with the company credit card, as the flight was nearly full and they were worried about weight. There had been over a hundred people in the queue in front of me, and at least another hundred followed. I'm not my sweet charming self at half past five in the morning, so finally they gave in. I had the painting in an Armani shopping bag under my coat, with the handles over my shoulder. But that still left my shoulder bag and my laptop and one more carrier bag. So the latter also had to go under my coat to get past check-in. When I answered the routine question on bombs, they remained suspicious, because I looked as if I was a bomb. On the whole, I was not beginning my new life with a great deal of elegance.

As I passed through passport control the man said, 'On your way to Russia?' And of course I set off the alarm when I passed through the x-ray machine. I thought it might be all those computer disks in my handbag. They ran them through the x-ray three times, probably zapping all the data. The problem turned out to be my six packets of Polo mints. The woman couldn't believe it could be the tinfoil they're wrapped in, so she kept whizzing that baton up and down my body. This meant that at least a hundred fellow passengers would peer at me on the plane with very sad and worried faces.

Once I was in the international departure lounge, I went straight to the coffee shop to partially disrobe and relax during the two-hour wait until flight time at seven thirty. I was beginning to feel human again when they announced a half-hour delay. I sat there practically holding my breath. Airport Control can look out of the window with no plane in sight. They may even know for a fact that it's broken down in Iceland. And they announce a short delay.

By the time they announced a further delay of an hour, I was sweating so much I must have looked like I'd been playing tennis for two hours. Well, maybe for fifteen minutes. Because even without further delays we wouldn't be leaving until nine, when Bas' secretary arrived at the office. When they finally announced it was time for boarding, I was so relieved I could hardly stand up.

Then my mobile rang. I wanted to ignore it, but I already looked so strange I couldn't afford to sit there beeping.

'Caron? I just phoned the office to say I'm going to be late and they said you weren't there.'

'Well, I'm not there, Bas. I'm here.'

'Where?'

'For heaven's sake, Bas, you're being ridiculous. Among other things, I went out to buy some Polo mints. Is that enough or do you want the full replay?'

'Don't be angry, honey. It's only that after what happened, it's important that we trust each other. Do you trust me?'

I couldn't believe he'd said that. 'Bas, I'm not the one who keeps ringing every few minutes. Look, I've got to go. And please stop checking up on me!'

'Sorry, Caron. It's just that I love you so much. I'd go to the ends of the earth to find you if I ever lost you. Can you understand that, honey?'

'Only too well, Bas. Look, I must go. Someone's calling my name.' I rang off, quickly turned back into a female Father Christmas and dashed for my flight. All the while they were urgently announcing my name. A celebrity type would have loved it as by the time I reached the plane every single person was watching me. People were probably offering to sit on the wing to avoid me.

None of this prevented the flight attendant from insisting that I had too much hand luggage. I couldn't hand over my shoulder bag which held my passport and money, and I was worried they would scratch the painting. So with great glee the bloody woman snatched up my laptop.

Once I entered the plane, I marched the final mile to my seat. I was still wearing my personal sauna bath. My nose was red. Probably the rest of me as well, but my nose was all you could see. My seatmate was adorable in the worst possible way. Sweet, pink, plump and smelling vaguely of baby lotion. A bit like a modern-day fairy godfather, in his early twenties. After five minutes of conversation, the seat belt sign was turned off and he quickly got up to sit on the armrest of the seat across the aisle. The other man seemed to know him. Well, if I'd known him, I wouldn't have chosen to sit beside him either. But at least that temporarily gave me two seats to myself to remove some clothing.

The food was amazingly good. A choice of Beef Wellington, Southern fried chicken and ribs, or English Sole Meuniere. It made me wonder what they were eating in first class. Previously, the only choice I'd been offered in economy was whether you got to sit down or not. I used to wonder if the standby fares meant you had to take turns using the seat.

I'd planned to use the flight to turn myself into a new person, to get comfortable with my new self-image of a Basless, bedless, beanless person. So, the first stage was that I decided that I hadn't actually fallen out of love. I'd simply been in love with a man who didn't exist, who wasn't the same man I thought he was. I wouldn't like to think of a world without love, so I needed a conclusion that wasn't simply that love stinks.

And the real culprit was the deceit, the lack of trust. I didn't think I could truly love a person I couldn't trust. People do. Lots of chronic liars seem to be married, and I suppose their partners make allowances. Maybe they knew in advance what they were taking on and didn't care. I saw this game warden on TV who loved bears. But a close-up of the bear's big teeth put me off bears forever. Love should be a warm comfortable feeling. And love should have the advantage over hate. I mean if someone hated you, at least you'd know at all times what to expect. Maybe Bas would find lies like murder: after the first one, the others wouldn't really matter.

My parents to this day absolutely adored each other. They'd always been besotted, which meant they didn't really need a helpless, totally dependent infant to love them best in the world. They were already number one to each other. And theirs was a very happy marriage. They were each so wrapped up in their own thing that they actually paid each other little attention. But maybe their love depended on that freedom. And maybe also on realising that they wouldn't really have suited any-one else. They loved me and treated me wonderfully, but they never needed me emotionally.

So when I fell in love with Bas it seemed like, for the first time in my life, I was the most important person to another human. You feel that way in love, when you don't know about the wife. So it was particularly awful to go from number one to number four, soon to be number five. And of course in another ten years I probably would have been number sixteen.

He had needed me for the business, too. I'd not only felt loved and needed but was also growing, learning, stretching. Working under Bas' tutelage had been like getting a graduate degree in business. And I'd travelled a good bit of the world and had a lot of fun. So while I hadn't ended up where I'd planned, I needed to think of it as being ahead of where I started. Somehow, you need to turn disasters into something you can live with. Even if it were possible, blotting out Bas would be a bit like erasing ten minutes of a Hollywood film. If you haven't totally distorted the plot, all your attention is still attracted to the blank bit, wondering about it, fretting about what might have been there. What's missing becomes more important than what remains. Of course the main problem with logic is that it moves at a different speed from emotions. All the above made perfectly good sense, but when I thought of Bas I felt like screaming and hurling half the passengers out of the plane. And then I felt like weeping enough to drown the other half.

The loudspeaker kept paging a Mrs Cockeral. The last time they asked if she'd push her call button when she returned. Quite honestly, I didn't understand where they thought she could have gone. A stroll? A fly? Perhaps Mrs Cockeral is a code for doctor? But who'd want the services of a doctor who could get lost inside an aeroplane for an hour? I really needed some coffee to dilute all the alcohol, but the attendant was nowhere in sight. When you've already got a drink, they're always there asking if you want a drink. But when you're parched, they become invisible. She was probably hiding in the cockpit and using my laptop to write a bestseller.

While my seatmate had been roaming about, perhaps pursuing Mrs Cockeral, I'd shifted myself and extra clothing and bags to his window seat. It therefore became important that I keep my eyes closed. Lowering my seat and shoving my legs under the seat in front, my leg scraped the edge of the painting frame through the plastic bag. It reminded me that not only did I love the painting, but it was also Bas' favourite.

My last thought before I dozed off was that I needed to work out some plans for my future pretty damn quick, because I'd just set my watch to London time and so I was five hours older.

3

'Caron, the only thing worse than failure is three failures. If you include yesterday, you might be up to nine failures.'

That wasn't the helpful sort of thing I'd hoped to hear from Flora, my new flatmate. Well, maybe that's the wrong way to put it. She owns the house in Hampstead, and I pay rent. To say we share would be like a Buck House live-in footman saying he shared a house with the Queen. On the other hand I couldn't say we don't share because we use the same kitchen and bath. With Flora often standing outside the bathroom mumbling that she hopes I won't use up all the hot water. But then the Queen goes around turning off lights in the Palace, which is sort of similar if the footman is trying to read.

I'm not usually so muddle-headed, but desperation makes your brain feel like dried parsley. I realised Flora was patiently waiting for me to say something.

'I'm not sure, Flora, that I would call it failure. Maybe practice. That sounds more positive.'

'But what's the problem, Caron? What are you doing and saying in the job interviews?'

'It's a challenge, not a problem. Anyway, nothing in the majority of the cases. Six of the nine times I didn't even get an interview.'

'Well, what are you putting on your application forms? Goodness, you've lived in the States and after college you practically ran a large company. And look at you! Blonde, slim, long legs to die for. You wear expensive clothes. And those gold bracelets don't look like they came from a Christmas cracker. Unless you're trying for Chief Executive Officer, I should think you could at least get interviews.'

I offered to make us both a cup of tea to gain some time. We were getting onto dicey territory. I'd only been in Flora's house for two days, and getting past her interviews had been a bit like trying to win Miss Universe. There had been lots and lots of other houseshare applicants. Well, she'd inherited the small house in Hampstead from an aged aunt and it needed doing up. So the rent wasn't as high as it could be in that part of London, where I'd spent my childhood. I had so much other crap on my plate at the moment that living in a familiar neighbourhood that I loved seemed very important.

There had been the first meeting, to get on Flora's list. Then the shortlist included a visit to a coffee shop so she could view me in a different environment. She actually asked me what my hobbies were, although fortunately she didn't want to hear me sing. The truth was, I couldn't afford to lose my place in her house. And I couldn't afford to pay Flora if I couldn't find a job.

Returning with the tea, I said, 'What a lovely dress, Flora. Is it new?'

That didn't work. She said, 'Listen, Caron, maybe I can help. I do work in a human resources department.' She went to her desk. Well, *our* desk, as she has assigned one drawer each to the other tenant and me. 'Here's an application form from Chambers' Emporium. It's fairly typical. I brought home a copy for a friend of a friend to make an application.'

'You mean there's a vacancy where you work? Right now?'

Flora got my implied criticism. Surely a tenant had priority over a friend of a friend, especially if the hot water was rationed. She said, 'Well, in a large department store on Oxford Street, there often is a vacancy at some level. And I didn't mention it because from what you said I thought you'd be applying for top management. The vacancy is only in accounts.'

'I love accounts,' I said quickly. Actually accounts sounded like as much fun as watching an oak tree grow, although it was definitely a step up from a brothel.

As she handed me the form, she said, 'Now, while I top up the teapot, you fill it in. Next, I'll try to work out what the problem, sorry, work out how to greatly improve your chances.' At the kitchen door she turned, 'And cheer up, Caron. It's not the end of the world.'

I refrained from saying it was very nearly the end of my bank account, although a date hadn't yet been set for the funeral. During my first two weeks back, while house-sitting for our old neighbours, I'd been so sure I'd get a job straight away, I'd sort of, well, spent some money. A bank robber could hardly have emptied my current account quicker.

My mother's lovely old friends, after they returned from their holiday in France, could only offer me the sofa. And finally I was feeling so miserable I went to a health farm for a week. The saunas and mud baths and pampering worked a treat until I wrote out the cheque. I spent more on carrot juice in a week than in a lifetime on booze. My savings account was still alive but losing weight daily. No one could afford to share Flora's house earning minimum wage, which meant the money had to stretch until I got a good job.

I gave the form to Flora who studied it carefully. She was a very pleasant sort of person. A pretty face, where her fringe wasn't hiding it. And slightly plump, from what one could tell. She had the dress sense of a weeping willow tree. Her flowing dresses were so roomy that a couple of boy scouts could have been camping out underneath.

'So far, so good, Caron. I mean you've got your name and address and phone number right. Now you need to fill in the rest.'

She made room for us to sit side by side at the desk. And then we both watched the blank space as if we were watching a slow starting video, waiting for something to happen. 'Maybe,' she said finally, 'You could dictate and I could write it down?'

We sat in silence, that sort of comfortable silence like when someone's facing the firing squad. When she began tapping the pen against the blotter I said, 'Look, Flora, I really did have that job I told you about. It just doesn't seem like a good idea to mention it there on that paper.'

I wouldn't for a moment accuse Flora of thinking evil thoughts, but after a moment she said, 'You know, in books, this sort of situation . . .'

I looked around the room at the bookcases. She'd given the other tenant and me a separate bookcase to share. And Flora's was arranged with five romance novels followed by one crime novel next to a biography. On and on, that was the sequence. Suddenly I felt sure she wasn't thinking of romance.

Huffily, I said, 'I did not embezzle and I am not on the run from the police.' That was perfectly true, but it didn't add anything to the blank space on the form. This was absolutely the only subject in the world I did not wish to discuss, but fear works like a magnet. If pink gremlins were your greatest fear, a couple would probably pop up out of your breakfast cereal.

To be honest, Flora came across as a bit prim and proper and I didn't want to risk being thrown out of the flat on a morals charge. And had she been a rampant nymphomaniac, I still wouldn't have liked to admit I'd been so naïve. 'All right, Flora. I guess I'll have to tell you. But I'll need more than tea.'

Surprisingly, Flora brightened up considerably as she dashed to the cabinet to pour us both glasses of brandy. 'You may not like what I tell you, Flora.'

Smiling, she said, 'Maybe not. But it's sure to be interesting. And the novel I'm reading has got to a long boring section. Do, like, start at the beginning.'

As I sipped the brandy, I told her the basic story, emphasising how Bas was gorgeous, tall, blond, sexy and rich, and describing the wonderful penthouse on Fifth Avenue in New York. Well, she did read romances. They must be full of women as stupid as me. But maybe not so stupid as those in the crime novels. Right before I got to Bas' wife's phone call, I took another sip of brandy and changed the subject a little. 'My parents hated him.'

Flora looked surprised. 'Why? If I had a boyfriend like that, my mother would start knitting him socks.'

I held up my glass for a refill. 'They were suspicious of him, thought he was a bit flash, all mouth and manners. But I loved him. At least I thought I did, was sure I did. What I'm wondering now is if you stop loving someone does it mean you never loved them in the first place? I mean, wouldn't the definition of love include permanence?'

Flora thought for a moment. 'Only towards the end

of the books, and only for the main characters. But did he bring you chocolates and flowers? Take you out, treat you well? I mean, he sounds terrific to me.'

'He was terrific. And I was young and stupid.'

'Do you mean stupid by not holding onto him and marrying him? And living happily ever after?'

I was finding it hard to continue. There's a sort of currency amongst humans, rather like in a poker game. And how you look, whether you can bluff, makes a difference to your number of chips, your actual wealth, as it were. But how you think of yourself, your self-image and self-belief is the bottom line in your actual standing. Mine at the moment was pretty low and I couldn't emotionally afford to take on the aspect of a victim. Job in the Bible felt a bit piteous, and look what happened to him.

Bluntly, I didn't want any pity. Flora might pity my ignorance and despise me. I'd been greatly advantaged in life because my parents never doled out pity. And one only had to look around to see that winners were never the ones who used pity like blusher, brushing lavishly and thinking it hid the blemishes rather than framing them in gilt.

Finally I said, 'He travelled a lot, because of his other companies. And it was four whole years before I realised . . .'

'Bloody hell, Caron. Was he already married? In books that's hardly kept secret for four whole years!'

'Thank you, Flora, for making my day.'

'Wait. In one book, there was a bigamist. That went on for twenty years.'

'Then what happened?'

'Both wives had children. And after the wives met at the hairdressers, they got together and murdered the man. They, like, used each other for an alibi. It worked because the policemen didn't know both women were married to him.' She looked at me thoughtfully. 'But that's not the same as your situation. I mean, his wife didn't suggest anything. Did she?'

'I rather got the impression that had Bas married us both, she would have murdered him by herself. Anyway, she lived in Chicago and I only found out when she got pregnant again. She rang and left a message. They already had three kids.'

I began really and truly to like Flora because she got as incensed as I'd been myself, which translated into my deserving better rather than poor little me. 'Bugger the man! Still, Caron, the least he owes you is a good reference. And surely he owes you money if you helped start up the business?'

I explained about sacking myself for severance pay. I expected an assistant manager of human resources to faint, but after some thought she said, 'That doesn't exactly fit the law. But it probably wouldn't pay him to challenge it. Any boss sleeping with his employees is at a disadvantage anyway. Was that all? Did you get anything else?'

'My clothes, personal stuff, odds and ends, a little picture.' I tried to make the latter sound like a Polaroid snapshot.

'But Caron, there must be something you can do. He actually mentioned he wouldn't give a reference?'

'He actually said he'd make sure I never got another job. If it was all right for me to sack myself, it's a pity I can't write my own reference. Dear Sir/Madam, I sacked myself but I'm rather good and would be an excellent addition to your firm.'

Flora laughed. 'It would be a first.'

Then we both laughed with relief. She – because I hadn't spent the last four years in jail and me – because it had really helped to air the situation. Flora's reaction had made it seem dramatic rather than sordid.

She looked again at the application form. 'Almost anything is better than blanks. You need to put something. Anything that can infer enough talent and ability to hold down a job.' She looked around the room. 'If push comes to shove, say you've been writing a book. So they'll know you can type.'

'I can't type. Well, not quickly touch type. But of course I can use a computer. Maybe I should say I've been a self-employed computer hacker. That would explain nice clothes without having any references.'

We laughed some more, but I must admit it was more due to the brandy than to my wit. I asked Flora if she could get me an appointment interview soonest. Saying goodnight, I took the dregs of the brandy and soaked in two inches of lukewarm water, thinking of the old days.

Actually, I wondered if Bas had been able to trace me. If he checked the credit card bill, he'd know about the ticket to London. I phoned my parents every Sunday, and so far they hadn't heard from him. My parents certainly wouldn't tell him anything, or not in any language he could understand. And what could he do anyway? He probably had a new girlfriend by now. I smiled and thought that was the most likely case. He was definitely the type to get on with his life, not try to find me. All that talk about messing up my life if I left him was undoubtedly bravado.

On my way to my bedroom, I passed the vacant room and wondered about the other house-sharer who was expected in a few days. Would I soon be hearing violin practice through the wall? Was she an athlete who'd need to soak in hot water? After I'd got in bed, Flora tapped on my door.

I shouted, 'Admission fee fifty pence!'

'I just wanted to say not to worry, Caron. Something'll crop up.' She glanced around the room. I thought at first she was wondering how long it would take before the peeling strips of wallpaper touched the floor. Then I wondered if she would object to my luggage sticking out from under the bed. It held my out-of-season clothes and the project disks. Fat chance I'd have to use those as a CV, as I couldn't seem even to get an interview. The lovely music box was gracing Flora's living room mantel.

I waited, and eventually she said, 'You've made it nice in here. Especially that painting. It's the best copy I've ever seen. It . . . well it looks exactly like an original Picasso.'

4

Flora rang me promptly at nine to say she'd made me an appointment for eleven. 'But Mrs Oakley, she's the head of human resources, has already taken two indigestion tablets, Caron. You've been warned. Would you prefer another time? She's usually very happy right before five o'clock on Fridays. But it would have to be next week.'

That would mean a whole extra nine days of intensive care for my current account. 'I'll risk today, Flora. Mrs Oakley might start eating curry on Thursday nights.' I thanked her and rang off and dashed to get dressed. I was careful to wear all black with little skin showing. It didn't seem the thing to wear anything bright that might have brought to Mrs Oakley's mind a fruit salad with lots of acid. She sounded a bit like a walking, talking funeral.

I arrived with an hour to spare. I'd been too nervous to eat anything, so instead of checking out Chambers' Emporium as I'd planned, I went straight to the coffee shop on the corner of Oxford Street. The apricot Danish, my absolute favourite, looked delicious. But I decided that the way I was feeling it might lead to the interview starting with my borrowing a couple of fizzy pills. Drinking three cappuccinos didn't exactly help either, as all the blood in my body felt like it was trying to escape.

I hadn't been into Chambers' since I was a child. My

mother had considered it too trendy. And by the time I was able to do my own shopping it wasn't trendy enough. As I made my way to the lift at the back, I decided their problem was that they hadn't actually changed in twenty years. One got the idea they were holding old stock and waiting for it to come back into fashion. That does sometimes happen, but usually only to the type of stock that sells in the first place.

Flora had said that the ground floor and the one above it were merchandise. And the next floor up was where I needed to go. The top floor held the executives. Someone like Bas would probably have had a little tent on the roof. But when I got out of the lift, I went from one end of the corridor to the other without finding human resources. No one had been at the reception desk in front of the lift, and most of the other doors had been open so I couldn't read their signs. It was mostly men trying to look busy with a few female PA types frantically working.

I'd made my way back to the lift for the second time when the lift door opened and a man stepped out. He was tall and slim with dark hair and cobalt blue eyes. His facial features were irregular enough to be interesting. He wasn't as handsome as Bas, which was greatly to his advantage. And he was confident enough to wear his Armani suit without resembling a coat hanger.

He smiled and said, 'Hello.'

His smile was such that I smiled back and was trying to think of something witty to say until I remembered I was off men at the moment. He broke the silence by asking, 'Are you lost?'

I said, 'Only if I fail the job interview.'

He laughed and turned to press the button to summon the lift. 'Human resources is on the next floor down.'

And then I remembered that while the ground floor in the States is floor one, in the UK of course it doesn't count. So I was on the executive level. I was about to explain my error, but just then the lift arrived. 'Well, good luck,' he said. 'Mrs Oakley is a bit . . .'

I must have looked alarmed, as he coughed slightly and finished, 'Well, the sort of woman who loves black so you should be all right. Perhaps we'll meet again? Well, more precisely, I hope we will. My name's James Smith.'

'I'm Caron Carlisle. And I hope we meet again, too.' I particularly hoped that the next time we met I would be looking for the payroll department.

I got lost again, but thanks to a bit of jogging I arrived exactly at eleven. I felt as if I needed to bend over and take deep breaths with someone pouring champagne over me for winning the race, but there wasn't time as Mrs Oakley opened her office door and beckoned me inside. Flora stood behind her desk, mouthing good luck and pointing to my clothes with a thumbs up and a smile.

A pleasant, pencil shaped woman with greying hair worn in a bun, Mrs Oakley didn't seem like an ogre, except that she was extremely brisk and short of time. She read the application form in about three seconds.

'Your references are all right for character purposes, the vicar and family solicitor. But credentials, Miss Carlisle? University, and then nothing. You don't appear to have any work experience at all. Girl Guides leading to amateur tennis in an attempt to make Wimbledon. Helping out in three charity shops in London that have now become defunct. Amateur modelling for Church fetes. Organising the jam sales for the Church repairs effort. And riding a horse to London to protest animal rights legislation.' She looked up. 'Were you on the side of the hunt or the animal rights group?'

'I was on the side of the horse. But Mrs Oakley, don't I even add up to having some leadership qualities? I mean it isn't easy to sell jam to people who don't like it or who prefer buying it from Fortnum's.'

'What you add up to, according to this,' and she waved the form through the air, 'is a lovely seeming young lady who has never had a job and who doesn't appear really to need one.'

She was peering at my Dior outfit. 'That is one advantage of working in charity shops, Mrs Oakley, buying designer labels cheaply. And I very much want and need this job.'

She wrinkled her mouth about as if she were cleaning her teeth without a toothbrush. Finally she eyed me closely and said, 'I understand you know Mr James Smith.'

My mind began firing on all cylinders. Or maybe erupting like Mount Etna. Who the hell was James Smith? And then I remembered the man I'd just met. Surely he hadn't had time to ring Mrs Oakley. But if he had, what had he said? That I'd gone to the fourth floor instead of the third? That Chambers didn't need people in accounting who couldn't count to five?

The main clue seemed to be that he worked on the top floor and Mrs Oakley didn't. I smiled. 'Oh, yes, I've met James Smith. Although I only know him slightly. Well,' I quickly added, 'not for example as well as I know my parents.'

For the first time, Mrs Oakley smiled. But she waited for me to continue. I tried desperately to work out what Smith's job might be, in case she expected me to mention that. He must work for Chambers as he hoped to see me again. I mean that would be a pretty feeble hope if he'd flown over from Hong Kong for the day.

'And of course I've known him longer than I've known you. Or anyone else I've met after meeting him. As the minutes tick by, I've known him longer and longer. And of course I'm not old enough to have known him for a hundred years. But then some people one gets to know rather quickly. And of course, those are the more memorable people. In short, it's a pleasure to know James Smith.' I smiled feebly and then kept my mouth shut, in spite of the ensuing silence. I'd screwed up so bad I could be used to uncork a bottle of claret.

I was startled by Mrs Oakley's loud gales of laughter. She was practically choking herself. All I could think to do was join in. After a few minutes of laughing, Mrs Oakley took a handkerchief from her desk drawer and wiped away tears. 'Well, you do have a sense of humour, Miss Carlisle. That is in such short supply in life I'm tempted to hire you merely for that.'

But she didn't look especially tempted. I knew had to do something. 'Mrs Oakley, I really do need this job. And I especially want this job with this company today. I first came here when my mother brought me as a baby. I'm a hard worker and I learn quickly.' She still resembled the white cliffs of Dover. 'I really know computers, and I'm good with numbers.'

I stopped to catch my breath, but Oakley still said nothing. 'Do you have some accounts I could add up for you? Like I learned in the charity shops? And spreadsheets, well I read those the way others read novels. In bed, in the bath.' I had actually done that while I was with Bas. He found profit margins as big a turn-on as others found whips and leather. But I didn't think Mrs Oakley's sense of humour would stretch to the erotica of spreadsheets. She just stared in silence for a while, the judge reluctant to suggest the gallows.

'What about this, Mrs Oakley? Hire me on six months' probation. If at the end of that time you do not consider that I've done a good job, I'll pay you back all the salary you've given me. I can get another job to do that.'

Mrs Oakley smiled and pointed at the form. 'You think that with these credentials you'll get another job at twice the pay, half to live on and the other half to repay this company? No. We don't have the facility for such an arrangement and it wouldn't be fair to you.'

There was another lengthy pause, during which I was holding my breath. Finally, Mrs Oakley said, 'I am going to offer you the job, Miss Carlisle, based on your having the gumption to approach us with so little on record to offer. And also based on your enthusiasm. Mr Chambers, our founder, has always stressed that we are a people company, that ultimately we are about people. Chambers' has been slow to modernise, and your computer ability may turn out to be especially helpful. You can start tomorrow and I wish you luck.'

Mrs Oakley then instructed Flora to explain to me about the pension and perks and salary and holidays. As soon as we were alone, Flora said, 'Well done, Caron! I got worried when I heard Mrs Oakley laugh.'

'So did I.'

We spent the next hour shuffling paperwork. If most people get to heaven, they'll probably find it lined with filing cabinets.

Flora said, 'Chambers' opens at nine, so we need to

be here by eight thirty sharpish. The door nearest Marble Arch is the only one opened early. Coffee, tea and doughnuts are free. Breakfast and lunch in the canteen are at discounted rates.'

As she stuffed all the forms into a folder, she added, 'The canteen's actually the same as the public café. Mr Chambers, he's the owner, thinks it a good idea for us to mix with our customers, keep in touch with what they're like, wearing, saying. But there's a separate section if we want to bring our own lunch.'

Flora took her job seriously and showed me everything from the ladies' room to the coffee dispenser, the copy machine room to the stationer's department. If we'd been in a hotel, we would have looked under every bed. The upper echelons of Chambers' had few modern open spaces, and as we turned corners and doubled back and went through offices only accessible by going through other offices, I began to wish I'd marked the route with breadcrumbs.

As we were finishing a tour of the fax machines, I was about to offer to buy Flora lunch. She said, 'New employees get their first lunch free. And you're, like, official now. I mean if you don't have other plans?'

My only other plans had involved employment agencies or leaping from Westminster Bridge. And the company wasn't looking so dusty as we made our way between the perfume counters on the ground floor, stopping to spray on the free samples. My natural optimism, which was almost obsessive and certainly occasionally blinding, loved the idea of a company that still believed in a free lunch. Mr Chambers was becoming my model of the perfect man, except that the décor indicated that he must be over a hundred.

The café cum canteen was quite large and in the

basement. The remainder of the bottom level was the executive car park. Of course I couldn't see any cars. I mean, the café wasn't a drive-in. I'd half expected a glorified soup kitchen, especially if staff got discounts. But it was the most modern and up-to-date part of the building. The cafeteria line had a selection of three hot entrees as well as a veggie dish. There were also grill facilities for burgers. Instead of the regulation plastic, sandwiches were made to order. A large separate table held an elaborate salad bar. The selection of sweets was so tempting I worried I might put inches on my hips by merely looking. Sorry to go on and on about the food, but my secret diet is my cooking. If I cooked for the world, we'd all resemble pencils. No one has ever asked for seconds. Well, no one at my one dinner party did.

I chose a large pasta dish with chicken and Parmesan. And a side salad. Well, all right, and a large slice of chocolate cake. Flora had the same. Even at full price, everything was a bargain.

Flora led the way to the other side of a row of tallish plants, where she said you could bring your own, although I couldn't see why anyone would bother. 'It's more private over here,' she said. 'And I want to hear how you got past Mrs Oakley.

'Often applicants are smug and patronise me on their way in, and then on the way out they're rude and horrid. Even the nicer ones tend to come out angry. Makes you wonder what she's doing.' She stopped to take a large bite of pasta, before adding, 'And I've never heard Mrs Oakley laugh out loud except on Fridays.'

Flora's voice was so dire I couldn't help but laugh before I realised she was serious. 'I don't know, Flora. Maybe I was the underdog of all underdogs. She didn't seem that bad to me. There was one thing. Do you know a James Smith?'

Flora stopped eating. 'Do you mean the James Smith? Our James Smith?'

'Probably. Well, Mrs Oakley asked me if I know him.'

Flora's face seemed to droop. 'Goodness, Caron. If you know James Smith, you didn't need my help with your application.'

'I don't know him. I only met him because I got lost. He said I was on the wrong floor. But I couldn't tell Mrs Oakley that, could I? What I want to know is how she knew about it? I'd really like to think I got this job without the help of a leg-up from a man.' I pushed my empty plate away and moved the sweet closer. Why, I wondered, do we eat free food faster?

Flora thought for a minute. Two minutes. 'He's very nice. He could have rung her. And I don't think that asking if applicants know him is part of her drill. But it's a bit far-fetched, isn't it? More likely she saw you talking to him.'

I had found the man attractive, but no way had I been so smitten I wouldn't have noticed Mrs Oakley standing behind him. Or walking between us.

Flora said, 'She'd only come in right before you, Caron. Maybe she'd been on the top floor. I must say, Mrs Oakley treats a summons to the executive area like an invitation to Ascot.'

Just then I saw James Smith join the cafeteria line. 'There, Flora. That's the James Smith I met.'

Flora turned around to look just as he looked our way. And caught both of us staring. He smiled and waved before the attendant behind the food counter regained his attention. 'Gosh, Caron, James Smith is Chambers' Chief Financial Officer, tipped for the top job if the rumours about Mr Chambers' retirement are true.'

'The CFO eats in the canteen?'

'Mr Chambers eats here, and anyone ambitious does the same. Those near retirement who aren't bothered like the prices.' She swallowed a bite of cake and added, 'Bet you can't spot Mr Chambers.'

'The loser buys the next two cappuccinos?'

Flora smiled. 'The next four.'

That clued me in that Mr Chambers wasn't obvious. I already knew he wasn't young. And he'd been described as a people person who believed in giving those like me a chance. So he probably wasn't sitting on a tall white horse and tossing crumbs to the peasants. After scanning the room, which at one point involved standing to look over a potted plant, I said, 'That one. Tall, military bearing, slightly plump, thick white hair. In the corner wearing the rumpled grey suit. With three other men.'

Flora's mouth gaped. 'Have you met him, too? When you were lost?'

I laughed. 'I wouldn't cheat, Flora. I would have said. Look at the group. He's wearing the least smart clothes, making the least effort. Yet the other three have their chairs angled slightly towards him. The three others are, probably subconsciously, mimicking his body language. The blond with his back to us has one leg jutted out into the aisle. Another has one elbow perched against the table. The guy nearest us is twiddling a fountain pen. Chambers is the only one doing all those things.'

'Gosh! Was your New York business a detective agency?'

I laughed. 'No. Bas bought small struggling companies and then we put them together differently and then usually sold them on. I read that body language stuff in a book.'

'I must get that book!'

'So must I.' Flora and I both looked up to see James Smith standing there. He smiled and said, 'Hello, Flora,' before turning back to me. 'I didn't mean to eavesdrop. I was waiting to ask how things went with Mrs Oakley?'

'Very well. I got the job. And thanks for directing me to the right office.'

'A pleasure. And how was Mrs Oakley's body language?'

When Flora and I looked blank, he added, 'I mean any revealing twitches? Any hints or suggestions?' He grinned and lowered his voice. 'I have the greatest respect and admiration for Mrs Oakley, but she reminds me of my old headmaster. I find myself thinking of ridiculous mischief, before taking her advice and escaping quickly.'

Maybe realising he'd given away quite a lot to two lowly members of the company, he quickly added, 'But she is of course indispensable to Chambers'.'

While he spoke with great seriousness, James Smith didn't look like he was the least bit intimidated by anyone, but he did come across as a bit shy. So I took his comments as dry humour and laughed. Shy types especially hate to venture out of their shells and toss jokes that nobody catches.

Flora said, 'Caron made Mrs Oakley laugh.'

She made it sound like I'd held a gun to Mrs Oakley's head and shouted 'Laugh, dammit, laugh!'

James Smith grinned. 'Quite an accomplishment. With your talents and knowledge of people, I'll have to watch out for my own job.'

He was so obviously teasing, I said, 'My new job is in accounts, and sounds terrific, lots of perks. Even today's lunch is free. So if you ever want to switch jobs with me, Mr Smith . . .'

He really laughed then. 'I've also read about the adventures of Tom Sawyer. Still, it worked for him.' With another glorious smile, one side of his mouth rising higher than the other, he said, 'Chambers' is an old family firm, and there's lots of scope for promotion, Caron. And do please call me James.' He glanced across the room. 'I'm expected over there, and I must remember to watch my elbows and knees.'

After he'd gone, Flora said, 'Goodness, Caron. Are you going to call him James? The CFO?'

'Absolutely. And if he'd agreed to switch jobs, I'd have done that too. Anyway, he seems very nice, and I seriously doubt he's worried about the new accounting person pinching his chair.'

'James Smith, age thirty-six, lives not far from us in Hampstead, tipped for the top job, unmarried although a woman sometimes answers his phone. Been with Chambers' seven years. Six foot, blue eyes, public school then Oxford.'

I laughed. 'Talk about detective agencies.'

'It's confidential, Caron. The employee files, I mean. Pity about the other woman, or you could snatch him up. He really is gorgeous.'

'Flora! I'm off men at the moment. And it's my experience that mixing business with pleasure leads only to the accounts department. Anyway, James was just being nice to a new employee.'

'Well, he's never, like, explicitly asked me to call him James.'

'You probably never asked him to switch jobs with

you. Anyway, he just seems a bit shy. It's surprising that someone so young should be tipped for the top job. I mean, Mr Chambers sounds a bit old-fashioned.'

'Mr Chambers knows the place needs modernising. And there's been talk recently that the company is going downhill and is ripe for a hostile takeover. But Mr Chambers insists that all the old-timers keep their jobs. He probably thinks Mr Smith, or rather James, won't sack anyone. You're right about him being a bit shy, and you really managed to draw him out. He would be such a good catch.'

I laughed. 'You make him sound like a fish. Anyway, doesn't Chambers' have a ban on inter-employee romance?'

'Not really. Mrs Chambers only recently retired. But she's a full partner and she and Mr Chambers set up the business together. So they could hardly have an explicit rule.'

'And in practice?'

Flora smiled. 'Practice is the right word. It's like almost everyone is in training for the London Love Marathon. It's all done discreetly, but everyone knows.'

'Including the top floor?'

Flora thought a minute. 'Only two of them are officially available. There's James Smith, and no one really knows about him. Just that woman answering the phone a couple of times when his the top floor PA tried to contact him. And then there's Jack Howard, recently divorced and no wonder. If all the rumours about him are true, he's been in enough bedrooms to qualify as a top adviser for Laura Ashley furnishings.'

All the while we were eating, employees stopped to greet Flora and were introduced. They seemed a warm, fun crowd, very welcoming. As we were finishing the chocolate cake, Flora asked, 'What about in the States? In that job Bas poached you from? Did they have a rule? About dating?'

'Oh, sure. Definitely a no-no. A company safeguard against harassment lawsuits.'

'Sounds a bit boring, like.'

'It would be if anyone paid attention. Just think, Flora, when someone says don't you dare think about sex, what's the first thought that enters your head? But in my first job, I was the only woman in the department. It meant all the guys made a play for me, and everyone else watched like hawks to see if they scored. So basic-ally, I had fourteen chaperones.'

Flora laughed and then asked, 'What did James mean about Tom Sawyer?'

'You'd love the book, Flora. It was a trick he played, making whitewashing a fence or a wall sound so intriguing he managed to get someone else practically begging to have a go.'

Flora leaned forward and lowered her voice. 'Caron, about that other book you mentioned, do you remem-ber if it applied to romance, and not just to business? I mean like measuring men's reactions?'

'You don't need a book for that, Flora. First their eyes glaze over, then they drool. Then a bit later their trousers inflate.'

'But, Caron, I wouldn't be comfortable watching a man's trousers.'

I reminded myself that Flora tended to take things literally. 'I was joking, Flora. But about the book, abso-lutely. There are lots of books with that sort of info. And the observations apply to anyone trying to impress you. Or not. Whatever. But do remember, reading that book didn't clue me in about Bastard. And of course, with any technique, you're up against everyone else who knows it.

'And it can get ridiculous. I was once talking to one of Bas' business contacts. She was copying my body language and also my speech. I said, for example, the financial report was looking good. Then she said she thought the financial report was looking good. I said I thought the business would really take off. She said I understand you believe the business will really take off. The idea, Flora, is to keep the other person talking, in her case to keep me talking. But soon I felt like I was talking to myself in the mirror. If she'd really known people, she would have realised I was eventually baiting her, shifting my elbows and crossing my legs rather furiously until she resembled a chimpanzee catching fleas.'

After lunch I went back to the house and rang my mother to say I'd got the job. At first I got the answerphone, but it was never safe to leave messages for my parents. Mother of course was good with machines. Well, married to Dad she had needed to learn. But it was Dad who always bought the new equipment, thinking himself modern because no one had succeeded in explaining otherwise. If Dad saw the light flashing, no telling what he would do. Spray it with fly killer? Ring the fire department?

It was nearly six o'clock before I got through to Mum. After Mum congratulated me, she said, 'Caron, that awful man Bas rang here. He wanted your address. He spoke to your father, who of course told him to do his own research. But later his lawyer rang.'

'Bas' lawyer?' My stomach felt like the Royal Ballet was inside doing Swan Lake. 'What did he want?'

'Your address. I must say, Caron, how like Bas – that

in romantic affairs he should use his lawyer to do his bidding.'

'But, Mum, there's nothing he can do. I mean, he can hardly sue for divorce when we're not married. And it's a free country. Sod him. And it's not fair for him to bother you. If anyone rings again, just slam down the receiver.'

'We keep our cards close to our chest, dear. But his lawyer was extremely persistent. Quite annoyingly so. I had a mind to ring Bas' office to tick him off and tell him to stay out of the game. Do take care, Caron, as a spot of bother may be on the cards. Bas' secretary said he wasn't available, that he was in London. And she had no idea when he would return.'

After ringing off, I began sinking into a sulk. And I opened the bottle of good wine I'd bought to repay Flora for dehydrating her bar for me the previous night, and for all her help. On the day I got a job, life should have also given me a win on the lottery. But oh, no. You make an effort, take a couple of steps forward, and whack, whack on your shins to slow you down. It's like having your guardian angel bite your ankle.

Still, no use blaming life. If you don't take responsibility in situations, you lose the power to do something about them. And believe me, taking the passive position with Bas was like offering a grizzly bear your last piece of chocolate. Better to eat the chocolate yourself and run like hell.

Hopefully, Bas was just in London for a one-day meeting with his Hong Kong agent. London was sort of a halfway rendezvous when papers needed signing and such. But surely Bas didn't really think he could get me back? Did he even want to? Or was he just raising general hell, wanting the last word. I agreed with Flora that he probably couldn't or wouldn't fight the severance pay. His lawyer would charge more for one hour than the money involved. So whatever Bas had planned, it would revolve around the painting. But that was my picture. And justice aside, if I returned it to him for peace of mind, to get shot of him forever, he would take it as weakness. No telling what claims he would make against me after that. Embezzlement? Harassing his wife? He could afford to hire a whole team of fiction writers to give him ideas. Well, no way Bas would read the books himself.

It was only after his wife's phone call that I'd realised the extent of my naïvety, how cleverly Bas had arranged everything, especially the finances, in his favour. And if one had to describe Bas in only four words, they would have to be, 'He likes to win.' He would start a war so he could win it.

Well, that was settled. I'd have to fight. It was time for Flora to return, even though she'd planned to do some shopping after work. So I quickly changed into jeans and a T-shirt for a walk on the Heath, to blow off steam. It wasn't fair to keep bothering Flora with my problems.

As I passed South Hill Green, I felt a bit like a mouse facing a tiger. But we'd once had a mouse that my parents and the exterminators took ages to get rid of. And even then we weren't sure it hadn't merely decided to go and live somewhere where they had better cheese.

As I walked, I wondered how Bas could actually find me. I mean, checking out London wasn't like looking over the passengers on a tour coach. Still, it's easier to spot a tiger than a mouse. Like any good mouse, I'd keep my eyes open and my head down for a while. The house and bills and phone were all in Flora's name.

And my front door wasn't exactly crushed with the media wanting to photograph and interview the newest employee in Chambers' Emporium's accounts department.

So that was sorted. Bas wouldn't find me and he'd get involved with other things and forget me. No need to worry. I'm not sure my argument was entirely convincing. As I walked across the Heath, I kept glancing around. Well, up actually. Bas never did his own walking. Helicopters were more his style. On the whole, I felt as safe as a couple of sticks of dynamite propped near a bonfire.

Walking always helps to calm my mind, or at least make me too tired to think. So I walked faster and faster. Finally, I had to slow down. Parents and small children fed the ducks on the lakes, elderly couples strolled, punks paraded their new ear and nose rings, people chased dogs chasing people. It all seemed so normal. But that's another trick of life. As soon as you let your guard down and relax, it sneaks up on you. There I was, happy as a lark, unworried for the first time since I'd returned to London. Health and wealth and happiness all possible. My future glowing like strobe lights in a disco.

Then a man behind me shouted, 'Caron!' and it was all I could do not to climb the nearest tree.

5

I wouldn't like to think of myself as a coward, but for some reason I had the urge to run as fast as possible without looking back. Life is full of choices, and while it was too late not to hear someone shout, there was plenty of time to ignore it. With luck, I could ignore it for the rest of my life. Or at least outrun it. Unfortunately, I could hear feet pounding on the path behind me.

I'm a regular jogger. Well, someone could say that if they faithfully ran only on New Year's Eve. At least I thought about it every day. And once you get into a steady lope, you get this rhythm and feeling of euphoria and the running is easy. I was going too fast for that, but not as fast as the person behind me. And you don't get that warm lovely feeling when you think your pursuer's on Bas' payroll. I was aiming for the edge of the Heath and hoped to race along the road leading to the High Street where there would be lots of people. I'd got to a high spot near some trees and realised the rest of the run would be downhill.

Sometimes it's when you think you've beaten the problem that you relax and get careless. Thinking ahead to possible traffic on the road and how I'd need to change my pace to dodge cars, I stumbled and went sailing through the air. I landed face down spread-eagled on the path. I was too tired to get back up and thought I'd better prepare to die, but I was too tired even to think of that.

'Caron, are you all right?'

I gingerly shifted my head and looked up. It was James Smith. I felt as stupid as someone who's just used a winning lottery ticket to light a cigar. And when you feel really truly foolish, it's sort of instinctive to lash out. 'Dammit, James, why were you chasing me across the Heath!'

He helped me to a sitting position but I felt boneless and my head drooped onto his shoulder as I gasped for breath. His arm was around me, supporting the upper half of my body. An onlooker would have thought he was holding a limp rag doll. And that a wild dog had been pulling out clumps of its hair. 'I wasn't chasing you, Caron.'

'Yes, you were. That's what chasing is. Running after someone trying to catch them.' He handed me his handkerchief so I could mop my brow. Why the hell wasn't he sweating? He didn't even seem out of breath.

He said patiently, 'My shout seemed to alarm you, and I wanted to catch you up so you could see it was only me. I mean there isn't any reason why you would run away from me, is there? So far as I know, our only point of difference is my not wanting to switch jobs with you.'

I looked up and saw that he was grinning. My heart-beats had slowed down to where they only sounded like the generator for the Royal Free Hospital. I took a deep breath and smiled. 'Have you changed your mind?'

He laughed and then became more serious. 'Are you hurt?'

'I don't know yet.' I stretched my arms and legs. 'I think I'm OK.' There was still a residual fear of being chased by Bas' commandos and I quickly looked around.

'It's all right, Caron. There's no one else about. I don't mean to be personal, but is it a stalker?'

'A what?'

'You know, a stalker. You look a bit like that TV newsreader who was being stalked.' When I said nothing, because breathing was using up all my strength, he added, 'I thought at first it was a game, a race. But I really had to stretch to catch you up.'

'Oh, great. I'm not only on the run, but I don't run very fast. Thanks a lot.'

We laughed, but I tried to get up. This was getting too deep. It's amazing that when you only have one subject you don't wish to discuss, all conversations lead straight to it. My elbows and knees were scratched, one knee bleeding. But I could live with that. I could even escape this conversation with that. I gingerly stepped forward and would have toppled over again had he not caught me.

'Dammit, James, my ankle's not co-operating.' Because we could both quite clearly see, I didn't add that my knee was leaking blood onto my track shoe.

He looked around, probably hoping the next passing joggers would be a doctor chasing a nurse. Although he gently touched and turned my ankle, it felt like he was bashing it with stones. 'I think it's only a sprain, Caron. But your knee needs attention. I live quite near. Do you think you can make it a bit further?'

He didn't live as near as my ankle might have hoped. But our slow progress was fairly comfortable, with me leaning heavily on his left arm with his other arm around me. I think he was mostly talking to distract me. Every other step I tended to mutter Ouch. 'Will your family mind, James? Your bringing home the wounded from the Heath?'

53

'My family?' Then he laughed. 'You must have heard the office rumours. The woman at the end of the telephone variety. Well, there is a woman, and I can hardly wait for you to meet her.' He grinned and added, 'Although I'm trusting you to keep the secret. The office rumour does suit me.'

When I looked blank, he smiled and added, 'When you know the company better, you might find yourself telling everyone you're married. You're not, are you?'

He was far more subtle than Bas, and more mysterious. Had he got some woman locked in his attic? Were they naturists and I'd need to leave my clothes at the door? 'No, I'm not married. The very idea makes me . . .' Oh, shit. I was about to say too much again.

James smiled. 'Makes you run quickly across the Heath? A rejected suitor? Actually, better that than an unknown stalker.'

Not really, I thought. I would have faced an unknown stalker and tried a few karate chops I've seen demonstrated on TV. With an unknown, you can shout for the police. Scream bloody murder. When it's someone you've been living with, everyone seems to think oh, a little tiff – unless he's actually bashing you with a tyre iron.

Still, my running had surprised me. It certainly hadn't been typical. Mum was generally so intrepid that perhaps I'd been more alarmed by her warning than I'd consciously acknowledged. But surely I didn't really think Bas would physically harm me? On the other hand, undermining my confidence and interfering with my chances for work were more serious, because it's harder to fight than a physical threat. Real power isn't about having larger biceps.

*　　*　　*

We reached the edge of the Heath and crossed the road. Not one single car, so the worry about traffic that had caused me to lose my pace had been unnecessary. My breathing was back to normal, and my ego had crept up from ankle level to that of my knee. Both continued to bleed. 'James, do tell me more about the telephone woman.' Well, he had treated that as a bit of a joke. Just in case she really was his lover, I quickly said, 'I'm sure she's lovely and charming.'

'Hmmm. Lovely and charming. I'll let you decide. We're nearly there.' He pointed to an elegant house on Well Walk in a terrace of white stone dwellings. Because of half basements, there were stairs leading to the front doors. As we reached the top step, he whispered, 'Prepare.'

The door opened just as we reached it. James mumbled, 'I think she watches from the window.'

Instead of a charming lover, there stood an ancient woman. Stooped and wiry with frizzy white hair escaping from a bun, she gave us that hearty welcome double glazing salesmen have come to expect. She stood bang in the middle of the doorway, glaring first at James and then at me.

'If you could shift slightly, Mrs Stone, my guest Caron Carlisle and I could come in.'

This comment didn't seem to have the desired effect. Then Mrs Stone noticed my knee. Whether it was because of my health or the possibility of blood on the carpet wasn't apparent, but she immediately backed up and motioned us in. Gripping my arm, she frogmarched me to the kitchen. After pushing me onto a wooden chair, she peered closely at my face. 'Looks like you're still alive.' She turned to James and said, 'Don't just stand there, Young James, get the first-aid kit.'

I suppressed a smile at hearing the Young James bit and looked at him. He rolled his eyes heavenward before opening a cabinet to retrieve the first-aid box. Then she began to issue commands, get this and get that, ending with boil some water. I hoped she wasn't expecting to deliver a baby.

She might have looked like the wicked witch of the west, but she knew what she was doing. After cleaning the cuts, she poured a purple medication on them, making me flinch. But I was sure my wounds would do as she intended and mend themselves instantly. Next she instructed James to carry me into the front room. Grinning, he literally picked me up and carried me. Then she placed my ankle, which was already beginning to swell, in a bowl of hot water. Fortunately it wasn't the boiling water.

Leaning close with another myopic stare, she smiled a cheeky smile and said, 'You're going to live.'

I thanked her profusely, and she smiled more broadly. Turning to James, she said, 'Brandy,' and mumbling 'Soup,' she turned and left the room.

'James, she's wonderful. Where did you find her?'

He grinned wryly. 'I inherited her along with the house. My bachelor uncle left a letter along with his will. I quote, "I trust, James, that you will take care of old Stone, let her work as long as she can stand up if that's what she wants. Send her out to pasture with funds if she prefers." My old nanny, you know, like her name, always been a rock in my life. The thing is, Caron, she's more like a pebble in my shoe. Not exactly lethal but hard to ignore.'

He handed me a brandy snifter and I took a sip. It was like fire sliding down my throat. If you ever wonder if you're still alive, try brandy. If you don't feel anything, ring the undertaker.

James settled in a deep leather wing chair across from where I was perched on the sofa. All the furnishings, including the paintings, looked as if not only James but also his uncle before him had inherited them. The room was just a tiny bit gloomy. I got the idea that if anyone tried to move a chair, it would bite a large chunk out of their hand.

James swished the brandy around in his glass. Mine was already too empty for that. 'My solicitor said we could get around my uncle's strictures, reinterpret them as it were, but I feel obliged to obey his intentions rather than the letter of the law. Although I do regularly, probably once a week, offer to pension her off.'

'But why, James? Your house seems well looked after, and she's certainly competent. Most people would die for someone like her.'

'That's because they don't have to live with her. Occasionally, when in prep school, I would spend holidays with my uncle. Mrs Stone was already old then and still treats me exactly like Young James. You are the very first person I've ever brought home that she hasn't tried to frighten away. Yet.'

'They probably weren't bleeding, James. If I ever come again, do give me a shove off the porch before she opens the door. I really like her. I wasn't much fussed over as a child, so having a bit of pampering has its appeal.'

James laughed. 'Pity about that. After hearing you talk about how to suss out people, body language and everything, I was hoping you'd think of a way to get rid of her. I've offered for her to retain the basement flat and receive an extremely generous pension, but she won't hear of it.'

Just then Mrs Stone walked in. 'I won't hear of retiring,

Young James, if that's what you're talking about.' Turning to me with a large smile, undoubtedly intended to irritate James, she said, 'He doesn't know how much he needs me. If I hadn't been here tonight, you would have died.'

'Mrs Stone, I do know how to use the first-aid kit.'

'That's as may be, but you can't make soup.'

She stood, hands on hips, waiting for me to taste the soup. 'It really is delicious, Mrs Stone. Absolutely delicious. I'm feeling much better already.'

She thought about that for a minute. Then she turned to James. 'I'd better prepare the guest room. She doesn't look well enough to move. May take weeks. Months.'

I choked and spluttered. 'I'm expected at home tonight, Mrs Stone, but thank you so much. I'm sure this soup will do the trick.'

'I'll be back to tape your ankle. And you, James, I suppose you'll be wanting dinner?'

'Soup will be fine. If there's enough?'

She shook her head sadly. 'Enough? What would you do without me?'

As soon as she had left the room, he said with resignation, 'Without her, I could die a happy man.'

I laughed. 'Cheer up, James. Keep a pair of crutches in your car for your guests to use. Or try faking an injury yourself on occasion. This soup is worth making an effort for.'

'I don't dare encourage her, Caron. Every night she places a cup of cocoa by my bedside. And whenever I have a nightcap, she mentions the AA. I can't really shout at an old lady. And she's stubborn as a mule.'

He smiled a bit sheepishly. 'The thing is, I can't get

really tough and make demands, tell her how it's got to be. I mean she's old enough to be my great grand-mother. And she shouldn't be waiting hand and foot on someone young and healthy anyway.'

I could hardly believe I was seeing this side of the Chambers' Emporium CFO. And James was obviously clever. You might get to be chairman or CEO or even a government minister by guile or accident, but never Chief Financial Officer. And to be tipped for the top job at his age was quite a coup. I wondered if he might be showing this weakness to be kind, having seen me run like hell from phantoms on the Heath.

I still couldn't help laughing. 'Anyway, James, you owe her. It's probably because of her that you've made your mark on the world. Not settled for being an idle playboy. The urge to be in charge somewhere. She's better than a nagging wife. Far better. You could hardly have a wife in her eighties. And nagging wives typically outlive their husbands.'

I really was enjoying this conversation, having James for a friend. My limited experience of men was that whatever the conversation, their thoughts were usually of sex. With Bas, it was business and sex – in that order. But here was James, seriously discussing how to get rid of an ancient family retainer. Maybe all men had something interesting to talk about once you got past the hormones. The dictionary says that hormones are tiny chemicals flitting about the bloodstream. But they're more like the Great Wall of China or maybe even more like the Wailing Wall.

As we ate our soup, and then our refills, with hot buttered rolls that tasted home-made, we discussed James' situation, while he focussed on the misdemean-ours of Mrs Stone. We were laughing so much we were holding our ribs. Well, not waving them about or anything.

Mentioning girlfriends to a man was a bit risky, as he might interpret it as a request for an audition. But if it worked, it could lead a relationship away from girlfriend to friend girl. I really liked James, and maybe he could become the brother I'd never had.

'I don't want to be nosy, James, but what about girl-friends? Does Mrs Stone throw them out at midnight? Or camp outside your bedroom door?'

'Probably both, if I ever tried it. I kept my old flat on after inheriting. Well, er, I wasn't, you know, living there by myself. Not exactly. I've only been here alone with the Stone for a bit over a year. And fortunately, it's quite acceptable to friends to go away for the week-end. Mrs Stone never sleeps or takes holidays. I'm think-ing of lending her to the Prime Minister as a secret weapon.'

After Mrs Stone had professionally taped my ankle, I asked James to call a cab. Before he could offer me a lift, she got in first, scowling and prompting, 'Young James!'

At the door after I thanked her, and she actually hugged me. Then she said, 'Now, don't go home and die, Caron.'

James said patiently, 'Mrs Stone, Caron's not going to die.'

'Everybody's going to die. Now, Caron, I want you to stop by again. Never mind him.' She stopped to glower at poor James. 'I'll be here, and there's always a cuppa waiting. I get lonely sometimes. Young James isn't very sociable.'

After another quick glance at James, she added, 'Did you know that statistically, as I have already got to such a venerable age, I've got a better chance of seeing in the morn than Young James here?'

Outside, James said, 'Bloody hell! Lonely? I'd actually pay people to visit her if she'd let them in. You know, Caron, I'm either going to have to go against my uncle's wishes or hire a hit man.'

As he started up his car, he said, 'Seriously, do you have any ideas?'

'I'll give it some thought. Wait! I know. You can marry her off!'

'Who do you have in mind? Brad Pitt? Hugh Grant?'

We were laughing so hard he almost missed the turning into Flora's street. I said, 'Well, then, you could get married.'

After James pulled up in front of Flora's house, he looked at me and grinned. 'Is that a proposal?'

'To get Mrs Stone out of your hair, I had in mind your marrying a widow with ten children.'

6

Fortunately, Flora was in bed reading by the time James brought me home. I managed to limp into my room before shouting hello and goodnight, so she didn't see my bandages. I could have used Mrs Stone's help in getting my jeans down over my swollen ankle, granted that she wouldn't have solved the problem with an axe. Efficient people can overdo it.

When my head hit my pillow ten seconds later, I was feeling surprisingly cheerful. My embarrassment at running away on the Heath seemed quite normal after hearing about James' dealings with Mrs Stone and meeting Mrs Stone myself. Anyway, I needed to get rid of my perfectionism. That was probably what caused me to plaster over all the cracks in Bas so diligently. With hindsight I wished I'd used fast drying cement.

So it was OK to be human. OK to be scared. As long as it didn't become an addiction. I fell asleep thinking of James helping me up on the Heath, with his strong arms around me, how it felt like snuggling up to a teddy bear – warm, nice, friendly, non-threatening, no romantic involvement, strictly platonic, perfectly safe. Talk about counting sheep.

I woke up the next morning feeling like twin elephants had tangoed all night on my body. I could smell coffee. Wrapped up in my dressing gown, I limped into the kitchen. 'Morning, Flora.'

'Caron! What happened?'

'I tripped jogging on the Heath. Just a sprain and a scratched knee. I'm fine. A bit stiff.' I needed to mention James as it might come up later. I didn't want to have to remember for the rest of my life not to talk about it. 'Guess who came by to rescue me?'

'Leonardo DiCaprio?' She had already put the kettle on for hot water to soak my ankle, bless her.

'James Smith. And I saw his house.'

Flora smiled brightly. 'Did you see the woman? The gorgeous lover who answers the telephone?'

Oh, dear. How to keep faith with both James and Flora. 'Well, I didn't actually see anyone of that description. But I did meet an elderly housekeeper.'

Flora said thoughtfully, 'The woman was probably still working. James is the type to go for high-powered executive women.'

I was surprised to hear this. 'Not housewives who bake delicious cookies on an Aga?'

'I shouldn't think so. Like I said, I think it was unusual his being so chatty with you. Word is that he's not one for small talk. I mean he's pleasant and says hello to everyone. But aloof. Keeps himself to himself. And believe me, no one messes him about.'

'But Flora, that could mean he's just a private person. Cold and aloof doesn't jive with your saying Mr Chambers thinks James can both modernise the place and also retain the old timers.'

Flora flushed slightly, and I felt badly, as if I'd criticised her. 'Caron, maybe it's just that he doesn't mix much, so no one knows much about him. I shouldn't go by gossip. I mean he was very nice to us at lunch. And he helped you out on the Heath.'

'You know, Flora, he just sounds to me like a man with ambition and brains. He must know that having a reputation like that VP you mentioned, Jack Howard, wouldn't help his career. And if you mix too much, you get forced into taking sides, and that doesn't help either.' Then I had to suppress a smile as I realised that the reason Mr Chambers trusted James to run his company was that he probably knew about Mrs Stone.

There wasn't time to soak my ankle long, and I wasn't entirely happy to limp on my first day on the job. Considering it necessity rather than luxury, I rang for a taxi to take Flora and me to work. I was trying to decide if I should wear a short skirt and advertise my wounds, so I wouldn't appear a slow moving slacker, or whether to wear a trouser suit and hope that if I ignored my limp it would give up and go away. I opted for camouflage. Surely people in an accounts department would just sit still in chairs all day, staring at numbers until cobwebs covered their ears.

Flora seemed pleased to be popping out of a taxi to join the group on the pavement waiting for the door to open. But I took it as my first mistake. That and my Dior cream silk trouser suit. It was my only outfit with really roomy legs, such that my bandages wouldn't notice them and take offence. The taxi driver had definitely noticed my bandaged ankle. Well, he would, constantly on the alert for guns and weapons tucked into passengers' socks. And he got out of the cab to open the door for me with a swish of his arm. It felt a bit too much like making an entrance for eight thirty on a Thursday morning.

The whipped cream on top of my arrival event was that just as the taxi drove away, rain came pissing down. Flora of course had an umbrella, but she had moved away to greet colleagues. I could feel my hair acting like honeysuckle, those new shoots that curl out and try to find something to grab hold of.

Flora came rushing over with her brolly. 'Here, Caron, there's room for both of us under this.' But she was so much shorter than me that when she tried to cover me she caught the rain herself.

'Thanks, Flora, but I'm already so wet it doesn't matter.' I shoved back my hair as its drips felt like a dog licking my face.

'Everything matters, that's what I always say to anyone who'll listen. You'll spoil your lovely suit, and on your wages you won't be able to buy another for ages.'

That brought me down to earth with a thud. I was no longer the big shot executive, but a lowly paid worker who was simply a bit overdressed. And very, very wet. I needed to get rid of any possible snooty feelings about a group of which I was now, only with great good luck, a member.

I did remove my jacket, as my black T-shirt was less formal. It was a bit tight across the chest, as I'd been lately overindulging in apricot Danish. Glancing down at my modest chest, I thought how unfortunate it was that pastries are not shaped like watermelons or even figs.

As the group moved inside Chambers', everyone seemed friendly. I know we're not supposed to go by first impressions, but on a first meeting there isn't much else available. And I don't know how I'd thought I could hide my ankle, what with Flora pointing to it and saying, 'Look, she hurt her ankle. Quite a limp. And her knee. But you can't see the knee.'

I almost said, 'Don't mention James!' Flora's previous day discussion of confidential facts about employees had made me wonder about her discretion, and I didn't want her to blurt out all the facts of my life. If the other employees wanted a soap opera, they could watch the telly. But I'd misjudged Flora yet again. Her crafty spot-lighting of my ankle and knee diverted people from asking the obvious: where I'd worked before. Instead they asked what had happened. One woman said, 'I hope the lorry got dented as well.' It was an old joke, but the laughter seemed to make me instantly one of the group.

The employees seemed to divide into two camps, the late middle-aged and downright elderly, and a smaller group of young employees. Chambers' desire to modernise must have come suddenly and recently.

The peek at the behind-the-scenes shop floor was fascinating. In films and on TV I'd seen how airlines and hotels and such had their own world, mostly unknown to the public. And Chambers' was a bit like that. Everyone moved quickly to their stations, the merchandising people donning badges. Greetings and quips were shouted across the large space, with lots of laughter. Even the moaning seemed to celebrate the fact that everyone knew everyone else and their little ways. Props were shifted, lights turned on, as if it were a stage onto which the public would soon be invited.

Maybe retail therapy means being on stage – the shop floor stage – becoming a temporary star and getting lots of attention. Even in places where staff tried to ignore customers, the places themselves had been designed for temptation. The punter was wanted, needed. Everything was geared to make you feel pampered: the smell of expensive fragrance, thick carpet, the well-dressed mannequins, and the more expensive items under glass. The magical spell was somewhat broken by a young woman with green highlights gulping her coffee and saying, 'Bloody hell, it's nearly time to let in the dawgs.'

Flora was introducing me to everyone along our route to the lift. The next woman, elegantly elderly, nodded towards green highlights and grinned. 'Seems like we've already got one dog amongst us.'

As we moved on, Flora said, 'She's the oldest on the ground floor and beats the socks off everyone else when it comes to sales.'

When we reached accounts, Flora introduced me to the manager, Mrs Brown. She struck me as the paradigm of a schoolteacher, friendly, warm and pleasant, but also stern and bossy. A kind heart cohabiting with a suspicious mind.

There were twelve people including myself in the department, a baker's dozen if you counted Mrs Brown. It looked like a group selected for a politically correct photograph. Two ethnic minorities, three candidates for a Save the Aged campaign, one punk with pink hair and a nose ring, one man, some tall, short, fat, skinny. The largest single group was composed of women about my age or younger who like myself probably wished they could have started on the executive floor.

The desks were arranged in rows and I was directed to the very back. Because of the filing cabinets, there were only two desks there. An elderly woman looked up and said, 'Please call me Melody.' Almost a stick figure in shape, topped off with a grey mass of ringlets, she patted her hair and touched the edge of her mouth, presumably to ensure no lipstick was smudged.

Mrs Brown had left me to 'settle in' and, with nothing actually to do, I turned to my neighbour. 'Well, tell me Melody, is it a good thing or a bad thing to be here on the back row?'

She had one of those smiles that wiped ten years off her as soon as her lips tilted. 'I suspect it's the bottom of the pecking order, Caron dear. But I like it. Out of sight, out of mind, you know. And it's a great advantage for Mrs Brown to forget all about us.'

I laughed but I think Melody was entirely serious. 'Don't you like the accounts department?'

She thought for a bit. 'I really don't know.' When I looked blank, she added, 'This isn't really accounts, dear. The real accounts are attached to individual departments. Import, export, forward planning, I really don't know exactly. I've never found numbers terribly exciting.'

Totally baffled, I said, 'Well, if this isn't accounts, what is it?'

'Well, it is accounts. I mean it's called that. And we sometimes input numbers and invoices and there are those things called spreadsheets.' She sniffed as if spreadsheets smelled exactly like skunks. Then she said proudly, 'I was once the star of the typing pool. Would you have guessed?'

'Well, yes, certainly. Actually, that would have been my first guess. But what do we do besides spread-sheets and the wicked numbers?' I could picture us sitting on the back row hemming garments sold in the shop.

'Oh, all sorts. Some of the older executives refuse to believe computers have taken over the world. And more power to them. So there is the odd letter to do. And because we do a variety of work in here, we are some-times lent out.'

'You mean like library books? We get borrowed? But we're not a temping agency. Are we?'

Melody smiled brightly. 'Temping agency is a good

description of our department. But only within the company, of course. And they cannot check us out for the merchandising floors.'

'So accounts at Chambers' is basically an admin department? A mixed bag?'

She smiled again and nodded. 'And speaking of bag, I'm so glad you aren't an old one. I do find elderly people tiring.'

Flora had said not much was expected of employees on their first day, but this was ridiculous. I checked all my empty drawers. I turned on my computer and tested that my telephone was working. My chair swivelled all the way around. Very exciting. I turned back to Melody, but she looked like she was sleeping.

She sort of coughed and sat bolt upright. 'Is it time for lunch?'

'I doubt it. Would you mind if I asked you some questions about Chambers', Melody? I mean you know all about it.'

I took her keeping her eyes open as an invitation to continue. 'I was wondering about the promotions policy. I mean, does it take very long to get a promotion?'

'Oh, I shouldn't worry about that, dear. We all get annual pay rises whether we get promoted or not. Would you believe I'm the highest paid non-executive in the company?'

'Easily. But I've not finished my first day. All things being equal, when is the earliest I could hope for promotion? I mean if I do a good job and get checked out often?'

'Assessments are every six months,' She looked me over carefully. 'In your case, I wouldn't be at all surprised if you moved up a row in accounts in January.'

'January? Nothing before then? And what about to another department?'

'Mr Chambers always says everything is possible. But in reality you'd need to find another empty chair. Where would you like to be promoted to, Caron?'

I was horrified to realise James was standing there. 'Oh, I can answer that for her, Melody. Caron has already laid a claim to my chair.'

Melody looked confused. 'Your chair? With you still sitting in it? Well, I suppose the top floor does have larger chairs. People often suggested that when I was in the typing pool, but it was always the men.'

I said, 'Melody, that's because women's chairs were always too small for company. Anyway, Mr Smith is joking.'

James said, 'James. And why do you think I'm joking?'

'Well, if you're not, do remember that there are two hundred and forty-two employees working in this building. And I'm two hundred and forty-one in seniority.'

'Are you leaving a space open for me?'

'Actually, I believe it's occupied already by the young man in his teens who goes about with the coffee and tea and pastry trolley. But my point is that if I'm at the bottom and you get to the top, we'll have the entire employee spectrum covered between us. That gives my job an unsuspected importance.'

'Absolutely.' Turning, he said, 'You see, Melody, with her sort of thinking she'll have my job in no time.' Turning back to me, he said, 'I wanted to welcome you on your first day, and also make sure your ankle and knee are all right.'

Melody, fully awake, said, 'I say. And what have you done to her ankle and knee, James? I was only making a little joke about sharing a chair.'

James' face turned slightly pink. 'Nothing, Melody, I can assure you.'

'Then how do you know about her knee? With what she's wearing, you'd need to take her clothes off to see her knee.'

I quickly said, 'I was wearing a skirt for my interview, Melody. Anybody could see my ankle and knee then.'

James looked relieved until I added, 'But then, Melody, I was out jogging and heard footsteps behind me. So I ran and ran, terrified. It was getting dark and I ran faster and faster. I thought it was someone big, a man – well maybe a big strong man like James here.'

Melody was wide-eyed, staring first at me and then at James.

I said, 'But it turned out only to be someone's pet.'

'And did it bite your ankle and knee?'

'No. It was a golden Labrador and it was trying to be friendly and leaped up and landed on top of me, causing me to fall against a tree. So really I was wounded by a tree.'

'Are you pulling my leg, Caron dear?'

I put on a mock serious look. 'No, definitely not, Melody. Not *your* leg.'

'Oh, good. Well, if you will excuse me, it's time for lunch. And good to see you, James. Do stop and visit us again some time. We're always here.'

When she was gone, James grinned and shook his head. 'I owe you, Caron.' He said it as if the pay-off would come after he'd had time to shop for fresh bullets. 'I was so busy with my own moans last night that I forgot about setting up a time to celebrate your new job. Are you free for lunch?'

I was imagining us walking into the canteen together,

nepotism gone nuclear. But James said, 'We could meet out front in ten minutes?' Smiling he added, 'If you prefer, we could meet by accident?'

I had to laugh. If there's anything I love, it's a man you don't have to explain everything to. The downside was someone who was able to read a mind like mine. Not that I had much to hide, but my thoughts weren't often overly reverent. 'I'll be there. But I can't walk very far.'

James was standing by the kerb and as soon as he saw me he flagged down a taxi. 'Faster than getting my car out,' he said. And once inside the cab he asked, 'Where would you like to eat?'

He went on to mention several new and very posh restaurants. Exactly the sort of places Bas would frequent. 'I only have an hour. So somewhere with fast service.' Desperately, I added, 'How about McDonalds?'

'You can't be serious, Caron. This is a celebration.'

'Oh, well, actually I like to go only to places I myself can afford. Which at the moment is well sort of limited to, well you know.'

'This is my treat, Caron. Besides I feel partially responsible for your falling yesterday. And you were so great listening to me grumble. And it was my idea so it's my treat.'

'Do you like Burger King any better than McDonalds?'

'Not really. Oh, has this got something to do with the reason you were running across the Heath?'

'That was exercise, James. I thought that was obvious. And eating burgers and fries is not exercise. No connection at all.' Thinking furiously, I added, 'What I'd really like is someplace where we won't see anyone we know so I won't need to keep explaining why I'm limping.'

Then I had a brainstorm. 'I know, James. We can get carryout sandwiches and eat in the taxi.'

He said patiently, 'Caron, this taxi is hardly a horse-drawn carriage in the park.'

'Use your imagination, James.' The taxi was stopped in traffic. We had only got to the end of the block. 'Goodness, it'll be time to return before we get anywhere. There, that deli. I'll have a tuna salad sandwich with a bag of crisps. And black coffee. And you get to decide where the taxi goes while we eat.'

The taxi driver had to move on when the light changed, so more of my lunch hour was used up before we returned to find James glowering on the pavement.

He had three bags of food and handed one to the driver. 'Regent's Park, thank you. We'll get out and you can wait with the meter going.'

There was no shortage of vacant park benches, but this was because the rain had returned. My hair thought it was a rose bush and began to grow. James fitted right into the scene, because he looked like a black cloud.

'Well,' I said, 'Isn't this lovely, James?' I quickly took a large bite of sandwich.

Then he began to laugh. 'It's certainly different. Definitely not the celebration I had in mind. So I'll take a rain check. And we can dine out another time. Fair enough?'

'Oh, absolutely.' As I opened my bag of crisps, I said, 'You know, James, you strike me as a bit shy.'

He brightened up, 'Thanks. I'm glad to hear that.'

'You, er, like being considered shy?'

'Oh, yes. When the alternative is being considered a cold bastard. I'm not very good at chatter.'

'You also don't seem the type to openly take out Chambers' employees. I mean, why me?'

He responded to this with a huge grin. 'It's different in your case, Caron. I met you before you began working for Chambers'. So I'm only taking out an old friend who happens to work at the same place.'

I laughed. 'James, that is feeble. You're skating such a thin line the ice will crack.'

He smiled. 'The truth is you're different. I realised that when you were talking to Flora about body language. So many women think of nothing but whether their thighs are fat and about clothes and makeup. But you don't mind? Being my friend?'

He looked worried and very serious. It didn't seem the time to mention that I'd spent an entire hour working out what to wear to work. 'Not at all, James. I really need a friend, too. A friend.'

'I assure you, Caron, that's all I had in mind.' He stopped and thought for a moment. 'I don't quite know how to put this. Well, I'm very good at my job. But the thing is you have people skills. And I was thinking . . .'

'James, what a lovely compliment. Thank you. But you haven't known me long. And not everyone would agree. But of course the more intelligent people would, certainly, I hope.'

James laughed. 'There. You've just done it. Turned a potentially embarrassing moment into fun.' He used his handkerchief to wipe rain from his face. 'I do realise one doesn't gain people skills by osmosis. But, well, I . . .'

James was so amazing. Here he was, clearly an ambitious man, wanting the top job at Chambers', yet honest enough to think he might need to improve, and trusting enough to mention it to me.

Bas had never once admitted any weakness. I of course wasn't particularly enamoured of weakness, but I valued honesty highly.

'You know, James, you're just fine the way you are. I should think people respect you enormously. And know you're honest, and do your job well. There's not much advantage in adding a shiny gloss to what is the real thing.'

He smiled. 'Thanks for saying that, Caron. But I find it easy to talk to you. For more than five minutes, I mean.' He turned to look at me for a few moments. 'And forgive me if I'm wrong, but I thought, after the Heath, that maybe you needed a friend too. I could practise being more sociable, and in your case, whatever.'

My first thought was to wonder about the live-in relationship he'd mentioned. Hadn't they talked, socialised? Well, hell, had Bas? Hadn't he been all business and bed? Maybe this wasn't about James wanting the top job, but about the reason his relationship failed.

James had given away so much it seemed churlish to continue denying I had any problems. And I really liked him, especially as a handsome sexy companion with no danger of involvement. A friendship with a bonus, as he could practise chatter and I'd have a bodyguard. I held out my hand to shake his. 'Friends it is then, James.'

We could see the driver hopping up and down and waving and pointing at his watch. As we got up, James said, 'And feel free to talk to me anytime, Caron. About whatever.'

I laughed and said teasingly, 'You'll know when my problem arrives, James. I'll want you to stand with one hand tucked menacingly into your jacket.'

He held my arm to take the strain off my ankle as we walked. 'I should be able to manage that, Caron, even with my modest social skills. What else?'

'Just don't be surprised if I introduce you as a Detective Chief Inspector.'

7

I got home that evening before Flora. For one thing, once you'd been at Chambers' for six months, you could work flexitime. And she was also putting in overtime helping to update the human resources computer data. I wanted to have a nice dinner ready for her, but I've almost turned being a terrible cook into an art form. I'd thought temporary poverty might be the spur to culinary skills, but it only determined how many frozen microwave meals I purchased.

I could already tell that Flora was used to taking the role of mother hen in her social dealings. So it was wonderful how her face lit up when she saw that someone else was wearing the chicken feathers. The opened bottle of wine and the steaming hot plates of lasagne looked delicious.

After we'd raised our glasses to survival of my first day of work, I said, 'Flora, do you mind if I bother you with another personal problem?' After my Mum's call the night before, she needed to be warned in case belligerent Bas arrived on her doorstep. I was half expecting that glazed look people put on when someone's about to describe their appendix operation, but Flora looked delighted. I wondered if she was considering me to be her personal letters to the editor column. Or more likely, letters of the lovelorn.

'It's about Bas, Flora. Mum said he's in London. And I thought you should know in case he comes snooping about.' I hadn't kept a photo, as it was hard enough forgetting him without it. But I described him.

'Caron, you know who he sounds like? That Jack Howard I mentioned before. Newly divorced, rumoured to sleep around? Tall, blond, good-looking, cool. You saw him on the day of your job interview. In the canteen, but he had his back to you. He was the one mimicking Mr Chambers' elbow.'

'Maybe you could point him out sometime, Flora. What I wanted especially to talk about is if there's any way Bas can trace me here. I mean with all the bills in your name and so far only my parents, their old neighbours, Chambers and you knowing where I live. I thought with your experience in personnel matters you might have ideas. So we can be prepared.'

Flora said, 'You don't think he would, I mean, attack you, do you? Blood and gore and murder?' Her eyes resembled two satellite saucers.

'I don't really know what he'd do, Flora. His nose could have been broken playing football. I mean not by a woman's stiletto heel.'

'Can you break a nose with that?'

'How would I know, Flora? Maybe it would only make a third nostril. And I've never actually seen him violent. Anyway, maybe he's only in London on business. He could have got a new account. More like Bas simply to want to mess up my new life. He wouldn't risk a lawsuit by ringing up Chambers' and giving a reference full of lies, but he could hint. I mean he could act all sorrowful and mention my mental state. What would Mrs Oakley do if he rang her?'

'Depends. If it was on a Friday, she'd probably just laugh. Unfortunately, most days it isn't Friday. Should we ring the police?'

'To say what? Tell me – how would you, knowing personnel records, go about tracing someone? Someone whose resumé was a bit dodgy?'

'We just wouldn't hire them. I probably know more from reading crime novels. Would Bas break the law?'

'Probably. Many men who've got rich quick at least bend the laws. And he's very rich. Still, London's too big to send random private eyes roaming the streets.'

'He'd have your USA social security number, but as you're using your UK one that wouldn't help. So I don't think he could easily trace you to Chambers'. The most obvious traces would be phone and e-mail or anyone you've given a change of address, like banks and such. Would he, like, steal your parents' phone bill? To see what numbers they've been ringing?'

'He wouldn't want to get caught, but yes, he'd not blink at having someone open my parents' post. And certainly my dad wouldn't notice if Bas spilled chocolate on it. I've had everything forwarded to my parents' address. But if he found out your phone number, could he get the operator to give him an address?'

'In crime novels, Caron, all the detectives could find that out. They all seem to have slept with a policeman or two, or they have a partner who works for the telephone company.'

'That's the kind of research Bas would love.'

Flora raised her eyebrows. 'If say he's been in London for three days, how many policewomen could he have met and slept with?'

I thought for a moment. 'They work shifts. And of course some would be married with kids and have no interest. Others might be suspicious. So maybe a dozen.'

'A dozen?'

'Maybe more. I mean he wouldn't approach them on the street and ask the time, Flora. He'd go into the station with some phoney question, get to talking, buy them a drink. He might even say I'm his ex-wife and amnesiac and he's got to find me quickly.'

'Right,' said Flora. 'Or he could say he suspects you're a serial killer. That would get their attention.'

'Yes, but it probably wouldn't get them into bed.'

'You know, Caron, in a book I think he would hire a private detective there who knew one here. The PI here would already have contacts. I don't want to discourage you, but with that scenario, it wouldn't take long for the UK PI to trace you.'

'How long?'

Flora thought deeply. 'In books? Maybe twenty minutes.'

'Shit! I mean thanks for your help, Flora, but the news is shit. At least forewarned is forearmed. So now I need a plan for when he finds me.'

'But if you don't, like, know what he's going to do, how can you have a plan? From what you've said, he could do anything, so you'd need a million plans.'

'The only thing is, Flora, having a million plans is like having no plans. But we need something concrete to do. For peace of mind.'

'We could have a drink.'

'I knew you'd think of something, Flora.'

We drank the whole bottle of wine, both of us tending to look often at the door. And several times Flora checked the windows 'in case it rained again', she said. I was glad the other housemate hadn't arrived yet, as it would be one more person to be nervous.

When I asked, Flora said, 'She's arriving tomorrow.'

We were in the kitchen putting chunks of cheese on crackers when the phone rang. 'Oh no,' I said.

'Relax, Caron. It'll just be Evelyn, about moving in tomorrow.'

Two seconds later Flora was back. 'It's a man. For you.'

'Shit, double shit!'

'Don't worry, Caron. In a book, it would be a double glazing salesman. A false alarm. Bas wouldn't possibly find out how to reach you on the same night we've been talking about him. It would take at least two more chapters.'

'Well, in case Bas doesn't know that, I want you to listen in. If it's him. So you can be a witness.'

As I picked up the phone, I expected Flora to huddle nearby, but she reached over and punched a conference call button. Only someone who worked in human resources would have a conference call button on a home phone. Well, she and my dad.

'Hello.'

'Hello, Caron honey. Bas here. I think you might have forgotten to leave me your forwarding address and phone number.' He words were as smooth as honey and potentially full of bee stings.

'So how did you get this number?'

He laughed. 'Just hypothetically speaking, someone could ring the phone company and complain about their bill. Say your mother's bill. And then go through the calls one by one to find out who your parents have been calling. You know the bureaucrats; it takes a long time hanging on waiting for them to get the information. And my time's pretty valuable.'

'What do you want, Bas?'

'Why, Caron honey, I want you. I told you before, I didn't want you to leave me.'

'I'm not coming back, Bas. You have a lot of nerve to think I would. And you don't really want me back. You just want the painting.'

He laughed. 'I want both of you back. In fact, if you come back, you can keep the Picasso.'

'Damn it, Bas, it's already mine! You bought it for me for my birthday last year. Only a sorry bastard would want a birthday present returned.'

'That little old painting's in the company name, honey.'

'Bas, you've cheated me out of my wages, out of my experience by not providing a reference, my morality by turning out to be married. You're not having me or the painting back. Just fuck off and don't ring me again. It's all over!'

'Wait, Caron! Don't hang up! It's not over. What's that saying, not until the fat lady sings? I told you not to be stupid. But did you listen?' He laughed again. 'Just believe me, honey, it's not over. And it's not going to be over until you pack up everything you took away, and I mean everything! Then get yourself the hell back over here.'

I was about to slam down the phone when Flora whispered, 'Ask him where he is and what he's going to do?'

'Where am I? Honey, I'm not far away from you this very minute. What I had in mind is that we could meet for dinner tomorrow night. We need to talk.'

'I do not want to talk to you, Bas! Have you got ice cream stuffed in your ears?'

He laughed. 'Dear Caron, always the wit. You asked what am I gonna do? I know positively, Caron, that you still love me. No one's ever left me before. You have to love me. But if you want games, we'll have games.'

'What kind of games, Bas?' I was trying to stop shouting. Flora was right, we needed as much information as we could get.

He laughed again. 'That's the game, Caron. For you to work it out. Be surprised.'

'Bas, surely you aren't physically threatening me?'

Another laugh. 'Now, Caron honey, you know me better than that. Would I touch you, harm you, lay a finger on you? I wouldn't dream of doing that ... myself. I mean not personally. OK? Know what I mean?'

'I know what you are, and that's a first-class bastard. But if you or anyone else touches me, Bas, you're dead meat. I mean it. Stay out of my life. Or I'll slap a court order on you so fast you'll think your balls have been in play at Wimbledon. Now fuck off!'

I slammed down the phone and shouted 'Shit!' Then I quickly punched in 1471 to find out where Bas rang from.

Flora was already reaching into her desk drawer for a pad. 'I bet the message says the caller withheld the number? Right?'

'Yeah. Anyway, he probably used his mobile so he could be anyplace. I know it'd be a bother for you, Flora, but do you think we should get the phone number changed?'

Flora thought for a minute. 'He'd probably just find out the new number. And maybe it's better to know what he's doing. I mean, each time he rings you might get a bit more information.'

She put pen to paper. 'I'm writing all this down and signing it, Caron. For evidence. Oh, this is so exciting!' Then she looked at me and added, 'Sorry, Caron. But you don't really think he'll hire a mugger, do you? Or someone who's been thrown out of the SAS? To, like, murder you?'

'I think Bas' flesh is composed of chicken shit. He's mostly bluff. What he really wants is to win, and having me dead wouldn't be much of a victory, would it?'

Flora said, 'Not if he couldn't tell everyone, no.' Then there was silence as she wrote everything down and I paced about with smoke coming out of my toes.

Flora stopped writing, looking puzzled. 'Caron, about his saying he wants back everything you took away? Did you take anything besides the Picasso?'

'Clothes. But I doubt Bas is taking up cross-dressing. A few books, my own CDs. I didn't even bring over my own CD player, as there wasn't room in my luggage.'

As Flora sealed the envelope, she said, 'Pity I don't have a recorder on the phone. But then when you came to stay, I'd no idea it would be so interesting. Evelyn's probably a bit boring, compared. She only does karate and dates men she meets through a dating agency.'

'Maybe she can teach us karate. And thanks, Flora. For being so brave and for being you. A lot of people would freak out, maybe throw me out. For being so much bother, I mean.'

'Oh, it's definitely no bother, Caron. But do you think you could help me shove some furniture across the doors? Just for tonight?'

After that, I went to the kitchen to make coffee. When I returned I found Flora standing in my bedroom doorway. 'I can't believe I have a genuine Picasso hanging here in my house. That's glamour, Caron.'

I handed her a cup of coffee with two of her biscuits

on the saucer. 'You don't happen to know a painter, do you?'

'Fine arts, like Picasso? I mean not for walls? Actually, I do. It's Mervin Thomas. You know Mervin, in the accounts section.'

'Medium height, slim, black hair worn in a pigtail? More precisely, the only man?'

'Yes. Mervin's lovely.' Flora was actually blushing. 'I understand he's very talented. Did you have in mind returning the Picasso and buying another painting for your wall?'

'How well do you know Mervin, Flora? Because what I have in mind is a copy.'

'Well, he may be awfully good, but I'm not sure he's as good as Picasso.'

'It doesn't matter. I suspect Bas' first move will be to steal the painting back. He wouldn't do that himself, and a hired burglar would only have a photo to go by. I doubt if even Bas could interest the curator of the Tate Gallery in a life of crime.'

'But, Caron, what good will that do? When Bas sees it he'll know the difference, won't he?'

'Probably not, but his art adviser will. The thing is, if Bas steals it or has it stolen, we'll have proof. Of the theft. And then I'll have some leverage to back him off. Keep him away from me.'

'You mean we'll set up video cameras, then tail the crook through the back streets of London until he leads us to Bas? Then confront him? And the police can rush in?'

I had to laugh. 'Flora, I haven't the money to do all that, and it probably only works in books. And we couldn't exactly tell the police that we think someone's going to steal a fake Picasso, but we don't know who or when. Half the people living in Hampstead would have police permanently guarding their homes if that were possible.'

When we were both sitting at the kitchen table, I asked Flora, 'Do you think that if I just gave Bas the picture he would go away and leave me alone?'

'Gosh, that would make a terrible plot. But no, I don't think it would make any difference. He sounded on the phone like he was enjoying himself, hoping to scare you. In a book, he would keep at it until you fell on your knees and begged him to take you back. Then in the last chapter he would scorn you and run away with a scantily dressed redhead.'

'He can forget the on the knees bit. And surely even in books, Flora, the heroine wouldn't go back to such a rotter? Who'd been giving her grief throughout the book?'

'You're forgetting all those chapters in between. First he'd be horrid. Then he'd repent, ask for forgiveness. Heroines are more susceptible to that than to the measles.' She stopped to consider. 'I can't recall a single heroine who had the measles. Then he'd try to make her jealous. Well, I don't know exactly, Caron. I don't write the books. I only read them.'

'You should have a go, Flora. You've pretty much summed up Bas in a nutshell. Of course, he might just have read the same books. It's too far-fetched to think he's slept with all the female crime writers.'

'Thanks, Caron. But I must warn you. Sometimes the hero accidentally murders the heroine. That wouldn't of course do for Mills and Boon. But crime novels use that sort of situation. The thing is, the heroine needs to die early so the plot can develop.'

'Well, I'd rather develop my own plot.' But somewhat

nervously I asked, 'Just in general, Flora, what chapter would we be in right now? Maybe chapter seventeen, past the danger?'

'Oh, no, Caron. We're only in about chapter two. Of a long book.'

'That's a book with the heroine already dead?' I looked closely at Flora to see if she were joking. She wasn't. I began to wonder if I'd have been better off discussing the problem with Mrs Stone.

I could tell the heroine would not only be dead but also dismembered with a chainsaw because, rather than answer, Flora seemed to develop an instant thirst. She rapidly got up and grabbed the coffee pot. 'More coffee, Caron?'

Dour as much of it was, the talk of books seemed to lift my spirits. I remembered reading an article that suggested imagining your problem and shrinking it. For example, if your male boss was giving you grief, you imagined him, then reduced him in your mind to the size of a peanut or marble. Well, two marbles. And Flora's references to books might be the literary equivalent, by turning Bas into a stock character on a page. You could later rip him from the book and burn up the page, or use him to wrap fish and chips.

'About that coffee, Flora. Better add some brandy.'

'You want the brandy actually in the coffee?'

'Well, it'd be too cruel for the heroine to die with only coffee. Think of the autopsy.'

8

It was a bit of a let-down the following morning to find that Bas and a team of commandos hadn't tried to breach the fortress. That would have cleared at least one door of the heavy furniture I needed to drag across the room back to its regular place. I'd woken up with my ankle better, but it was getting worse by the minute. I could almost hear it whispering, 'You're going to pay for this.' As I put the empty wine bottle in the recycle bin, I decided our wine-induced efforts at defence had really only helped to increase the drama. What was needed was something to decapitate the problem.

Wondering if that technique of imaging works, where you imagine what you want, I closed my eyes. I thought of flowers, gorgeous fresh flowers, the fragrant scent pervading the air, soft music playing in the background. With Bas lying there with his cold feet sticking out of a plastic body bag. Well, I don't always wake up very cheerful, or even very charitable.

It was just so awful thinking that any man on the street could be on Bas' payroll and stalking me. If he came himself, he'd probably avoid the obvious and maybe try to abseil from the roof. He hadn't tried that before, but even I could manage on Flora's house. Far better if he tried that bungee jumping, using a rope intended for the Grand Canyon. Unfortunately it'd be far more like Bas to work in the background and hire a flunky to be up front and get caught.

As I made coffee and spread toast with marmalade, I wondered if he were still in London. Because Bas' business interests were so numerous and widespread, he could run them from anywhere so he didn't actually need to be at his New York office much of the time. It would just be too awful if he'd flown to Singapore or Rome for a meeting while I was watching my backside in London.

Flora hadn't surfaced yet, so I took in a cup of coffee and put it on her bedside table. I didn't swish the curtains open like they do in films. Each time I see that, I half expect the sleepy character to rise up and strangle the maid.

I thought about how I'd jogged every morning in New York, but now I'd need to wait for my ankle to behave. I'd also waited until I went to that spa after I came to London. Then I waited until I found my own accommodation, and then until I got a job. I'd be in there with a chance to win a gold at the Anti-Olympics.

I was missing the frantic energy of New York. It charges your batteries just by being there. Everyone in New York seemed to rush about hell for leather. There was this chronic feeling that if you didn't hurry, everyone would get ahead of you. And they did – on the job front, the jogging path, clogging the roads, filling the sidewalks.

People in London seem to get just as much done, so I thought the difference might be due to those taller New York buildings. London has the same crowds and pavements, but you see more sky. So the frantic feeling of being closed in is reduced. You know unseen people in London surround you, but it doesn't feel like they're all breathing down your neck. The thing about anxiety is it's a mindset, more about psychological space and mental freedom than actual muggers creeping up behind. When there's a real grizzly bear chewing on your arm, you don't have time to be anxious.

While I was thinking these thoughts, Flora got up and beat me to the bathtub. That's the downside of philosophy. While it massages your brain cells, you forget about time. Probably all the amateur philosophers in Britain were now brushing their teeth at the kitchen sink.

As I tried to unsnarl my hair, I shouted through the bathroom door, 'Flora, you never said how well you know Mervin Thomas. You know, the painter in the accounts department.'

Flora shouted back, 'Thirty-three, university degree in fine art from Reading. Salary enhancements every six months. Five foot nine inches, brown eyes, dark brown hair. Changed his surname by deed poll to that of the Welsh poet. Except now he's into painting. He does poetry readings sometimes, but mostly he paints.'

'That'd be fine for his tombstone, Flora. But I need to know if you trust him. So I'll know how much to say about copying the painting.'

There was a long silence, which turned out to be equal to the total time she'd ever spent talking to Mervin.

'Well, he's always surrounded by girls, Caron.'

'Of course he is. Everyone else in accounts is a girl. When you said hello those three times, what happened?'

'He said hello once, how are you once, and repeated hello the third time.'

'Oh, great, Flora. So we can trust him with our lives, is that it?'

'He really is wonderful, Caron. Haven't you noticed?'

'I haven't actually met him.' This was a bit warbled as I was pulling a T-shirt over my head. 'He's on the front row next to Mrs Brown. And Melody suggested we avoid her.'

Flora laughed. 'Old Melody isn't as dozy as she acts. She notices everything and has hotlines into all the Chambers' gossip.'

'Great. Then maybe I should ask her about Mervin?'

Another long silence. Long enough for me to put on my trousers and shoes. 'Flora, do you by any chance fancy Mervin?' Another long silence. Forgetting the hot water, or lack of same, I shouted, 'What about if I arrange for the three of us to have lunch to discuss the copy? Kill two birds with one Picasso.'

The bathroom door opened abruptly to reveal Flora wrapped in a towel, with another around her head. Her eyes were blinking rapidly. 'I don't want to appear forward. Do you think . . .'

'Flora, if I ask him, I'll be the forward one.' I grinned and pulled a face. 'Well, hell, Flora, whoever would have thought? I mean you and Mervin? That's terrific!'

Her face went pale and she looked so serious. 'Do you really think . . . ?'

'Leave it to me, Flora.' My ego plummeted when she seemed to be frowning. I quickly added, 'Don't worry. It won't turn out to be you out of a job, with Mervin trying to get revenge and breaking down the door. Really. I'm sure I can arrange your life better than I've done mine. More objective, you know.'

Flora smiled brightly. 'It would be the happiest day of my life if Mervin tried to break down my door.' She dashed into her room to dress and shouted over her shoulder, 'But I've got a meeting over the lunch hour and can't eat until late. So not today.'

'Perfect, Flora. Gives me time to do a bit of ground-work.' I started humming 'Here Comes the Bride' until Flora opened the door and threw her damp towels at me.

When I even thought about taking another taxi to work, I could almost feel my chequebook trying to climb out of my handbag and swat me across the jaw. Flora preferred the bus to the tube. Like the tube, the bus required one change but it was far easier on my ankle. The Underground seems to have a keep-fit conspiracy that it feeds by keeping some of the escalators out of action at all times. And they probably have a psychic on the payroll, as they seem to know in advance my personal route.

As we made our way through Chambers' to the lift, green highlights repeated her joke about letting in the dawgs, as did the elderly top saleswoman. It made me feel like I belonged without encouraging much thought as to what I belonged to.

I arrived in accounts a few minutes before the nine o'clock sit-down, thinking to introduce myself to Mervin. But Flora was right, he was surrounded by women. Not as I'd thought in the sense of wallpaper but rather like butterflies. He was practically holding court, a tight knit group of women circling him, listening avidly, laughing. I sincerely hoped I hadn't misled Flora about her chances.

Melody was already in her chair, with that fierce look of defending it from ambush. Flora had said that Melody had been the Chambers couple's first employee, and that her job was probably safe until he retired. Or until the end of the world, I thought, as she had the same sort of tenacity as James' housekeeper. With his head start, my mind boggled at the thought of a geriatric Bas. That reminded me of the painting, so I turned to Melody.

Motioning towards Mervin, I said, 'Well, Melody, what do you think of our only man, Mervin?' I am so subtle.

She put on her glasses and peered. 'There's more to him than meets the eye.'

That didn't seem likely as his all black clothes were on the snug side. 'Like what, Melody?'

'I shouldn't think he's very similar to James Smith, that nice young man who called on us yesterday. And certainly not like Mr Chambers. He's the one to die for. It keeps me awake at work, just hoping he'll stop by. Have you met him, dear?'

'Not yet. But what were you saying about Mervin?'

'He's very intelligent, not at all flashy and arty as he tries to appear. And I understand he has talent. But he doesn't take his job here the least bit seriously.'

I suppressed a smile, or I hope I did. 'Not like us, then?'

'Definitely not. You have ambition, Caron, a wonderful thing for a woman. And I see no reason why in thirty or so years you shouldn't have James' chair, so long as he's not still sitting in it. And I'm already a great success.'

I was speechless, imagining thirty years in accounts, so she carried on. 'Success depends entirely on one's goals, dear. I never wanted to head up the company. I wanted to be loyal and supportive. And I'm still here doing just that. You wouldn't believe the number of employees who have come and gone, some permanently gone to the great Chambers' in the sky, and I'm still here.'

I smiled. You couldn't help but like Melody. And

her definition of success was spot on. Of course that philosophy led directly to those with no ambition at all having immediate success. Or the less ambition, the more success. It wasn't particularly helpful for those who loved unlimited hot water.

'Melody, do you happen to know if one of those women Mervin's talking to is his girlfriend?'

She put her glasses back on and looked at me. 'Why? Are you interested?'

I'd already cottoned on to her wearing her specs to think rather than to see. Most of her work she did without the glasses, but the minute she became interested in something, on they went. Perhaps in some weird way the ear stems nudged her brain and triggered her memory.

'What? Oh, no. Not me, not personally. Just curious.'

'Good. Well, I don't think so. He probably enjoys the attention, but basically he just humours them. My best guess is that he plays the part of the struggling artist at work, then goes home to a semi in the suburbs and watches the telly. Of course, if he sticks it out here like me, he can then afford discos and nightclubs.'

I was trying to prevent my eyebrows from tangling in my hair. I would have loved to request her potted history of me, but it didn't seem wise without a couple of stiff whiskies under my belt. Before I could ask Melody which clubs she frequented, Mrs Brown arrived with some work. She gave me a stack of audiotapes of letters to type and handed Melody a mountain of spreadsheets. It left both of us feeling mutinous.

'At times like this, I wonder if there's a bounty on my head, payable to whoever can secure my retirement.'

I laughed. 'Two bounties, Melody. Do you think we

could switch? You the letters and me the spreadsheets?'

'My dear! Perhaps you'll get to the top in only twenty years. Oh, dear me yes. But she'll see us.'

'We both dump the stuff on the floor, Melody, then pick up the other stack. Do you think there's something on our computers that tells her which machine did the work? If so, I could probably fix it.'

'Mrs Brown wouldn't know about it. She delegates everything but breathing. Still, she probably wouldn't mind if it speeds up our work rate.'

'It'll do that,' I said. Well, we were going from nothing to something so the increase would be difficult to avoid.

The coffee wagon arrived in accounts each day at eleven. Apparently Mrs Brown went to a regular meeting and the moment she was gone everyone got up and milled about, chatting and laughing. Again, Mervin was surrounded. Feeling like an adolescent groupie, I edged my way through his fan club and introduced myself.

Leaning close and lowering my voice, I said, 'I was thinking of commissioning a painting, Mervin.'

He smiled, took my arm and angled me towards the coffee trolley and away from the crowd. 'Thanks for the rescue, Caron. Being the token man is exhausting. I think they just use me to practise their chat-up lines.'

I laughed. 'I had a job once where I was the only woman, but it didn't seem like it was chat they wanted to practise. Anyway, before Mrs Brown returns, is your style anything like Picasso's?'

Mervin had a lovely smile. And he seemed far nicer on a one to one than as king of accounts. Lowering his voice, he said, 'At the moment I'm doing anything likely to sell. You know, a bit of sheep fur floating in a pool of pee, balanced by the school of chocolate box saccharin.'

He reached into his pocket with difficulty, while trying to ensure his trousers didn't slip down they were so tight. When he pulled out a slip of paper, he said, 'I've got my first exhibition coming up. It'd be brill if you could come to the private view. And you could get a line on my range.'

Quickly I said, 'Can you spare two tickets?'

While I checked the date on the invitation, he reached into his trousers again, then gave them a sharp upward tug. I'm sure I heard fabric split. 'Mervin, I'm going to need a painting copied before your show. As in urgent. Can you do Picasso?'

'I'm willing to try anything except going to jail. I mean it's perfectly legal to copy a painting, even exact copies if you're capable, so long as you don't try to, I think it's called, "pass it off".'

'I don't plan to sell it or anything illegal. I promise. Would it take long, do you think?'

'Depends. For a genuine fake, you know, one that'll fool the punters, well, maybe forever.'

'Nothing like that, Mervin. You could do a computer scan, print it out and slap some paint on top. Just a little something to hang in my bedroom. Think of it as a stage prop.'

I could see Mrs Brown coming down the corridor. 'It's Picasso's *Green Shoelace*. You know the one? Where there's one chartreuse eye in the toe of the shoe and a hot pink eye looking the other way from the heel? The orange shoe shaped rather like an opera singer's body when she's in her death throes and trying to make it until the aria's finished?'

Mervin laughed. 'That's not exactly the way the art books describe it, but yeah I know it.'

'Would a copy be terribly expensive?'

'Well, not for a colleague. And not if I just splash a bit of paint. I mean that's not art, is it? Tell you what. I can get the exact measurements and a photo off the web. I'll do a mock-up and if that's good enough, you can buy me a drink.'

'Mervin, these woman aren't just practising. They love you because you're wonderful.'

'Yeah, well. Not one's ever mentioned painting, know what I mean?'

Remembering Flora, I said, 'Maybe we can meet up in the canteen for lunch sometime?'

He smiled over my shoulder and said, 'Did you enjoy your coffee break, Mrs Brown?'

Back at my desk, I rang Flora. 'Surprise, surprise.'

'Well,' she said, 'What is it?'

'That's what it is. I have a lovely surprise for you. See you out front after work. Do I hear someone laughing?'

'Mrs Oakley. I told you she does that on Fridays.'

'But who's she laughing with?'

'She's in her office alone. About the surprise, could I have three guesses? So I'll have something to think about during my meeting? And don't ring off until you tell me if you met Mervin.'

'Later, Flora.' I quickly added, 'And thanks for sorting out those personnel records for me.' I smiled at Mrs Brown just as nicely as Mervin had.

I became so engrossed in the spreadsheets I almost missed lunch. The thing about numbers is you put them on a page and they stay there. And you know what they're going to do next. You can shrink them, increase them, or get rid of them. They can be as absorbing as crossword puzzles. It's of course not the same as work-ing with your own numbers, say with your bank balance. And I was already getting the impression that poor Chambers was sort of like a grandfather to my own bank account. Everything's relative, and while my account was sliding off a sand dune, Chambers' was nosediving off the Matterhorn. Maybe James should forget about people skills and set to work crunching numbers with a sledgehammer.

I looked up and realised James was standing there and everyone else had gone to lunch. Amazing. I'd thought the only way to conjure up James was to men-tion getting a promotion.

'How's the ankle, Caron?'

'Much better, James, thanks. I've really been missing my daily jogging.'

'Terrific. Maybe we can jog together? On the Heath. I try to get in five or more miles each day.'

Shit. 'Well, I don't want to rush things. I'll just carry on waiting, you know, for things.' I took a deep breath. 'Well, if it's not one thing, it's another. That I'm waiting on, I mean.'

'Yes. Well, then perhaps we could walk. Or we could sit on a park bench and watch others walk, if you prefer.'

Goodness, his wit was so dry I was surprised he wasn't on intravenous cough syrup. 'I looked for you in the canteen, Caron. To check on your ankle. Better not leave lunch too late, or they'll close.' He glanced at his watch. 'I'm due at a meeting. Oh, and Mrs Stone's been asking after your health.'

'Not my death?'

We laughed as I quickly put away my work and then walked with him to the corridor. As he turned in the other direction, he said, 'Perhaps we can meet up this weekend?'

'Great,' I called over my shoulder, rushing as I remembered the canteen lunch was cheap, and thinking how much my bank manager would like for me to eat there.

Melody was so pleased at our swap of work that she returned from lunch with a couple of Harrods chocolates for me. 'You're the first ever person to sit beside me who likes those wicked spreadsheets, Caron.'

After another hour, I was more intrigued than ever. If this was the sort of stuff they delegated to the internal temping agency, the top floor and real accountants must be working out estimates for Saint Peter for his Entry Gate. I skipped ahead and came to a sheet marked confidential. Either to keep its confidentiality a secret or by error, it was on the very bottom. I stopped working and looked at Melody who was happily humming as she typed letters so fast she outpaced a machine gun.

'Melody, do you think these spreadsheets might have been meant especially for you?'

'Yes, dear. I told you already someone has it in for me.'

And then I twigged. Either they were sent to Melody because of her long-standing loyalty or because she wouldn't recognise their significance. Possibly both. 'Melody,' I whispered leaning towards her, 'I think I ought to tell you these papers are extremely confidential.'

'I know, dear, so please don't mention them to anyone. And don't even think of giving them back to me.'

'Do you know which office they come from?'

'From the little code at the top I know they end up with Mr Chambers himself. But they couldn't possibly come from him, as he doesn't wish me to retire.'

When we'd both finished, I must admit with Melody winning hands down on speed, I took the lot up to Mrs Brown. She raised her eyebrows and looked at her watch. 'Impressive, Caron. You must be providing a catalyst for Melody.'

'Thank you, but it's really the other way around. She's really lovely.'

'Well then, as you've got quarter of an hour before leaving, why don't you take her a cup of coffee? And one for yourself. The machine's in the corridor and I take milk and one sugar.'

When I met Flora after work, I waved the invitations and said, 'Ta-da!'

She reached for them and said, 'Gosh! These are tickets to Mervin's private viewing! Kathy in the office next to mine has one. She showed it to me. Oh, my God, I think I'm going to faint. You've actually talked to Mervin.'

'I did say I would.'

'Yes, but so fast. I thought like maybe next month. Oh, I can hardly stand the excitement.' She clasped the ticket to her chest. 'This is like Christmas coming early. Pickled Onion here we come!'

'Is Pickled Onion sort of cockney for your true love for Mervin? Or what?'

'It's the pub around the corner. Mervin goes there two days a week. But not Mondays. So we could, like, go after work next week for practice. I can hardly wait to really talk to him. I mean, get to know him better before the exhibition. You will come with me?'

'I suppose a practice run in the pub would be OK. You have been to a pub before?'

The bus arrived and as we climbed on, she turned

and said, 'Of course I have. Well, not often because I don't like to go alone. Anyway, you're a single girl, too. Maybe you'll meet someone. The pub's popular with singles and especially with the Chambers' Emporium crowd.'

The bus was too crowded for us to sit together, so Flora looked at her private view ticket and sighed. And I looked out the window to see if any strange men were chasing the bus.

When we got home, before Flora had even got the key into the lock, I heard music. We hadn't left the TV or radio on, so someone was definitely inside. But before my blood pressure could cross the Alps, Flora said, 'Sounds like Evelyn has arrived.'

Evelyn had bright red, close-cropped hair, a beautiful face and a wide smile. But that wasn't what you noticed first. Her most distinctive characteristic was her size. She looked like a long slimline sofa had been set upright and turned sideways. I mean she wasn't fat, more well proportioned, but solid. A walking, talking Amazon. She and Flora and I looked like those graduated paper doll type figures they have in catalogues with the words 'choose your correct size'. If Bas should suddenly appear, she would definitely get the job of opening the door.

She was off the sofa in a flash, and brandishing two open beers she kicked straight out and sent a small block of wood flying across the room. At the same time she boomed out, 'Eeeeugghh!'

Flora said, 'Careful, Evelyn. If you'd hit the table, you might have broken it.'

'Flora, if I'd kicked the table it would now be out on the front pavement. And it would be sliced in two parts. You two ever think of taking up karate?'

She handed us each a beer, which was kind and generous but I don't much like beer. I glanced down at the table and decided maybe I could cultivate a taste.

She and Flora of course knew about each other due to Flora's auditions for the rooms. So Evelyn and I spent a few minutes swapping personal info. She was a real temp, meaning not the Chambers' variety, and had spent the day dressed in a milkmaid costume handing out free samples of cheese in a supermarket.

'Perks of the job, ladies. Tonight, let them eat cheese!'

Flora said we could use what was in the fridge to make up a meal to go with it.

'Not necessary. There were forty-two varieties and the shop manager gave me some free packets of biscuits. And there's cherry tomatoes and pickled beetroot. I'm telling you, it's all in hand.'

'There's one thing I ought to mention, Evelyn. There's this ex-boyfriend of mine who might come around. Well, might try to break in, who knows what. So be on guard. Or he could send someone, maybe a fake meter reader or census taker. So do keep an eye out for any strange men.'

'All men are a little bit strange. What's this bloke look like?'

Flora described him, making him sound like the hero of a romance, which sort of counteracted my attempts at making him resemble the devil. 'Where is he? I'd love to meet him. I mean since you don't want him anymore.'

'Evelyn, he's a real bastard. And he's got a wife and will soon have a fourth kid. You don't want to know.'

She laughed. 'Oh, I can handle him. I can see there's a lot I can teach you two. This bloke, he'd be free, no fee to the dating agency. And I suspect lots of those blokes aren't bachelor of the month either.' She swigged some beer. 'I'm not looking for a husband, just an evening out. Some fun. And I can help. He sounds like a high roller, so I'll keep an eye out in the posh hotel bars.'

Flora had her wide-eyed look. 'Do the dating agency men take you there? I thought it was just coffee shops or a pub.'

'Not if they want me to finish the first drink, it isn't.'

Evelyn said she was hungry and went to the kitchen for the cheese. Flora and I looked at each other, both trying to take in our new Amazon friend. To be honest we were just a tiny bit overwhelmed. Then we heard a shriek. By the time we got to the kitchen, our heroine was sitting on the table with her feet kicking in the air saying, 'A mouse. Bugger it all, I saw a fucking mouse!'

Flora was highly incensed. 'Calm down, Evelyn. I do not have mice in my house.' She had her hands on her hips as if daring Evelyn to mention mice again.

'Yes, you do,' Evelyn shrieked. Once onto a shriek, she stayed there. 'I saw it. It's gone under the cooker. What happens when it comes out?'

I'm not terribly patient with hysterics. 'Maybe, Evelyn, you could give it a karate chop.'

Flora smiled, and Evelyn, reminded of her courage, shut up. But she wouldn't get off the table. 'It was probably just a large spider, Evelyn,' I said.

'*Bugger it.* Spiders are second only to mice in scare factor.'

'Well,' I said, 'what aren't you afraid of? It can be that. You know, under the cooker.'

When she didn't answer, Flora said, 'Honestly, Evelyn, you can't be frightened of everything.'

Evelyn said hesitantly, 'Well, on the whole I prefer living things if they only have two legs.'

Flora said, 'Well, we've all worked hard all day and we're hungry. So you've got to get off the table, and you're too big for Caron and me to carry.'

I tapped my foot gently against the cooker. 'I'm an expert, Evelyn, and if anything were under the cooker it would at least peek out.' That seemed to reassure her. And as she stepped onto the floor and sprinted back to the front room, Flora and I looked at each other shaking our heads.

Not one to frown on opportunity, I called out, 'And one more thing, Evelyn. I wouldn't spend too much time in the bath. Spiders absolutely adore bath-tubs.'

'I'm sorry, Caron. I should have asked about mice and spiders at her interview.'

'Nonsense. You couldn't have known. Anyway, Evelyn's OK. It must be hard for her arriving after we've already become friends. She was just trying to impress us.'

'With her phobias? She probably doesn't even belong to a dating agency, and probably doesn't know karate either.'

'Well, I suggest we don't test her karate just yet. And let's give her a chance. As you said before, she could turn out to be interesting.'

When we took Evelyn a plate of food and settled ourselves onto the sofa with our meal, she looked full of remorse and mumbled sorry. But she took one look at her plate and set it as far away from herself as she could on the coffee table.

'What's wrong now?' asked Flora.

'You've arranged those slices of red peppers in the

middle of the salad to look like a spider. To get back at me.'

'Damn it, Evelyn, no she hasn't! She's done it specially to make your plate beautiful. So eat it. Every damn bite.'

She immediately obeyed, making me wonder if her aversion to mice was caused by her own temperament being so closely related to one.

Later we watched a video we'd all seen three times already. But it was fun and cosy. It did show the stereotypes are all wrong. People tend to think that once you're a couple you settle into a domestic life, whereas Bas and I were out nearly every night, although much of that was business entertaining. As for singles swinging away the weekend, you had only to look at the three of us to realise that overwork and undermoney wasn't always enough to get the swing to swing.

While I was thinking this, the phone rang. Flora didn't seem too happy when Evelyn beat her to it. 'It's for you, Caron.' Before Flora and I could even think of moving all the furniture, she added, 'It's only a woman.'

It was my parents' old neighbour. 'Just a quick word, Caron. There's been a man asking around about you. A few days ago. He hasn't been to us, but apparently he says he's an old chum looking you up. The thing is, he doesn't sound your sort. Wrong age for your childhood, and terribly scruffy so I'm told. Just thought you'd like to know.'

After some general chat, she rang off and I told the others. 'What we need to be on the lookout for is a middle-aged man, brown hair, no distinguishing marks.'

'That could be anyone, Caron,' said Evelyn. 'Anyway, he sounds boring. I'll watch out for your good-looking wealthy blond ex. And you two can watch for the other bloke.'

'Look, Evelyn,' I said huffily, 'I'm not asking you to sleep with him, marry him, or bury him hoping he'll grow into a tulip. All I'm asking is that you warn me if you see any strangers about, OK?'

Flora said, 'Honestly, Evelyn! You and me and Caron are living together, sharing the house. If you don't co-operate and act more friendly, I'm going to buy some spider food and encourage them.'

'Yeah, Evelyn, and I'm going to buy you a pet mouse.'

9

I did my usual wake-up with the birds the next day, but when I remembered it was Saturday, I made a cup of coffee and took it back to bed. The house was quiet, and the next thing I knew I was waking up again at ten o'clock. I could hear Flora and Evelyn in the kitchen. Attracted by the smell of coffee and bacon, I wandered in with my empty cup for a refill. I was surprised to see champion cook Flora sitting at the table while Evelyn bustled about by the cooker, along the counter and back, like a cookery video on fast forward.

Evelyn turned and said, 'Good morning, Caron. I don't know exactly what I did to upset you two last night, but I'm going to make it up to you. Harmony in the home, that's my new motto.'

I sat across from Flora who said, 'Evelyn's cooking us breakfast.'

Flora tried to smile but it had the conviction of a month-old lettuce. I'd already gathered that while Flora accepted that our rent money included kitchen privileges, our actually using it was tantamount to borrowing her toothbrush. That suited me, as my idea of the perfect kitchen is a red phone box with a working phone and a long list of catering company numbers.

But even a lousy cook can recognise the smell of burning and that having to peer through clouds of smoke is not a good sign. My eyes began to water, maybe thinking they'd need to put out a fire. I blinked a couple of times and said, 'Morning, Flora.'

Eventually Evelyn whisked plates onto the table. At first I thought it was a joke, or more precisely an act of revenge. The bacon, mushrooms, and tomatoes were all nearly black, while the fried eggs had white rims with edges so stiff they could have been used as frisbees. The coffee was fine, but probably Flora had beaten Evelyn to the pot.

Before we could say anything, Evelyn sat down and began tucking in ravenously. 'Oh, this is delicious. I was starving.' She handed around a plate of burnt toast and said, 'Why aren't you two eating?'

I tried to move the egg around the plate, but it seemed to have grown a root. 'This was really nice of you, Evelyn, but I, er, don't usually eat breakfast. Just coffee. But this looks delicious.'

With great difficulty, Flora said, 'Yes, it does.' She was scraping burnt bits off the toast which meant that when she finished the slice was as thin as a wedding veil. But definitely not the same colour.

'Well,' I said, 'now that we're all together, maybe we should discuss house rules. I'm willing to help with the shopping and stuff if someone else will do the cooking. Or I'm quite happy not to eat. And I was thinking . . .'

'I'll do the cooking,' said Evelyn.

'Yes, well, I was thinking maybe the owner of the house should have first choice. Flora? I know it's a lot to ask, but you're a very good cook.'

Evelyn reached across for my plate. 'If you're really not going to eat it, well it's a shame to waste it.' As she scraped my food onto her plate, she said, 'And I'm surely the best cook. You wouldn't believe how much practice it took for me to get this good.'

'I believe it, Evelyn,' I said.

'Me, too,' said Flora, shoving her plate across the table. 'Sorry, Evelyn, but I think I've got a bit of a stomach bug.'

'Bloody hell, don't mention bugs!' As she scraped more food onto her plate, she said, 'Well, you two don't like my cooking, is that it?'

Flora said weakly, 'Your cooking's fine.'

'No, it isn't,' I heard myself saying. 'Someone's got to tell you, Evelyn. This is the worst breakfast I've ever seen in my whole life.'

Evelyn slammed her mug onto the table. 'And I suppose you cook cuisine bluevell?'

'It's nouvelle, and I'm a horrible cook. But I know better than to cook a meal this complicated. I would have cooked one thing at a time, and after we'd eaten that, cooked the next thing. Well, actually for breakfast I would have done peanut butter sandwiches.'

Flora said, 'Caron, Evelyn's uh, you know, made an effort and she's, well, she's trying.'

'Flora's right, Caron. You're a bitch.'

'No, I'm not. Since we're living together, I just thought we needed to be honest and upfront. Before you kill us all off.' I could tell my spiel wasn't going down very well, so I tried another tack. 'Look, Evelyn, I'm just trying to help. If you kill Flora and me, you'll go to jail. To protect you, I nominate Flora as chief chef, commander of the kitchen. Let's vote on it.' I held my hand high.

Flora sort of twisted hers, not knowing what to do. But Evelyn held her hand up. 'I vote for Flora, too.' Then tears washed over her face and she spoke jerkily, in hysterical soundbites. 'I'm a failure. I know it. Thank you for your honesty, Caron. And now I've eaten a load of what you think is rubbish. I'm going to die. A real friend would have told me before I ate it.'

'Evelyn,' I said, 'You're not going to die. Well, you might get indigestion or maybe stomach ache. And the calorie and cholesterol levels were quite high. It was only one meal. Well, three meals.' I didn't even like conversation at breakfast, let alone melodrama. The reason Verdi's operas aren't staged as breakfast shows is the audience would jump on stage to help with the murders.

Flora was first to the paper towels, and as we patted Evelyn on the shoulder she drowned the entire roll. When her tear ducts reached drought level, she said, 'I really wanted to be a good cook. And the breakfast tasted all right to me. Don't you think with more practice?'

I wasn't diving headfirst into shit again, so I smiled sweetly at Flora. She said, 'I haven't got any formal training, Evelyn, but if you want some lessons?'

This was getting a bit boring for my taste. I got up and said, 'Well, now that's settled. And no offence was intended, Evelyn. I'd better go get dressed for the day.'

Once in my room, I collapsed on the bed, far more tired than when I'd got up. I remembered a self-help book that said anyone could change their life. But that probably meant buying the book changed your bank balance. If Evelyn continued having a drama a minute, I'd be totally wiped out. I didn't recall the book mentioning a type like Evelyn, but there had been a girl very like her living in my dorm at university. I tried to remember what eventually happened to her.

All I could recall was our discussing the problem at a dorm council meeting. After lengthy futile debate, someone suggested we have her put down. I thought it was a joke until I saw all these hands going up to second the motion. She probably just grew out of her behaviour or got a job with the tabloid press. Or maybe she became a politician. Perhaps Evelyn would settle in, but it would be a hell of a lot easier to avoid her in a dorm of two hundred than in a house with three bedrooms.

My ankle was much better so I thought I'd go for a gentle walk. I put on a fresh bandage and shouting goodbye headed for Hampstead High Street. After another cup of coffee and an apricot Danish pastry at Louis', I strolled along window-shopping. My handbag began vibrating when my chequebook got nervous. I exchanged smiles with people who were sitting outside some of the other cafés and enjoying mid-morning cappuccinos. Then I stopped to look at an outdoor fruit and vegetable stand. It was a veritable work of art, all the colours and shapes and various fragrances. I leaned close to smell the lemons. At the end were bouquets of cut flowers and I decided to buy one for Mrs Stone. She'd been so wonderful about my ankle.

After a pleasant five-minute walk, I rang the doorbell. Immediately the door opened and Mrs Stone peered out. Then her wrinkles crinkled into a big smile, which widened further when I handed her the flowers.

'Come in, Caron. I'd better get these into water immediately.' Rushing towards the kitchen she said over her shoulder, 'Did you know flowers die the moment they're cut? That these are already dead? It just shows that dead can be beautiful. My word, they are lovely.'

She had a pot of tea on the hob, so strong it could have walked over unaided and jumped into our cups. After we were seated at the old pine table, she opened a tin of home-made cookies. 'American brownies, Caron.

I made them hoping you'd stop by. Go on, they're fresh. I've been making a batch every day. You can take the rest home with you.'

As I took a bite and sighed, she said, 'Are you going to ask where James is?'

'Well, actually I came to visit you. To thank you for fixing up my ankle and knee. I'm pretty much back to normal now.' Before she could say anything, I quickly added, 'And very much alive.'

It turned out Mrs Stone was an avid gardener and soon she was showing me the back garden. 'I planted this tree my first year here.' That seemed perfectly reasonable, as the tree was about seventy feet tall.

'And the shrubbery, many of the shrubs are from cuttings.'

It was a delightful garden, lots of evergreen to cheer the winter and perennials adding colour and fragrance. A shed at the very back was nearly covered with jasmine, giving the impression that the shed was a camouflaged perfume factory. As she showed me her herb section, she kept snipping off pieces for me to take home. I'd need to hide those from Harmony in the Home.

I thanked her and said I'd best be going. 'I mean coming unannounced like this, I don't want to take up your time.'

'Nonsense. We'll have another cuppa first.'

'Well, maybe a glass of water. And another brownie.' The calories didn't count when you were being polite.

We found James sitting at the kitchen table reading the newspaper. Mrs Stone said indignantly, 'Young James, what are you doing here?'

Surprised, he said, 'Well, actually I live here.'

'Not in the kitchen. And it's me Caron's come to visit. Look. She brought me flowers.' She proudly held up the vase, whose flowers weren't a patch on those in her garden.

James said, 'Hello, Caron. I'm glad you stopped by.'

Mrs Stone said, 'That's enough now. I don't intrude when you have guests.'

Hoping to prevent an argument, I said, 'Actually I was just going.'

She said, 'See that, young man? You've just messed up my social.'

'Sorry, I meant I was just about to have another cookie.'

James said, 'Please have two or a million. Do Americans actually eat them for breakfast? I tried to explain to Mrs Stone . . .'

'Oh my goodness, I promised I'd be back to make lunch. Oh, dear, this has been so pleasant I forgot the time.' I again thanked Mrs Stone as she handed me the herbs, the large tin of brownies, and a pot of non-dead flowers.

James said, 'I'll see you to the door, Caron.'

I made a face at him and he said, 'Actually, maybe I won't.'

Mrs Stone gave me a big hug at the door and said to please come again, anytime. 'You need to come while you're still alive. I understand it's more difficult once you're dead.' She smiled and we both laughed at her joke. I quickly walked down the path to the road and wasn't surprised to find James waiting around the corner.

'Sorry, Caron.'

'James, Mrs Stone is lovely. Why don't you ever bring her flowers?'

'Well, I've tried that, but she goes on about how I killed them. And the damn garden's full of flowers I bought her. I've arranged an unlimited account at the nursery. And for them not only to deliver, but also to collect her and bring her back as well.'

James and Mrs Stone, and perhaps Flora and me with Evelyn as well, were all cases of chalk and cheese not blending. But I wasn't the least bit sure who was the cheese, or if it was better to be chalk.

'There's something I wanted to ask you, Caron. I'll just walk along with you as I know you're in a hurry to get home and cook.' He turned and smiled. 'I'll bet you're a marvellous cook.'

'Don't bet more than a fiver.'

He laughed and I thought about how tangled life gets when you tell the truth and people think it's a joke. 'About that rain check, Caron. I know it's short notice, but how about tonight? Are you free for dinner?'

Thinking about Evelyn, I said, 'Oh, yes.' Then thinking of Bas, I said, 'Oh, no.'

'Do those add up to a maybe?'

'I know, James. What about a picnic?'

'I was thinking more of trying that new restaurant on the Thames. It's got pretty good reviews.'

'Then it'll be crowded, probably with visiting Americans. A picnic on the Heath would be great. It's sort of like after a fall, getting back onto a horse.'

'Is it?'

'I mean after that scare on the Heath. Well, really I mean that surge of adrenaline when I was walking that caused me to bolt.'

'Oh, yes. The exercise, as I recall your earlier description.' He was looking suspiciously amused so I limped a bit.

'Wouldn't you prefer to eat indoors, Caron?'

'It's a rain check, James. We have to eat outside.'

He smiled. 'This afternoon, then? Or early evening, since you're doing lunch?'

'Well, I had in mind after dark. A night picnic sounds better.'

'With the long summer daylight, Caron, it would have to be nearly midnight.'

'James, you are a genius. What a brilliant idea, a midnight picnic on the Heath. Yes, I'm agreeable to that. We'll have the picnic under that exact tree where I fell off the horse. I mean fell off my ankle.'

'Caron, but I meant . . .'

'Now James, don't put yourself down. It's a brilliant idea. We each bring pot luck and then we have the added mystery.'

James laughed. 'The mystery of maybe having nothing but strawberries?'

'I love strawberries. That's one thing I cook really well. You take the berries from the punnet and wash them and put them on a plate. And let everyone sugar their own. And I pour cream with real panache. They charge a fortune for those at the Ritz, so it must take a lot of talent.'

When I got to Flora's house, she was alone. 'Where's Household Harmony?'

Flora grinned. 'Harmony's gone to the dating agency to look at photos of prospective talent. For tonight. I asked if she couldn't bring the albums home, but she said they won't allow that.'

'But I thought your heart belonged to Mervin.'

Flora coughed slightly. 'I'm just curious. It'd be fun to look, to see who dares be in them. And, er, um, of course we could see if any of them look like Bas' man.'

She was delighted at all the loot I'd returned with, and she also seemed very impressed and delighted that

I was seeing James. After tasting a brownie she said, 'His housekeeper's got serious talent.'

'I know. That's why I need your help, Flora. James and I are each supposed to bring a hamper, and the one Mrs Stone does is going to make my contribution look like a compost heap.'

'I've got a hamper.'

'I meant the food. Could you make a shopping list, and when I return give me a hand?'

'No need. Mum stopped by earlier with loads of stuff. She does it every Saturday. This is my first time living away from home and she seems to believe that single girls live on crisps. And I love making up hampers. I often do them at Christmas for gifts.'

I gave Flora a huge hug. 'Absolutely brilliant, Flora. I'll do the laundry and the shopping and dust. Well, I never notice dust so scratch that.'

Flora laughed. 'I owe you for getting Harmony out of the kitchen. When I tried to explain to her that she needed to fill the kettle with water before using it, she said not to bother with details. That Delia Smith on the telly taught people to cook in half an hour.'

I settled happily at the table with a cup of coffee and the newspaper. I didn't ask whose it was in case it belonged to Evelyn and she might not like my filling in the crossword. Flora chatted merrily as she put together the picnic. It was a difficult crossword, I mean fancy Evelyn taking *The Times*. Whoever buys that on Saturdays except for the crossword, anyway?

So I didn't pay much attention to Flora's chatter. Although I did laugh when she told me about her mother. I'm always curious about other people's mothers. When Flora was packing to move out, her mother had said, 'Well, if you insist on the single girl life in a scruffy house, expect all handouts to be on that level. Baked beans, tinned sardines, white bread, bags of crisps.'

Flora said, 'Mum is a brilliant cook and has terrific reverence for food.' She laughed and added, 'So that was Mum's worst insult.'

Because Flora had done the hamper and the lunch, I made us some delicious tinned tomato soup for dinner. If you add a few drips of milk to the water it says to add, it makes all the difference. Just as I was taking a large bite of one of Evelyn's cheese samples, she returned and went straight to her room.

An hour later she came out looking like a model, and she'd done her hair beautifully. Well, to me that means that it isn't all sticking out. Hers was well behaved, making me think she slept with a swimming cap stretched over her head. Which could account for her brain being a bit shrunken.

Both Flora and I complimented her looks and she seemed pleased. Well, even a tiger would be pleased to hear that. It's just that no one trusts a tiger enough to wait for it to think it over.

Then she started fussing about and looking everywhere, grumbling, 'Bugger it. Where's my copy of *The Times*?'

Shit, and double shit. 'I thought you'd know today's news by now so I threw it away. I'll buy one tomorrow for you. A fresh one.'

Cursing, she rushed to the kitchen and returned with the paper. 'Who the bloody hell did the crossword?'

I said, 'It wasn't Flora. Anyway, I thought you had a date.'

'That's what the bugger's for, you idiot.'

Flora asked in her sincere and curious voice, 'Is that

what you do with the men from the agency? Read the newspaper to each other?'

Evelyn shook her head in exasperation. 'No we don't. The paper's a bit of window-dressing. The idea is that the bloke arrives and sees me filling in all the answers.'

I must admit I was really impressed and prepared to like this Evelyn. 'Goodness, Evelyn, can you do it that fast?'

'Bugger doing it. I just fill it in with any words. I mean guys don't pay the agency so they can proof-read the answers, do they?'

'One who would be impressed that you could do *The Times* crossword might. Anyway, I've done you a favour. If he checks, the answers are right there.'

You could tell that Evelyn hated for things to turn out simple. Looking at her watch, she moved towards the door and had one last stab. 'I usually write them in with green ink. This black looks a bit common.'

As midnight approached, I kept telling Flora she didn't need to wait up. But I think she liked the idea of a man coming to her house and wanted a glimpse of James. She said, 'Do you realise, Caron, that we've had three phone calls either from men or about men since you moved in? And that's in less than a week.'

'Goodness, Flora, one was an outright threat and the other two about likely danger. Or were you thinking crime novel rather than romance?'

'You have to admit it would be less interesting if this was about a woman and not a man.'

'Only if the woman were Evelyn.'

The doorbell rang, and unsurprisingly Flora got there first.

James said, 'Good evening, Flora. I'm sorry to ring the bell so late.'

'Oh, that's no problem, and well, have a good time.'

That one sentence had cost her two hours' sleep and an extra bath. I really hated leaving her there but thought I'd just embarrass her more if I asked her to go with us. I'd really got to give some thought to her and Mervin.

As we set off, James mentioned my ankle and ended up carrying both hampers. He looked a bit like a beast of burden that someone was going to report to the RSPCA. 'Surely, James, one hamper will do?'

He quickly agreed and handed mine back. 'No, James, we'll leave yours here, as it'll be a surprise for tomorrow.'

Before handing over his hamper, he grinned and removed a bottle of champagne. Flora opened the door while I was fiddling with the key. I said, 'Ta-da! Tomorrow's lunch!'

'But Caron, I went to a lot of trouble.'

'No, no, it's the one James brought.' She was already peeping under the cloth covering it, so I said, 'Why don't you have a look? And put anything perishable in the fridge.'

A few minutes later we were on the Heath. The sun had long gone and the dusk seemed thick and murky, mist rising from the ponds. A slight breeze shifted the tree branches, causing shadows to move across the path. I'd got unused to the British dusk, which lingered for hours, mostly at the dark end of the spectrum. One man and his dog passed by but no one else was in sight. But I could still hear sounds of leaves being crushed, soft footpads, maybe a fox or a rabbit. Maybe Bas' henchman. I began talking in a very loud husky voice.

'Er, Caron, is there any particular reason why you're shouting?'

'An old trick. Whoever else is out here is probably

worried too. So if we sound big and tough, well that will stop them getting any negative ideas.'

With a crooked grim James said, 'Don't tell me the intrepid Caron is frightened of a little dark?'

That smacked of devilish insult. 'Not me, James. Never. It's just, well you see, if anyone attacked us, you would feel the need to act big and strong and maybe get beaten up.'

'Would I? Feel the need to act big and strong?'

Speaking even more loudly, I said, 'It isn't necessary. I have a karate black belt.'

James laughed. 'I'm glad I've been warned. Do you really have a black belt?'

Whispering, I told him, 'I have several. All in leather, different widths. Italian.'

It occurred to me then that if we were being followed, no one would attack while I was with James. So I relaxed, thinking better the devil you can see carrying your hamper. Shifting the basket to his other arm, James asked, 'What have you packed? Bricks?'

Not having actually looked inside the hamper, I tried to recall what Flora had been saying. 'The usual deluxe house-share fare. Tinned baked beans, sardines, sliced white bread. I forget what else. Oh, yes, single girls practically live on crisps.'

James said, 'In that case, I hope you forgot to pack the tin-opener.'

Would Flora have forgotten that? 'I'm sure it's in there. Or you can use your teeth, James.'

Laughing, we reached the designated area. 'Not that tree, Caron. This tree.'

'I don't think it was that tree, James.'

He said, kneeling, 'Perhaps I can find where our feet crushed the grass.'

'James! It doesn't matter which tree. Just pick a tree. I'm starving.'

We spread out the tablecloth that had been covering the food in the hamper and set out various items. There was enough room on the cloth for both of us to sit as well. 'Can you see which things are which, Caron?'

I heard the pop of the champagne cork just as my fingers felt the shape of the wineglasses. Strange, Flora had put in the best crystal instead of plastic. They certainly weren't the ones that lived in the kitchen. 'It's too dark, James. Aim that champagne carefully or I'll get drenched.'

We leaned against the tree drinking the champagne. 'I don't feel very hungry,' he said. 'Perhaps just the wine. Or we could collect my car and go to the Savoy later?'

'Don't be rude. You can't just turn down my hospitality like that. So eat.'

Reluctantly, James picked up a parcel. 'I shall begin with that famous delicacy, the sardine.' A few moments later he spoke again in a greatly cheered voice. 'This is the flattest sardine I've ever seen.'

'It probably got mashed in the hamper.'

'It's not only flat, but it's pink. And do you know, it's smoked salmon flavoured. Now, would this be a bean? An olive flavoured baked bean? Here's a little bunch of connected beans, purple like grapes. And this white bread is exactly like the crusty French variety.'

I laughed. 'That's much better, James. You're a good sport.' Then I reached for a sardine and piece of bread and said, 'Oh, my God, this is smoked salmon. I mean it isn't a flat sardine. I thought you were joking.'

James laughed until he was choking. Spluttering he said, 'Talk of joking. Are you saying this is a magic hamper? That you put in sardines and out came smoked salmon?'

'And roast beef. I've just found some slices of that. Even a little container of beef juice to dunk it in. And some mustard.'

As I put a sliver of smoked salmon between my lips, James stopped laughing. 'Caron, did you or did you not pack this hamper, prepare this picnic?'

'Absolutely. I did or did not.'

We both ate in silence for a while, occasionally saying, 'Delicious,' or 'The best picnic ever.'

James picked up a tart and asked, 'Do you want to guess whether this is apple or cherry before I take a bite?'

I reached over and grabbed it and took a mouthful before handing it back. 'I can say with certainty that it's apple. With maybe a little added rhubarb.'

'You know, Caron, if I didn't know for a fact that you only recently began work in Chambers' accounts and live in a house-share, I would think you'd gone into the delicatessen on the High Street and asked them to make you up their best hamper. I don't think you had time to get to Fortnum's.'

'I can confirm that about Fortnum's. But I did ring them to change the address for my regular order. You know, for breakfast and dinner delivered each day. Except of course when I'm having dinner parties for thirty in my bedroom.'

Satiated with the non-sardines, we leaned back against the tree and each other sipping champagne. After a while James said, 'Remember we're friends, Caron. So if you want to talk about anything? Falling off your ankle sorts of things?'

I held my glass out for more champagne. 'It's your

idea, so you go first. I mean if, say, you wanted to discuss, well the four-year period before giving up that flat. Oh, James, it must have broken your heart.'

'No, no, my heart's fine. It was just, well some things that were said. And your horse? Sorry, ankle? Did that break your heart?'

'No, no, my heart's fine, too. In my case, it wasn't what was said, more what was done. Or said about what was done. Or the fact that the horse didn't actually talk, if you know what I mean. About what was done. Before I met the horse.'

'Well, I'm glad we've both got that off our chests, Caron, made everything clear.' It was so ridiculous that we both laughed until we were holding our sides. But neither of us broached the subject of relationships again.

'You know, James, I find it a bit worrying that you're relying on my people skills. They're a bit like the British weather, very changeable – although definitely more sunshine than rain.'

He laughed. 'I find you delightful, Caron. And what matters to me is that I trust you and find it easy to talk to you. I'm sure that would remain the case even if you began to snow or hurl hailstones. Do you have a line in thunderstorms?'

'Lightning's my speciality, although I've yet to set fire to a barn. And what's your weather, James?'

'Mrs Stone might say I'm more sunrise than sundown, bearing in mind that she treats me like I'm thirteen. And, well, I've been described as quite competent as ice. And perhaps boring as rain.'

'James! That's awful and it can't be true. You're warm and kind and extremely generous spirited. And you have a good sense of humour. Surely you're a warm summer day without any of those high or low pressure thingies creeping in from the West!'

James laughed. 'I'd quite welcome the Gulf Stream coming along to warm me up a bit. But what you've just said is a good example of why I like you. And I fervently hope the one you see is the real me.'

'Of course it is. But you know, James, maybe for at least a while we should stick to other topics, not previous, well horses or ice cubes. As friends we could discuss other things. Such as work.'

'You don't throw things when men mention work?'

'I love to discuss work. People spend most of their lives working, and if they find it too boring to discuss, then they're in the wrong job. I mean my current job isn't exactly fascinating. But there are still hilarious moments.'

'I couldn't agree more, Caron. Here, hold up your glass.' He poured out the last drops. It was such good champagne I would happily have helped him by squeezing the bottle.

'This is a little delicate, James, so please don't take offence. About work, could our friendship be a little discreet? I don't plan to spend my career as the carpet, and well, I would hate it said I rose up by, well, er, bouncing the mattress.'

James laughed and then said seriously, 'I doubt if anyone would think that of you, Caron. In any event, people can only bounce so high on a mattress. Did the, er, horse have a, er, mattress?'

'Probably one just like that of the ice cube. So it's agreed, James? No really personal questions until things are, well, you know, sorted?'

'I don't really mind your asking me questions, Caron. I'm just not very good at answering them.'

'Well, when you get my answers to questions, you may not like me anymore.'

I could sense him grinning as he said, 'I might surprise you about that.' After a short silence, he said, 'Oh, dear. Dear Caron. I should have realised. There is a sort of short-term amnesia, a psychological disorder, not important of course, I mean who cares what you thought you packed in the hamper, and I . . .'

I said heatedly, 'Dammit, James. I'm not mental in any way! That was not amnesia. It was merely an unanswered question. And I . . .' I stopped talking when I realised he was laughing and reached over and thumped his shoulder. 'But that's agreed? About the questions?'

'Absolutely, Caron. Now to make it official, we need to seal the agreement.'

'What? You mean swear on a Bible?'

Before I had time to decide whether it was a good idea, he leaned over and held me close. 'Actually,' he said, 'I was thinking of a friendly kiss.'

10

Although I hadn't arrived home until after two a.m., I still woke up early the next morning. With the minimum noise in case Evelyn had survived the night, I made coffee and returned to bed. It seemed strange that Evelyn, who hated creeping things, was causing everybody else to act like we'd grown six extra legs.

I thought about James and the kiss. It was definitely a friendly kiss. I mean, after it went on so long we were gasping for breath, I could hardly say it was unfriendly. And considering how I was off men at the moment, the kiss certainly had my full attention. It was so warm and lovely and wonderful it nearly scared me to death, because I could feel my hormones tuning up like the London Symphony Orchestra.

Then James began packing up the hamper with no attempt at a second kiss. Hadn't he enjoyed the first one? Or had he planned the single kiss as just a teaser? It had been like eating only one strawberry or one peanut. Tantalising.

We held hands on the way home, which was just more of being friendly, as it was so dark we needed to watch our step. It was of course possible that James was as couple-phobic as I and thus equally alarmed by the kiss. But the only way he could really believe that kiss was a little token peck was if his ex had been the mama of all hot tamales.

I tiptoed to the kitchen for a refill. No smell of cooking, although there was a paper bag full of croissants with a note, 'Harmony in the Home'. Next to it was a jar of gooseberry jam with a printed label saying the same thing. I couldn't work out if Flora had bought it as a joke, or if Evelyn's motto had been pinched from a label in the supermarket.

The bathroom was empty, and I quickly dodged in and bolted the door. But not before I heard Flora asking from the front room, 'Well, did he notice the crossword puzzle?' Obviously trying to pump Evelyn about her date. Better to use some hot water and hear about it later.

Hot water is total bliss, and I returned to my room feeling absolutely refreshed and not a little bit guilty. It would be midnight before the water heated itself up again. I spent some time tidying up my room. Never did I leave clothing lying around. My efficient mother had believed anything left about was a discard and took it to the Salvation Army.

Dressed in jeans and a T-shirt, I'd just stretched out on the bed with one of Flora's books. It was a romance and I'd checked the last page to make sure the heroine stayed alive before beginning to read. Then I heard Flora call my name, followed by Evelyn doing the same in a louder voice.

I rushed in before Evelyn could warm up her vocal cords. She and Flora were flanking a very short, wiry, middle-aged man. Evelyn said, 'We've got your man, Caron. Not as tall as you said, and you didn't mention bald. Anyway, you can't say I'm not co-operating.'

The man said, 'What's going on? I'm looking for a Caron Carlisle. Got a delivery.'

This little man was not at all the type I'd imagined Bas hiring. Well, I suppose I'd thought he would pick

James Bond. Or that type. Then I remembered he'd probably hired him second hand, through a local agency. It was almost a relief at last to know what I was up against, although my first impression was that the guy looked a bit intimidated, as if we might be the bullies. Pulling myself together, I said, 'That's not very likely on a Sunday. Flora, Evelyn, make sure he doesn't go into my bedroom.'

'Look, what's this about? We deliver twenty-four hours, round the world. Are you going to sign this or what?'

Flora said, 'In books you never sign anything not checked by your lawyer.'

Evelyn said, 'You don't seem to have a parcel. What are you delivering, a singing telegram?'

'Look. Either sign this and I'll go and get the goods, or forget it.' He was looking extremely nervous as Evelyn moved her belly button closer to his eyes.

Just in case he was genuine, I said, 'Why haven't you got a badge or uniform on?'

'In the lorry all day I'm supposed to wear a costume? Sign this or I'm outta here. This is your last chance.'

This guy really invited suspicion, going so much against the Hollywood stereotype of a villain. I asked, 'Why have you got a bit of an American accent?'

'Why do you? We probably watch the same films. All right, I'm off.'

Evelyn said, 'No, you're not.' She moved closer.

Flora said, 'Caron, should I call the police?'

'If you don't get this Amazon off my neck, I'm calling 'em myself.'

That surprised me. Bas might try a bluff like that, but certainly not a genuine crook. 'Well, he hasn't tried to get into the bedroom. Maybe I'd just better take a look.'

Evelyn blocked the door while Flora and I looked at the paper. 'You know, Flora, it looks pretty much like any old delivery slip.'

'It's certainly not divorce papers or one of those pre-marital contracts.' Then Flora whispered, 'Sign it with one of those film star autographs or like a doctor's prescription, Caron.'

I whispered back, 'Well, that might make it useless in court, but it'd still have my fingerprints.'

'Lady, there's nothing wrong with my ears. You can wear gloves when you sign.'

That was so embarrassing that I just signed. Well, scribbled. The man took the form and practically ran to the door. Evelyn said, 'I'll go with him in case he tries to escape.'

The man stopped. 'I'm not carting in the parcel if you're gonna hold me hostage after. That's final. One more word and I'm leaving it in the middle of the road. Then I'm gonna drive the lorry over it.'

A few minutes later the man returned carrying an antique rocking chair, with a small parcel tied with string to the armrest.

I felt positively queasy. 'Shit! That's the wooden rocking chair Bas and I bought. This has got to be some sort of trick.'

Evelyn again blocked the door and said to the man, 'You open the parcel in case it's a bomb.'

Flora said, 'And open it outside.'

The man shook his head until it looked like it would completely unscrew. 'The bloody thing's come halfway around the world. It's been on boats, planes, in the back of a lorry. If it were going to blow, it would have blew.'

Evelyn said, 'Even I know the word's blowed.'

I said, 'I think he may be right, Evelyn. Blew is the past tense of blow.'

'No it's not. Blue is how you describe those cheesy films.'

'That's a different spelling of the sound,' I said.

The man said, 'Ladies, I'd like to retract my statement. Instead I'll say that by now the fucking parcel would have blown up.'

Flora said, 'Anyway, I've read about bombs you can put in a letter. It'd be a waste to use a parcel that size. And anyone who hired a hit man would know that.'

The man said, 'You know, I've been here more than fifteen minutes, and according to the union I get a coffee break.'

Flora said, 'Sorry, I didn't mean to be inhospitable.'

'I mean this bloody woman's got to let me outta here.'

Evelyn said, 'Not until you open the parcel.'

The man stared at her, then returned to the chair. With one quick motion he untaped the parcel and tossed it onto the floor and then sat on the rocking chair.

Evelyn, Flora and I stared at the package, waiting for something to happen. We probably should have been running away, but we were like those rabbits that get hypnotised by headlights. Slowly counting, I'd got to fifty before I realised the delivery man was talking.

'I'll have my coffee here, then. Milk and five sugars. And two biscuits. You don't happen to have any doughnuts, do you?'

Flora started for the kitchen, but I said, 'No, it's all right. He's proved the parcel won't explode. He can go now.'

'I'm not moving. Not until I've had my elevenses. And now I'm curious about the parcel. You three must have some weird friends.'

I really didn't like touching any parcel sent by Bas. But I couldn't ask anyone else to do the honours in case the bomb would only go off the second time it was attacked. I unwrapped it very slowly and very carefully. Flora was returning with a coffee tray just as I pulled out a box of chocolates with a note on top.

The man said to Flora, 'Are these genuine American brownies? Delicious. I'll just put one in my pocket for later. Are you gonna open the chocolates or what?'

But first I opened the note. In large black block letters it said, *Trust Me.*

Flora said, 'I knew it. The chocolates are poisoned.'

The man said, 'Do you women hold down ordinary jobs during the week? All normal like?'

Evelyn said, 'Maybe the delivery man would like to test the chocolates?'

Flora said, 'That wouldn't prove much, I mean if he lived. The poison could be in the last one.'

The man said, 'Would you mind terribly if I had a second cup? This is better than the truck stop on the motorway. Is this just your usual weekend?'

'Bas has to be up to something. These're my favourite, soft orange centres dipped in bitter chocolate.'

Flora said, 'The bitter chocolate might disguise the taste of the arsenic.'

'I really doubt if Bas would want to poison a whole crowd. There are twenty-four chocolates here, and he knows I only eat one occasionally. Well, one at a time. Well, certainly never twenty-four at one go. And as he knows about this address, he'd know I was sharing.'

'That's true,' said Flora. 'And like we discussed

before, he couldn't really ring the BBC like the IRA does to take credit.'

Undecided what to do with them, I put the chocolates on the top shelf of Evelyn's and my empty bookcase. I didn't want anyone to risk eating them, but in case they'd been tampered with they might be needed as evidence later. Then we had the most awful time getting the delivery man to leave. He seemed quite prepared to remain all day.

Evelyn finally got him to the door. As he was leaving, she said, 'You know, if you weren't so short . . .'

I had really loved the rocker. We'd spotted it in an antique shop. It was almost exactly like the one we had in my childhood home before it got scratched and Mum donated it. And it was mine, not Bas'. So I sat down to gently rock and think things over. Flora was fussing over lunch and Evelyn was still seeing the delivery man out. He'd been quite nice, when you considered what we'd put the poor man through with our suspicions. And I began to wonder if Bas wasn't doing more harm, making life so crazy with his games, than if he simply walked in with a rifle. But of course he could be saving that for later.

When Evelyn returned, Flora called us to the kitchen where she'd spread out the contents of James' hamper. Lemon flavoured chicken breasts, home-made rolls and butter, strawberries and Devon cream, tiny artichoke tips with a container of lemon butter for dipping. And lots of salady finger foods like carrot and celery strips as well as radishes and spring onions.

Evelyn thanked Flora, who said, 'It's compliments of Caron.'

'Double bugger. I wish I couldn't cook the way you can't cook, Caron.'

I had to say something because Flora was looking at me. 'Well, actually it was a gift hamper.' Then they were both looking at me. 'Actually, a spare one from the picnic last night.' Now they had stopped eating to look at me. 'Well, James and I had both got one, you see. Flora was wonderful to do mine, but then we had two, and it was midnight and they were heavy.'

Evelyn pointed her fork at me. 'You had a midnight picnic with a bloke? I thought you said you were off men.'

'He's just a friend, that's all.'

'Is he as good-looking as the other bloke, the one we're watching out for?'

'They're different, but yes, I think rather more attractive.'

Evelyn waved a chicken breast in my direction. 'Well, let me know if he wants more than friendship, will you?'

Flora quickly said, 'You never finished telling me about your agency date.'

Evelyn frowned at me. 'Just as well you did the crossword. The bloke checked it out.'

'Glad to be of help, Evelyn.'

'It's only a help if you like to spend half the bloody night talking about words.' Flora and I were eating faster, as Evelyn had already had seconds.

'Next time, Evelyn,' I said, 'why not choose a prop to do with something you're really interested in.'

'You think that'll work better?'

Flora said, 'It's worth a try, Evelyn. And you know, Caron, your rocker is beautiful. I love the way it's really painted. Not just a design along the edges, but an actual landscape on the seat, the seascape on the back, and flowers on the arms. I'm not an expert, but I think it's called primitive art. It must have cost a fortune.'

Evelyn said, 'Yeah, it looks quality. Is this what the bloke's going to do? Send furniture over bit by bit? And then try to move in himself? It would save us having to look for him.'

We all laughed. Maybe all Evelyn needed was a better diet. 'I don't really know. I doubt the chocolates are poisoned. Right now I think he's just trying to make me, well us, nervous. Throw us off balance. Sometimes Bas sent adversaries a present, flowers or something to do with their business, if they were competing for a contract. It tended to throw them off guard or unnerve them, giving Bas the advantage. Usually he did that before he sprung a trap, pulled a rabbit out of a hat.'

Flora said, 'Could you tell by the present what he was up to? I mean if the competition knew him as well as you do?'

'Sometimes. But Bas' brain is like a three-ring circus, so much going on at once. And you don't know if you're dealing with the clown, the elephant, or the tiger.'

'If they had those choices at the dating agency, I'd choose the tiger over the clown any day.'

Flora said, 'It would be your last day if he ate you up, Evelyn. So what would Bas do next, Caron? If he were negotiating?'

'Who knows? Probably what we least expect.'

Evelyn said, 'A rich, handsome bloke like that, surely some gorgeous gal's going to snap him up, keep him busy. Then he won't have time to bother with tricks. Just remember, I'm available.' She looked at her watch then got up. 'Got a coffee date. And I need to stop on the way and buy some strawberry flavoured condoms.'

Flora looked shocked. 'Before you've even met him?'

Evelyn looked surprised. 'It was Caron's suggestion, like when he arrives I have them on the table.'

When we heard the front door close, Flora said, 'Do you think Evelyn's joking, Caron? Winding us up?'

'I'm beginning to hope so.'

And then Evelyn came barging back into the kitchen. She looked happier than I'd ever seen her. 'I've got another one! And I bloody well hope this one's a genuine fake. That'd be a fake florist. Shall I show him straight into your bedroom, Caron?'

At first I didn't know what she was talking about. 'Repair doorbell' was on Flora's 'To Do' list, after 'replace hot water boiler', which meant we didn't complain. And you couldn't hear a knock on the door from the kitchen.

Evelyn said, 'Hurry up before he escapes. You said to keep the other delivery man out of the bedroom, so you must have thought that's where he was aiming. I can take this bloke in there and check him out.'

Flora grabbed her rolling pin and rushed into the front room. She returned disgusted and angry. 'Evelyn, that's James, Caron's friend. And my friend, too. Don't you dare touch him.'

'Bugger it. You say to keep an eye out, then you say don't. How am I supposed to help?'

This exchange was carried out at full volume, so I hurried into the front room. James was standing there holding a bouquet of flowers and looking a bit sheepish. 'Sorry, Caron. I seem to have started something. I mean Flora was brandishing a rolling pin, and that other woman . . .'

I shouted out, 'Flora, Evelyn, look who's here! It's James.'

It didn't exactly get things back to the starting line because they'd started somewhere outside the stadium. I couldn't help but think that if Channel 4 put one of those *Big Brother* cameras in Flora's house, none of us would ever need to work again.

Soon Evelyn was saying, 'Pleased to meet you I'm sure.' I mean that is an exact quote. And dear Flora set about welcoming James.

Soon Evelyn had gone and Flora and I were drinking coffee with James. He still hadn't sat down and was making 'I'm sorry if I've come at an inconvenient time' noises. And then he saw the rocker.

'This is beautiful. Will it hold my weight if I sit down?' He did sit when we both reassured him, with me hoping it would crash to the floor and divert him from further questions. Well, a painted piece of furniture like that was not called a conversation piece for nothing.

When he complimented Flora on her good taste, she pointed to me. Shit, shit, and double shit. It wasn't the sort of thing one could buy with my current pay. It wasn't even the sort of thing I could have bought alone with the pay Bas didn't pay me. 'Thanks so much for the hamper, James. We all just had it for lunch, and it was terrific.'

He smiled. 'Mrs Stone's doing, as I'm sure you know.'

Turning to Flora, he said, 'Mrs Stone's my house-keeper, Flora. Well, actually now she's called Stoner. And the flowers, Caron, she sent you those. You've really made a good impression.'

When Flora went to the kitchen to refill the pot, I grinned and asked, 'What's this about Stoner?'

He smiled. 'It's all thanks to you. When I saw you managing it, I decided there had to be a way to talk to her. So I assured her it was not about pensions and asked her if we could speak frankly. Then I asked what it would take to get her to stop calling me Young James. I offered first to get her a second cleaning woman to come in. Next I mentioned another pay rise. She still refused. So what would it take, I asked.'

'Did she bite?'

'First she said it would probably take death and she didn't plan to die first. Then she relented and said she was going to keep on as long as I called her Mrs Stone. That it made her feel old, so I might as well feel young. So Stoner it is.'

'Will she want me to call her that, too? I mean calling an elderly woman Stoner?'

'Absolutely. She says she wants a new image, a new lease of life, and she's planning to plant another tree.' He smiled wryly. 'Do you think she has another seventy years in mind?'

We were laughing when Flora returned with a plate of brownies. James got up to shift a table for her to place the tray on. And when she offered the brownies, he declined, making a rueful face at me. Admiring Flora's books while sipping his coffee, he saw the box of chocolates. Flora and I exchanged worried looks as he looked at them.

'These are my favourites. But of course you're probably saving them for Christmas?' That was the sneakiest way to say I want one that I'd ever heard. It was many moons until Christmas.

'Well, actually, James, I don't think they're fresh. I'm sure they've gone off.'

'In that case you won't mind if I take one? I mean if you don't plan to eat them yourself?'

He'd got the damn thing nearly to his mouth, when Flora and I both jumped to our feet and I said, 'Stop, James! They might have been tampered with.'

He raised his eyebrows and looked at us. Flora said, 'You know, James, like with arsenic. You wouldn't know if you got the poisoned one until it was too late. Or they might all be perfectly safe. And you're our friend.'

James said, 'And that makes a difference?'

'No, no,' I said. 'We wouldn't let anyone eat them. They're just sort of there to keep the bookcase company.'

'Caron, am I missing something? I mean is this some sort of game?'

'Probably, James, but it isn't my game.'

He was looking at Flora and me exactly as if we were those old ladies in that film who kept killing off people who'd come for tea and burying them in the basement. Flora quickly got up and said she thought there was some shortbread in the kitchen. I'm sure that if a doctor told Flora she was going to die, she'd move her bed between the cooker and the sink.

She wasn't even out of the room before James saw the folded paper by the chocolate box. Philosophy had let me down badly. I should have remembered that if you put things in the middle of an empty space, there's a law that says a person will become very interested. That's exactly why museums surround small but rather bland and gloomy paintings with six-foot wide frames.

Without even asking he unfolded the note and read it.

'Caron, if this message came with the chocolates, how did you interpret *Trust Me* to mean that the chocolates were poisoned?'

'I should think that's a reasonable way to see it.'

'Well, what would it have meant if it said *Don't Trust Me*?'

'The same. Surely you've seen people in films say trust me. It always means to hide your money.'

'But we're not in a film. So there must be some other reason why you took it like that.'

'Honestly, James. Think about it. When someone says trust me, you have to take into account what he or she is planning to do. There's a hell of a difference between someone saying trust me to repay a five quid loan on Friday, and someone saying trust me to fry you in fish batter.'

He sat beside me on the sofa and took my hand. 'Caron, were the chocolates sent by, well, by horse, as it were?'

'I don't want to talk about it, James. I mean, I feel so stupid.'

'You don't sound stupid, just a bit vague and mysterious.'

'Well, it's complicated.'

He looked at his watch. 'Take your time. I probably have about forty years.'

'OK. It's to do with my previous live-in. When the horse turned into a jackass. He says he wants me back, but he probably doesn't. I mean he's probably angry because I left because he prefers everything to be his idea. It's his idea of a game. I mean I don't think he'll really do anything. He sent my chair from New York. It just got here. With the chocolates and the note. We thought he'd sent the delivery man, you know, as a sort of burglar, and you should have seen the poor man as we surrounded him. That's what Evelyn thought you were, another fake delivery person. Well, you were carrying flowers. Now, that should be perfectly clear.'

James was silent for a few minutes, looking at me intently. Finally he said, 'No, it isn't clear. I'm just trying to think of another approach that won't take you the remainder of my forty years to answer.' Finally he said,

'Why a burglar? I mean why would he send a burglar?'

Shit. James would make an excellent lawyer. Throw a thousand words at him and he homes in on the one word hidden in the crowd. I smiled hesitantly and then spoke very slowly so my mouth wouldn't get too far ahead of my brain. 'I guess it's like any split-up, James. You even argue over who gets the cobwebs. I only took my clothes and whatever would fit in the airline's luggage allowance, give or take a bit. But it wouldn't make any difference if I'd left my clothes or even had movers clean out the place. He just wants the last word.'

'Yes, Caron, but what is the last word? I suppose what I'm really asking is if you're in danger?'

'Look at it this way, James. If your previous sent you a box of chocolates, would you eat them and offer them around to your friends?'

He thought for a minute. 'If she sent them, they probably would be poisoned. But your situation is different.'

'No, it's not. Except that you didn't get sent a chair.'

'The bastard's got you in a state of siege, Caron. You must admit, Stoner and I don't greet delivery men with rolling pins.'

'I'm being cautious, James. He's sure to meet someone else and forget all about me soon.'

'It's hard to imagine he could ever forget you, Caron.'

James was right in there for Friend of the Year, until I realised his comment was probably an insult. While we'd been talking, Flora had been in and out, and at one point there was a loud grinding sound coming from the kitchen. Then she sat down.

James said, 'Flora, what do you think? Is there any danger?'

'Not from the chocolates. That's definite. But I think

he's still in love with Caron and wants her back. That's what I really think. So I doubt if he'd really hurt her. Not on purpose. Not, like, personally.'

James thought for a moment, then said, 'If you two aren't levelling with me, I'm going to eat the whole bloody box of chocolates right now.'

'No, you're not,' I said. 'I'm going to do it so we can forget this whole thing.'

'You're both too late. I, like, took care of them already.'

I was horrified, as was James. I could hardly get the words out, 'All of them, Flora? All twenty-four?'

She nodded. Then she suddenly seemed to feel our tension. 'Surely you don't think I was stupid enough to eat them? I put them all in the waste disposal unit in the sink. But I saved the box, Caron. You can put it back on your bookcase if you like.'

James glanced at his watch, and I quickly, hopefully said, 'Have you got an urgent appointment?'

His next question was sure to be why Flora got rid of the chocolates if she believed there was no danger.

Instead, he said, 'I've got to pick up a couple of items for Stoner at South Hill Green. Do you want to come, for the talk? Sorry, walk?'

As South Hill Green was only a couple of hundred yards away, he cut to the chase re his walk talk. 'Caron, we're supposed to be friends. So why do I believe there's a danger you haven't mentioned?'

'Because you have a suspicious mind?'

We went into a shop where he bought milk and butter. Back outside, he said with concern, 'Would you like me to walk you back? Just in case . . .'

'James, it's so close you could almost throw me back.'

He looked at his shoes for inspiration. 'What I actually

came to your place to tell you is that during the next few weeks I've got to make some short business trips. So I won't be around all the time. I mean, as we're friends, I thought I should tell you so you wouldn't think, well, whatever you might think. I suppose I'm trying to communicate better, I mean by telling you that.'

I felt like I should comfort him by saying he communicated well already, but I wasn't even sure what he was telling me that very moment. The words were clear enough, but like crosswords, each one seemed to have more than one meaning.

'Is this about your previous, James? I mean did she say something awful like maybe she got more conversation out of an ice cube?'

'No. She said iceberg. Although she was only meaning communication. Well, my verbal communication, if you know what I mean?'

No I didn't, but then he gave a demonstration, although I doubt if it was intended as that. He tilted up my chin and then ran his hand up to hold the side of my face with his fingers touching my ear. It felt like I'd just run across a synthetic carpet and then touched a metal doorknob. Then he leaned over and kissed the tip of my nose. That must have been where he was aiming, as I was holding my mouth where he could have found it wearing a blindfold.

'I'd be happier, Caron, if I thought you'd ring me if anything else happens.'

'You mean if someone delivers a sofa or a piano?' I was just being difficult.

'Anything suspicious, Caron, anything at all. And if you want to discuss anything, well just remember two brains might be better than one.'

I was still holding my head back so far I could see a blue patch of sky. But nothing happened and I was getting a crick in my neck. I couldn't last much longer. 'James, it's also probably true that four lips are better than two.' And I leaned up to kiss him.

He put his arm around me and I could feel the milk carton pressing into my back. It felt wonderful. The kiss just felt so warm and good and affectionate and comforting and safe, so different from all the worrying and hysterics of the past few days. His hand fitted so snugly around my side. And I could smell his aftershave. I'd got to that stage where my emotions were shouting go for it girl, and then my logic whispered asshole. I quickly pulled back.

'Oh, James, I'm sorry. I mean we're friends and I shouldn't have . . .'

He grinned. 'That didn't strike me as an enemy attack. To be perfectly honest, I'm not certain what female friends actually do. The limits, I mean. When it's not a relationship or a lover sort of thing.'

'The same goes for me about men who are strictly friends. But I somehow don't think it's this.'

Well, hell, this friendship was moving faster than my relationship with Express Train Bas had done. And it was scaring me half to death. I hadn't really got rid of Bas yet, and certainly couldn't deal with it on the rebound if I was with another man. Maybe I was just cowardly, switching my dependence rather than learning to do my own dance.

'James, in films don't pairs of "strictly friends" just talk about their current romances with others and cry a lot on each other's shoulders? Or maybe play Scrabble?'

'I haven't tried Scrabble. And I'm not sure I want to

take on another lover just yet. In order to retain my friendship with you.'

'Oh, I didn't mean that. I meant, well, not the opposite but something very like it. Maybe chess would be better so we could declare a stalemate.'

'Well, we've already agreed not to go into detail about previous stuff. I'm quite happy with that. Well, absolutely delighted with that. Is there anything you want to cry about? On my shoulder? It's here and available. It's even already warmed up.'

My logic wanted to set definite limits, such as only meeting once a week for an hour. With a chaperone. A night in the cinema would be all right, sitting on the front row. But my feet didn't seem to want to move.

'The thing is, James, when I'm around you I don't actually feel like crying. Even if I felt like it before, not that I ever feel like crying. I mean I'm a fighter and not a crier. Mostly.'

He smiled. 'It's the same for me, Caron. You make me laugh.'

'James! That's not very polite.'

'I mean in the sense of feeling happy. Cheering me up. Making me more alive.'

My logic was making my feet itch. I held out my hand to James and we shook hands. 'So we're still friends then, James? And we can sort of make our own rules? And no one takes offence when we draw lines? I mean if anyone felt this was necessary?'

He grinned, still holding my hand. 'Absolutely. And here's my mobile number if you need to contact me while I'm away. If I can't get back fast enough, I can get you some other help.'

As I took the card, he added, 'And don't forget, you can laugh or cry on my shoulder anytime. What about

Samuel Johnson's words, "The enduring elegance of female friendship"?'

I smiled. 'That's flattering, James. But we need to be vigilant. I prefer, "Thy friendship oft has made my heart to ache: Do be my enemy for friendship's sake." William Blake.'

He laughed. 'I'll stick with Johnson. He also said, "If a man does not make new acquaintance as he advances through life, he will soon find himself left alone. A man, Sir, should keep his friendship in constant repair." You just let me know, Caron, if the friendship's getting any rips or anything, in time for me to do something.'

'And you do the same, James.' After a quick peck on the cheek, he left. As I walked the short distance home, I decided James had hidden depths. Bas' idea of a poem was roses are red and violets are blue, and his only quotes came from the financial pages. But I was also a bit nervous. 'A woman's friendship ever ends in love.' (John Gay)

11

It was almost a relief to get back to my desk on Monday morning to relax. Well, everything is relative and there was life with Evelyn as well as the spirit of Bas haunting us at home. And then there were my somersaulting emotions with James. Compared with all that, holding down a full-time job seemed a breeze. As soon as we reported for work, Mrs Brown was called to an urgent meeting. This meant those who hadn't got leftover work from the previous week were left on idle until her return.

I used the time to balance my chequebook and gave up after thirty seconds. With no prospect of a promotion for many months, and with my short time at Chambers' already seeming like eternity, the only thing moving quickly in my life was my money. It was like I'd stumbled at the starting line, whereas my cash was running fast enough to win Ascot.

Because I'd begun my before-Bas working life on the bottom rung of management, it had never occurred to me that work was not an actual ladder where you worked from bottom to top. Management was, or could be, like that. But at the non-management bottom, it was like your feet were stuck in quicksand. You could move sideways in the swamp, or in my case up a chair in accounts, but the largest effort was undoubtedly from the swamp to a tree. Then swinging from tree to tree was comparatively easy. That's probably why monkeys always seemed to be smiling.

The main problem was that the swamp was too far from top level for any special talent to be spotted. And the really awful thing was that there wasn't the slightest chance in hell that Mrs Brown thought I was a diamond hiding in a coal mine.

I got coffee refills for Melody and me. She was reading a magazine. I'd learned that she only tended to doze off faced with spreadsheets. So she was remaining awake for much of the day now.

My thoughts were interrupted by Mrs Brown's return. And I soon realised I could drop the concept of peace at work. Due to a company crisis which she didn't mention but which had added wrinkles to her forehead, she had a mountain of work so tall it made Everest look like a pimple on a pig. Accounts were being redone, and a general inventory seemed to be in progress, maybe more, but I could only go by my own stack of work. Well, Melody's stack. As for my stack, some computerphobe had sent audiotapes with enough official memos to keep Melody happily humming for a week.

No confidential stuff this time, but I certainly got a feel for the company I hadn't got from just waltzing through the merchandising areas en route to my desk every day. Apparently Chambers' was hugely into import and export. Some items were partially manufactured abroad and then brought to the UK for finishing. Other imports arrived ready to sell. Chambers' had a large mail order business, and some orders were filled from London. Other orders were handled from manufacturers abroad who might have got merchandise from the UK or from other manufacturers abroad. It was amazing that the garment labels didn't say 'Made in England, China, Singapore, Italy, and Texas'. Or maybe just labelled, 'Hell, I don't know.'

I couldn't believe there were so many size double D bras in the entire world. Japan, with all the women wearing Chambers' double D? And half of Australia wearing green silk knickers?

Mrs Brown had mentioned overtime, so Mervin took orders for sandwiches from the canteen and we all worked through lunch.

Melody said, 'Do you know, dear, that one hour of my overtime now is more than a full week's pay when I started here?'

Mine wasn't even equal to the taxi fare I'd used in New York to get to the bank. And by the end of the day, the numbers on my computer screen seemed to melt together and resemble mashed potatoes. It was with great thirst that I was looking forward to meeting Flora to go for that drink.

But then she rang to tell me her mum had got the flu. Flora was going to see her and wouldn't get home until late. So I stayed on at work for an extra hour overtime. Most everyone else did, too. That made me wonder if the front row was getting much higher pay than the back row. Well, me on the back row. Melody was probably planning to buy a yacht.

While Mrs Brown hadn't declared automatic coffee breaks every two hours, she seemed well aware that if personnel didn't take breaks from their computer screens their eyes would meet in the middle and get stuck. So it seemed perfectly acceptable for staff occasionally to get up and wander around. During one of his eye rests, Mervin brought me a large cardboard-backed envelope.

He smiled. 'We'll all be rich or dead by the weekend, if this keeps up. Here are the Picasso *Green Shoelace* mock-ups. Want to take a look?'

I didn't want the entire office to gather round, so I suggested we go into the corridor. 'Mervin! These are terrific!'

He grinned. 'I've tried different tints and thicknesses of paint. Pick the one you like best and I'll tidy it up.'

'But Mervin, these are fine.'

'Only for an extremely myopic viewer at a hundred yards.'

'That suits perfectly. And I'll have all six.'

'But Caron, that'll be six drinks.'

'A done deal. You don't like to drink six drinks all at one time, do you?'

He laughed. Mock seriously, he said, 'I don't know. My interest rates are pretty high. If I haven't been paid off by Christmas, that'll be seven drinks.'

I was eating yoghurt that evening when Evelyn arrived home all excited. 'I'm off to Manchester, Caron. This could be my chance!'

I grinned. 'A man?'

She seemed miffed. 'I do think of things besides men. Occasionally. And if I get discovered, I won't need a rich man.'

'What are you going to get discovered doing, Evelyn? Robbing a bank?'

'I wish. It's a three-week assignment with forty-two kinds of cheese. But it's a trade fair. Not just housewives shopping. Hollywood producers could be there.'

'Evelyn, I'm the last one who'd want to rain on your parade, but ... Well, hell, you may be right. Who knows? Just stand close to the Stilton and Brie. Do you want to be a film star?'

'A model. I'm tall enough but not skinny enough.

But one woman of seventy-two just got taken on by a proper agency for TV advertising. Maybe I'll come into fashion.'

'Well, you're not fat, Evelyn.'

'It's just large bones. But when you stop to think about it, don't you think I'm really average, normal? More people like me than the current catwalk models?'

I looked up and out at her and said, 'Well, people are evolving larger. You hang in there, Evelyn. And good luck.'

I made her a yoghurt dinner, strawberry followed by apricot, while she packed. She actually came into the kitchen without putting on her mouse-proof boots. I was beginning to think her phobias were a bit like her karate, in that her practice of the latter was looking more and more as if she planned to audition for cabaret. I doubted the truth of that old adage about familiarity breeding contempt, as I was beginning to really like Evelyn.

We took her bags to the waiting car of a friend on the same assignment. Evelyn took more stuff for those weeks than I'd brought from the States for the rest of my life.

Later that evening, James rang. 'Caron, I'd planned to ask you to dinner this week, but things have come up at work.'

'That makes Chambers' top floor staff the Americans.'

'What?'

'Don't you know that old saying, that when America gets a cold, Britain gets pneumonia? Accounts has practically been converted into a field hospital.'

He laughed. 'Well, actually it wasn't taking you to dinner that really mattered. I mean anyone can eat. But you have a very special way of saying goodbye.'

'Oh,' I said. 'Then you like the idea of getting rid of me?'

'Over and over and over again.'

There was e-mail from my mother. My laptop now resided on the top of Flora's desk as I let both her and Evelyn use it for e-mail. Well, Flora and I used it for that, but so far Evelyn seemed to think she was supposed to keep her snail mail there. Mum's message said hello and asked how I was doing. Then bless her, the message said, 'Are you managing, Caron? You needn't ever feel the need to throw in your cards, dear. We cannot of course afford an ace, but we can certainly send you a pair of clubs to improve your hand. Do let me know. Love, Mum and Dad.'

I appreciated it, but telling them I was short of funds would be second only to the horror of Bas knowing I wasn't chief ape on a large tree. So I typed out, 'Haven't played out all my cards yet, Mum. But thank you. Lots of love, Caron.'

Flora arrived home after eleven. Even though she looked tired, I didn't think she'd appreciate a yoghurt dinner, however many courses it was. So I offered to make some delicious tinned cream of mushroom soup with buttered toast.

'Thanks, Caron. I ate at Mum's.'

When I asked how her mum was, she said, 'Not too good. I offered to stay over but she said it was only the flu.' She smiled. 'It's strange. First she didn't want me to leave home. Now she doesn't want anyone meddling with her house. Anyway, she's got good neighbours and I'm sure she'll ring me if she needs anything.'

'Want a glass of wine?' I looked at the remains in the bottle. 'This looks like the bit they decant out and throw away.'

'That's fine. I'm too tired to taste it, really. And I just want to unwind a bit before going to bed.'

I'd never seen Flora tired, or at least admitting to it. Thinking to cheer her up, I said, 'Guess what I've got?' I dashed into my bedroom and laid all Mervin's copies out on my bed. Leading Flora to the room, I made her close her eyes until I switched on the light and said, '*Voila!*'

She grinned. 'I must be more tired than I thought.'

'Hallucinating Picasso? That would be more than exhaustion. What do you think?'

Reverently she picked up each one in turn. 'They are so lovely. But why six?'

'Bless him, Mervin made six to give me a selection. But I'm going to hang them all up. It's going to be one confused burglar.' When I get my overtime, I thought, and could afford the frames.

But Flora said, 'Oh, Caron, could I buy the frames?'

'Flora, you're so tired you're dreaming.'

'No, it's just that Mervin might want to come and see his work hanging here. And he might think me a philistine, you know, because I don't have lots of original paintings. The least I can do is show him I have good taste in frames. Maybe at his show I can afford one of his works?'

'You can loan me the dough for the frames, then, Flora. And after the burglar's been, you can have your pick of the copies. What I thought was I'd hide the original, turn it face to the wall with a magazine page or something showing. Hang it in the bathroom. Then put the other copies in various frames. If the thief does know a Picasso from a hole in his shoe, he'd feel more confident pinching one he's selected.'

'But wouldn't a fake be more convincing in the original frame?'

'I don't want to lose that. Just the frame represents many moons at Chambers'.'

'That's a bit complicated for me to take in at the moment, Caron. But I'm sure it's a good idea.' She didn't sound very sure, but then I was tired, too.

As we sipped the dregs, I said, 'Flora, what the hell is Bas up to? I've been thinking about it all day. I can see the point of the chocolates and note. That was sheer menace, although not a provable one. Well, it might have proved something if we'd eaten them and died. But the chair? Bas is a brilliant strategist, and he rarely wastes time or effort. So the chair must mean something, but what? He could've hoped it'd cause me to let my guard down, see it as an act of kindness. But surely not along with a note saying trust me.'

Flora gave this serious thought. 'Not even in bonk-busters, where they do it everywhere, have I read about a rollicking rocking chair. And well, I guess in crime novels they do it everywhere, too. Except of course they aren't doing the same thing. But I don't recall any rocking chair murders. On the whole, beds seem more popular. In both genres.'

After another sip of coffee, she said, 'Do you think there's a connection between the chair, the note, the chocolates, and the Picasso?'

I frowned, and if you do that too often you get those horizontal brow lines that resemble train tracks. 'Not really. The Picasso's pretty much break and enter. Get it back, laugh like Father Christmas. I mean it wouldn't make much sense to send me the chair and then steal it back.'

'None of this makes much sense to me, Caron.' Smiling, she added, 'But it's interesting.'

'Yeah. Bas probably knows that Chinese proverb, or more like hex: "May you live in interesting times."'

It was really weird how for the next few weeks the office got more chaotic while it seemed like a gentle rain of Prozac had fallen on home. The previous week, I would have been grateful, but with all the overtime I was so tired I was usually in bed before Flora returned from her mum's. And I heard lots of mysterious sinister creaks and screeches as I lay there, often too tired to sleep. Flora said they were just an old house going to sleep at night. But it sounded more like a werewolf waking up hungry.

In the third week, I finally got checked out of accounts. Caron the library book. By the real accounts department, well – I mean where they have real accountants. It was pretty much the same work, but the change of scene was welcome.

It was after the overtime was slowing down, while I was back at my own desk, that I or rather Melody got something really interesting. There was the confidential sheet on the bottom, and the rest included a summary for the past six months. But while I was actually doing the work, I noticed some errors. Or the possibility. I couldn't be sure, because from my desk I couldn't see the forest for all the little bushes.

I wasn't sure what to do. I mean there was little point in telling Melody. But I couldn't possibly in all good conscience and professionalism ignore it. But neither did I want to get caught out and return to doing letters. In the end, I wrote a little note and put it behind the confidential sheet. All it said was that there were some large invoices that needed to be checked out for duplication. It looked like there was a pattern of their having been paid twice. Although I didn't state it explicitly in the note, each amount was large enough to purchase about a million double D bras.

If I was wrong, they'd probably think it was Melody, who would be delighted. I mean she would have fouled up spreadsheets with camel piddle if she could buy it at Harrods.

Anyway, it was probably just a mistake, as Chambers' was such a nice, dozy family company. On the other hand, that would only make it easier for a villain to fiddle the accounts to a different tune. It was only after I'd turned Melody's and my work in to Mrs Brown that another thought stabbed my brain. If it wasn't simple honest mistakes, it could be dangerous for someone like me to know about it. As I cleared my desk, I told my brain to go take a nap. Nobody could be expected to worry about chairs and bras and Picasso all at the same time.

After work, Flora and I were walking towards the tube when she stopped. I waited for her to do something, fish in her handbag for coins, or remember something she'd left in the office. But she just stood there as though she had run out of petrol on the motorway. 'Are you all right, Flora?'

'I have a confession to make. Or an announcement, I'm not sure which.'

'Do you want to go to the coffee shop to talk about it?'

'No. I want to go to the Ritz.'

'Goodness, Flora. We'll have to order one Coke with two straws. Or a glass of free tap water.'

'No we won't.' Her face was turning red – either a blush or she didn't like tap water. 'Caron, the thing is I've made a date for us.' I was about to say great, who with, try to show some interest and get us off Oxford Street where homeward bound people were bumping into us. But she added, 'With Bas.'

I was thinking it wasn't a lack of petrol, that her whole engine had stalled or been hit by a lorry on the A5. She turned to me and began talking quickly. 'He rang me at the office and was ever so polite. Charming, really. And all he wants is to talk to you, to sort things out, like.'

I took her elbow and edged her towards a shop window where we wouldn't get run over by pedestrians. 'Flora! It's a trick! Of course Bas is charming. Handsome and sexy, too. That's what I fell for, and now he's got to you.'

'But Caron, I thought it would help. You know, sort things out. Better than living in a state of siege. And if things don't get sorted, then at least I'd know what he looked like, who was after us.'

Suddenly I felt horribly selfish, realising how I'd dragged Flora into something that could turn really sour, dangerous even. 'Sorry, Flora. You're absolutely right. So when am I supposed to meet him?'

'Us, Caron. I made it a condition that we both come. So I can protect you, if need be. Since I was the one who agreed to meet.'

I almost laughed. Having Flora for a bodyguard was a bit like telling an intruder in your bedroom not to come near, that your teddy bear was going to get him. 'Well, I can't stretch to a taxi, so it'll have to be the tube, Flora.'

'No it won't.' By then she'd moved back to the corner where she'd originally stopped. And then a stretch limo pulled up to the kerb. The driver left the engine running and quickly got out to open the door for us.

Once inside, Flora smiled hugely and said, 'No way would I agree if it would cost us money, Caron. Just look at all this.' She opened a cabinet door that revealed a complete bar, including champagne in an ice bucket. 'It's got TV, Caron. And a mobile phone. Gosh!'

I was furious at Bas for using Flora like this. And really concerned that he was trying to win her over to his side. She said, 'Can you believe people can't even see us through the tinted windows? And think somebody important's inside?'

'We are important, Flora! Anyway, how did the driver recognise us? Has Bas given our photos out all over London? Is he watching our every move?' As the limo edged up to the taxi rank at the side entrance of the Ritz, I was feeling horribly nervous, even scared. I didn't think he would have a sawn-off shotgun. But I'd already fallen for his charm once. It was just so much easier to dislike him from a distance.

He was standing right inside the entrance and smiling. He took Flora's hand and shook it, then quickly leaned down and kissed her cheek. The Queen wouldn't have received more reverence, although I've read that if anyone actually touches her, it's straight to the Tower and the chopping block. Flora's face turned the colour of pickled beetroot, and she smiled like an angel. I braced myself as he shook my hand and repeated the cheek kiss. The Ritz was entirely on his side, as I would have simply looked stupid if I'd jerked my head away or said something rude. A seduction manual would have called that step number one: get victims into a situation where it would be uncomfortable or impolite to demur.

Bas escorted us to the room used for afternoon tea, which had finished, and the room was half-filled with people having before dinner drinks. I'd been there for tea as a child, intrigued with the décor, all gilt, mirrors, statuary, and small tables surrounded with gilded chairs with pink velvet seats. It was royal theatre, but as a kid I'd thought it was like Hollywood without the cowboys. As a child I'd thought royalty itself was part of Hollywood. By choosing that room, Bas had made a mistake, as we all seemed like actors in a BBC costume drama to me.

The waiter rushed up and led us to the corner. One table had two chairs and the one nearby one chair. As the waiter pulled out a chair for Flora, Bas did the same for me at the second table.

'Bas! That's rude! You can't expect Flora to sit by herself!'

Flora, watching the waiter pour champagne, said, 'I'm quite happy, Caron. Really.'

As the waiter poured champagne for Bas and me, I said, 'I think I'd prefer a gin and tonic.' If it had originally been a G&T, I'd have ordered champagne. Anything to gain a bit of control in the situation. My drink was brought so fast I suspected the waiter had been holding it behind his back. Probably Bas had anticipated my reaction. 'Make this fast, Bas. Flora and I have other plans for the evening.'

He laughed. Flora had probably told him we were free for the rest of our lives. Then he leaned over the table and started to take my hand, then seemed to think that wouldn't work. 'Caron, honey, I love you and want you to come home. I've just missed you more than I can say.'

He needed a better scriptwriter. 'Bas, I'm not coming back. And I'd like for you to stop all your tricks.'

Laughing again, he leaned back in his chair and said,

'Honey, I thought you loved your rocking chair. And your favourite chocolates. And you are as beautiful as ever.'

'I haven't had time for my hair to turn grey and my teeth to fall out, Bas. You've got five more minutes, so say what you want to say.'

He narrowed his eyes and his body tensed. In a film that would be when he knew he'd have to have a shoot-out at high noon. 'You can't possibly like that little job, honey. It's beneath you. And that little house you're living in. I'll send movers tomorrow to pack up. You don't need to do a thing, honey.' After a short pause, he slapped his hand on the table and said, 'Godammit, Caron, I don't have time for all this. I want everything back like it was!'

Immediately Flora was standing there. 'I just wanted to see if you had bowls of cashews and olives like I do.' Then she sat back down.

'Dammit, Caron!' Bas whispered. 'Do we have to have the gooseberry here?'

I grinned. 'I don't recall a comparable American word for chaperone.'

'If they haven't already, they'd make gooseberries illegal, honey. Capital punishment, the electric chair.' He was all charm and clotted cream again. 'Let me ask you, Caron, why did you take the particular things you took from our flat?'

'Because they were mine, Bas! Why do you think? And that includes the Picasso.'

'That's not a good reason, Caron. Everything belongs to both of us, to our life together. But why those particular things? We have other really prettier valuables. And you didn't take all your clothes.' I took a big gulp of my G&T, draining the glass, a hint that I was about to leave. This whole conversation was crazy.

Then he said with real menace, 'I want you back, honey. And I'm going to get you back!'

Flora appeared again and said, 'Have you tried the olives?'

I was about to get up to go, while Flora was already standing. But Bas stood first and said, 'If you'll just come back, honey, give it a try for at least two weeks? Then if it doesn't work, I'll leave you alone.'

I got up and said, 'You can start leaving me alone now, Bas. It's not really me you want back. You just have to win all the time, be in control. Thanks for the drink.' Flora and I headed for the door. As we went down the few steps to the main corridor, Flora looked back. 'He's still standing there, watching us leave.'

When we got outside, the limo driver quickly got out and opened the car door. Flora said, 'Should we take the tube instead? In case Bas rings the driver and says to kidnap us or something?'

We both laughed. 'No, we'll enjoy the limo, let Bas pay. I wish I'd had a plastic bag to bring home the cashew nuts.'

'I could see you were too busy to eat, so I wrapped some in a napkin. I wanted the napkin for a souvenir, anyway.' Once we were seated inside, Flora whispered, 'Do you think it's safe to talk in here? I mean is the limo bugged?'

I was about to laugh, but had a second thought. I whispered back, 'I wouldn't put it past Bas. To get my reaction so he'd know what tricks to try next.'

We rode in silence, and just as the driver pulled up in front of Flora's house she said, 'Now I wish we'd spent the trip home drinking up the champagne.'

As we got out, I took the iced bottle of champers and waved it at the driver. 'Thank you so much!'

Once we were ensconced at the kitchen table with glasses of champagne, Flora said, 'He's very charming, Caron. I can see why you fell for him. The man exudes power and confidence. But why does he miss your clothes so much?'

I laughed. 'Bas never had any small talk, it was always about business. I suppose he just means he wants everything the way it was. That, or he's cracking up.'

'Is there any chance at all, Caron, that he'll just go home and leave you alone now? Give up?'

'That'll happen the day hell freezes over and pink elephants go there to ice skate.'

'It's strange he didn't precisely make a fuss about the Picasso. He only mentioned other valuables. It was you who said the word Picasso.'

'People like Bas are always thinking of more than one thing at a time. That's why they get ahead in life twice as fast. He doesn't want us to know exactly how much he misses that painting.'

'So are we back to square one? I mean about what could happen next?'

'Square one has now had a bonfire lit in it, Flora. One that could get out of control. Your idea was good, to find out what Bas was thinking. But now he's been rejected again.'

'Oh, dear. I still think he's in love with you, Caron, and wants you back. He's going to an awful lot of trouble, even playing tricks is a bother for him.'

'Playing tricks is Bas' greatest pleasure, Flora. I'm realising now that sex and love are just the salt and pepper, whereas power is the meat that keeps him going.'

'Goodness, Caron, if this Bas stuff was in a book, I'd need to take it off the romance shelf and put it with the crime novels.'

'I'd rather be a detective than back with Bas.' I emptied the bottle into our glasses and then took a sip. 'We'd make a good detective team, Flora.'

'We would?'

'If it's either that or become victims, then yes, absolutely. So cheer up.'

Flora sipped her champagne. 'Thank goodness we're not drinking beer. That type of detective usually gets beaten up, tortured, and sometimes captured. Bullet wounds, knife scars on their cheeks. And their romances always fail.'

'What happens to the ones who drink champagne?'

'Well, for a start, they do drink champagne. And they sit in stately homes and think a lot. But I can't recall any who have nine-to-five jobs at a department store.'

12

At last the day of the Pickled Onion arrived. The pub was crowded, but some of the tables were free because so many punters preferred standing. Flora and I sat near a fake coal fire with electric lights flickering like the real thing. A few people had tossed cigarette stubs on it.

Flora offered to get the drinks while I guarded the table. 'A G&T please, Flora. Make that a double.'

'But Caron, won't that use up a lot of your overtime?'

'Yeah, but it might help me think of another way to make money.'

I was actually too tired to think at all. I tried to cheer up and remembered some advice I'd seen in a get-ahead book that to gain promotion or whatever, you needed to think and act positively. Behave 'as if', sort of role-play. So if I smiled and sat up straight maybe I'd feel energetic. Then I remembered how in such a short time I'd begun to think like a member of the accounts section, instead of a high-flying executive. Heaven help me if the as if worked in reverse.

Soon my positive thinking ran out, and our conversation was mostly just poor Flora listening to me moaning. Fortunately for Flora, a tall athletic chap leaning over the table interrupted this. He asked if we would like another drink. I quickly said no, but Flora just as quickly said yes. When he returned with the drinks, he pulled a chair from another table and sat down. It was such a blatant come-on that I remained silent and bored, wishing he would go away. Therefore it was the polite Flora who answered all his questions.

I hadn't been paying much attention and then suddenly realised the man was sort of sending up Flora to get my attention. He'd tell Flora she had lovely hair, or figure, or whatever, which she'd take at face value and thank him. All the while he kept trying to nudge me and once actually winked. This was a guy who seriously needed to be buried alive.

I leaned across the table and said, 'My dear friend Flora is leading you on. She's the VP of Information Technology and has guys like you drooling over her all the time.' Then for good measure, I added, 'And she obviously thinks you in particular are a shit and a bastard.' I was so furious my face felt like a bonfire.

The man looked taken aback, then smiled sarcastically. 'Why don't we let the charming young lady speak for herself.'

Flora said hesitantly, 'Well, I wouldn't say a shit, I mean that's not one of my words.'

I looked at her, wanting to shake her, while the shit began gloating.

Then Flora added, still in her hesitant voice, 'But yes, I can say you definitely are a bastard.'

The man's face flushed and he mumbled what sounded like fuck, fuck, and more fuck, as he wandered off.

'Well, done, Flora! That was brilliant!'

Flora smiled happily. 'Do you really think so? Gosh, it's a good thing my mother didn't hear me.'

'Well, your mother's not here, and anyway, she would have been proud of you. And your mother won't be with you when you go out with Mervin, either.'

Flora blushed. 'I did realise, Caron, just for the record, that he was winding me up. But I don't really know what to do besides be polite.'

'Well, you're learning fast. And keep on learning. If you lie in the road with a sign saying drive over me, there are a lot of people who'll rev up their engines. And before Mervin's do, we're going shopping. Get you some new clothes to wear to the private viewing.'

Flora looked crestfallen and glanced down at her latest tent. 'I paid quite a bit for this. It's really quite stylish. Don't you think?'

'If we're both polite all the time, then we won't make much progress, Flora. Your dress is fine, but it doesn't suit the brief. I mean, what's under there, anyway? There must be some curves somewhere?'

Flora laughed. 'What's under there is an awful lot of me. Anyway, I want a man who loves me like I am, then he can see the hidden bits.'

'Nonsense, Flora. That only worked in the old days in small communities where the choice was limited and inevitable. Now you have to advertise. Flaunt it. I mean you have to create a bit of interest.' After a minute I added, 'Anyway, it's quite like your habit of being polite. How the hell is a man going to know the real you if you keep yourself sprinkled with icing sugar?'

Flora grinned. 'Maybe I can switch to chocolate icing. But you Caron, you don't wear really tight clothes. They sort of, like, sway off your skinny body. Sorry, I mean, you know, slim and lithe.'

I laughed. 'Nothing wrong with skinny. If I wore tight clothing, I'd be all ribcage and knees. You obviously have a cleavage, Flora. Accentuating that might distract from other bits if you think that's necessary. Men on the whole love big boobs. Women spend a fortune buying them.'

'But I'm so round. A bit fat, really. Don't you think this dress hides it?'

'It isn't clear what it's hiding, and men tend to imagine the worst. Make the best of what you do have. Stop slumping and trying to blend into the woodwork. I've seen women a lot heavier than you strut and dare the world to get in the way.'

'But that's not me, Caron.'

'Maybe not yet. Just wait until we hit the shops. Make out a budget, decide what you can afford to spend.'

'You can shop, too, Caron. You'll have more overtime by then. In spite of Bas, wouldn't you really like to find a husband?'

'Bas being one has quite put me off. Anyway, there's plenty of time. When the guys are all forty plus and on their third divorce, maybe they will have learned a thing or two.'

Flora laughed. 'That might suit me. I mean it would be easier to catch one when they've slowed down.'

I spoke carefully. 'You know, it's not good your constantly putting yourself down, Flora. You've got a lot going for you. Mervin's not going to know what hit him.'

As I sipped my drink, I noticed a man in the far corner looking at us. 'Do you know that man, Flora? The tall blond in the navy linen suit. Looks like a real smoothie? He's staring at us.'

Flora turned and then saw the man. 'Jack Howard, Chambers' Emporium VP, aged forty-two, six foot tall, Cambridge first-class degree, has probably slept his way through half of Chambers'. That's the Romeo I mentioned earlier, who mimicked Mr Chambers' elbow.

Look, he's doing it again, and Mr Chambers isn't even there. Do you think he's practising?'

I laughed in case she was joking. 'Don't tell me you got the Romeo info through his personnel records.'

'Pat told Anne who told Dorothy who told me. But I don't doubt there's truth in it. And talk about a good catch. He's tipped to take over from Mr Chambers.'

'I thought you said James was.'

'Both of them. Even if Jack Howard started his own rumour himself, no one's tried to shut it up. Word is that there's bad blood between him and James and that whoever gets the top job will, like, sack the other. Gosh, he's coming over here.'

I couldn't believe how much the man resembled Bas. Flora had said before that he matched Bas' description, but as she hadn't actually seen Bas I hadn't given her comment much weight. He even had the same sauntering walk with one hand stuck in his jacket pocket with only his thumb showing. All the anger and resentment I felt for Bas seemed to colour my perception of the man until horns seemed to be sticking out of his skull.

It must have been exhaustion, because even my recent gruelling work pace seemed to be this stranger's fault. I wanted desperately to stand up and bash in his chin. It was absolutely the wrong time and the wrong place for me to fall head over heels in hate. But I couldn't seem to regain my equilibrium.

'Good evening, Flora.' Turning to me, he said, 'I don't think we've met. I'm Jack Howard.'

'I'm Caron Carlisle.'

He held out his hand to shake mine. Laughing he said, 'James Smith's a lucky bastard. Haven't I seen you talking to him?'

There must have been so many people in the corridor on my interview day, I'm surprised they didn't set up benches and sell tickets. 'James directed me to the personnel department for my accounts interview, and we met then.'

He laughed again. 'Not a bad idea, meeting people on the executive level before going for an interview.' It was only a joke, and coming from a woman I might have laughed. But after Bas the idea of my getting somewhere hanging onto a man's coat tails was still fresh in my mind. So I took his comment as a slur.

Uninvited he sat in the empty chair recently vacated by what I now considered the first blond creep. That made Jack the second one and Bas the King of Creep. He offered drinks and again I said no and Flora yes. But instead of going to get them, he waved down a young man in a business suit, probably middle management, and sent him to fetch them. He also ordered me another G&T even though I'd said no.

Jack Howard was very good-looking and exuded sexuality, but he was totally ignoring Flora and gazing at my chest and sitting far too close. I said, 'That's not my best bit. Look up.'

He settled his eyes on my mouth. 'Quite pretty mouth, too.'

'Keep going,' she said.

'And gorgeous eyes.'

'Still not quite there.'

Jack laughed. 'I love it. A woman who puts brains first. That makes you a very exceptional female.'

'And you'd bloody well better not forget it.'

Flora looked stricken and Jack turned gratefully to retrieve the drinks from his flunky. I noticed that he didn't give the guy any money for the drinks. Then Jack stood up. 'It's been a pleasure, ladies. Now if you will excuse me.' He turned back and said to me, 'So you're in the accounts section. At least for now. I won't forget you, Caron. I love a challenge.'

After he'd gone, Flora said, 'My God, Caron, what did you think you were doing? Most women would die to have him. And what did he do wrong? That man's got power. He could get you the sack in ten seconds flat.'

I said a bit too loud, 'For what? Not succumbing to a pass made in a public bar? I'd hightail it to the employment tribunal so fast you'd think my hair was on fire!'

But already I was admitting to myself that I'd over-reacted horribly. As they said in New York, men making a pass were a dime a dozen. And I wasn't even certain he'd made one. I wasn't wearing a revealing outfit. He could have been admiring the fabric, or the buttons, or just focussing his eyes, and then played the game I set up.

'Sorry, Flora. It's not your fault. It's not even Jack Howard's fault. He just reminded me so much of Bas. And now I can't exactly go apologise and say, I'm sorry I thought you were staring at my tits. Double, triple shit! I can't afford to lose my job over something so ridiculous.'

Flora said, 'He wouldn't get you in such a way that you could claim harassment. Chambers' goes by all the rules religiously. But when a VP has it in for you, they can always find something. And you're still on probation. They don't need to give a reason for letting you go. Jack Howard can just snap his fingers. Click, and you're out.'

I imagined Jack clicking his fingers and it sounded

like a guillotine. It was really shitty to think of Bas gloating that he didn't need to ruin my job chances because I did that better myself. And Mrs Oakley had trusted me, had even laughed. And a reference from a job I'd held for such a short time would be worse than an envelope full of buffalo droppings.

Another man stopped by our table to ask if we wanted a drink. Flora smiled at him and said, 'We'd really like you to go away.'

'I feel dreadful about ruining your night out, Flora. But everything will be all right, believe me.' I took a deep breath and realised positive thinking could be so exhausting it was almost counter-productive.

'It's me who should be, like, reassuring you, Caron. But I can't think of anything helpful to say. Well. Maybe Jack Howard will be run over by a bus?'

'Anyway, Flora, you heard what Jack Howard said. About his liking a challenge. He won't be so unsubtle as to charge my desk tomorrow morning shouting, 'Out into the cold, cold snow.' And while he thinks of a strategy, OK, more likely a torture, it gives me time to think of something.'

Flora looked enormously relieved. 'Oh, I hadn't considered that. Of course you can think of something. I'd pit you against Jack Howard any time. It's not really an advantage to fight from the accounts department, but look what happened with David and Goliath.'

I nearly spilled my drink when I thought of David and Goliath. The mountain pitted against the molehill. None of which would have mattered much if I could've had that smug feeling of being in the right. There wasn't a precedent in legend for the guilty little guy beating the righteous giant. There were simply lots of little dead moles cluttering up the base of mountains.

'I know what I can do, Flora, I'll write Jack Howard a note. Head him off at the pass.'

Flora thought for a moment. 'You want to be careful. I mean a full confession. If he wants to get rid of you, well that would provide evidence at the trial. Wouldn't it?'

'I don't mean anything specific, like saying "I thought he was on a scavenger hunt looking for my breasts." Something more like Bas, trust me, that could be taken more than one way.' By this time I'd got out a pen and pad and begun scribbling furiously. I turned the page and did some more writing.

Flora said, 'Remember, it's got to be something that doesn't make matters worse.'

'Yeah,' I said, still writing, scratching out bits, adding more. 'And I have to take into account that his secretary will probably read it first.' Finally I shoved the paper across the table.

Flora read aloud:

'Dear Mr Howard, I feel I owe you an apology. You reminded me of an old flame and I suspect I took out on you what I couldn't level at him. Sincerely, You know who, and if you don't then you are probably guilty as previously charged in which case no apology is needed.'

'Well, OK, Flora, so it's not Shakespeare.'

'It's not what I would call a traditional apology, either.' She considered for some time. And then, surprisingly, she said, 'But you know, Caron, it might work. There's a hint of the old, "Have you stopped beating your wife?" You know, the question a person can't safely answer either way? And it doesn't actually have your name on it. And if his sex life is really rampant, well he might be into that sadomasochist stuff.'

'You mean it could make him angry as hell? You

know, Flora, all this would be infinitely easier were he guilty.'

'Maybe you shouldn't do anything. Just wait and see what happens?'

'I have to take the initiative, Flora. That's the little guy's only chance.'

'Try it, Caron. It wouldn't work for me or anyone else I know, but it just might work for you,' she said, looking again at the note. 'If the worst comes to the worst, maybe he'll get really angry and try to shoot you.'

'And that would improve matters?'

'Well, you said it would help if he were guilty.'

'Sure. I'd be in the right, but I'd be dead.'

Flora smiled. 'One thing's for sure. His reputation's too well known for him to pass this note on to a job tribunal.'

When we got home and Flora was unlocking the door, she said, 'I don't know him very well, but it'd be really helpful if Jack Howard has a sense of humour.'

I grinned. 'Then we might be in luck. I don't think Romeo had much of one, or the Marquis de Sade for that matter. But I think the Devil's is supposed to rather well developed.'

13

Once in bed, it was hard to sleep. And it wasn't just the fear of losing my job. I'd done something so stupid it made me wonder if I were cracking up. Well, more precisely, if the cracks I'd already got were getting wider. Jack Howard quite simply wasn't Bas, so my reaction might have had to do with a different worry. When my thoughts get tangled and stuck together like cold noodles, it sometimes helps me to write furiously, to try to catch the stream of consciousness. Just slap everything on paper, let my brain spew like ticker tape. I'd got to page four before I could see a pattern.

And then it hit me. My real fear, or the deeper one, might be exactly how far my brain had depended on my skirt over running Bas' company. Could I have been just a glorified secretary sleeping with the boss, both of us leaning on his talent? Were my hopes of promotion even in the accounts section not realistic?

I made a list of our various assets. Obviously, Bas had the money and the contacts. He actually chose the companies to buy and did the sales pitch to backers. I did the computer stuff, helping to crunch the numbers and work out viability. And I did the cosmetic bit, figuring out what we needed to do to improve our buys to sell them for a profit – that included landscaping, interior decorating, general prettifying. I suppose I was like a mortician dressing up the corpse, except I had to make sure the corpse could later get up and slink along the catwalk.

Of course I didn't actually plant trees and lay carpet, but the hired experts had followed my designs. And when I remembered some of the actual results, I felt much better. Bas might have paid for my scooter, but it wasn't his third leg that had propelled it along the pavement.

So my current problem was probably that I was suffering from self-pity. And the incident with Jack Howard was only a self-fulfilling manifestation of my belief that I'd got a rotten deal with Bas. Think rich and you make money, think poor and someone steals your loaf of bread. Think pitiful and evidence grows like hairs out of your ears.

Well, Bas might have kept my money, but I still had my todays and tomorrows. And if I drowned in self-pity, that was my lookout and not his. My fears weren't simply a matter of feeling poor and helpless and humiliated by someone with power and wealth. I was intimidating myself, reducing my self-worth to such a low level that someone else's power and money seemed a problem. But Bas had started out with nothing, and at my age probably had not much more than me. And in his late twenties, Bas must have turned a lot of powerful people into turnips. So it wasn't only about him and not me having the power of money. Money didn't make the woman, rather the other way round.

Getting a bit of perspective helped, I thought, as I gazed at the loosening wallpaper and remembered my bank balance. Sure, I needed my current job, but I needed to think further than that. One thing was for certain. Being so bitter about Bas meant I wasn't rid of him psychologically. I needed to get really involved in something more engrossing than revenge. The accounts section obviously wasn't providing that. In fact, just thinking about it was probably what made me fall asleep.

The following morning I woke up feeling like I had a hangover, making me wish I'd had the pleasure of more than two G&Ts to deserve it. Even a hot soak in the bath went pretty much unnoticed, except for my wondering if it would be my last. I dressed all in black, the same clothes as for my interview, although I didn't think they were what had made Mrs Oakley laugh. If I'd had a nun's habit, I would have worn that.

The post arriving with a postcard from Paris didn't help matters. On the front was a depiction of a painting by Picasso, although it wasn't the same as my painting. But there was no time to think about it. I crammed it into my shoulder bag and set off for work. It was still early, and I wondered if I were the only human who, when expecting a firing squad, would actually arrive early.

I tried to look cheerful as I reheard the two dawg jokes. And I sprayed on a Dior sample. But even the lovely smell didn't lift the gloom. I really needed a job where my midnight highs could be put to use. One that didn't involve standing on street corners.

I remembered where the mailroom was from Flora's orientation tour. When I told the man I'd like to buy some stamps, he said they didn't sell them. So I had to keep asking questions until one of them caused the man to turn his back. I think he looked up the airmail rate for Tibet just to get rid of me. Then I slipped the envelope addressed to Jack Howard into the 'incoming' pile. After that, I rushed to my desk while speculating whether I should have taken Flora's suggestion and done nothing. Waiting was waiting, and it was beginning to seem like all I'd done was load Jack Howard's gun for him.

By the afternoon, my nerves had turned into mint jelly. And then I heard Mrs Brown saying, 'Caron, if I might have a word.'

I followed her to her desk station. Mrs Brown never hurried and it was only after she had resettled comfortably in her chair that she spoke again.

'This is most unusual, Caron, for such a new employee. But there's been a specific request for you in particular to work in another office this afternoon.' She coughed slightly and added, 'I noticed that you had lunch at your desk. It isn't necessary to tire yourself out and work too hard. It will all come in time, my dear.'

'Er, which office, Mrs Brown?' It had to be an important office because Mrs Brown's added solicitude was obvious. And of course welcome. Except that it was really too late. But it meant she didn't know the request wasn't exactly a compliment.

'Vice President Jack Howard.'

'Is there any reason why he asked for me specially?' I wanted as much information as I could get.

'Oh, it wasn't for you specially in that sense, Caron. Mr Howard said he'd heard you are good with figures.' She blushed slightly. 'He actually said he'd heard you have a good figure, but of course that was a slip and we both laughed. Quite entertaining, our Mr Howard.'

So it was going to be slow death by stale jokes, I thought as I made my way to the top floor. The receptionist was at her desk by the lift this time, just when I would have relished getting lost again. But as I went slowly along the corridor checking the names on the doors, I came to James' door first. He was standing beside his PA's desk giving her some instructions. When he saw me, he came to the door.

'Hello, Caron. Lovely to see you.' He lowered his voice and grinned. 'Lost again, or have you come to use my shoulder?'

I said, 'Honestly, James, if I used it today you'd need a lifebelt.'

He laughed. 'Go ahead. I'm a good swimmer.'

I smiled. 'Just joking. I'm looking for Jack Howard's office to do some temping.'

Flora must have been right about the bad blood, because for a moment it looked like the two of us would need a whole lifeboat. 'Two doors down on this side, Caron. I'll be away for the next couple of days, but you've still got my number?'

I assured him I had, and then he seemed to watch anxiously as I went down the corridor, making me wonder if they kept Jack Howard in a cage.

His secretary's desk was unoccupied, and when I knocked on his door, he came personally to open it. 'Julie is running errands, Caron. Do please come in.' I did so and then stood like a robot with a rundown battery, until he added, 'And please sit down.'

There was a silence as I gathered mental bullets without any idea where to shoot them. Then Jack Howard limply held up my note and just let it dangle for a few moments between us.

He smiled. 'As you can see, I got your apology. If it is an apology?'

Still I said nothing. Well, I didn't want to own up to having anything to do with it until I knew his reaction. He dropped the note onto his desk, and it seemed as if it clanged a bit when it landed.

Then he leaned back and relaxed. 'If it's any help,

Caron, I haven't called you in to sack you. For a start, it isn't that easy. And it happens it isn't in my own interests at the moment in any case.'

I realised I'd been holding my breath, and I slowly let it out. 'Well, that's welcome news. Look, Mr Howard, I . . .'

'Jack. We're an old family company.'

'Jack, then. I'd like to say I was way out of line in the pub. And I'm sorry. Is that better?'

Surprisingly, he said nothing but appeared to be thinking furiously. 'Do you think we might be able to start again, Caron?'

I really was relaxing, because that struck me as hilarious. I mean, what would the poor man have done if I'd said, 'Look up, Jack, further, not my tits.' I smiled. 'It would be easier if you didn't want to leave the sword hanging over my head. I mean, if it doesn't suit you to sack me today, what about next week?'

He again seemed to be thinking furiously, weighing his next words carefully. I half expected his eyeballs to start whizzing around like a pinball machine. Then he matched my smile exactly. 'You can take it that it won't suit me next week either.'

Then he stood up and put the one hand in his pocket as he paced about. But he no longer resembled Bas except superficially. In his shoes, Bas would have had a charcoal barbecue smoking and asked if you preferred to be cooked rare.

'I'm sure you've heard rumours, Caron. Your note indicates as much.'

I laughed. 'The Romeo of Chambers' Emporium variety?' At this point, it seemed like I needed to reassure him more than vice versa, which was puzzling.

He also laughed. 'Exactly. Well, I began work at this

firm in a far lowlier position. It didn't matter then. But in my current position, that behaviour would be seen as taking unfair advantage. And quite right. But it is easier to change the man than the gossip.'

I couldn't believe it. He was in effect apologising to me. It had to be a trick. Maybe he really was like Bas. Maybe he wanted to use me to get word out that he wasn't Romeo, that he was only Mickey Mouse. He kept sort of glancing at me to see how I was taking his words. Not the actions of a completely sincere and honest man. Well, hell would turn into a parcel of frozen shrimp at Iceland before I'd assist another Bas. But I needed to say something.

'Thank you for sharing that with me, Jack.' Those mimicking books always mentioned the word 'sharing' a lot. 'I admit I was totally out of line.'

'In that case, would you mind if I asked what the hell this guy who reminded you of me did? And what you did in return?' He picked up my note. 'This isn't exactly the work of a humble woman. Surely you didn't murder him? Or anything especially interesting?'

We both laughed. 'It was because I couldn't slaughter him that I attacked you. But I only ever use words, Jack.'

We then exchanged a few pleasantries, about whether I was enjoying my job and did he like his. Then he said, 'You're sure to go quite a lot further than the accounts section, Caron. And you're obviously an intelligent and interesting woman. I don't wish to repeat the pub fiasco, but would you consider allowing me to take you to dinner?'

Surprised and somewhat caught off guard, I said, 'But wouldn't that break your personal rule about company dating?'

'Only if either of us jumped the other and dragged

them into bed. And then told everyone about it. But I personally doubt either of those events would occur with you. I would sincerely like to get to know you better. And we could put the pub incident completely behind us, then. The truth is, your being in accounts doesn't matter because it is so blatantly obvious you won't be there long. Just your facility with numbers should ensure that.'

My first thought was how did he know I was good with numbers. He'd mentioned that to Mrs Brown as well. Did the whole the top floor realise I was doing Melody's work? That seemed unlikely. And the stuff I did for the real accountants was pretty basic.

And what the hell should I do about the date? With both of us carefully choosing every word, it'd probably be less effort if we took along a translator. I still wasn't the least bit sure I should trust him and that precluded my liking him. On the other hand, he'd handled the situation with a certain delicacy and most assuredly in my favour. That was what the self-help books called a win/win situation, but only if I accepted his invite. Because he'd so craftily put my acceptance on a par with wiping the slate clean. I thought of all this quickly enough not to cause an embarrassing silence. Well, maybe by then a translator would've been thumbing through a dictionary.

'That would be lovely, Jack. But could we wait a few weeks? I've just moved and it's taking all my spare time to get things sorted out.'

Hanging between us in the air was the fact that I hadn't been too busy to go to the pub. And how was I going to go there with Flora on Mervin's nights without compounding the crime?

Then I smiled. 'You see, Flora in personnel has been

helping me out with some complicated forms. And of course I think it only fair to buy her a drink while we talk. But do, of course, if you are ever in that pub again when we are, join us. I owe you a drink.' That should keep him away from the pub, the notion that Flora would be witness to his every move.

That seemed to do it and he smiled in a friendly manner and said, 'Excellent.' Looking at his calendar, he added, 'Shall we say in two weeks then? Is that convenient? Perhaps the theatre and dinner to follow?'

Looking at his watch, he added, 'You've been here long enough to satisfy Mrs Brown. We can leave it that I wanted you to double-check some figures for me. There really isn't any work. But you are welcome to stay.' He smiled brightly and flashed his blue eyes.

I grinned. 'I'm going back to my desk while we're still at square one. And thank you, Jack.'

I felt great relief as I went along the corridor. On the other hand, I didn't relish going to the sorts of places frequented by Bas on the arm of his lookalike. And what about my dear friend James, if I went out with his enemy? By the time I got my life sorted out, my teeth might be sleeping by my bedside in a glass.

I rang Flora as soon as I reached my desk. 'It's all right, Flora. I've kept the job.'

I could hear Flora sort of gulping. 'Fantastic, Caron, that's so wonderful. I can hardly believe it. I was more worried than I dared tell you. In case, you know?'

'I do know, and thanks. Gory details later. Mrs Brown's coming. And I'm treating us to pizza on the way home.' I was going to start thinking rich until it either worked or my bank manager became homicidal.

'How did it go, Caron?'

'Very well, Mrs Brown. Just double-checking some

figures. Not my figure of course.' I waited until Mrs Brown had a delicate chuckle. She had seemed to like the other version of that joke. 'It was just faster for me to read out numbers from one list while he checked his accounts.'

After Mrs Brown returned to her desk, Melody asked what was going on.

'I can't tell you, Melody. You said not to mention numbers.'

She was blowing on her fingernails to help the varnish to dry. 'Well, you watch out for that Jack Howard, Caron. He's too crafty for his own good. There's little that young man won't do to get advancement. And I've also heard he has a very large ding dong.'

The Italian place smelled terrific. The garlicky smells were certainly tickling my appetite. I ordered the basic cheese and tomato pizza with added pepperoni and anchovies.

While waiting for Flora to decide, I touched the soft tallow of the candle sticking out of the old wine bottle. I'd only been to Italy once, but I hadn't seen red checked tablecloths or candles in wine bottles. It made me wonder if it'd only been in a film, branding the Italians for life. Probably all the tables in Naples held dusty empties by now.

Flora ordered extra mushrooms and green peppers. We'd ordered a whole bottle of house red, and she began filling our glasses. With a big smile, she said, 'Now, Caron, tell me about Jack Howard. I can hardly wait to hear.'

I gave a pretty much verbatim account of the meeting, adding on what Mrs Brown and Melody had said.

Flora's mouth was nearly hanging open. 'My God, the man's in love with you! Maybe more than James.'

I was amazed. 'James is just a friend, Flora. And he's your friend, too. And he's our neighbour. As for Jack, he hardly knows me. What on earth gave you an idea like that? Certainly nothing he said in his office, or even in the pub.'

'What? And here's me thinking you're a woman of the world. A man doesn't have to jump up and down, I mean, like, flashing a diamond and falling onto his knees, you know, to be in love. I know that much from reading romances.'

She took another small bite of tomato. 'He didn't sack you, and he asked you to dinner and the theatre. In all the books, that adds up to true love. I mean it's obvious. In romances the men have to choose between sex and love. Cocktails might be for sex, but theatre's always love.'

I laughed. 'I'm afraid I don't quite follow your logic.'

Waving her fork that had speared a mushroom, she said, 'Name me one romance with the hero and heroine at the opera or the theatre or in a stately home that isn't true love?'

I combed my brain. Nothing. 'That's not fair. The whole point of a romance is true love. So wherever they go, they fall in love.'

Flora positively beamed. 'Gotcha! That's presuming, if you know what I mean, that there's only two characters. The other woman gets only sex. The other man doesn't usually get even that.'

I must not have looked convinced, so Flora continued, 'If your meeting with Mr Howard was in a romance, believe me, it would mean true love. He's a VP, and yet you say he spoke hesitantly. Would a man just wanting sex do that? And more serious, he keeps stressing your intelligence. That's a sure sign of love in romances, although the actual action doesn't make that completely believable: that they only want a woman to talk to, sort of thing.'

'But Flora, the only choices aren't just sex or love. He could've been hoping I'd gossip and change his image. Look how it's worked with you.'

'Yes, Caron. But anyone can look at you and tell you aren't going to gossip to the accounts section. I wouldn't have been surprised if you hadn't even told me, you know? I never expected so many tasty and interesting and fascinating and juicy details. You aren't, well, leaving anything out? A little kiss or anything, before the mention of the theatre? Hardly any heroine gets dinner and the theatre before a kiss.'

I could hardly talk for laughing. 'No way! He wouldn't have dared touch me after my note.'

Flora said adoringly, 'That was so clever, your note. No one else would ever have thought of writing a rude note for an apology.' Smiling, she asked, 'Do you think Mervin would like a rude note?'

'Actually I suspect Mervin would love it. He seems to have a terrific sense of humour, more than one could say about Jack Howard.'

'When men fall in love, humour's the first thing that goes. But what about you, Caron? In books you would need to have serious doubts, but in real life most women would snap him up.'

'Would you, Flora?'

Flora carefully refilled our glasses. Although the wine wasn't an expensive one, she was treating it as the arm and leg it was costing me. Which goes to show that the cost of arms and legs is relative. 'He's a terrific catch, you know? Not just because he's got money, well, he must have, working on the top floor. And he could, just could, get the top post. But I suspect he would attract women if he weren't rich. He may have slept his way through Chambers', but no one complained and most of them would love encores.'

'You still haven't answered my question, Flora.'

'Well, to take me. I probably would go for him, if I couldn't get Mervin, that is. But that's because my choice is sort of limited, you know? But if I could choose from the whole world, I don't think I'd choose him.' She smiled brightly. 'I guess it is possible for me to change. Whoever would have thought at the pub last night that I'd turn down Jack Howard?'

'Well, I don't want him either. And if you're right, Flora, and I don't agree you are, it's a serious problem. If it gets to the point of turning him down, I might really get the sack. In those books you've read, how long could the heroine stall, put off the dire moment?'

'Sometimes for three hundred pages. But I don't know. I don't see Jack taking more than fifty pages. Maybe fewer. You would just be on page three at the moment. And that's only if there was a long description of his office curtains. He might be out buying the diamond as we speak.'

I choked on my wine. 'When exactly is Mervin's show? Isn't that in a few weeks? Maybe I could steer Jack towards that. Surely at the exhibition he couldn't jump up and down with a diamond between his teeth.'

Flora laughed. 'More's the pity. And it's the right timing. Do you think he would go? Wanting to change his image? I mean, all of accounts will be there. He'd have to be very sure of himself, kind of thinking of you as a prospective trophy wife and wanting to show you off.'

She became serious while taking a sip of wine. If Flora were a weathervane, you'd know exactly when to go get your raincoat. 'You don't think the accounts crowd just considers Mervin a poor substitute for Jack Howard, do you? I mean, you don't think Mervin's slept with everyone?'

'Honestly, Flora! I believe it'd be far easier to get Jack into bed than Mervin. Maybe that's what's unappealing about Jack Howard, that it all sounds too easy. Wouldn't mean much, probably not to him either. Anyway, I'm sure he isn't in love with me.' I added to myself that I couldn't possibly be that unlucky.

I took the Picasso postcard from my bag and set it on the table. Flora had seen it in the morning, but we hadn't had time to talk. 'What the hell do you make of it, Flora?'

She picked it up and turned it over. 'No message. Well, not anything written out. A reminder, maybe? That he hasn't forgotten about it?'

I thought about that. 'If that's all it is, Flora, it probably means the postcard doesn't connect to the chair and the chocolates. I mean this is explicit.'

Flora turned the card back to facing Picasso. 'It's been about a month since the chair. Could that, like, mean something?'

I laughed. 'It would give me great pleasure to think Bas was beginning to have periods.'

The waiter returned and Flora and I ordered a zabaglione between us. 'Did you notice, Flora, that there's no mention of our meeting him at the Ritz? Because it involved rejection, he's probably going to act like that night never happened. What do you think?'

Flora smiled. 'I think we're going to need a very large bus, what with all the people we want it to run over.'

'In the meantime, we need to keep a lookout for runaway buses ourselves.'

14

Flora and I were going into work at the same time, so we had breakfast together. Evelyn had returned during the night from Manchester, and her coming into the kitchen interrupted our civilised silence, the early morning yawn and sip coffee period. It wasn't that she was particularly noisy, but when she makes an entrance, the room shrinks. I said, 'Well, how did it go, Evelyn? And when you get to Hollywood, don't forget me and Flora.'

Flora had been excited when I told her about Evelyn's hopes and now she said, 'Caron and I especially like sailing in yachts.'

'It's modelling. I already said I wasn't aiming for Hollywood.'

Flora smiled. 'But you wouldn't exactly turn Hollywood down? I mean like break their hearts?'

'Well, you know from my efforts with you two that I don't like letting anyone down.'

I asked, 'And did you meet some helpful men?'

She poured corn flakes into a bowl and managed to sprinkle bits in both Flora's and my cups of coffee. 'Believe me, the only men who made suggestions wouldn't have wanted a camera within a zillion miles.'

Flora grinned. 'At least that saves on fees at the dating agency.'

'Surely, you two don't think I go out with men I know nothing about!'

Flora's and my eyebrows waved at each other. But there was no time to discuss Evelyn's love life further as work called. In fact, it was practically shouting. Later, as Flora and I made our way through the racks of clothing and passed two dawgs, Flora whispered, 'One day we need to bring a couple of poodles to work.'

'To end the jokes, we'd need to bring Alsatians.'

Just as we started up the stairs we bumped into Mervin. That was so unusual I'd begun to wonder if he came to work through a window. But it was probably because whenever I didn't think anyone was watching I used the lift.

Flora said, 'Good morning, Mervin.' And he said, 'Good morning, Flora.' I just smiled and nodded at Mervin, not wanting to interrupt the love scene of the year.

That day's work was the usual spreadsheets, numbers to the right, to the left, a few strays under the desk trying to bite my ankles. Finally Melody stopped to take a break, and I got us coffee. Her completed work stack was so tall I began to wonder if someone on the top floor was writing his memoirs, the great *Chambers' Emporium Exposé.* How to fit the bra to the customer, with maybe a chapter titled The Bra Bites Back.

'Caron, did you by any chance write a letter to Mr Chambers?'

That caught me so off guard I wondered if she had just come across a love letter on the audiotape. 'Me? No way. Why?'

'Are you sure?'

'Oh, maybe I did. You said those confidential bits go to him. One day I added a little note. Just about some figures needing checking out. But, Melody, I definitely didn't begin, ''My dearest darling Mr Chambers''.'

She smiled. 'That must be it, then. He rang me at home last night.'

'Oh, no. Don't tell me I have to switch back to letters.'

'No, no, dear. As I told you, that's entirely out of the question. I told him you are perfectly discreet.'

'And that's all? Just carry on?' Life does sometimes blow you a kiss.

'Yes, dear. And he said he liked your note and please to send more any time. That's why I thought it might have been something interesting, and not just about spreadsheets. That and the fact that he wanted it kept quiet.'

I felt incredibly relieved. I must not have been entirely mistaken about the spreadsheets smelling a bit fishy. And this precluded the possibility of Mrs Brown trying to switch Melody's and my work back. On the other hand, if the discrepancies had been simple errors, why the secrecy? It was one thing for Melody to be sent confidential records, but quite another to ask a lowly employee you don't even know to keep her eyes open and her mouth shut. It seemed awfully like he was trying to second-guess someone else on the top floor. And I found that a bit worrying because James, as the Chief Financial Officer, ranked somewhere near the top floor rafters.

The next morning Flora woke me up at six o'clock with a cup of tea. 'Thanks for the tea, Flora, but didn't you know it's against the law to wake up early on Saturdays?'

'We're going shopping.'

'Well, we can't go to the shops until they open, surely?'

'We can be waiting when the doors open.'

It was pointless arguing when I was already awake.

And bless her, Flora banned Evelyn from the bathroom until I had my turn, her way I suppose of saying thanks about the shopping. People do sometimes kick my shin one day and pat my back the next.

Our first stop was our own place of work on Oxford Street, which seemed rather a shame on our day off. And when I led Flora to the cosmetics counter, she whispered, 'Even with a discount, I can't possibly afford . . .'

'Shush.' I'd never met the elegantly dressed and made-up model type behind the counter, as her station wasn't on the express route for late to work employees. But Flora knew her and introduced me.

I said, 'She'd like the free sample make-over.'

As the woman indicated where Flora was to sit and unfolded a clean large white cloth to put around her shoulders, she said, 'What look are we after?'

'The kind of look where it doesn't appear she's wearing any makeup at all.'

'Ah. That would be the Cosmetically Natural Uninhibited Fashion Mode Number Fourteen.'

Fidgeting and looking apprehensive, Flora asked, 'What's look number one?'

'Debutante Balls.'

Hesitantly Flora asked, 'Have you got a number for going to art exhibitions?'

'The National Gallery or The Tate?'

I repeated, 'The natural look. Listen, Flora it's always best to have everybody thinking we'd look better if we made more effort, not knowing we'd already done all possible.'

Gone were the heavy foundation, the overly outlined eyes, the purple eye shadow, and the bright red cheeks. Instead Flora looked a bit more pale and delicate, the contours of her face accented where she now had some angles. The faint grey shadowing around her eyes made them appear a deeper green. The blusher, very near the foundation colour, made Flora appear as though she spent time outdoors, a natural blush from exercise and health. From tart to toot in one hour.

Flora didn't seem too impressed. 'It doesn't look like me.'

The technician said, 'Actually, my dear it does. And you look far slimmer this way. Give yourself a chance to get used to it. Now, about the purchases . . .'

I said quickly, 'As Flora's not sure, I think we'll go have coffee and discuss it. You've made a really lovely job of it.'

Outside Flora said, 'Even if I loved it, it can't possibly last until Mervin's show.'

I laughed. 'We're going straight to Boots the Chemist while you're made up to exactly match everything. What you really pay for, Flora, is that woman's expertise. And we just got that for free.'

Still undecided on her new look, Flora said, 'Well, at least it takes far less time than what I usually do every morning.'

She noticed I was practically growling at the street display windows of Chambers'. 'What's wrong, Caron?'

'These displays. I've seen charity shops with better windows. And why don't they ever change them?'

'I admit they don't really make your eyes pop out. But soon they'll change for Christmas. That should brighten them up. Anyway, the art department's small, maybe that's the best they can do.'

After Boots, I led a protesting Flora to an extremely expensive hairdresser. As I'd anticipated, they were already booked up. 'We just want to use your computer to decide on the style for a later appointment.'

The man looked sceptical. 'We don't let customers loose on that by themselves. Still, the hair washer could help. But she may be called away. Need to dash back and forth.'

'Excellent,' I said before Flora could protest.

Flora's bush of brown hair resisted being tied tightly back, but the computer camera needed to see all of her face. After that, we simply indicated various styles which appeared before us on Flora's image.

Flora said excitedly, 'It's like being on television. I had no idea you could do this. I mean I've read about it, but this!' She smiled brightly.

But the smile dimmed with each choice of style. 'I cannot possibly do that! I look like a punk!'

I thought she looked terrific with the short cut, slightly spiky on top with a smooth as butter fringe, which included highlights in auburn that went well with her natural dark brown. 'Why ever not? Mervin wears a version of the punk.'

'Does he?'

'Well, his style isn't exactly pinstripes and bowler hat.'

'But I've always had long hair. And it would take such a long time to grow it back.'

'Make sense, Flora. When you're eighty, do you want your only claim to fame to be the fact that you've never had your hair cut? Everybody would swoon with envy.'

'You're pulling my leg.'

'Absolutely. Just look at that screen and forget it's you. What would you think of that person?'

She looked carefully. 'Well, she looks richer than me, for a start. And certainly people would notice her. You can see her ears. I don't know if that's good or not.' Then she stopped talking and looked at me for a long moment. 'You know, Caron. If she were wearing a bright pumpkin-coloured dress, with a bit of purple glitter woven in? Very long earrings, maybe with parrots in bright colours? I can sort of imagine Mervin talking to her at his show rather than to me.'

I smiled, inwardly flinching at the clothing description. I turned to the hairdresser and said quickly, 'We've decided. Can we please have a printout of this one.'

As we left, I told Flora, 'You can take that photo to your own hairdresser. The cut's the main thing with hair, and it really is worth spending a bit. When do you think they can fit you in?'

She was still peering doubtfully at the printout, closing one eye then the other. 'Maybe today. Before I lose my courage. It's only around the corner. One of the cutters is Mum's neighbour.' She smiled brightly. 'And you'd be there making sure I went through with it. You're absolutely positive it's the Mervin look?'

'It's the Flora look we're after. When you feel you look terrific, Mervin and the rest will follow, sure as the taxman chases money.'

Flora's mum's neighbour-cum-cutter looked at the photo, then waved it in the air. 'Brill, Flora. Really, really brill. No more awful bush. And your face! You look a good ten years younger! Really, really brill!'

Flora looked horribly embarrassed, but I felt terrific relief. All the stuff I'd been spouting to Flora mostly came from self-help articles in magazines. I myself had actually worn the same hairstyle since college. It made me wonder if a hairdresser would exclaim with joy if I changed it, if she'd sort of run at me with the scissors.

While Flora got her locks chopped, I glanced at the magazines on a table near the door, but they didn't have my full attention as I kept glancing outside. Finally

I stood at the window and looked out. It had worried me how that limo driver on the night we met Bas at the Ritz recognised Flora and me. General descriptions didn't seem enough when we were in the after-work crowd. Of course the driver could have simply waited to see who came to the car.

As I watched the passers-by, everyone looked suspicious. But it's like when someone has their leg in a cast, suddenly the world is full of casts. Because people tend to see whatever they are looking for in life. The men looking at the hairdressers looked suspicious, but so did the ones who looked the other way.

By the time we left the hairdressers, Flora was practically stooped, extremely withdrawn. 'Buck up, Flora. Stand straight or you'll get backache. What's wrong? You look terrific.'

She looked almost tearful. 'I love it, Caron. Really I do. It's just that I'm so horrified that I looked so drastic before. I had no idea.'

I put my arm about her shoulder as we dodged through the shopping crowds on the pavement. 'You didn't look horrible. You just looked different. The old look was fine for what you wanted then. Now you want something else.'

But I could well see Flora's point. The main difference was that you could actually see her now. There's something a bit fearsome about a person you cannot actually see, so her appearance was greatly improved. But maybe now she was feeling horribly exposed.

As we made our way along Oxford Street looking at clothes, I hopefully told Flora about Jean Muir. 'As such a successful designer, she can afford anything she wants, but you know what? She wears all navy.' The result of this was that should Flora ever win the lottery, Muir couldn't count on her sales figures to rise. As we went from shop to shop, Flora favoured a Chagall palette while I tried for Rembrandt. We compromised on Matisse, and Flora kept one new outfit on.

'Does this look all right? Such a tight, skimpy camisole?'

I smiled. 'Absolutely. When Mervin sees that outfit, he might decide to do a portrait of your chest.'

Flora just laughed, gave me a big hug and thanked me. 'You've changed me into a new person, Caron!'

'Oh, no. People change themselves. It was just time for you. And I'm so proud of you, Flora.'

When we got home, I quickly eased off my shoes. There should be a law that all shopping has to be done barefoot. After I wiggled my toes to make sure they were still functioning, I rummaged around in the fridge for a yoghurt. When I got back to the front room, Flora was just closing the outside door and was holding a parcel.

'It's for you, Caron. I went ahead and signed for it. It wasn't the same deliveryman. This one was driving a Parcel Express van. And of course it isn't a chair. '

The return address was Chambers', but I was holding my breath as I opened it. We couldn't ring for the bomb squad every time we got a delivery, but if Bas merely wanted us to have nervous breakdowns he was batting home runs. Then I opened the inside package which was covered with pink paper tied with pink ribbon. As I lifted the lid, Flora and I just stared.

Finally, Flora said, 'Even in a Mills and Boon, I don't recall anyone being sent a pair of pink and chartreuse silk knickers. And they've got the Chambers' label.'

'Could it be a mistake, Flora? Or a lampshade in disguise?' I looked for a card. 'Nothing. I guess the Prime Minister must have sent them.'

'What do you think this means, Caron?'

By then Evelyn had heard us talking and come into the front room. Fingering the pink wrapping paper, she said, 'What's this? I thought you said Bas was the villain? So far all he does is send you presents. One of the sods at the trade fair in Manchester wanted to buy me knickers.'

'It's a trick, Evelyn.'

'Well, I know that. You have to take off the old ones to put on the new. And in between, well you have to be careful. But this Bas isn't even here. Knickers for nothing.'

'All I can think of,' I said in answer to Flora, 'is he's reminding me he knows where I work. And we know he knows that, because he rang you about the Ritz. He's just menacing me.'

Evelyn said, 'But it's silk. Leather, that might be menacing. You know, with chains?'

Flora said, 'Has any man, you know from the dating agency, ever given you those?'

'Nah. A girl my size, nobody gives leather. Or chains.'

'Anyway, Evelyn, I think you're in luck. You're the only one these knickers will fit. But just don't let your guard down. Bas is one tricky bastard. The more he sets us up with these silly things, the worse whatever he's really planning is.'

Flora said, 'But Caron, that makes a rocking chair with chocolates, a Picasso postcard, and a pair of Chambers' silk knickers. If the postcard is separate, what's the connection between a rocking chair and a pair of knickers?'

Evelyn said, 'If it was a bra, it could stop your boobs bouncing if you rock too fast.'

'That sounds more like a mattress, Evelyn. Anyway, I don't know, Flora. But I have a feeling Bas is arranging things so that by the time we've worked out what he means, it's going to be too late.'

15

'Caron,' said Mrs Brown, 'You're wanted in another office at half past nine, so there's little point giving you an assignment here.'

I smiled at Melody, and said reluctantly, 'If you need some help on those letters?'

She smiled. 'No thank you, dear. This memo is so interesting.'

'Oh, yes?'

She chuckled. 'Apparently someone at the perfume counter has been answering the phone by saying, "Hey!" and upstairs is worried this means the customers are horses.'

I laughed. 'Eating hay instead of greeting hey? But do they really handle that on the top floor, Melody?'

'Only because the caller was the VP's wife.'

The mention of VPs reminded me that I needed to try to change my date with Jack Howard from dinner and theatre to Mervin's do. If I simply rang him, his secretary might start gossip. Another note.

No salutation. Then: 'Previous commitment. Willing to substitute previous plan for attending arty function same date?' Could his secretary conceivably take that to mean a business conference? Maybe she would think arty meant party, as in the Conservatives? Maybe it was so vague even Jack wouldn't know what it meant. I left it unsigned and put it in an envelope. There was just enough time for me to dash to the mailroom before reporting to the real accounts department.

It was a pleasant morning, in a private office. The work was a bit more complicated than my regular work, except of course for the private stuff meant for Melody. So that was promising. Soon maybe they'd be on their knees, 'Oh please Caron, please, please, switch to real accounts with double pay!' And I could reply, 'Only double pay?' Actually, when I thought about, it seemed like they were on to a better deal borrowing me. Even when library books were late, you only paid a few pence a day.

I had lunch in the canteen with one of the accountants, Harvey Harris, who had been supervising my work. He looked like he was auditioning for the bookkeeper part in a play. Middle-aged, shy, quiet, steel-rimmed specs, thin body and thinning lank hair, old-fashioned suit. He tended to state the blatantly obvious, but then he had probably been saving up things to say for ages. Still, he was nice and tended to treat me as an equal. He'd probably not met many women who knew numbers and therefore thought I was really a man.

Over the tuna casserole, I said, 'Harvey, do we use a different accounting system from the Americans?' Some of the Chambers' methods had struck me as strange.

'Oh, no, not really,' he said. 'Not so's you'd notice. Not any more. Big business is just that global now. Our system at the moment seems to have a slight blip.' He sort of shivered as if that were the ultimate sin. Then he quickly sealed his lips, after which he realised he needed to say more. 'I don't mean a problem as in a problem.'

'Of course not,' I helped him along. 'And my question wasn't really a question as in a question.'

He coughed in a way that seemed to indicate that the next information was stuck in his throat and it might be better to swallow it. 'We are simply getting used to the bigger and better system.' After a large bite of tuna casserole, he added, 'Fancy your noticing anything in one day.'

He had stopped eating and was staring at me suspiciously. 'Oh, I didn't mean at Chambers'. I haven't noticed anything here. I mean, I'm just a beginner. But I'm thinking of taking a night course and was reading this textbook.'

He sighed deeply with relief. 'Good idea that. You can go much further as an accountant than in your present clerk's job.'

After he finished the casserole, he said, 'Admirable your educating yourself further, Caron. Perhaps I can assist. Divulge a few secrets of the trade.' As we got up and he put his jacket back on, he added, 'Help pave your road to success.'

I patted his shoulder and thanked him profusely. His face turned red as a sunset. As we made our way back to his department, I hoped his blush would disappear. There were some things you couldn't blame on a tuna casserole

I returned to my own desk right before five, and there was a bouquet of flowers so large that my computer had needed to be shifted to accommodate it. All stops had been pulled out. A yellow balloon floated above it on a string connected to the vase. Roses in red, yellow, pink, and gladioli, carnations, chrysanthemums, and irises. It was a bold and garish statement. Everyone's eyes were pinned on me as if I were naked. Particularly Mrs Brown who was trying to hide a smile.

I considered waiting until everyone had gone before

opening the card. But oak trees were more likely to waltz. Had James lost his senses? Had Bas?

I removed the florist's envelope with the card inside. Unsealed. Usually florists were religious about that. Surely no one had looked inside, everyone else would have been watching. But someone could have opened it with unanimous consent. It was like being on one of those TV programmes where the slightest slip could cost you a million. Two seconds more and ding, you leave with only a fiver and a potato peeler.

'*Yes. Six o'clock. YKW.*'

Who the hell was YKW? And then I twigged. You Know Who. The same way I'd signed the first note to Jack Howard. And I'd thought the man hadn't got a sense of humour. I couldn't help but laugh. I stood up and waved the card.

'It's from my old auntie. She got my birthday wrong, but remembered the time. Her name's Yardley Katherine Whitehall. Well, isn't this wonderful!'

Melody reached over and patted my arm. 'Lovely, my dear, although your beau has unusual taste. But you really are special. See you tomorrow.'

Everyone had laughed at my announcement, and of course no one else believed me either. As they began to leave, Flora arrived.

'Gosh, Caron, what's going on? I came to see the flowers.'

'How did you know about them, Flora?'

'Practically the whole company's been ringing me to ask if we have an employee with the initials YKW.' She pulled over Melody's chair and sat down. 'So who sent them?'

'I think YKW stands for You Know Who, which is how I signed the first note to Jack Howard. And this morning

I sent another note switching the theatre to Mervin's do, although of course I didn't mention Mervin.'

'No, all you said was . . .' And she quoted my note verbatim.

'Shit! This place is going to put British Telecom out of business. And Jack Howard needs a more discreet secretary.'

'It wouldn't have been her, no way. Probably the mail room.' She fingered the flowers. 'It proves I was right. The man's head over heels.'

I pointed to the bouquet. 'This isn't about love, Flora. He's sending me up. It's a joke. Just look at them! They are so far over the top I'm surprised they aren't sticking up through the roof, getting in the way of aeroplanes.'

'All I see is the most gorgeous bouquet imaginable. I'm changing my mind. If he proposes, I'll accept. Woooo, Caron, how can you not be over the moon?'

'Please believe me, Flora, it's not true love. Just from our short acquaintance, I'm positive Jack would not consider these my sort of thing. What I will concede is that I was wrong about his not having a sense of humour.' I admitted to myself, a really magnificent sense of humour. Something I adored in a man.

Flora laughed. 'You can think what you like. But Jack just skipped lots of chapters and is near the end of the book. Just imagine them brightening up your room.'

'There's no way we can carry those home, tube or bus. We'd be the joke of London. And I can't work with them here. I know, I can put them on Mrs Brown's side desk for everyone to enjoy. As they've had so much enjoyment already.' But I was beginning to think it was a good joke.

We both looked up as James arrived. I said, 'Don't tell me you've heard as well?'

He smiled. 'Gossip, like ground mist, tends to rise.' He faked serious concentration and moved around the bouquet, looking from every angle. 'That bouquet is amazing, Caron. Is there a coffin under it?'

After he'd gone, I noticed Flora was still giving the bouquet adoring looks. 'Why don't you select a few stems for us to take home before I move them? And then tell me if anyone noticed your new look.'

'Thank you,' Flora said as she removed the brightest flowers. 'Notice? I could have been wearing a sign saying "Look at Me." '

'And was that all right?'

Flora smiled. 'I'd never, well you know, have imagined how lovely it would be. My boss, old Oakley, was the best. She avoided making it sound like I'd been so gross before.' Although we were alone, she looked all around before moving her chair closer. 'There's been a development. You know, with Mervin.'

'Brilliant.'

Flora was still looking cautiously around. 'I did what you said, about the rude note. I brought it for you to vet, but you weren't here. But when Melody said how nice I looked, it gave me courage and I delivered it. Here, I made a copy.'

'Dear Mervin, I'm really looking forward to your show. I would be really, really looking forward to it if you'd invited me yourself, but I'll forgive you seeing as we hadn't really met properly when you gave out the invites. Flora Finton, Personnel Department, Fourth Floor.'

'Well, it was as rude as I could think of, not having had much practice. And you said I should say what I really think, and that was what I was really thinking. It hasn't of course got the zing of your rude note, but then Mervin doesn't work on the top floor.'

I was delighted and amused. Perhaps I'd been underestimating Flora. 'And has anything happened?'

Flora beamed. 'He sent me my own invitation. Now I've got two.' She proudly waved them about. Then she turned bright pink. 'And he sent a note. It said, "Dear Flora, sorry I haven't got this invitation to you sooner. There's sure to be a crowd going for supper after my private viewing, and I wonder if you might join us?"'

'Flora, that's terrific!'

She said hesitantly, 'You don't think he's just being polite? That I embarrassed the invitation out of him?'

'Ha!' I thumped Flora's arm. 'The truth is you're already on chapter four, you skipped two chapters, and next we'll have to shop for . . .' Then I started humming the wedding march.

'Oh, stop, Caron! I shall faint.'

'Have you actually seen him today?'

'Oh, no. If he'd come into my office, I would have hidden under my desk. I can't think up something to say every minute.'

'Absolutely perfect, Flora. Keep your distance a bit, so he can only admire you from afar, and contrast you with those too easy to get.'

'Is that what you plan to do with Jack Howard?'

'Not exactly. I'm going to avoid him like the plague until the private viewing. I'm going to latch onto you the minute we get there, so he won't have much time alone with me. After that, I plan to run like hell.'

But Flora didn't laugh. 'You know, Caron, even if you don't love him, well don't love him yet, I mean, things always change in the last chapter. He could be really helpful in getting you a promotion.'

'You mean so I could sit in his office all day? No thanks.'

'I mean by his asking for you that day. No one else knows it wasn't for work. You've already been requested to other offices. That could lead to promotion.'

'Flora, I'm not riding piggyback to promotion, period. Anyway, with hundreds of people employed here, surely there will be some vacancies soon?'

'It may look like lots of people, but there're so many jobs farmed out these days, like the cleaners and the security and such. They work for concession firms and not directly for Chambers'.' She frowned and thought for a moment. 'But,' she continued, 'someone could die.'

I grinned. 'Well, I'm not riding behind a hearse to promotion, either. If I can just come up with one good, really good idea, I might raise the money to start my own business. That's the only way to wealth. Every other job just makes the bosses richer.'

The following morning I arrived before Melody and saw an awful mess on her desk. It looked as if it had been spread with honey. Well, it looked like thick pee but smelled like honey. Stuck on top was cardboard cut to the size of a greeting card, blank but with a thick black rim around the edges. Like a death announcement without any words. I was using wet paper towels to clean it when Melody arrived.

She looked at her desk, then put on her specs to talk to me. 'Not again. The other day someone spilled coffee all over the audiotapes.'

'Have you reported it? Complained?'

'I told you. Someone wants to get rid of me. It's better to ignore it.'

'Someone needs to be fried in a chip pan, Melody.'

'That's as may be, Caron, dear. But if I kick up a storm, it'll just make someone happy.'

When Mrs Brown came around with our work, Melody's was in a large sealed brown envelope. Thinking it must be personal, I handed it to her. She opened it, took one look and handed it back. 'Numbers, Caron.'

Well, it was, but they were at least six months out of date. The confidential stamp was on the bottom as usual. As I flipped through the pages, I wondered if an official audit was taking place. That would explain going over old stuff.

But as I thoroughly checked the data, I again found unlikely and large amounts sort of disappearing into the sunset. No double D bras, but huge consignments going to Austria. There couldn't be that many women yodelling while wearing red flared trousers. Handing in the day's work was a bit tricky, as I hadn't actually produced anything. I'd only been checking. I put the lot back into the envelope and sealed the packet with tape. I also enclosed a note pointing out the suspect bits and adding that it would probably be necessary to go over a complete two years of records to pinpoint anything further. It was sticking my neck out a bit, but I have a long neck. And if Chambers' went bust, I'd be out of a job like everyone else.

The next morning Melody seemed nervous. She usually typed like a machine gun and hummed, but instead she would type a few words then look at me. Finally, she said, 'Are you a prodigy, Caron? One of those child geniuses?'

I laughed. 'I've always thought and said so. But I'm not sure the opinion is general. Why?'

She put on her specs and began touching up a nail with polish. 'Would you mind if I asked what you did before coming to Chambers'?'

Uh-oh. She wouldn't have been able to see my personnel file. So how would she know I hadn't previously worked in accounting? Well, maybe I wouldn't have begun so low in Chambers'. Thinking quickly, I decided I'd better trust Melody with a little truth.

'Well, the truth is, Melody, I worked before for an American company. But I didn't approve of what they were doing so I quit. But I didn't think they'd give me a good reference so I'm, well, sort of starting again.' Well, hell, I couldn't really say that I hadn't approved of my boss sleeping with his wife.

'Well, that's a relief, dear.' Then she took off her specs and attacked the computer while humming 'Greensleeves'.

I couldn't remember any words to that song, so couldn't use Freud's help in working out what that had been about. Even I couldn't work out a theory connecting 'Greensleeves' to spreadsheets.

But it all became clear the following morning. First Melody asked if I'd get us coffee, which I did. Usually I waited until we'd worked a half-hour. Then she reached over and took my shoulder bag and stuck something in it. I've got about the same patience as a mosquito, so I quickly went to the loo. Inside the small envelope were four unlabelled floppy disks. That was all.

Back at my desk, I said, 'Melody, you know Mr Chambers? Does he, well, you know, have a working relationship with computers?'

She smiled. 'He's a bit like me. I gather he considers

it's only TV without the soap operas.' She added in a soft voice, 'But he's sharp as a razor. And he knows what to do with the results.' She sort of nodded towards my handbag.

'Well, it might take a few days. Even a week.'

'I'm sure that'll be fine, dear. Some soap operas last for twenty years.'

After work, I stopped by to see Stoner and have a chat. She asked me to stay for dinner, and I sat at the table as she played Delia.

James came in, and before Stoner could banish him, I said merrily, 'James, lovely to see you. Sit down and watch Stoner with me. She should have her own cookery show.'

'So she should,' he said. 'Do you know of any vacancies?'

'Now, would I leave you James? Even for glory? I'm staying here until they carry me out.' It was the first time their darts seemed to have a little strawberry jam on them, instead of vinegar.

James said, 'I've been meaning to ring you, Caron. To arrange a time to take you out to dinner. But everyone on the top floor is working flat out, and I never seem to get away in time.'

'Well, this is dinner, James. And no one cooks better than Stoner. I prefer it to large fancy restaurants any day. All those crowds and American businessmen.'

To change the subject, I said, 'I don't know if this is supposed to be confidential, and you don't need to answer, but there are lots of rumours about Chambers' being subject to a hostile takeover.'

James frowned. 'When you hear the rumour saying which company it is, I'd love to know.'

I laughed. 'That bad, is it?'

'Probably worse.'

Stoner cooked the most delicious roast dinner. Chicken with stuffing and roast potatoes and mashed potatoes and three other vegetables plus fresh green salad. And the sweet was fresh strawberries with loads of cream all sat on a home-made Madeira cake. If I were James, I'd bow every time Stoner entered the room.

He walked me home across the Heath. 'Pity you're not wearing jogging clothes, Caron.'

'Yeah, well, if I remember correctly I did my ten miles before breakfast.'

He laughed and took my hand. 'You could probably outrun me tonight. I seem to be desk-bound all the time.'

'Surely things will settle down soon? Then you can rest up.'

'I was thinking about that, Caron. Maybe soon we could go away together for a weekend?'

Surprised, I said, 'As friends?'

He laughed. 'Well, I didn't mean as enemies.'

'James, don't you think it's a bit well soon? I mean horse and ice maiden?' I couldn't recall exactly how we were supposed to refer to what we weren't supposed to talk about. 'Or ankle and iceberg?'

He grinned. 'I'm feeling pretty much like the Gulf Stream has found me. Really defrosted. What about you?' And then he stopped and said, 'You aren't still having problems with, well, with deliveries and things?'

'They come and go. Well, they just come, and I wish they'd go. Nothing since the pink and chartreuse silk knickers.' I clamped my mouth shut, but the words had escaped.

'Silk knickers? Caron, are we dealing with a psycho?'

I couldn't resist a slight tease. 'Don't you think pink and chartreuse knickers are in good taste? They had the Chambers' label.'

'I'm sure you'd look good in anything, Caron. And if I'm ever in a position to see, well, what I mean . . .'

'In a position to see which knickers I'm wearing?'

'Yes, actually, I did mean that. Well, those colours wouldn't be my first choice. You aren't now?'

'James! I wouldn't be caught dead in knickers sent by the horse's ankle. And do I look like a chartreuse and pink person? Anyway, about the psycho bit, I hope not. But it'd be a bit rash for me to completely ignore it. I mean everything must be leading up to something. I don't actually feel in any personal danger at the moment.'

'I should hope not. Not while you're standing here talking to me. But you will let me know? And then I won't risk making you anxious by bringing the subject up so often.'

'Of course I will, James.'

When we reached the edge of the Heath, he said, 'Well, whose turn is it?'

'Turn for what?'

'That must mean it's my turn.' He turned me slowly to face him and then gently put his arms around me. At first we just stood there in the most heavenly warm embrace. Then he raised my face and kissed me. It was one of those kisses where you don't know where you end and he begins and won't know until you try to walk. In fact, it was so nice that when we finished I decided on an encore.

When we came up for breath he said, 'So, when things settle down, what about that weekend?'

'Well, we did decide we'd make our own friendship

rules. And what with your working late so much, you'll definitely need some R and R. Just remember that stands for Ravioli and Reading.'

He grinned. 'And not Romance and Rip Van Winkle?'

'Rip Van Winkle?'

'Well, he did spend a lot of time in bed.'

16

The following Saturday was warm and sunny. Flora, Evelyn and I were lingering over lunch while trying to think of something to do. When someone knocked on the door, Evelyn got up saying, 'Flora, when are you going to get a doorbell like normal people?'

Flora seemed a bit put out that someone like Evelyn didn't consider her normal. I said, 'Don't worry, I've decided to get Flora a doorbell for Christmas.'

Seconds later Evelyn returned. 'Another delivery. But don't worry, the delivery truck's from Harrods and it's for Flora.'

Flora said, 'But I haven't ordered anything from Harrods. Or from anywhere else.'

The deliveryman said he was delivering garden furniture, a barbecue grill, and a hamper with provisions and champagne for twelve. 'Me and my mate have instructions to set it up for you. But you'd better put the perishables in your fridge. Where do you want me to put this hamper?' He stepped inside, making way for the other man with a similar hamper.

'Wait,' said Flora. 'It's a mistake. I mean it's not really for me.'

The first deliveryman smiled. 'If you're Miss Flora Finton, it is. The instructions were quite precise. Wait until the first dry, sunny Saturday and deliver and set up in time for the barbecue. And this is the correct address.'

Evelyn said, 'You must have entered a contest and won, Flora. Shift yourself so the men can come through.'

'But I would know if I'd entered a contest, Evelyn. I didn't. And if this is a mistake and we eat everything up, I'll have to pay for it.'

I said, 'Flora, could you have entered a competition without realising it? Sometimes in the small print, when you buy or order something, it says your name will go in for a prize draw.'

Flora thought for a minute. 'I recently subscribed to the Romance Book Club.'

'That's it, you silly bugger,' said Evelyn. 'Romance, champagne, Harrods, hampers. It all fits. Pity they didn't send along a few men as it's romance.'

The deliverymen looked nervous, so she said, 'I meant dates, not just any old men.'

Flora still wasn't convinced and asked the deliveryman if there was a card. He looked through some papers and said, 'Sorry, I didn't see it before.' He handed her an envelope of that thick cream paper you'd use if you could afford both that and the stamp.

Flora took out a page of the same paper and read aloud, '"Dear Flora Finton, Congratulations! We take great pleasure in delivering to you the treat of a lifetime because . . ."'

We waited in silence for a moment. I said, 'Because what, Flora?'

'That's all. There's no second page. I mean surely there should be one. I've never heard of the Because Prize.'

We all laughed. The deliverymen assured Flora the prize was hers, that Harrods would absorb any possible error. Evelyn said, 'I'll show them to the garden.'

Before she could take one step, Flora said with a mischievous grin, 'But what about spiders? Bugs? I only said there weren't any in the house.'

Evelyn shrugged. 'I don't care if there's bodies buried in the garden. If there's going to be a feast, count me in. Maybe if I get accustomed to eating their food, Harrods will hire me to give out samples. That'd be better than forty-two cheeses.'

As Flora and I put the perishables away she said, 'I just had to say something. It annoys me her checking for spider webs every morning.' She picked up a ham. 'Goodness, Caron, there's enough for an army.'

'Yeah. If Harrods thinks this amount feeds twelve, they probably had starving soldiers in mind. We'd better have a party. You ring Mervin. I'll ring James and invite Stoner as well, if that's all right?'

'Of course it is, Caron. But I can hardly tell Mervin I've won a romance prize, can I?'

'Just say book club. There's that Booker Prize, so this can be the Because Prize.'

She made me ring James first, to see how the Because Prize went down. James said, 'You want Stoner there? I'm sure she'll love it. I can have her there in ten minutes. Should she bring an overnight case? I mean I can manage without her. Overnight. For a week. A year?'

'James, that's terrible!'

He laughed. 'Hang on while I ask her.' He returned to the phone and said, 'She's delighted. I can come over fairly soon, but Stoner's garden helper Henry's here at the moment.'

'What's Henry like? Maybe he'd like to come, too? For Evelyn.'

'What sort of men does Evelyn like?'

'Anyone between eighteen and eighty? And we have a lot of food, so bring him even if he's a hundred.'

James laughed. 'Henry's what your friend Evelyn might call a hunk. A pre-med student who gardens part-time to help pay his university fees. He'd probably enjoy a free meal, and he might even like Evelyn.' He offered to provide the wine, but I told him just to get as thirsty as possible instead.

After we'd rung off, I told Flora about Henry. 'And James didn't even ask what the Because Prize is.'

'But you mumbled.'

'Well, you can mumble, too.'

Evelyn joined us. 'What can I do next? Now I've got the deliverymen sorted.'

When Evelyn offers to help, people often begin to cry. I said, 'You can watch out the front window for your new boyfriend.'

'I wish you two wouldn't joke about important things like bugs and men.'

Flora laughed. 'She's serious. His name's Henry, and he's a pre-med student.'

We'd drunk half a bottle of wine when James arrived. 'Stoner would sooner die than arrive empty-handed. So her toyboy will be here in a minute with some flowers. Then he's returning for Stoner, who's quite keen to ride in his van.'

'This bloke Henry is your housekeeper's boyfriend?' If disgusted looks could kill, we'd need Stoner's flowers to lay on top of James.

He laughed. 'He's her garden helper, but after she changed her name to Stoner . . .'

Evelyn said, 'Well, if this bloke's a mature student doing pre-med, he's sure to like me.'

Flora said, 'But you're never sick.'

'Well, bugger it, you don't think doctors like sick people, do you?'

Flora said indignantly, 'Yes, they do.'

I said, 'Maybe Evelyn's right, Flora. If they liked sick people they'd leave them alone and stop trying to make them get well.'

James said, 'He's nice and well-behaved, to use Stoner's description. And Evelyn, he's large enough to pick you up and carry you away. So be careful.'

'Sod careful. But can you lot give me any advice? Tips? I mean usually the dating agency does that.'

I said, 'I don't suppose playing hard to get would be helpful?'

'How can I play hard to get when I've never even met him? You've got to think harder. And faster.'

Flora said, 'I think, well, I suggest you don't put the condoms on the table this time.'

We heard the van arrive and Evelyn said, 'He's here! I'll go and help him with the plants.' And then she broke the world record for the fifty-yard dash. Flora and I rushed to the window.

'Gosh, Caron, Henry's tall, broad, and sexy, with red hair and beard and a lovely smile. I bet he's got sky-blue eyes. He reminds me of a doctor in a Mills and Boon romance.'

James asked, 'And did that doctor fall for a woman like Evelyn?'

Flora laughed. 'None of the romances have a woman like Evelyn. One crime novel did, but she died on page twenty-three. Do you think she's going to scare the poor man to death?'

James said, 'Not if he's going to be a doctor.'

Evelyn came rushing in carrying three gorgeous pot plants. 'You won't believe it. Henry is serious talent!'

'We believe it,' said Flora and I together. Then Flora added, 'Why didn't he at least stop for coffee?'

'He had to get back to Stoner. He's bringing her over, then going home to change. So he won't be here 'til late.'

James winked at me and said to Evelyn, 'As I said before, be careful. Maybe Henry is waiting to appear after dark. As vampires do.'

Mervin arrived carrying a bottle of wine and some flowers. He said, 'I've also brought my video camera. To take some footage of this special event. Congratulations, Flora!' He took a look at Flora, who was wearing one of her new outfits – wide-legged cream trousers with a matching skimpy camisole. 'You look great, Flora. Why don't you use that style for work?'

Flora smiled. 'You mean wear my new clothes?'

'Yeah. And I'd wear the hair as well.'

The Harrods' men were nearly finished by then. I'd read about how the rich simply order a party. An entire party. The men had brought fake grass carpet, which they laid over Flora's weeds. After assembling the gorgeous teak garden furniture, they surrounded the area with pot plants and set out hurricane lanterns. They lit the charcoal in the barbecue and even seemed prepared to stay and do the cooking. Flora said no thank you. And she was right; the garden area was so small that what with the furniture and guests, the men would have needed to act like garden gnomes and stand by the fence.

When Stoner arrived, I leaned down and gave her a hug. 'Thanks so much for coming, Stoner. Are you sure you want us all to call you Stoner?'

She laughed. 'You should have seen James' face when I said that. A good thing. You know, Caron, it wasn't normal for a man his age always to be thinking about pensions.'

Henry arrived and was introduced around and thereafter had Evelyn acting like twining ivy to his oak tree. Flora set out the smoked salmon starters, which we ate with the first of the champagne. The men volunteered to do the barbecue bit. I don't much like gender role playing, but neither did I want to offer to cook. We sat cheerfully, smelling the sizzling steaks, sausages, and burgers. There was even a supply of veggie burgers. Platters of raw vegetables and olives and dips had been provided, along with a selection of condiments. Champagne corks were popping every few minutes. It was like heaven in Hampstead for a day.

As Henry was helping to cook, Evelyn did the same, dropping steaks, spilling drinks, breaking one of the Harrods champagne glasses. But Henry was laughing, so maybe he'd gone off the efficient nurse types and preferred Evelyn instead. He probably already realised she was Eliza Doolittle in need of a make-over.

When Stoner congratulated Flora on winning the prize, Flora said, 'Well, I was just lucky. Caron's the really brave one. She wants to do things, and she's willing to do any job, take a second job, spend every minute working, even at the weekends. She welcomes overtime, too.'

I realised Flora wanted to distract from talk about the Romance Club, but she was making me sound like superwoman, an image hard to live up to. Well, I could try. 'Thanks, Flora. What I figure is if you want a tan, you've got to show skin. It's the same with luck. Like your recent luck. The more you're out there, the better your chance. I've never heard of one single person winning the lottery while sitting in a cave in the Hebrides.'

Flora said, 'Do they have caves there?'

'Well, if they don't, it makes it even harder. What do you think, Stoner?'

'She's right, Flora. We're born not knowing anything. That's why age, with all that experience, is so valuable. Like I keep trying to tell certain people.'

I grinned. 'You know, he really does appreciate you, Stoner. He's just not very good at showing it.'

She grinned. 'Maybe he needs to show skin.'

We laughed, and I said, 'I'm happy to work all hours, Flora. Like someone said, "The harder I work, the luckier I get."'

Flora asked, 'That sounds like what a hopeful workaholic would say.'

'Actually, it was Henry Ford.'

Stoner said, 'Well, I agree with him, too. In spite of certain people, I'm planning to die going full blast. I've seen them on telly, sitting in chairs in a row on the porch of a nursing home with knitted rugs wrapped around them, waiting.'

Flora said, 'Waiting?'

'Death's going to get us anyway, but it's not a good idea to issue invitations.'

Flora said, 'Well, I did read that the only risk-free state is dead. Maybe that's true.'

Stoner said, 'That's as may be, but the only test is lethal.'

The first grilled food was ready, and we sat around the table. Stoner's flowers had pride of place in the middle. Evelyn reminded Mervin to use his video camera and record us for posterity. So we all smiled for that. After that, everyone tucked in. Then Mervin said, 'This is one terrific party, Flora. I have to admit I'd never heard of the Because Prize before.'

James said, 'I thought at first you said the Booker, but of course that's for writers.'

Flora was blushing furiously, obviously anticipating having to explain about the Romance Book Club. She wouldn't want Mervin to know all her experience came from books. I said, 'The Because Prize has to do with readers, not writers.'

'Yeah,' added Evelyn. 'Flora here has her nose in a book all the time. She was certainly the right person to win.'

Mervin said, 'What kind of books, Flora? I mean what exactly did you do to enter for the prize?' Even Flora's ears had turned purple by now.

I said, 'Flora joined a book club. She has very catholic taste.'

Evelyn said, 'Yeah, Flora reads the kind of books where some of the characters actually go to church. One had a picture of a vicar on the front. So if I had to say, like for the television, I'd say they were all books about Catholics. Maybe some dicey priests, too.'

I quickly said, 'Not religious books, Evelyn. Catholic in the sense of a having wide taste in literature.'

James said, 'It's surprising the sponsors would provide such a lavish prize without wanting publicity – to send round photographers and have mentions in the press.' Flora coughed, or possibly choked. She said, 'I've read that publishers are having a hard time at the moment. Well, maybe they didn't want the public to misunderstand and think I'm not just the best reader, but the only reader.'

Evelyn said, 'Also, Flora probably ticked that little square that says no publicity. Like you can do when you win the pools. What do you think, Henry?'

He smiled the smile that might bring patients back

from the dead. 'About books, publicity, or the pools? I approve of them all, especially as they've brought us all together and provided such a lovely party.'

'I like men who like everything,' said Evelyn. 'And you look the lucky sort. Flora here should give you the address of her book club and you can enter for the next prize.'

Flora got up and said, 'Evelyn, do you think you could, without breaking or spilling anything, help me bring out the strawberries and cream?'

Later, Evelyn put on some music and suggested dancing. There wasn't anywhere to dance except along the edge of the fake grass carpet or on the weeds beyond. But dancing is code for touching, and nobody complained. And nobody really danced besides Evelyn and Henry. If that was dancing.

After dark, we lit candles and the hurricane lanterns. There was much patio to kitchen traffic. At one point, when I was making a cup of tea for Stoner, Flora came in.

'Well, Flora, it looks like Evelyn is scoring. They make a good couple, but how's that for speed?'

Flora smiled. 'Evelyn is definitely a short-story person.'

The kettle had boiled, and I poured hot water over a tea bag. Flora was wrapping packets of surplus food for the guests to take home. 'Have you noticed James and Stoner being friendly, Flora? Saying nice things to each other?'

'That's really good. In books they always wait until someone dies and weep too late.'

At some point in the evening, Mervin asked if he could take a peek into my bedroom to see his Picasso copies. Flora agreed instantly, and I could tell she was

222

hoping he liked simple frames. James leaned close and said, 'I'd love to see your bedroom, too, Caron.'

'James! Remember, we're friends.'

'Of course, Caron. It shouldn't be a problem to go in there with half a dozen other people. Anyway, all I had in mind was checking that the deliveryman wasn't hiding there.' He sounded about as convincing as the Marquis de Sade claiming he was planning to play bingo at a community hall.

'Oh, sure, James. He's probably sitting up in bed reading a book.'

'Sensible fellow.'

Then he saw the pictures. 'And just look at that, Caron. A copy for each of us to admire.' Everyone was laughing at all the Picassos. Well, I suppose it was different.

Stoner seemed amused, if laughing out loud was anything to go by. And she admired the rocking chair in the front room and tried it out. Then she said, while standing in front of the mantel, 'That music box is beautiful.'

'Lift the lid, Stoner. There's nothing personal inside. Just spare packets of Polo mints.'

When she did, we all listened to 'Yankee Doodle went to town, riding on a pony . . .' That got a laugh from everyone.

Later, James and I were in the kitchen alone. By happenstance. You didn't need to actually reserve the kitchen.

We had a long, lovely, suspiciously gritty charcoal kiss, and after holding me close for a while, James said, 'I've been thinking about our friendship, Caron. Do you think we might take it up a step?'

'Well, what exactly is the next step up for friends,

James? We've held hands, we've kissed. We're planning a weekend away together.'

He feigned seriously thinking and then said, 'I'm not sure. Perhaps golden wedding anniversaries?'

We both laughed, but it was a scary thought. 'I'm thinking maybe we should back off a bit, James.'

'Agreed,' he said quickly. 'Which kiss do you want to back up to?' And he didn't even wait for me to answer his question.

Suddenly we heard Evelyn shouting, 'Eeeughah!' That's apparently karate for get out of my way. Then we heard Henry shout. James and I got to the front door at the same time as Stoner, Flora, and Mervin.

'The fucking bugger's escaped!'

Flora said, 'No, he hasn't, Evelyn,' as we watched a breathless Henry walking towards us from down the road.

'Sod that for a lark, Flora! I don't mean Henry. He was leaving and I walked him to his van.'

Henry joined us, doubling over to gasp for breath. When he straightened, he said, 'I saw this bloke at the window, between the bush and the house. He'd got the window open and his feet were still hanging out.'

Evelyn said, 'You should have seen Henry tackle those feet. I thought he was going to bite them off.'

'Evelyn, I was shouting to get him off guard. But he kicked out and I fell backwards onto the ground. By the time I got up, he was running away.'

'I tried to trip the bugger, but he wouldn't come near where I had my foot ready.'

'Then I chased him.' Henry stopped to take another breath. 'But he had an accomplice, a getaway car parked at the corner.'

Flora said, 'We'd better ring the police.'

Henry indicated a mobile strapped to his belt. 'I rang them. I'm going to stop by the station and give a statement. But it won't do any good. He was medium tall, medium wide, the only thing not average was his ability to run.'

James said, 'I don't suppose you saw his face?'

'Nah. Like I said, I was flat out when he went by. He had a cap pulled way down, and he was wearing gloves. What about you, Evelyn?'

'It was dark. And I was looking at my foot, to make sure it was positioned correctly.'

James said, 'Are you sure he was going in and not coming out?'

When Henry didn't answer, Evelyn said, 'Yeah, we're sure. It was my bedroom window. And we'd just come from there.'

Henry said, 'Uh, Evelyn thought there might be another bottle of champagne in her cupboard.'

Stoner said, 'That's a strange place to keep champagne. Was there any there?'

James coughed and said, 'Do you want me to come to the station with you, Henry?'

'No thanks. Evelyn might want to come?'

She grinned. 'Maybe there's some champagne in the van.' Mervin had been pretty much staying in the background during this conversation. Evelyn turned to him and said, 'You missed your chance, Mervin. You should have caught that crook on your video.'

'He forgot to tell me what time he was coming, Evelyn.'

James insisted on searching the house before taking Stoner home. And she asked if we wanted to go home with them.

I said, 'He's not likely to return tonight, surely. But thanks so much.' Back inside, Flora and I made sure all the windows were closed and locked. And we also checked that the brownie recipe was still hanging in the bathroom. She said, 'Do you think the burglar was, you know, after the Picasso?'

'Yeah, I do.' And then I started laughing. Finally I managed to stop and say, 'Flora, It wasn't the Booker Prize! Or the Because Prize! It all makes sense, now. The Harrods' delivery, their instructions to deliver on a dry, sunny day, the hamper with perishables, the missing second page of the enclosed note. It was the Bas Prize. The whole thing was intended as a distraction for the burglary!'

Flora smiled. 'That makes sense to me, too.'

'And it means we won! Tonight we won the Bas!'

'I hope he doesn't try to steal back the garden furniture.'

'He wouldn't do that. It would indicate that he'd lost. No, he'll have to think of some way that this all led to victory.'

Flora looked alarmed. 'Is it really good that we won then, Caron?'

'Of course, Flora. It's always good to win in a fair game. Why?'

'Well, if we'd been the losers, we wouldn't turn violent and want revenge. It sounds like Bas is going to be angrier than ever.'

'Yeah, there's that. A good point. Well, not good in the sense of likeable. But the only way to stop a bully is to stand up to him. We've done that, now.'

'In children's stories, or even those for adults, that disarms the bully. It makes him leave you alone in future. I don't remember any cases where the bully just gets worse and worse.' She looked quite sad as she added, 'And I always believed those books.'

'Me, too, Flora. But Bas probably wouldn't know that Little Red Riding Hood's supposed to win.'

'Maybe he'll decide it would be easier and cheaper simply to buy back the Picasso.'

'He'd join a monastery before he'd do that.'

'You know, the burglar tonight could have, like, really hurt Henry if he hadn't been able to kick him out of the way. I mean if they'd fought. He might've had a weapon or something.'

'Yeah, Flora. That's the problem. Hiring a crook is one thing. Controlling a crook's another. Did any of the books you've read cover that situation?'

Flora thought for a minute. 'One did, but I didn't finish it. I decided to read a romance instead. Well, after five bodies in three pages.'

17

The days before Mervin's show passed quickly, mostly because they were interesting. Which isn't to say that obstacles didn't leap at your throat. Some good news came in an e-mail from Mum:

'Dear Caron, Sorry I haven't answered your last two msgs. We won the tournament. Your Dad's fine. Some news. Bas has been in the papers, something to do with a merger. Sounds like his game will keep him in New York for a few weeks. Thought you'd like to know. Love, Mum and Dad.'

That was a relief. I mean even Bas wouldn't get involved in a merger just to get me off guard. So maybe the problems with him were over. Ha. Fat chance. Never mind. In a few weeks, Rome could be built several times over. And part of New York could land on Bas.

Also, Harvey Harris, true to his word, got me transferred to his department for three separate days. Delighted to have my attention focussed on his beloved work, he began by trying to educate me, but soon he was positively showing off. Amazingly, he had copies of some of the confidential papers I'd been sent via Melody. Either Mr Chambers sent them about like greeting cards, or old Harvey was a good enough hacker to give Microsoft a migraine. There was no way a humble bookkeeper, which he delighted in calling himself, would have access to the high-level passwords he would have needed.

It even occurred to me that Mr Chambers might have told Harvey to tutor me, but there was something too sly about Harvey for that. In those films where people get tortured, Harvey would be the one who for one cigarette and half a bar of chocolate immediately spills the beans. I don't mean I'd prefer to see him tortured, but there was something about him that made your instinct shout if you even told him your brand of tooth-paste. I personally liked him fine, and I use whichever toothpaste is on sale.

Melody had more irritations. Little things, but enough for me to begin to agree that someone had it in for her. Another coffee spilled on her desk. The electric cord was removed from her computer – but then she might have done that herself, or at least have wanted to.

It had taken some time to run Mr Chambers' disks through the computer programs I still had on my laptop from Bas' days. A computer ace had helped me set it up, and I used to run the accounts of companies we were thinking of buying through it. It was a sneaky, sophisticated audit. I finally came up with basically the same sort of data I'd sent Jim Chambers before, except this time there was more of it, with the pattern of fraud more obvious.

The next step would be to find out whose passwords had accessed the files. But of course the master lists weren't on the floppies, and my own password couldn't access such data. Anyway, I hoped Jim Chambers could take it from there. Surely Melody had been exaggerating about him and soap operas. As I didn't hear anything more I figured it had just been an interesting interlude.

Then one day after a sandwich lunch at my desk, I

looked up to see James helping a very distraught Melody to her desk. I quickly got up and took her arm. She was pale and her whole body was shaking.

'What's happened?'

Melody sort of fluttered her hands and took out a lavender-scented linen handkerchief to wipe her forehead. I looked at James. He spoke in a serious manner, but sort of grimaced and looked doubtful while Melody wasn't looking.

'Melody says someone tried to push her in front of a bus. That someone's trying to kill her. Just down the road from Chambers'. It was apparently a close call. I was returning from a business lunch when I saw the crowd gathered around. Someone had called the police. But in spite of the crowd, no one had actually seen anything.'

'James, could you or someone get Melody a cup of tea? While she tells me about it?'

Melody said, 'Thank goodness James came along. I must say, Caron, I was in a state. But he doesn't believe me. The police didn't, no one did.' She sniffed at her hankie and then said firmly, 'It just goes to show that the world is full of idiots.'

'I believe you, Melody. So what happened?'

'What James said. I was standing there waiting for the light to turn. Next thing I was shoved from the back and stumbled forward. If I hadn't grabbed hold of a man with a briefcase, I'd be dead.' She glared at me. 'I'm sure there's a bruise on my back, if you want to see.'

'I believe you, Melody. I already said. But why? Who?'

'Well, you may believe about the bus, but you obviously don't believe me when I tell you repeatedly that someone wants me out of here.'

'I'm trying to understand it, Melody. It's just hard to credit that they'd risk murder to accomplish it. Why don't you have lunch in the canteen with Flora and me for a few days? Give going out a rest?'

'Well, with the enemy within, I should have thought I'd be safer without. If you take my point.' She was smiling, and by the time James returned with the tea she was pretty much her old self. But she didn't hum as she worked that afternoon. Maybe someone merely wanted to stop the humming.

Flora and I left sharpish on the day of Mervin's do. On the bus, as we stood swaying and hanging onto those nooses that dangle from the ceiling, she asked what I planned to wear. 'I don't know. The usual, I expect.'

'Not to worry. I mean you always wear the same. Such understated classics.'

I could feel my eyebrows levitating. 'Are you hinting, Flora, that basic classics can end up looking a bit frumpy?'

'Gosh, no. You're such an understated person, anyway. I mean, who would have imagined you'd blend in so well in accounts? But now you're one of the gang.'

Not entirely cheered at this image of myself, which had a bit of James' ice queen about it, I said, 'I do have a bright red suit.' Well, I had lots of clothes I never wore, because I could only afford to go to the corner shop to buy crisps. And that's on the big nights.

'Never! Oh, wear that, Caron. It's such a special event with, you know, Mervin.'

'I just might, Flora, I just might.'

We got off at Tottenham Court Road to change buses. Fortunately, the right bus was coming. And amazingly, we found two seats together.

'Is James back in town yet, Caron? Mervin would love it if he showed up.'

'He was in New York when he rang yesterday. So he's probably still there. Anyway, unlike Mervin, I'd need to explain what I was doing there with Jack Howard.'

Flora grinned. 'Is this an announcement that the friendship is off? Or that it's sort of graduated? Chapter three, page forty-two?'

Huffily, because I'd been trying not to think about that, I said, 'Not at all. But even friends might balk at your going out with their enemies. You did say they were enemies.'

Flora smiled. 'That was before. At some point it's sure to turn into outright war.'

'With me as the hand grenade to toss back and forth?'

Flora grinned. 'Wouldn't that be what they call making a splash?'

I imagined that most of the guests would be wearing Mervin gear. Ripped jeans and novelty T-shirts and leather aviation jackets. But I couldn't imagine Jack wearing that. And I didn't want him embarrassed, being the only suit, after having agreed to go for my sake.

Most of the private views I'd attended had been on workdays – the gallery's attempts to get the working spending crowd on their way home. People too busy to attend on the weekend. That had entailed office wear, although sometimes a dressy version. So the red suit might just be all right.

When Flora and I got home, there was a small florist's box sitting by the door with my name on it. I picked it up before thinking it might be from Bas. But while I knew about letter bombs, I'd never heard of a flower bomb. And I could see clearly through the cellophane top. There was only a standard, unsigned card, which said *To*

My Favourite Person. There was a corsage consisting of two gorgeous gardenias with ivory-coloured ribbons.

As we went inside, Flora said, 'Jack Howard's turning out to be quite the gentleman. A real corsage!'

'Not only a gentleman, but a bit old-fashioned. Still, I guess I'll have to wear it.'

I hadn't remembered the skirt of my red suit being so short. And so tight. Never mind. Jack couldn't get ideas in only a couple of hours amidst a crowd. In case I'd misled Flora with the low-cut tops, I needed to wear one as well. Maybe, I thought as I pinned the flowers to the dress, they will distract everyone from the décolletage. As I stood on the bed to look in the mirror, I smiled. Just let anyone try to think ice maiden tonight!

Evelyn got home before Flora and I could escape. And hearing us talking about the private view said, with long pauses between each sentence, 'You two have a good time. I don't mind staying here by myself. Dying of boredom. Wearing old clothes. Fighting off mice and spiders.'

'All right, all right, Evelyn,' said Flora. 'You can come too. But you can't wear that tracksuit. And I've got to go early to help set out the wine.'

'I'm leaving in about ten minutes, Evelyn. And I can't tell you how much I'd love for you to go with me.'

'Well, you'll have to wait, then. It takes longer than that to put on my eyelashes. Why are you wearing those funny flowers?'

'She's got a date, Evelyn. And her flowers are a lovely present. Here, take my invitation. And come when you like. Mervin will be glad to see you. I mean we'll all be glad.'

Too late I realised my sartorial mistake. When I

233

opened the door, Jack looked like he'd died and gone to a brothel. He tried to come in for a quick drink, but I scotched that. He gripped my waist on the way to his car. You would have thought he'd got hold of a Zimmer frame. And the car was a soft-top, vintage E-type Jaguar where our knees were almost touching when we sat down. His aftershave and the last of my Dior mingled, smelling too much like the Garden of Eden for my comfort.

Before he started the car, he said, 'You look absolutely gorgeous, Caron.'

I wanted to reply, Thank you Mr Howard. Anything to create a little distance. Instead of a hard-nosed and brutal businessman, he looked like a soppy teenager in love. Flora was going to die laughing.

As he zigzagged through the traffic in a hair-raising manner, he said, 'Did you get the flowers?'

'Of course I did. I'm wearing them.'

He glanced at me and said, 'Those look terrific. But I meant the ones I sent.'

It took a moment for me to realise that James must have sent the corsage. I said, 'You know I got your bouquet, Jack. The entire company knows.'

'I hoped you'd like them. I wasn't sure if you wouldn't have preferred something more understated. Say, a large cactus plant. That's what the florist, whom I used to know, er, rather well, suggested.'

I turned my laughter into a cough. He not only hadn't intended a joke himself, but hadn't recognised that of the florist. His sense of humour would fit in an egg cup.

'It was very kind of you, Jack. But I'd really rather you didn't do it again. I mean, the accounts section will make the connection.'

He seemed disappointed. 'I just wanted to make sure you didn't forget me. A few weeks can be a long time. And as you seem to like notes, I didn't think a phone call would be the right thing.' He stopped talking to swerve sharply around a corner. Then he laughed. 'All right. I wanted to impress you and it didn't come off. Back to square one again?'

'Agreed.' I could tell Flora he was back to the title page.

'Anyway, Caron. I don't care any more if everyone knows. You're so special that Chambers' doesn't come into it. I can be a bit arrogant, and you were the first person to tell me off in years. In the pub. Also with your first note. I need that.'

Horrified that he was going to add that he also needed me, I quickly said, 'Goodness you made fast time. We're almost there.'

'I can go a bit faster if you like? We're running late.'

The venue in Camden Town was a large warehouse. Maybe it was an antiques depot. Various pieces of both valuable and simply elderly furniture were dotted about at random. The walls were covered with fabric on which hung Mervin's work. But none of this was obvious at first glance, because with upwards of two hundred people crammed into the room, it was difficult to see further than a few inches.

Mervin was at the door and greeted us in his artiste guise, kissing air above each of my ears. He shook hands with Jack Howard. Mervin shaking hands with a suit? He seemed astonished to see Jack Howard. As Jack introduced himself to Mervin, I realised he hadn't connected Mervin with Chambers'. As we moved past him, Mervin whispered into my ear, 'I'd thought YKW was one of the Royals.'

Jack and I bumped into Flora, who was carrying a glass of wine. 'For Mervin,' she said. 'I hope he hasn't already got any. Evening, Jack.'

'Hello, Flora. Good to see you.'

I turned to Jack who was practically glued to my side, although this could have been partly due to the crush. 'You're taller than me, Jack. Can you see the drinks table? I'll wait here, if you like.'

He took his cue like a good boy. I turned desperately to Flora. 'Don't mention the corsage to Jack. It must be from James. And, Flora, please stick with us as much as you can. Except when you're with Mervin, of course.'

'I'm taking your advice – hard to get, you know? I'll just pop up every so often so he won't forget me. You look terrific, Caron! Jack Howard is going to be in the first chapter of the sequel after tonight. The man's nearly drooling.'

'Flora, what am I going to do? I should have worn a flour sack. But I thought he might be the only one dressed up and I didn't want him embarrassed.'

'Mervin's friends are casual. Well, some sort of look like they might pass the hat for a few coins, you know? But that's probably just the scene. Thanks to you, I feel just right. I would never have worn such a low-cut bodice if you hadn't suggested it. And I'm glad that I didn't go over the top. The accounts section's dressed like Christmas trees.'

After Jack returned, we sipped wine and wandered the walls trying to see the paintings. Some were garish and modern, resembling fireworks and burnt out buildings. A few others were more traditional and rather beautiful. I was relieved to see that some of the frames had red dots in the lower left-hand corner. Thank goodness they were selling – two of the creepy ones but more of the representational.

As I was admiring a small seascape, somewhat impressionistic but no mistaking the blustering waves and movement of the water, Mervin joined us.

I said, 'You're a marvellous painter, Mervin.' But as I turned towards him, I was shocked to see James some distance away looking at the paintings and slowly working his way towards us. I didn't think one could hallucinate after only two sips of wine, but I'd rather have seen a pink elephant than James at that moment. He looked all too real, and Jack was too large to hide in my handbag.

Mervin grinned. 'I have to do the others, for street cred. To get anyone to give me a show. But the trad sells better. Hope no one thinks I'm stale bread. I should probably do more of the dead sheep in a bottle that's so much in vogue.'

Flora said, 'You should, like, paint what you want to paint, Mervin. I read that in a book last night. And I believe it.' Mervin smiled so broadly Flora looked a bit dizzy.

Helpful as ever, Flora wedged herself between Jack and me. Although he treated her pleasantly, joking and teasing, he wasn't having much luck getting her out of the way. He turned to me, 'Well, are you ready to leave, Caron? Go on to dinner?'

I wanted to say for him to go by himself, that he looked embarrassingly hungry. 'We've only been here five minutes, Jack. Don't you want to buy a painting?'

'Oh, er, yes. Who do I tell?'

'Which one do you plan to buy?'

'Any of them. Sorry, I mean why don't you select one?'

Flora quickly said, 'There's a smashing one over there. It's named *Pot*. Probably the most expensive, but it's the most, you know, representative of Mervin's work.'

Good for her, I thought, until Jack said, 'Splendid, Flora. Thank you so much. If I just give you my credit card, perhaps you could take care of it for me?' He handed her the card quickly.

As we made our way through the crowd, Jack put his arm around my shoulders and said, 'Now this is more like it. A crowd can be awkward unless one puts it to good use.'

To prevent James seeing us, I'd swivelled such that I was practically hiding behind Jack. And the heat was stifling, so I'd earlier removed my jacket. Jack's hand edged to the part of my neck and shoulder that was exposed. 'It's awfully cold in here. I'd better put my jacket back on. And do you think we could have another glass of wine?'

He took my arm firmly, 'As I remember, the bar's this way.'

'No, you get the wine, Jack, please. I'll just try to find your painting.' When he hesitated, I said, 'That was a magnificent gesture, buying Mervin's painting. It'll get around that you're an art collector and strong supporter of Chambers' staff. An excellent public relations decision. You do know the entire accounts section is here tonight?'

'Actually, I didn't know.' He smiled a more business-like smile and began to thread his way to the drinks table. Anything, I thought, to get his ambition focussed back on the office. I quickly worked the crowd, to greet my workmates while I was on my own and to find James while unattached to superglue.

Passing Mervin, I whispered, 'Jack Howard's buying a large painting, and if you tell anyone we came together he's sure to return it. If I don't murder him first.'

Mervin grinned. 'I wouldn't in any event. At the office, I mostly listen. Thanks, Caron, about the picture.'

'Flora was the saleswoman, actually.'

He smiled. Leaning close he said, 'Here comes Jack, you'd better shift.' He grinned and added, 'I'll head him off at the pass and give you a breather.'

I turned quickly away and bumped into James, who was wearing khaki trousers and a sexy bomber jacket. 'Caron!'

'James! I didn't realise you were coming. I mean you didn't mention it.'

'I hadn't planned to. But Jim Chambers tries to attend anything put on by staff, and he couldn't make it. He asked me to stand in for him, so I returned from New York early.' He leaned down and kissed my cheek and took my hand. I could see Jack nearby with Mervin. The James/Jack situation was like counting your cash from under the mattress while the Inland Revenue banged on the door.

James was using the crowd to better avail than Jack had. He kept turning to chat such that I bumped into him. 'I rang you when I got back. It's a real treat finding you here like this. And looking so gorgeous. I like the flowers. What are they?'

'Don't you know?' It didn't seem like James to tell the florist to send just any old blossoms.

'Stoner would know. But while she tries to teach me, the flower names skip out of my head. But they are a lovely old-fashioned touch, Caron, with such a modern suit. Nice.'

'Thank you.' If neither Jack nor James had sent the corsage, it must have been Bas. The flowers were probably concealing a cyanide capsule, and just one bump in this crowd and the fumes would get me. I'd probably been breathing it in already and was half-dead without noticing. I realised James was talking.

'And perhaps, beautiful lady, you would allow me to escort you after the ball to dinner?'

'James, let's go see a darling little painting. Over there.' I was trying to unpin the corsage without bringing attention to it. I would have felt like a person in the desert who'd just found an oasis, if there hadn't been a jackal lurking in the sand dunes. And another jackal taking action from a distance.

'Of course. Which one?'

I almost said any one. 'I'll know it when I see it.'

As we edged along, he repeated his invitation. 'That sounds like Cinderella, your mention of balls and beauties, James. So why don't we meet at midnight?'

He laughed. 'And do what? Eat pumpkin sandwiches? We've already done the picnic thing, Caron. This time I get to choose.'

Soon we were tucked into a corner. And fortunately the crowd was pushing us the right way, which was towards each other. With my help and not a little from James. We were standing comfortably with our arms around each other's waists looking at the wall – unusually, as it was probably the only bit of wall without a painting. I casually dropped the corsage, but James saw it and picked it up.

'Here, Caron. Do you want me to pin it on better?'

'No! I mean no, thanks.' I took it back and held it behind me.

'Caron, I've never liked crowds before, but I could

easily become addicted.' He smiled and ruffled my hair with his free hand. 'When you've finished looking at the paintings, I mean, anytime you want to leave? You have come on your own?'

I was horrified to see that Jack had freed himself from Mervin. Probably bit his hand. And he wasn't far away. 'James, wouldn't you like some wine? I would.' Like Jack, he took my arm to take me with him. Probably basic training for the top floor. 'Er, James, I'll just stay here. To keep an eye on the painting.'

He looked at the blank wall. 'Whatever. It's a bit too modern for me.' I watched as he ran into Jack and they greeted each other with all the warmth of a Popsicle meeting a Cornetto.

I quickly went to find Flora. 'James didn't send the corsage either. It must have been Bas!'

Flora peered at my face. 'Do you feel any swelling? Itching? Do you think you're about to throw up?'

'Flora, I'm still alive as we talk! I need to get rid of the bloody flowers.' I looked around and said with relief, pointing towards the wall, 'There's a rubbish bin over there.'

'No, no, that's one of the exhibits. Let me have them. There's a bin behind the bar.' She carefully held the corsage by one of the ribbons.

I took a deep breath and tried to relax just as Jack handed me the wine. I detected a small change in his manner. Maybe my reminder that other Chambers' people were there had done it. He smiled and said, 'I'm sorry if I've seemed to be rushing you, Caron.'

'Well, you have, and I don't like it.' I smiled to make the words less brash.

'I wasn't thinking. It's just that when I saw you in

that outfit, so different from your usual conservative clothing, well, you do look absolutely stunning.'

He was now standing a more reasonable distance from me, about two and a half inches. So I said, 'Thank you.' He took a sip of wine and smiled at me over the glass. I had to admit he was extremely good-looking, at least when he stood far enough away for me to focus my eyes. But I'd always thought tigers were handsome, without wishing to invite them home.

'You know, Caron, I don't want us to be a short play-ing record, like for instance a cassette tape.'

I laughed. 'What did you have in mind? A CD?'

'Actually I was thinking more of a round-the-clock radio station. Preferably owned by the BBC so it would never go out of business.' He was back to being the man I had seen in his office after the apology note. I hoped this was the real one, who might be stalled for the next twenty years. Or the necessary minutes before James returned.

I'd considered his more subdued manner a stroke of luck, but then I hit the jackpot. The entire accounts section arrived and circled Jack like vultures. One, in a friendly manner, nudged me and said, 'You've already got to talk to him. You wouldn't consider pissing off, would you? I mean you've had your chance.'

I laughed. 'Go for it. I've warmed him up.' Well, that was the truth. As I moved away, I saw even Mrs Brown very delicately aiming for Jack.

Over the heads of the crowd I saw Evelyn. By the time I made my way over to her, Flora was already there handing her a glass of wine. 'Evelyn,' I said, 'I've got just the man for you. Tall, blond, handsome, probably rich, single and quite possibly a sex maniac.'

Evelyn looked puzzled. 'But I thought I was supposed to avoid him. Report to you if I saw him.'

'No, no, it's not Bas. It's Jack Howard. Flora thinks he's nice, too, don't you Flora?'

'Actually, Evelyn, he's an extremely good catch.'

'What is the catch? You two being so generous? Does he use cheap deodorant? Eat garlic for breakfast? Remember, I'm supposed to be your friend.'

'That's exactly why we're going to introduce you, Evelyn. After that, it's your own lookout.'

'Point him out and I'll decide.'

Flora said, pointing, 'That one surrounded by girls.'

'And it's not the British Garlic Club, Evelyn.'

Evelyn smiled. 'All right! Yesssss!'

As we approached the crowd around Jack, I whispered, 'Softly, softly, Evelyn. You don't want to scare him.'

She smiled. 'He doesn't look like he scares easily, but it'd be fun to try.'

Flora and I made the introductions, telling Jack she lived with us. And whether it was because of love at first sight or to please us, he turned to her with a large smile. While Flora and I escaped the glares of our colleagues, Evelyn took his arm and led him apart from the group. None of the other women seemed inclined to argue with her.

I barely managed to return to the blank wall before James caught me up. But as he handed me a glass of wine, I realised I was still holding the one brought by Jack.

James saw it and grinned. 'I suspected that bastard was looking for you. Well, he won't bother you any more.' Taking a sip of wine, he added, 'I told the accounts section he was here.'

I must have looked impressed because he smiled broadly. 'Men who spread a load of shit shouldn't be surprised by a large crop of flowers.'

'I really need to stay here until the end, James, for Flora and Mervin. Why don't you come over later? I mean you could go home now if you want to leave.'

He smiled. 'And do what? Change into something more comfortable?' We laughed and then he said, 'Actually, I could unpack before Stoner gets into my cases.'

'Why? Have you got someone hidden in there?'

James blushed slightly. 'Well, I got you a small present. And it would be just like old Stoner to decide it was for her. More likely confiscate it in case it wasn't.' I walked him to the door, and could only hope he took my delighted expression to mean I was looking forward to beating Stoner out of the present.

When I found Flora, she was giddy with excitement. 'What did you say to Mervin, Caron? He kissed me on the cheek. Twice. I mean both. He said you'd spoken to him.'

'Just that you'd sold a painting for him, which is true.'

Flora smiled. 'And I saw James Smith leading accounts over. He looked like the Pied Piper. I wonder how Evelyn's getting along with Jack?'

'I hope they're planning their wedding.'

Flora laughed and said, 'I don't think so. In books she would make you jealous. Hardly ever in books does the heroine try to match up the hero with a friend.'

'There probably aren't many people in books like Evelyn. Oh, dear, here she comes. And without Jack.'

She looked furious. 'You set me up!'

I said, 'That was the idea. What happened?'

'All he did was ask about you, Caron. I think he would have listened if I'd said what you ate for breakfast.'

'Shit and double shit.'

'Don't worry. I didn't tell him.'

'No, I didn't mean that. I really don't want him, Evelyn. It's too complicated what with working with him. I'm sorry.'

'No problem. Why don't you try talking about breakfast, to get rid of him?'

Flora said, 'In books breakfast always means after the bed part.'

'Yeah, well. You don't have to love him. I mean couldn't you just think of him as exercise? Think of me and keep him in the family?' She said this as a joke then spotted more prospective talent across the room. 'See you two later.'

Flora said, 'You know, Caron, all that's left is for you to have a headache or need to wash your hair. Have you ever said that to a man?'

'No. But it's not the sort of thing that needs a lot of rehearsing.'

As the crowd began to thin, it became more and more difficult for Jack to break away from the office workers and escort me out, without being more obvious than even he wanted to be. Someone suggested we all go out for pizza.

As the group, including Mervin and Flora, moved towards the door, Jack managed to grab my elbow. He leaned down and whispered, 'I'm sorry.'

I smiled brightly. 'I don't mind.'

He grinned wryly. 'It's me I'm feeling sorry for.'

I then managed to get to the tail of the crowd. There was only room for one passenger in Jack's car, and I didn't plan to be it.

After numerous girls tried to edge into the Jaguar, I watched cheerfully as Jack Howard drove off to meet the others with Mrs Brown waving happily from the passenger side. With great laughter, Mervin, Flora, and

I set off in a taxi. 'My treat,' said Mervin. 'After Flora sold my most expensive painting ever.'

'Thanks, Mervin. Where did you arrange for the painting to be sent, Flora?'

'To Jack Howard's office to hang on the wall. Help like to advertise Mervin.'

'Wonderful. I never got to see it. Named *Pot*, I should imagine it's crockery? Maybe with a sunset behind?'

'Oh, no, Caron,' said Flora. 'It's a whole plantation of marijuana.'

At the pizza place, I said, 'Congratulations again, Mervin. And if you two don't mind, I'll keep the taxi and go home. Flora, would you mind telling Jack?'

Mervin said, 'Aren't you feeling well? Flora and me can protect you from Jack Howard.'

'It's all right,' said Flora. 'She has a headache and needs to wash her hair.'

'Flora, maybe it would be better to tell Jack that I broke a heel on my shoe, or laddered my tights?'

As I unlocked the door, I felt exhausted. I'd believed I was free from worrying about Bas for a while, and only needed to deal with James and Jack. My muse was working overtime, or she was drunk. My wishing to ditch Jack was pretty equally balanced by my fear that I liked James too much. For strictly a friend. And I didn't want to lose him. But there was no way I was ready to get really involved. I had absolutely got to pull myself up a notch or two, because it was completely out of the question to have a repeat of big powerful rich man and little me.

After opening a bottle of wine, I took a glass and sat on the front steps. The nights were shorter, but there was still some late summer warmth in the air. The sky was sprinkled with stars. There was a large moon, the kind that looks so close you could poke it with your finger and take a bite. And then I saw James walking towards the house. He stopped a few feet away on the pavement and smiled.

It was as if I hadn't seen him for years. We both rushed forward and wrapped our arms around each other. With my cheek pressed against his and one hand touching his bare neck, and one of his hands running through my hair, he asked, 'Did you miss me?'

'A bit. Did you miss me?'

'Rather.'

It was just too comfortable and wonderful to shift, so we stood that way for a few minutes. Then James said, 'We'd better get you inside.'

Puzzled, I asked why.

'Well, you need to get some clothes on. I mean, that skirt and tiny top. I did notice earlier and rather hoped you'd only been to . . .'

'Church?' I suggested. As we made our way inside, I said, 'I thought men loved this sort of outfit.'

'Exactly.'

I hadn't realised he was carrying a bottle until he asked if I had some glasses. 'Save that, James. I've got an open bottle.'

'But this is champagne. I thought, well, New York seemed awfully far away.'

'Oh, I see. It's duty free, is it?' I was grinning mischievously.

'Yes. No. Well, that isn't exactly the point I was trying to make.' He reached into his jacket pocket and took out a large gift-wrapped bottle of perfume. I smiled and set it aside to open later, but there was no delay in planting the thank you kiss. It was long and delicious and made my blood boil, and we hadn't even drunk the champagne yet.

As I held up a glass to be filled, I asked, 'What did you do in New York? Did you have a good time?'

He grinned. 'Does this mean we can both ask questions?'

I also smiled. 'Absolutely not. I shall reword that. I want to know if you met any gorgeous women.'

Reminded of New York, he sort of forgot himself and began to speak rapidly. 'You wouldn't believe the women. I don't know if it's just New York. A colleague did say there was a shortage of men there. They ask you for dates, ask straight out if you want to go to bed.' He stopped and blushed slightly as he added, 'Sorry, Caron, I don't want to bore you.'

'Bore me, James? You must be joking!'

He held out his glass for me to refill it. 'Well, the men called me Jim, and the women called me Jimmy. And a beautiful blonde put her hand on my thigh. This was in a large group at the dinner table. Rather embarrassing, I thought.'

He stopped to sip champagne and then wiped his chin with his handkerchief. 'One of the PR women after dinner asked outright, did I feel like fucking her.'

'Well, I suppose you thought it rude to say no?'

'Well, it would have been rude. So I said I was engaged. But then she said that meant I needed to sow wild oats. Finally I said I'd used up my quota of fucks for the day.'

I laughed. 'Did she then say you can never have too much of a good thing?'

'Actually, she did.' He took another sip of champagne. 'The women were beautiful, especially some from the South who had names like Lucy Sue and Clara

Bell. They seemed to have double-barrelled Christian names rather than surnames. And the clothes they wore, they were . . .'

'Like this?' I asked, wiggling and showing a lot of leg.

James smiled. 'Very like that.'

I asked in an offhand manner, 'And was there anyone in particular?'

He grinned. 'I could perhaps have coped with one, but it seemed like hundreds. Don't misunderstand, when I say could have coped I . . .'

We were sitting on the sofa. 'I do misunderstand. You need to demonstrate, James. Move closer.'

I lit three candles and turned off the lamps. Soon we were back in each other's arms, and it seemed quite natural to lie back, as it was so late and a person gets tired. I was slowly unbuttoning his shirt while his hand moved along my leg, gently touching the soft flesh as his hand moved up.

'I did warn you about this skirt, Caron.'

He was kissing my neck. I smiled and said, 'If the skirt bothers you, James, we need to get rid of it.'

'In that case, it's bothering me very much.'

My hands were inside his shirt, rubbing up and down his back. He had moved my elasticised top up and his hands were cupping my breasts. At the same time we were making our previous kisses resemble infants playing Postman's Knock. James leaned back. 'Caron, before I forget. Are we still on for that weekend away?'

'Absolutely. Name a date.'

'Is there the slightest chance you would be free this coming weekend?'

'Definitely. But do carry on with the preview.'

We both sat up quickly at the sound of knocking on

the outer door. 'Oh, no, James. I wasn't expecting Flora back so soon.'

'Doesn't she have a key?'

'It could be Evelyn. She acts like this is a hotel and often leaves her key at the desk.'

We both rushed to make ourselves presentable. He grinned wryly. 'In a way, Caron, our friendship has been saved by the bell.'

I smiled at him then opened the door. Shit! Shit! Shit! It was Jack Howard.

'I've come to apologise for not seeing you home, Caron. And to make sure you're all right.'

What could I do? If, against all odds, I managed to send him away, James would already have heard his voice. Well, hell. If Jack was going to cost me James, I might as well hope James would return the favour.

18

James and Jack spoke softly at first, a bit like quiet and deadly spiders would if they could talk while sneaking up on Evelyn in the bath.

'Good evening, Jack. I take it this is a business call?'

Jack grinned smugly. 'Caron was my date this evening.'

James hid his surprise well. 'So you took Caron out but didn't even see her home? You may be voted gentleman of the year.'

'There were reasons . . .'

'For deserting Caron? I suppose death would be a reasonable excuse.'

'Fuck off, Smith. What the hell are you doing here, anyway?'

'That's not your concern, but as you ask, Caron and I are dear friends.'

'Then why don't you do as I do, take her out in public instead of sneaking around at night? As we were together earlier,' he quickly smiled at me before turning back to Jack, 'you can't have been here long.'

'I'm glad I am here. I don't actually know what a man would be planning, ditching a date then turning up later.'

'I didn't ditch Caron, damn it. And I came to apologise, well, for the mix-up.'

'Look,' I said. 'It's late. Why don't we call it a night?'

Quickly both men sat down. James said to Jack, 'You

were last in. It won't help your image to stick around and play gooseberry.'

'But she's my date!' Jack was losing it.

'You're history, Jack. Caron's my date, now.'

I could have strangled them both. It was like two bulls fighting over a cow, and of course that made me the cow.

'Jack, I understand about the mix-up. And thanks for coming to tell me. So, well, goodnight.'

'Caron, I'm not leaving until James does. Hell, the man's dangerous.'

James laughed. 'Coming from the Trousers of Chambers', that's a bit much.' He slowly sipped champagne, making it obvious that he was the guest and Jack the intruder. Finally, Jack stood up.

'Then we should both go. Have some consideration for Caron, who after our date must be exhausted.' He grinned wryly at James with as much innuendo as he could muster. James' smile could have turned hell into a ski resort.

'I don't think you should leave together.' I didn't want to have to sweep up dead bodies off the street. 'Jack, as you came by car, you go first. Then . . .'

'How the hell did he get here? Fly?'

James smiled beatifically. 'I walked. Caron and I are neighbours.'

Before I could see Jack to the door, the phone rang. I snatched it off the table and said, 'Hello?'

'Don't hang up, honey. It's Bas and I want to really talk, maybe sort something out.'

I practically shouted, 'How dare you ring me in the middle of the night!'

Both James and Jack were looking at me expectantly, as it was too late for a normal call. And as if it wasn't complicated enough with the two of them, now they'd think there was a third man. James said in a low voice, 'Is there a problem, Caron?'

I put my hand over the phone and said, 'It's just a double-glazing salesman.'

'Sorry, honey. I forgot all about the time difference. It's only six in the evening here. Did you get the flowers?'

'Yes. Don't you think they're a bit old-fashioned?' To Jack and James I said, 'The French doors with stained-glass windows. Half price.'

Bas laughed. 'I wanted you to know I'm a changed man. So are you gonna come back to me?'

'Never. So stop ringing me.' James reached for the phone and asked if I wanted him to handle it. I said loudly, 'I'm not a woman who needs men to handle everything!' James looked embarrassed and sat back down.

Bas said, 'Cool it, honey. I've never thought of you as a weak woman. I wouldn't want one of those. But I need a decision soon, Caron. I'm not waiting forever.'

'The answer's no. So stop bothering me.' And I slammed down the phone.

Fortunately, before either man could ask questions about double-glazing salesmen, Flora and Mervin came in. Mervin laughed. 'Is this a meeting of the board?' He was obviously trying to defuse the situation, as James and Jack looked like they'd eaten a dozen worms each.

Flora said brightly, 'I'll make some coffee. Would you like to help, Mervin?'

'Thanks, Flora,' I said. 'Jack is just leaving. I'll see him out.' He leaned down to kiss my cheek as though everything were perfectly normal.

'I'll be in touch, Caron.'

That was not the best way at that moment to say goodbye.

When the car was gone, James came up behind me at the front door. I tried to reach up and kiss his cheek, but he brushed quickly past me. 'I can explain, James!' But once outside he began jogging away without looking back.

Flora and Mervin came from the kitchen. She said, 'Sorry, Caron. We didn't know Jack was coming here after the pizza.'

'Heavens, Flora, it's not your fault.'

Mervin thanked me for coming to his show and said goodbye, while leaning over to kiss my cheek.

'It was a super evening, Mervin. They'd better start making room in the Tate.'

When he'd gone, I turned to Flora. 'Well, I've managed to mess up everything. That was Bas on the phone. And I didn't want Jack and James to think I was involved with yet another man, so I acted like he was a salesman and shouted for him to leave me alone.'

'Well, that's not the first time.'

'No, Flora, but I think he wanted to work something out. Maybe negotiate. Then after I was so rude, he said he needed a decision. It sounded like an ultimatum. He was ringing from New York, so nothing should happen tonight. I don't think.'

'I'm not sure what ultimatum would follow two gardenias. Did he explain them?'

'Only that he's a changed man.'

Flora laughed. 'That could be very good or very bad. What about James and Jack?'

'They were both so angry they'll probably start sending mysterious presents themselves.'

Flora smiled. 'In that case maybe we can open a gift

shop.' But I could tell she was really worried. She gave me a big hug and said goodnight, and said to call her if anything happened during the night.

In my room, I tried to ring James. His mobile was turned off, and I didn't want to ring the other number and wake up Stoner. The next day, Sunday, the mobile was still turned off. That time I left a message asking him to ring me.

By Monday morning, I was resigned to the fact I was on the shit list of both men, and that Bas was looking on the internet to find out how to make bombs or hire army tanks. The upside was that it cleared the field of men in one fell swoop. The downside was that without James in it, the field would just be a patch of weeds.

Unfortunately Jack made a play. Mid-morning a small, elegant vase of delicate flowers was delivered. No name, no message. But surely James would not ignore my phone calls but still send flowers. And Bas would be so angry any flowers would wilt before I got them. I gave them to Melody, not wanting flowers on my desk in case James should pass by. But every day a new bouquet arrived. The second lot went to Mrs Brown. After that I began to pass them out to the pool, going counter-clockwise. What I'd do when there were flowers on every desk I couldn't imagine. Still, I was grateful they weren't cactus plants.

I joined Flora in the canteen. 'Caron, wait for it! You remember, after the pizza, Mervin took me home? Just me. And he came this morning to my desk to ask if I'd be willing to help, like, manage his career. What do you think of that?'

'That's wonderful, Flora. How manage?'

'The business side, you know? Think up some promotional ideas. And he's going to use the graphics programme on his computer to make brochures so I can pass them out within the company. That was my idea. And I asked Mrs Oakley and she said it would be all right being as he's an employee. Isn't that brill?'

'It is, Flora. Really terrific.' I was trying hard not to let my black cloud cross the table and rain on her.

Just then Mervin arrived and asked if he could join us. Already he seemed quite protective or proprietary of Flora, touching her shoulder as he sat down.

'Have you two heard the news? Jack Howard's got my painting on his wall.' He spread his arms wide. 'This size, right behind his desk. His PA told me she asked about the painting, and he said, "It only looks like pot, it's really lettuce." '

We all choked up with laughter. I said, 'I wonder if we can get the drug squad to bust his office?'

After forking a bite of lasagne, I said, 'Flora says you're going to make some flyers to advertise your art work. Terrific idea. But how do you get that programme up on your computer? I can't get anything interesting with my password, not even Solitaire.'

Mervin looked a bit nervous. 'Well, actually, I copped a password one day when I was lent to the top floor.' He was studiously shifting a noodle around his plate.

'I hadn't thought of that. Well, more to the point, I haven't had a chance.'

He brightened immediately, realising that I seemed unlikely to grass him up or even tick him off. 'It's not a top-level password, but enough to know this company's got problems. And I, well, I like to keep in touch in case we need to look for jobs.'

That didn't seem the least bit likely. More likely Mervin, like most of us, had a well-developed snooping streak. 'Well, do warn Flora and me.'

Flora said, 'Mervin's quite good. Tell Caron how you hacked into your school computer and found out the exam questions, Mervin.'

'Flora! I nearly got kicked out of school for that. And well, I didn't access the right papers, anyway.' He grinned mischievously with wide-eyed innocence. 'Surely you two don't think I'd do anything like that now that I'm grown-up and respectable, do you?'

Flora and I both laughed. Then I said, 'You mentioned company problems, Mervin. Have you really looked at the new shop window Christmas displays that were installed on Sunday?' They both said they hadn't particularly noticed.

'That's my point exactly. I've never seen such bland displays. What they need, Mervin, is some of your artistic expertise. You work well with lots of colour. So who wants to barnstorm the windows?'

Flora said, 'The actual clothes looked all right.'

'Yes, but a large part of Chambers' business is lingerie and the new cashmere line. Where are they displayed? If people like us wouldn't stop to look at the windows, they certainly wouldn't come in. I mean, where are the new customers? Soon all the regular clientele will have died off.'

An enthusiastic discussion, mostly between me and Mervin, ensued for the rest of the lunch hour about how the windows could be improved. Mervin looked at his watch before getting up. 'Well, I'm game for a midnight onslaught.'

'But you'd get the sack,' said Flora.

I gave it some thought. 'I doubt it. When I did some work for old Harvey upstairs in accounts, he mentioned that sales had dropped. If we did something that was helpful, no one could object, could they? Anyway, the only way to make real money is to be self-employed. If we did a good job and got the sack, we'd get some attention. Maybe we'd be offered better jobs. Or we could make a stab at being self-employed.'

'But that would mean you no longer, like, worked here.'

'I'm not bothered,' said Mervin. 'I can always get another job like this. Brain dead and bill paying. And with you helping me, Flora, I might not need an outside job much longer. But if you're serious, Caron, we need to make a move before the public and staff have time to get used to the crap that's out there now.'

Flora took a deep breath and sort of held it. 'The art department head will probably murder you, I mean us, because if you're going to do the deed, count me in. Could we just, you know, think about it overnight?'

Mervin smiled. 'I'll chat up the shop floor and find out how best to access the windows. Just in case we decide. Caron, could you somehow recce the night security?'

'Absolutely.' I suppose if I tried to break in, I'd find out soon enough. 'I especially need to check if our taking security tagged cashmere sweaters into the windows will set off the alarms.' Anyway, we went away greatly cheered. Well Flora probably went away with indigestion.

It would certainly help if I could get back in James' good graces before trying such a stunt. And back in his friendly arms would be nice, too. Another bouquet arrived along with Mrs Brown and a mountain of spreadsheets. When she'd gone, I remembered James and my weekend away. Well, that was probably cancelled.

I smiled as I figured out how to contact James. Ring

his mobile while he was at work. He'd have to answer or walk about with his pocket going pip pip. Bingo!

'Don't hang up James! I just want to know if our weekend away is still on?'

He sounded like he'd slept in the fridge. 'I'm the sort of man who keeps his word. But could we delay it a week? Would it mess up your, er, other plans?'

Hotly I said, 'It suits me fine. And when I explain everything to you, James, you'll be crawling around and feeling like a worm.'

'I shall look forward to that. Thank you for calling.' And he rang off.

What an icy monster! So that was it then, he'd simply put the weekend off each week indefinitely. Keep me dangling, tease me along. I couldn't possibly sit back and let this go on. What was so bloody frustrating was, what the hell could I do about it?

That evening after a quick sandwich, I staked out the Heath. I'd read a book and wait until he jogged by. I would block his path. He was too much of a gentleman to knock me down.

But he wasn't too much of a gentleman to jog around me and keep going. I began to jog along behind him, not really able to catch him up. Just thinking about exercise doesn't keep you in very good shape. This went on for some time, until I was gasping. In frustration, I picked up a pebble and threw it at his back.

Before he could turn, I stretched out flat on the ground. Well, that was easy because I could hardly stand up I was so exhausted. James said, 'Well?'

'Can't you see I'm dying, James? I'm out of practice. Couldn't you at least help me up?' When he didn't move, I said, 'It's either that or call an ambulance.'

James, with a slight smile, immediately reached for

his mobile. I called his bluff, until he was punching in numbers. Then I shouted, 'Shit!'

Still breathing heavily, I got up and brushed myself off. 'Well, go on then. Please don't feel you have to wait for me.'

But he stood there, gazing into the distance at the ponds. When I was beside him, he began to walk, but more slowly. Well, more slowly for a man with such long legs. It still took a bit of huffing and puffing on my part.

'James, don't think my running after you on the Heath was personal. I just wanted to ask you about Chambers' security.'

He looked surprised, even a bit wary. 'Security?'

'Surely you know what security is. I mean what's to stop someone breaking in at midnight and stealing all the cashmere sweaters?'

'Oh, that security. Surely you aren't planning . . .'

'I'm not a thief, James! I just meant generally. But I suppose you wouldn't know.' That works with most men.

'Of course I know, Caron. There are alarms. There's a night guard. The police do regular patrols of the area. Stuff generally gets stolen during the day. It's called shoplifting.'

'I know that!'

'Well, if you know the answers, why are you asking the questions?'

'I don't know all the answers! Anyway, it's a mark of intelligence to ask questions when you don't know something. I was thinking more about ram raiders bashing a truck through the shop windows. If they took things out that way, wouldn't it set off the alarms?'

'That's why the security devices are only around the

doors. People do, on the whole, try to steal merchandise that way!'

He really did look angry. And surprisingly, this made him look sexy. Well, friends can look sexy. After five minutes of silence, I reached and touched one finger to his bare upper arm, below the short sleeve of his T-shirt. After a minute, I added another finger, sort of pressing in his arm. Then I rested my knuckles against his arm. Still without looking at me, he reached down and took my hand. And we walked on hand in hand during more silence. It wasn't exactly like Scarlett and Rhett, but it was better than a war film.

'James, I'd been terribly rude to Jack Howard in public. To make it up, I agreed to a date. But we really weren't alone, certainly no, er, touching.'

'I'll believe many things, Caron, but never that Jack Howard didn't touch a beautiful woman.'

'Well, he might have touched. Nothing important. My waist, well then my shoulder.' Desperately I added, 'You know, the same bits you touched at Mervin's show.'

'I was only touching second-hand, used bits? Well, that's flattering. Maybe I could send Jack on stage first to warm up the women for me. And then?'

'There was no and then. I escaped and made my own way home. So I could meet you.' That should do it, I thought happily.

'And that makes everything better, Caron? As I remember, we had to eat lunch on a park bench in the rain as you obviously didn't want to be seen in public with me. But with Jack it didn't matter that half of Chambers' would see you together?'

'It wasn't like that, James. Don't be so obtuse. I managed it so that no one realised we arrived together, and you know we didn't leave together.' When he said nothing, and dammit still wasn't looking at me, I added, 'At first it was supposed to be dinner and the theatre, and I got out of that by suggesting the exhibition.'

'Dinner and the theatre? You must have been exceptionally rude.'

I was reduced to holding his hand with both of mine so he couldn't run off. 'It was in the pub where I went with Flora. I'd heard his reputation so I thought he was making a pass. I ticked him off. Then I wrote an apology, but somehow that came out rude as well. Matters just seemed to get all tangled up.'

James said, 'Your department has so many floral deliveries it resembles a hospital ward. Are you rude every day?'

I yanked his hand until we were stopped. Facing him, I said, 'You are a pig-headed stubborn mule, James. I've been as rude to him as I could be without getting sacked. Do you want me to lie down on the ground and grovel?'

'No. Does this mean we can begin to be seen together in public? For example, dinner and the theatre?'

'I've agreed to go away with you for a whole weekend. Isn't that enough?'

'Perhaps. Don't you want to cancel? Enjoy the limelight with Jack Howard?'

'I too keep my word, James. I'm coming on the weekend with you.'

He still hadn't looked at me and his next words were drier than the first and last cake I baked. 'How honourable, Caron. I can't tell you how much I'm looking forward to it.'

I dropped his hand and stood back and yelled, 'I'm looking forward to it, too. It's going to be the best time I've had in ages!'

Then I stormed off, not looking back to see if I'd finally got his attention.

A few minutes later, I turned aggressively when someone touched my elbow. The return of James. 'I just thought, Caron. Well, I thought it a bad idea for friends to part in anger.' He quickly kissed me, the way politicians kiss babies, before jogging off into the sunset.

19

I'd reached the stage of who needs men, anyway. All my leading men were simply playing human poker with me as a chip. Only a tiny chip. So little that after you won you'd use it to tip the waiter.

The weekend away was beginning to sound awful, but I wasn't about to cry Mercy first. And heaven only knew what Jack Howard was planning. Fresh flowers continued to arrive daily. It was surprising that the entire accounts section hadn't developed hay fever.

Even worse, I seemed never to get checked out of accounts anymore. And there had been more rumours about a possible hostile takeover bid. I'd seen Harvey in the canteen and tried to chat him up, said how much I missed working in his office. But he only said, 'Not a very good idea at the moment, Caron.'

'Because of the problems?' I'd risked asking.

'Excuse me, but I don't know of any problems.'

'Of course you don't. I must have been thinking of something else.'

It was a few days before Mervin joined Flora and me for lunch again, as he had needed to use his lunch hours to help dismantle his show in the gallery. And Flora hadn't mentioned the shop windows, probably hoping that if the idea wasn't watered and fed, it would begin to resemble a vase of three-day-old tulips.

By the time Mervin finally did join us, I was feeling a bit reckless. The combination of tedium and no prospects in sight for promotion made any kind of risk seem less extreme. And of course we wouldn't get caught.

'Sorry I haven't been able to make lunch. Loads of work. Well, are we doing the deed?'

I said, 'There's one restriction. If we get caught, and of course we won't, but if we do, I take the flak. You two weren't there. Agreed?'

Mervin said, 'Sure, we agree, don't we Flora? Why don't we just take Caron out now to the firing squad?'

'I'm serious. Otherwise it's no go.'

A heated argument ensued until Mervin touched Flora's hand and said, 'Let's agree with her. She can't blame us if we default, when the heavies are twisting the thumbscrews.' He smiled, but Flora choked on her Diet Coke.

Flora said, 'We still have to decide. Why don't we be democratic and have a vote, a private vote?' So we tore a napkin into bits and got out pencils. The vote was two to one for. Mervin and I sat staring at Flora who didn't know where to look. The next vote was unanimous.

There was a special on macaroni cheese and as we forked the steaming creamy pasta, we huddled in the corner.

Flora asked, 'What do you want me to do?'

'You be lookout,' suggested Mervin.

'Fine. But there isn't much time to, like, read up on the subject.'

'Flora,' I said, 'all you need to do is hide in the shop and come and tell Mervin and me if someone's coming.'

'And not knock anything over or make a noise,' added Mervin. 'You're a natural, Flora – neat and tidy and meticulous. Anyway, anyone who can sell Jack

Howard my pot painting for his office can easily play watchdog.'

'You're not frightened of the dark, are you Flora?' I asked.

'Who? Me?'

'I've got all the gen on the windows, and where the light switches are, Caron. Don't you think we should work in the dark, not attract attention from the street?'

'Good point, Mervin, and I think I can manage security. If Flora tips us off soon enough.' I was imagining the guard pushing a button that set off the alarm and caused hot water to sprinkle from the ceiling right before the cops rushed in.

Mervin leaned further across the table. 'So it's all go? Midnight Saturday night?'

'Either that or Sunday night,' I suggested.

'But Caron,' said Flora, 'that way we'd be too exhausted to work on Monday. They might send police around to check out, like, which employees were the tiredest.'

Mervin said, 'The new forensic fingerprints, check those eye bags!'

We all laughed, and then agreed Sunday was best. 'Upstairs will be more reluctant to change the windows back if a crowd's gathered on Oxford Street, Mervin.'

Flora said, 'Has anyone worked out how we can get into the building?'

Mervin and I said together, 'We won't leave.'

I amplified, 'We can hide out in the staffroom, drink wine, eat a picnic. It should be fun.'

'That will be a long picnic, Saturday night and all day Sunday. And how exactly do we, you know, get out when we've finished? If we use the fire doors, it will set off the alarm.'

Mervin said, 'By then it's too late Flora. And the

whole point's to get attention. So. Sunday night then?'

Flora's last bite of macaroni cheese slipped off her fork onto the table. She quickly said, 'Is that a sign?'

I said patiently, 'Flora, I rather think it's only a very antisocial piece of pasta.'

The next day, Friday, a complication arose. Flora rang and whispered furiously, 'They're planning a skeleton crew to man your department this weekend, on standby basis, being as there's some sort of meeting on the top floor. I heard them ask Mrs Oakley to arrange it. She was going on about rules and not wanting accounts to form a union what with weekend work. That it's too short notice. I volunteered. And suggested you as "last in" employee, and Mervin as he's the only man. Could you sort of quickly go and mention to Mrs Brown that you'd like some overtime?'

'Absolutely. Well done, Flora.'

'That means that it's us who'll have the staffroom keys and outer door key instead of Mrs Brown.'

I didn't know how to mention to Flora that her Sunday scenario might simply point a finger in our direction after the windows were done. It would hardly do for us later to say we'd forgotten to lock the outside door.

Mrs Brown seemed quite relieved when Mervin and I volunteered to work the weekend. On our way back to our desks, I mentioned the possible problem to Mervin. He grinned. 'No need to worry. That's too obvious. To think it's us. And if we all stick together on our story?'

I could just imagine Flora saying later to the authorities, 'No, it wasn't us three who stayed late. We didn't hide in the staffroom, and creep up to the window before switching off the lights, as we couldn't have known where they were.'

All day Saturday we had mostly sat around, occasionally being required to send a fax. We'd left promptly at five p.m. When we got home, Flora flipped through a pile of post on the desk. Evelyn was engrossed in a mail order catalogue and without looking up, said, 'Mostly bloody junk mail. There's a letter for you, Caron. Probably from your mum.'

It was airmail from the States with no return address. Inside, with no dear anybody or signature was the message: 'If you don't want to talk, we won't talk. But I know what you're up to, honey, and it won't work. I taught you everything you know, and believe me, honey, I'm always one step ahead.'

I was practically spluttering as I said, 'What I'm up to? What the hell is Bas talking about?' I showed the letter to Flora and Evelyn.

Evelyn said, 'I thought your mum said the bloke was busy with that merger thing. I could have told her that no man could behave himself that long. Usually not even for twenty-four hours.'

'I'd forgotten all about the merger. But there have been the gardenias and the double-glazing phone call already. So maybe the merger fell through.'

Flora said, 'Could Bas' letter just mean you're making it difficult? About the brownie recipe?'

'But that's overt, and he already tried to pinch it.'

Evelyn said in a bored voice, 'You two keep forgetting that Bas is a man. He's just tired of your playing so hard to get. He's probably got a new girlfriend and wants out.'

'Out of what, Evelyn? As far as I'm concerned, he's already out.'

Flora said, 'Could it simply be bluster? Because the garden furniture thing didn't work?'

'I don't know. Bas isn't exactly the bluster without bomb type. We'll just have to wait and see what comes next. He sent the threat by ordinary letter, so there's probably no hurry.'

'That's just what that bloke Bas would want you to think. I'd say if anyone asked me that Bas is about to strike again. Any minute we'll probably all be dead.'

Flora said, 'Thank you for being so helpful, Evelyn. I think you should peel the potatoes tonight.'

'And do the washing up,' I added.

By the next day a sense of excitement had taken over, and I didn't give Bas any further thought. I was not a little concerned that my shop windows idea could get my pals knee deep in shit. We mostly talked about how terrific it was to be making the extra money. My bank account had become positively anorexic. We'd get time and a half for Saturday and double for Sunday. Plus free lunches and transport. If we ever formed a union, we'd definitely want Mrs Oakley to be in charge.

There was practically nothing to do. Every hour or so, a call came from the top floor for someone to come and send a fax. Mervin seemed the keenest, so Flora and I let him go.

The first time, he returned gleefully and said, 'Almost the entire top floor's up there. No secretaries or assistants. No one saw us come in. I could have smuggled in the Crown Jewels, not just my duffel bag.'

Flora said, 'I did wonder about that, why they didn't just give the work to their secretaries. They even take them travelling, so what difference would a weekend make?'

Mervin said, 'Obvious. It's top secret. They couldn't get rid of the secretaries between faxes, like they can with us.'

'But they must know how to send faxes themselves?'

Mervin grinned. 'But which one of them? Next thing they'd be asked to make the coffee. That's the whole point of being important, telling someone else what to do.'

I asked, 'Did you overhear anything interesting, Mervin?'

'They see me coming and clam up. The last fax was just asking for info from the New York office.'

'They're probably, like, planning next year's strategy,' offered Flora. 'That's what Mrs Oakley was told when she asked.' She carefully measured out half wine and half water into our plastic cups, much to Mervin's and my annoyance.

'Do you think, Caron, it would be all right if we left Mervin here and went and checked out the shop? All the stuff I'm not supposed to fall over in the dark?'

The entire hour we'd been gone, Mervin hadn't budged. Then he got called to send faxes to Hong Kong and Milan. 'Just asking for more numbers,' he said when he returned.

I glanced at my watch. 'Well, it's five thirty, time they went home.'

But the next summons was for Mervin to go out for sandwiches. Flora went with him, as they needed to purchase quite a lot. I remained sitting at my desk at the back. I looked up and saw James standing near Mrs Brown's desk. He was looking around. Dammit, he was looking at all the flowers shared around the desks.

'Hello, James,' I said standing up. 'If you need anything, I'm here on standby. Anything at all.'

James seemed startled, not having seen me. 'No, thank you, Caron. Should you be on standby here alone?'

'Why? What are you planning to do?'

'I'm serious, Caron.'

'Oh, yes sir, sorry sir.' He just stood there waiting. 'Flora and Mervin are getting sandwiches. Anyway, there's a crowd on the top floor.'

'Yes, I know. I'm on my way up. But that isn't much help in the way of safety for you down here.'

I smiled. At least grumpy James didn't want me dead. 'I'm fine, James. Not exactly helpless.'

'No, you aren't that,' he said as he turned to walk away.

As usual with James, I couldn't sort out the compliments from the chaff. I half wished I could ask him what was really going on. From working with Bas, it was just the sort of thing I knew a bit about, although our company had never been subject to a hostile takeover. But I didn't want to put James in the embarrassing position of having to tell me it was confidential. Pity Mr Chambers hadn't strolled by. On the other hand, he might not have recognised me. Our communication was similar to putting notes into bottles before tossing them into the sea.

Soon after James left, Mervin and Flora returned full of laughter. They were carrying bags from the deli. 'Caron, you won't believe what Mervin did! When we took up the food, he said we wouldn't dream of leaving until the top floor did, in case they needed us, like.'

Mervin punched the air. 'From five o'clock, and we're still on double time. All night maybe. And if push comes to shove, we can say we changed the windows on company time, trying to help out.'

Alarmed, Flora said, 'But I thought we were going to, you know, keep it secret?'

'I said if push comes to shove, Flora. If we get caught.'

Flora said, 'But do you think the top floor will work all night?'

'Who knows? Or cares?' said Mervin. 'You don't think anyone will actually remember to tell us if they leave in five minutes, do you? They're looking a bit grim up there.'

Mervin started taking food out of the bags. 'Don't worry, Caron. This doesn't come out of our meal allowance. Upstairs is paying. I'm sure they would have said yes if I'd asked. I didn't risk it in case they insisted we go home for dinner.'

'Goodness, this looks delicious,' said Flora.

'Smoked salmon,' said Mervin to me. 'And there's roast beef and mustard, turkey, ham, cheese and salad. Piles of crisps. Cokes. We didn't think the top floor would be wanting plain economy cheese.'

Between six and midnight, there were two more summons, both to send faxes. I said, 'Pity the answers to the faxes aren't coming to us. It must be interesting.'

'They're going straight to Mr Chambers' office. That's where everyone is.'

Flora said, 'As they haven't gone home yet and could call us, do you want to put our plan off until next weekend?'

Mervin and I nearly shouted: 'No.' Me because I wasn't going to miss my weekend away, if James didn't postpone it again. And Mervin seemed to be thriving on the prospect of mischief.

Strangely, Flora said, 'I agree, we should carry on. We've come so far already.'

As I munched a sandwich, I got up and gave her a hug. We could of course all get the sack. But Flora was the bravest of the three of us, as her aversion to risk was so much greater.

It was decided we'd go by the original plan, leaving accounts deserted, hoping to finish the windows in an hour. We could always say we'd been on a break, or had gone home, or had been in the photocopy room. Even better, we could say we'd heard some noises. But the windows would take too long, greatly increasing the risk, if one of us remained behind to man the phones.

When we reached the deserted shop floor, Flora squeaked, 'Gosh, all those mannequins look like ghosts.' We left her near the lifts as we made our way to the windows. There was enough heavy gear to bog down a couple of camels and we stopped often to rest and listen and look for the guard. Mervin began on the first window as I quickly collected various items from the display counters.

Mervin and I had worked out the various details during our department coffee breaks. And extremely unrealistically, we'd thought the windows could be done in an hour and a bit. We should have asked Flora, who would have said it'd take a month, causing us to revise our estimate.

Each window took nearly an hour. We'd just finished the last window, believing we'd got away with it, when suddenly Flora came rushing up. 'Someone's coming.'

Mervin said, 'Hide!'

Flora asked, 'Where?'

'In the window,' I said. 'Quickly. Stand still and we'll look like mannequins. The window lights are still off.'

We waited for a time in silence, but just as we thought we were in the clear, we heard someone trying to open the door to the window display. I stood stiffly, my arms flung out in a dramatic pose, my back to the door. The streetlights cast eerie shadows on the display. I didn't dare turn to look at Mervin or Flora.

Slowly the door opened. I held my breath. A voice said, 'Caron? Is that you?'

I quickly turned. 'James! Dammit, what are you doing here?'

I thought he was smiling. Hoped he was smiling. 'I should think it is I who should be asking you that question.'

My foot got twisted behind a prop as I tried to get out of the window. As I fell into his arms, I reached behind me and shoved the door to. 'Thanks, James. Well, lovely to see you. Would you like to go for coffee?' I had his arm and was trying to lead him away.

I'd got him to the centre aisle when he said, 'But what were you doing? Have you always dreamed of being in a shop window? Perhaps a fetish?'

I could barely make out his features in the dark. 'Certainly not.' Thinking furiously, I finally said, 'I was getting some exercise, just walking about. I noticed the shop window light was off. And I was looking for the switch.'

He started back towards the windows. 'I know where it is. Just a moment.'

'No! I mean, I found it. But I messed up the window a bit and need to straighten it up first.' He hesitated, and I added, 'Why did you come down here at this particular moment?'

'I was looking for the night guard to tell him there's personnel on the third floor tonight, to keep an eye out. He didn't answer his bleeper. And I noticed the window light was off.'

'Well, you carry on looking for the guard, and I'll take care of the window.'

'I'll wait. I don't like leaving you alone down here.'

I grinned and whispered, 'Would you hold me tight and maybe kiss me if you thought I was frightened?'

After a short silence, he said, 'I might.'

I put my arms around his neck and hugged him. Remembering Mervin and Flora, I tried to think of hugging James as martyrdom for the cause. After a moment, James returned the squeeze. He'd been acting so much like an ice cube, it was surprising I didn't get wet when he defrosted. Soon a kiss followed. Then a more serious kiss. I was halfway to forgetting the plan and the fact that Mervin and Flora were still trapped in the window.

When we came up for breath, James said, 'This reminds me about the question you asked about security. About whether Chambers' had any.'

'Isn't it an amazing coincidence that we talked about that? Shall I check your pockets in case you've been shoplifting?'

James laughed a bit nervously. 'I rather need to get back upstairs at the moment.'

I laughed and tried to lead him further from the windows. 'It's like a dream, alone here in the shop, in the dark, James.'

James said, 'I don't often dream of standing about in empty department stores. Do hurry with that window. I'll wait here.'

I assured him I was all right. That on finding the guard he could send him to check that I'd made it back upstairs.

'And James, er, if there's any future comment about, say, the windows, could you keep quiet? I mean sort of forget you saw me down here? If by chance I don't get the window put back exactly the way it was?'

'If you insist. I had hardly planned to say we had an assignation here.'

'Oh, thank you, James.' That would have to do.

As soon as he was out of sight, I told Mervin and Flora. We grabbed our equipment and dashed up to accounts, wanting to be there should the guard arrive. And he did arrive immediately after. Some guard. He said he already knew we were working late, that he had been checking on us regularly.

Mervin said, 'We appreciate it. I think I saw you once or twice. But each time, you've probably found us all talking. Don't you check about every hour? More often?'

'More often than that, like as not,' said the guard, before leaving.

'Great!' said Mervin. 'He can alibi us, if the plan backfires. He probably sleeps the night away in the guard room.'

'Should we make the calls with my mobile?' I asked.

'Brill,' said Flora. 'It might make them like harder to trace. I've got the numbers here,' she said delving into her handbag.

I made the first call, to one of the tabloids. Trying to sound like an elderly woman, I said quaveringly, 'I couldn't sleep and was walking my dog. Well, bless my soul, you wouldn't believe them Chambers' shop windows. A scandal, I calls it.' It was the sort of accent a Martian would acquire by living twenty years in Alabama.

After a couple more, Flora took over, this time ringing TV newsdesks. 'Have you seen those obscene shop windows? At Chambers', you know, the best shop on Oxford Street? Gosh, I could only look for a minute, so shocking.'

Mervin rang all the same numbers, which had included the broadsheets. 'I say, how fabulous. Those effing windows at Chambers'. Can't wait for them to open the shop. If I was you chaps I'd be out with cameras.' All in all, using different voices, we made thirty calls.

'What happens, Flora, if they ring here to check?' I asked.

'Well, they wouldn't bother with the shop closed on Sunday, would they? And there's no way the switchboard has been diverted to the top floor.'

'But how would the villains presumably have got out? Which door? I mean we can't leave yet and set off the alarm.'

Mervin jumped up. 'I'll go and unlock the side door. With the top floor here, it could have been one of them who left it open.'

'Great! And you, Flora, ring the guard and say you think you saw someone. That he'd better check the doors. So he can lock it back up. We'd be in real trouble if burglars or even reporters got in.'

When Jack Howard arrived in accounts, he apologised for our having been kept so late. And he handed each of us an envelope with a hundred pounds' cash bonus in it, in addition to our scheduled pay. Either Jack earned a fortune, or he grew his own flowers and minted his own money.

We stalled a bit outside, to ensure that the top floor was also leaving. And with great relief we noticed that after using the side door, not one of them turned towards Oxford Street. Then we made our way there ourselves, standing back to admire our work. We moved away quickly when a TV van arrived and watched from a distance as the window was surveyed and lighting set up. Another car arrived, with a newspaper logo on the side.

We all hugged each other and punched the air with our fists. We were practically jigging on the pavement. 'My friends, it's too late now for anyone to change the windows!'

'Well, they'll probably still change them,' said Flora. 'The art department, well the head will probably faint.'

Mervin said thoughtfully, 'They might not change them back.'

'Exactly,' I agreed. 'If there's enough publicity, and if more customers come into the shop, the top floor might decide to say the displays were intentional.' I added, 'It just shows what a stuffy reputation Chambers' Emporium has, for the press to come here in the middle of the night.'

The following morning, we three arty musketeers, as Flora had branded us, met before work for coffee. 'Did you see the telly?' Flora asked Mervin, her words tumbling out in excitement. 'One station said Chambers' had joined the new millennium.'

I said, 'They made it sound like the Queen Mother going out in public wearing hot pants.'

Mervin said, 'The station I watched said it was the coup of the century, that it would give Chambers' a head start on Christmas. That it was amazing there'd been no leak that the company was changing their image.'

'Did you see the live interviews of people walking

past the shop, Mervin? Flora and I could hardly stop laughing. The punks of course said they'd try the shop. But one elderly lady said women didn't need to grow old today and she was going to give Chambers' a fling.'

There was a large, noisy crowd in front of the shop as we made our way to the staff entrance. And managers were already bustling around the shop floor bossing the salespeople about. Two dawgs were nearly barking. All the upstairs staff, young and old, seemed cheerful, delighted that they worked for a company getting so much attention. Even Mrs Brown seemed invigorated.

I sat frozen to my chair, fingers crossed, wondering what would happen next. But I didn't have to wait long. I saw James talking to Mrs Brown and then I was called to the front. James escorted me to the corridor to speak in private.

'I, uh, Caron, I don't really know what to say. I, er, well . . .'

'If you're planning to call off our weekend away . . .'

'No.'

'Or if you have regrets about last night, the kiss in the shop . . .'

'No. But it is about last night.'

'It's simple, James. Amnesia. If it gets past that and there's blame, I worked alone. If there's glory, more than one.'

'I don't know if glory is the correct word, Caron. But blame doesn't come into it.' He looked slowly and carefully around before speaking quietly. 'It's just that the top floor needs to make a statement. A statement to the press. And they, well, need to be assured no one is going to come forth and claim it was a joke, if you take my meaning. And I said I thought perhaps I could help to clarify that point.'

'I speak in confidence, James,' I said with my biggest grin. 'But if, say, the people in question were on double pay at the time, I mean working for Chambers', then whatever you're talking about would surely be official.'

James sighed with relief. Before turning to go, he asked, 'Where on earth did you get the idea, Caron? Certainly those original painted canvas backdrops have brightened up the windows no end. And Father Christmas wearing hot pink and sporting sunglasses and dreadlocks. But where did you get the idea for the other changes?' He smiled wryly. 'It's all there. The mannequins dressed in the best silks and cashmere. The new Christmas line of lingerie. But whatever made you think of putting the bras and knickers and camisoles on the outside of the clothes?'

20

When I returned to the pool, Mervin raised his eyebrows, but I nodded no, to indicate nothing had happened. With James it was rarely obvious what had happened, and it was too early to get anyone's hopes up. Word had got out that the three of us had worked standby over the weekend, and we were swamped with phone calls asking if we'd seen anything.

Melody said, 'Caron, the new window displays make such a nice change, dear, and the underclothes should be worn on top, considering what they cost. Well, what they cost at Harrods.'

I grinned. 'Melody, you didn't think the displays were a bit risqué? Or anything?'

Melody laughed. 'Oh, no. We might get a few old biddies complaining. But mostly when you reach a certain age, you wish you'd lived a bit more. Had more interesting things to remember. Anyway, complaints should be few. It isn't the in thing to appear old-fashioned.'

I didn't know about Flora, but Mervin and I certainly weren't being pushed too hard to get much work done by Mrs Brown. When Mervin told her how many hours we'd worked over the weekend, she looked shocked. Then she smiled. 'Good for you, dear.'

The three of us had of course planned to meet for lunch, but before we could get away from our desks, we each received a phone call direct from Mr Chambers' secretary asking if we could come to his office straight away.

Meeting in the corridor outside, Mervin said laughing, 'It's break or bust time.'

Flora said hopefully, 'Maybe it's about something else?'

We both laughed and she joined in, as if she'd been joking.

Mr Chambers' office was delightfully old-worldly, with the oak panelling, the original oils, the three-piece leather suite in the corner. A full-size conference table to the side. If the man was like his office, he was certainly capable of playing the old-fashioned fuddy-duddy, defying all to reverse the window displays.

'Sit down. Please sit down.' He turned to his secretary and said, 'Please bring us some coffee, Jo.'

Once we were all seated, with the three of us perched on the edge of straight chairs facing the desk, and Jim Chambers in the huge executive chair behind it, I relaxed. He seemed to be trying to suppress a grin. 'I wanted first to thank all of you for your giving up your weekend to help out. That was very kind indeed.'

This was followed by such a long silence that Flora began to fidget, as if that was all and we could leave. Then coffee was brought in on a silver tray that also contained a plate of biscuits. Mervin and I took several each, slipping the extras into our pockets.

'Now,' said Jim Chambers. 'As you were here at the weekend, I wanted to enlist your help. There has, as you know, been a little incident, or happening, whatever. I would like you to read the proposed press release and tell me if you think it is inaccurate in any way.'

The secretary passed out a copy to each of us before retreating to her own office. The press release said:

'We would like to thank the press and the public, especially our loyal customers, for such a splendid reaction to our new image. We wanted it to be a surprise, so three employees were given carte blanche, under auspices of working overtime for other purposes, to make the changes. We took a risk, but then Chambers' has always been known for leading the field. Of course where and how our shoppers actually wear their purchases is entirely up to them.'

Mr Chambers said proudly, 'That last bit is intended as a laugh line. I shall be speaking to the press myself in due course. And to the television. Now, do you see any inaccuracies?'

I said in a fairly loud voice, 'I think the press release describes the situation nicely.'

I turned to Mervin who agreed. And we both looked at Flora who said, 'And me. I mean I agree.' Mr Chambers seemed to relax, and then he laughed.

'Well, now I'm sure the old-fashioned part has been overplayed by the media, but you have done Chambers' Emporium a service. Therefore, you will each receive a bonus.' He smiled, before continuing, 'I mean to say a hefty bonus, so don't worry about stinting on your Christmas shopping.'

After we said thank you, he added, 'And you can all count on an incentive increase at the usual six months' assessment. Have you any questions?' I wanted to ask what size hefty was in plain English, but didn't. And it didn't seem at all the time to say how much I enjoyed sending secret messages back and forth to him through Melody. I mean MI5 agents didn't make public announcements unless someone was trying to shoot them.

He stood up and thanked us again, indicating that

the meeting was over. He walked us to the door, and then said, 'Oh, by the way, Caron. I haven't had a chance to welcome you to Chambers'. I hear you're doing an excellent job. Do please let me know if you need anything . . . else?' He sort of raised his eyebrows and grinned while the others couldn't see us.

Outside the boss's office, Mervin jumped up and shouted, 'We bloody well effing did it!'

Even Flora punched her fist into the air and hugged Mervin and me.

Chambers' secretary, who was older and certainly more staid, said, 'Well done. We're all so proud of you.'

'Do you think everyone's going to know?' Flora asked eagerly as soon as we were in the corridor.

'Probably before we get downstairs,' said Mervin. 'I vote for the canteen for lunch, do our fan club a favour.'

'And I vote,' I said, 'for staying there as long as we like. Mrs Brown won't dock us today. I could use three cappuccinos.'

Before we got off the top floor, James called to us. When he caught us up, followed by Jack Howard, he said, 'Congratulations!' Turning to me, he grinned and said, 'You should have my chair soon.' Then speaking to all of us, he said, 'Perhaps we should add a penthouse for you three!'

We all responded with those smiles such as when someone's playing your song.

Jack also congratulated us. Then he said, 'And Mervin, by displaying your work in the window, you've certainly upped the value of my painting. Some-one mentioned it to the press, that I'd bought one for my collection, and they plan to come and take a photo.'

James said, 'You know, Jack, before the press arrives,

maybe you should, with Mervin's permission of course, change the name of the painting from *Pot*. Maybe to *Green Grows the Grass*.'

We all laughed and Jack, trying obviously to top James, said, 'Well, Caron and Flora, you two are certainly not just pretty faces. Not that I'd ever thought that.'

Mervin laughed. 'Does that mean that I am just a pretty face?'

As we moved away, Jack placed his hand on my arm and leaning close, he asked, 'Are you free for that date we never had? Theatre and dinner?'

'Oh dear, I haven't had any sleep for ages. Perhaps later, Jack. But thanks.' And I quickly caught up with the others. Well, I was running like an antelope, so I almost passed them.

'I thought you both knew by now it's your job to protect me from that man!'

They were both laughing. 'We had to escape before we cracked up about the next press release saying Chambers' is so modern we have marijuana plantation paintings in our executive offices,' said Mervin. 'But still, at least Jack Howard's modern enough not to mind.'

I said, 'Yeah. I doubt if Bill Clinton would have hung it in his office when he was President.'

Flora said, 'I am so glad I met you two. Before, nothing much ever seemed to happen in my life. Now it's a scare a minute.'

We weren't even allowed to pay for our lunches. The cashier said, 'It's the least we can do. To celebrate your triumph. Enjoy!'

Basking in the glow of nice food, wonderful friends, and delightful attention, I thought it so wonderful that

Chambers' really did believe in a free lunch. With a hostile takeover that would be the first thing to go. After our jobs.

Old Harvey ambled up and mumbled congratulations. We thanked him, and when he'd shuffled away, Mervin leaned across the table. 'You know, Caron, I'd steer clear of that bloke. I know he's given you work in accounts, but . . .'

'Not lately,' I said. 'But even though he's a bit odd, I quite like him.'

'Well, discourage him a bit. Stay clear of his office. At the moment he's, well I guess he's sort of walking in a shadow, if you know what I mean.'

'That's because of his cobwebs,' I said, and we all laughed. We were in such a good mood that we'd probably have laughed if a cop came in and gave us tickets for parking at the table too long.

Soon colleagues from accounts stopped by to ask for details, how we'd thought of such a ruse, and managed to get away with it. Alone again, Mervin said, 'I don't know about you two, but I plan to be headhunted by an advertising agency. Big bucks there. And maybe I can take over their art department.'

'Think big, Mervin. Let's take over the world.'

Flora said, 'I don't know, Caron. If we're going to be surrounded like rock stars, well, I guess I could learn to sing.'

Mervin gently put his arm around Flora's shoulder. 'Flora, we can sing duets. And Caron can lead the orchestra.'

With a straight face, I said to Flora, 'Well, I must say, I think that's chapter fourteen and near the end of the book.'

Fortunately for Flora, the cashier arrived at our table

carrying three large slices of chocolate cake with cream. 'Might as well do this right,' she said.

After that, the conversation was on headhunters. 'Actually,' said Mervin, 'it might embarrass Chambers' if I went too public. But I can get word around through my art friends. Jim Chambers was brill, but that could change if we started trying to upstage him.'

'Oh, I don't know, Mervin. If the bonuses are over a million pounds, we might want to stay right here.'

Mervin said, 'I'd settle for splitting a million three ways, as long as we got the penthouse on the roof.'

'With a helicopter pad,' added Flora. 'My chances of learning to fly are better than my chances of learning to sing.'

It was too much to hope that Jack Howard could continue using restraint, and that afternoon a replica of the first garish floral display arrived at my desk. Everyone broke into somewhat hysterical laughter. I also laughed and immediately carried the damn bouquet to Mrs Brown's side table.

Half an hour later, a small posy arrived, tiny delicate flowers. A perfect gardenia surrounded by lily of the valley. The card said only, *J.* But I knew which J. All afternoon, between short spurts of work, I picked it up and smelled the glorious scent.

Just as Melody and I were clearing our desks, an elegant older woman arrived. She was carrying a bunch of flowers and two gift-wrapped parcels. Melody immediately got up and hugged her. 'Caron, I want you to meet Betty Chambers.'

She was charm personified, but she also seemed to be discreetly looking me over, not my clothes or looks, but trying to peer inside me, subtly. 'It's a pleasure to meet you, Caron. I've heard so much about you, all good. And congratulations. It was such a clever idea. And I couldn't resist doing some shopping myself. I've brought you flowers and a little present.' As she handed me the parcel, she also gave one to Melody. The flowers she handed me were far more James than Jack.

I began to thank her, but Melody cut in. 'Caron, dear, do please pull a chair over for Betty. And sit back down yourself. Honestly, the way we work, you don't want to miss any gossip.'

Betty Chambers laughed and sat down. 'Fire away, Melody.'

'Well, what did Jim really think of the windows. Tell all.'

She laughed again. 'Really, truly, it's been such a grand day, with everyone ringing. Well, about Jim. He only heard right before leaving for the office. Usually the media contact him when a story's about to break, you know how it is, courtesy and for confirmation. But this time they obviously thought it was a joke and didn't wish to alert him, have him undo it, as it were, before they could have some fun.'

Melody said, 'Go on.'

'Well, he had his driver stop the car in front so he could have a look. He rang me on his mobile and said, 'Bloody hell, Betty, you won't believe this!' More curses. Of course he maintains now they were compliments.'

We both laughed before she continued. 'There were already crowds there, in front of the shop, and he had believed they were an angry, shocked mob. So he asked his driver to take him to the side door. But inside, staff and customers began to congratulate him. Well, as you know, my dear Melody, Jim is pragmatic. The bottom line for him is profit. And by the time he got to his office and rang me again, one might easily have thought the idea was his.'

I laughed. 'And when, Mrs Chambers, did he find out who did it?'

'It's Betty, dear. The top floor didn't know anything at first, Caron. And they were very worried. Of course you three had been in the building, and that drew their attention to you. But to be honest, they didn't actually think a personnel assistant and two accounts section employees could make such a splash. And they called in the duty night guard who claimed none of you three had left your office during the night.'

It was so extraordinary that the boss's wife was telling all this in front of me, especially talking so frankly about her husband. It made me wonder about her agenda. Was she saying that she trusted me, that Jim Chambers did, and in a big way? Or was he so widely known as last year's suit that it didn't matter?

'Anyway, Caron, I'm not quite sure how they worked out it was you three. I think someone made a wild guess. Or for some reason the guard's statement was suspect. When Jim called you, Flora, and Mervin to his office, he still wasn't at all certain. Although I do think at that point he was a bit desperate. They couldn't answer the media until they knew the facts.'

She surely knew about James playing the detective, but she left that out. Only confidential stuff about her husband. I was beginning to feel like I was debriefing a spy.

When she didn't say more, Melody said, 'Well, do go on.'

Betty laughed. 'I'm sure you know more than I do

about the rest, Melody. About these splendid flowers, for example.' She was referring to James' posy, as Jack's embarrassment was on Mrs Brown's desk.

Melody said mysteriously, 'No giving away secrets.'

Betty laughed, and I wondered if Melody could possibly know who sent them. I mean she'd have needed to replace the buttons on James' and Jack's jackets with police tracker gadgets.

Thinking they might like to talk privately, and dying of curiosity about what was in my parcel, I excused myself. Betty stood up and shook hands. She gave me a very straight and non-frivolous look and said, 'Thanks again for all your help, Caron. And do please let us know if you need anything else. To help you get on with your job.' She finished smoothly with, 'It's been such a pleasure meeting you.'

Flora had been waiting in the corridor and when I came out, she said, 'I got one, too.'

'What is it?'

'Go on. Open it. I don't want to ruin the surprise. Oh, it's so nice.'

Inside was a roll-neck cherry-red cashmere sweater with a matching cardigan.

'Terrific, Flora! Absolute bliss! If this is the extra, what on earth will the bonus be?'

Flora laughed. 'I don't know, but I think our helicopter should be blue with white trim.'

As we got on the bus, I said, 'Things seem to be developing with you and Mervin. Compared with you, Evelyn's driving a snail.'

I was obviously teasing and she blushed. 'Like you said, Caron. Bliss.'

Evelyn was waiting for us when we got home. She'd heard about Chambers' on the evening news, and could hardly believe it had been us. 'Bugger it. Why didn't you let me help?'

Flora said patiently, 'Evelyn, you don't work at Chambers'. You would have been arrested for breaking in.'

'Well, then I would have been on TV for sure.'

When we showed her our loot, she said, 'Well, I suppose I can enjoy looking at the flowers. If you two weren't such shrimps, I could borrow the sweaters.'

Flora turned on the TV to see if there was any more mention of Chambers'. When I sat down to watch, Evelyn said to me, 'Do you only watch the tube when you're on it?'

'Evelyn, we're not on it. The windows are on it. Anyway, I got out of the habit in the States. The programme segments are so short you need the attention span of a flea.' I was trying to shut her up so I could hear the television.

'They can't be that short.'

'Well, maybe the commercials are longer.'

Then she said, 'I almost forgot. Another parcel for you, Caron. A neighbour signed for it and caught me when I came home. So no bomb. It had most of the day to blow up the neighbour's house. I put it on the kitchen table. I'm really disappointed in Bas.'

I really didn't want to dampen down such a wonderful day. All I could see on the kitchen table was a carrier bag from Tesco containing a box of cornflakes. I considered putting the bag straight into the rubbish bin. But that would only mean I'd be getting up at midnight to see what was actually in it.

When I took it to the front room, Evelyn said, 'I know it's a fiver for delivery as well as the cost of the cornflakes, Caron. But sod it, I'd ditch a man who's that cheap.'

I said as patiently as I could, 'I have ditched him, Evelyn.'

'Well, it's like I said about the letter. He's bankrupt now.'

'What do you think, Flora?'

'You know, I can't remember seeing cornflakes mentioned in a romance novel. In the crime novels, I don't recall anyone eating them, even in prison.'

'You bloody wouldn't. It's porridge that's slang for prison, everyone knows that. No one's ever been sentenced to ten years' cornflakes.'

Flora said, 'It could just mean he's keeping an eye on you. But it's awfully soon after the airmail letter. Only two days.'

I shook my head. 'I don't know what's going on. Evelyn's at least right about this being different. Bas could be saying it's the last straw. Well, the last cornflake.'

Evelyn had gone to the kitchen and returned with bowls, milk and sugar. 'Anyone else hungry? I'd just forget it, Caron. Even if it's only cornflakes, it's still free food. Bloody hell, the bloke does nothing but send you presents and all you do is grumble.'

'It's like the Trojan horse, Evelyn, presents that aren't really presents.'

'Well, bugger it, Caron. I know about that horse. Once they took it inside the castle walls, it turned out to be full of men. I mean what's wrong with that?'

'Well, nothing, Evelyn, unless you consider everyone ending up dead a problem.'

21

I'd been giving a lot of thought to the confidential work I'd been doing for Mr Chambers. Especially after meeting his wife, Betty. Her manner convinced me more than anything that something serious was going on. And as I was involved, that meant opportunity. I don't know if guardian angels and muses actually exist, but I suspect they do. And if I had one, she would need to have been listening to loud rock music with earphones while jumping out of aeroplanes without a parachute to have missed what my goals were. At its simplest, I'd been someone's daughter, followed by being a rich man's partner, and now I wanted to be a somebody. Not just anybody. I wanted to walk on my own feet as far up the hill as I could go. I was willing to stumble, although I wouldn't exactly welcome some of the mountain falling on top of me.

And about opportunity, what I figured was, you can tell your muse where you want to go, but you can't stipulate the route. For example, if I said I wanted to go to Chicago, without my realising it the most direct route might be through a mud puddle. So it's no use floundering in the mud and shouting at your muse to cut out the rain.

Whatever the hell was going on, Jim Chambers was trusting me. And there was a somewhat distorted mirror symmetry to the situation. I mean after my trusting Bas and learning that trust sucks, here I was being trusted by someone who didn't really know me. It was flattering and seemed in some way to make up for Bastard Bas. The bottom line was that the situation could catapult me out of the accounts section, although hopefully not all the way to Chicago.

And if there was danger, well what the hell. There was chronic danger of something falling out of the sky and braining you if you got so bored you forgot to walk fast. With what I'd sent him already, Chambers should have been able to carry the investigation through. But his comment to me on window day, along with what Betty had said, made me wonder if he had two problems. One, Melody hadn't been joking and he couldn't use the computer that well himself. And two, maybe he didn't sufficiently trust anyone on the top floor, and an outsider like me was preferable. So the very next time I got one of Melody's confidential envelopes, I returned it with a note: 'Higher level password.'

I don't know whether I really expected anything to happen. From the start there had been this horrible feeling that he would show up at my desk laughing his head off and saying, 'You, Caron, have one hell of a sense of humour.' The whole confidential thing could have been a private joke between him and Melody. But I'd take my chances. If he said that, I could always laugh. If I got sacked, I could cry.

Flora and I got home late because we'd stopped off for some healthy, non-fattening, good jogging substitute pizza with everything from tomatoes to pepperoni on top. We entered the house laughing to find a very hysterical Evelyn.

'I'm going to have to move out. Sleep in the street. Oh, I don't know how things can happen to me all the time. It's a wonder I haven't karate chopped all the furniture waiting for you.'

I said, 'Don't pack, Evelyn, until you tell us what happened.'

Flora said, 'And you wouldn't have had time to do the furniture using the saw.'

Evelyn ignored the insult, so it had to be serious. She said, 'I think I'd better tell Flora and let her tell you, Caron.'

Flora said, 'Is it really that bad?'

'No, bugger it. You never take me seriously. It's worse.'

'Flora, I'm going to go change. Shout if you get some sense out of her.'

Two seconds later I returned yelling, 'The Picassos are gone!' I quickly ran into the bathroom, then shouted, 'Yesssss!'

Evelyn said, 'I don't get this. You wanted the Picassos stolen?'

'Not exactly wanted, but definitely expected. It was the framed recipe for brownies in the bathroom I wanted to keep.'

Flora said, 'But we were supposed to be here and follow the thief. You know, Caron, with the police and cameras?'

'That's a complication, I'll admit.' Suddenly I turned to Evelyn and said with suspicion, 'But why are you so upset, Evelyn? I mean you didn't steal them. Did you?'

'Yeah, kind of. Well, I mean it was my fault.'

Flora said, 'If I pour you a drink, Evelyn, could you, like, limit the explanation to fifty words?'

When we'd all had a drink, Evelyn calmed down a bit, but only a bit. 'It was the dating agency. I met this bloke at the coffee shop. Super talent. Then he suggested we go to a club, so we came back for me to change.'

After holding her glass out for the second refill, she continued. 'I was in my bedroom when I remembered I'd left my makeup bag in the kitchen. After I got it, I was coming back when I noticed the bloke had gone, but Caron's door was open.'

She held out her glass again, but Flora said, 'Not until fifty more words.'

'Well, bugger it, I didn't know what to do. I mean here I was in the house alone with a maniac. So I did the only sensible thing.'

Flora and I waited with bated breath to hear what Evelyn considered sensible.

'I tiptoed to the hall cupboard and got in it. Except I'm too big, so I couldn't. And all this damn stuff, boxes and bed linen, fell on top of me. So I was flat out in the corridor half buried. He heard me and came rushing out. He was carrying all your pictures, Caron. Well, not the brownie recipe.'

'Was he, like, wearing gloves?'

She thought for a minute. 'I don't think so, Flora. But fingerprints wouldn't be any help. They were only on the frames, so he stole his fingerprints, too.'

Flora said, 'Pity you didn't video him.'

'I did. Oh, double bugger. Now you've tricked me.'

Flora and I just waited. And waited. Then Evelyn said in a pitiful voice, 'If I change my story, are you going to think I lied?'

'It's better than thinking you're crazy, Evelyn,' I said. 'So what really happened?'

'It was the only likely weapon in the cupboard.'

'The video was in the cupboard?'

Flora said, 'Mervin forgot it, Caron, the night of the

Because Prize. So I put it there to keep, well to keep anyone from breaking it. I've never broken a bloody video in my life. At least I think it's still working.'

'Why don't you finish telling us, Evelyn?'

'Bugger it, I don't like to say this bit. The truth is, when I crushed myself into the cupboard and was trying to close the door behind me, I heard this whirring sound. I thought it was a mouse. That's really why I got out so fast. And turning around caused everything to fall. So I didn't actually video the bloke, but the machine was on. I mean, sorry, Flora, it wasn't mice.'

Flora was already sliding the video into the player.

The three of us stared intently at the screen as if it were Judgement Day and we wanted to know if we'd passed Life. First we saw nothing.

'Shit,' I said. 'Something's blocking the viewfinder thingy.'

'Wait, Caron. There's some light. That must be Evelyn falling out of the closet.'

'Bugger it. The camera's pointed the wrong way and I'm not in the picture.'

I said patiently, 'Evelyn, it's the thief we want in the picture. So we can forgive you and not make you pay for next month's wine.'

The only sounds were crunches and crashes, stuff falling, footsteps in the corridor. Evelyn shouting, 'Bugger, bugger.' The sound was a bit muffled, maybe something was partially over the camera. Well, maybe Evelyn was on top of the camera.

'Look, Caron! A man's shoes. He's stopped. Now he's turning back to Evelyn.'

'Yeah. Now we get to see his left knee, Flora. Police love that kind of description.'

The screen went black, then Flora said, 'There's his other knee.'

Evelyn said, 'I saw more than his knees. I can describe him.'

While we watched the flickering black screen, she said, 'He looked a bit like that bloke at Mervin's do.'

Suddenly we got sound but no picture on the video. The man said, 'I haven't got time to sort out the clones from the real thing, so I'll just take them all. It still leaves one hand free for 'Yankee Doodle Dandy'. Hope you enjoyed the date, honey.' Suddenly my blood turned to Bloody Marys.

'Rewind it, Flora. That sounds like Bas.' I looked at the mantel. 'And my music box is gone.'

'Bugger you, Caron, don't blame me. The bloke said he was French, and you know that foreigners speak English with an American accent.'

Flora played it three more times. I started laughing. 'We've got him, Flora. I'm sure that's Bas' voice.'

Flora smiled. 'In crime novels they can check that out. And surely some of the police read crime novels, so they'd know how.'

Evelyn said, 'I didn't much like those pictures, so I say good riddance.'

Flora asked, 'But, Caron, why did he take the music box?'

'Yeah, why did he take that?' Evelyn repeated. 'I liked that music box. It really cheered me up to hear it play 'Yankee Doodle Dandy'.'

'I don't know. I'll have to think about it. Probably pure spite, as he knows it's one of my favourite things.'

Evelyn said, 'Maybe he would have needed both hands to take the rocking chair. Anyway, Caron, have you thought of trying to steal the stuff back? Then you'd have his fingerprints.'

'Thank you, Evelyn, for making a contribution to this serious discussion.'

Evelyn said, 'Sod you, Caron! You won't admit I ever do anything right. It might have been better if I'd videoed his face. But you and Flora didn't even video his shoes. So admit it, I've finally done something right.'

I gave her a big hug. 'Definitely, Evelyn. No packing and sleeping in the street.'

Flora said, 'Should I ring the police now?'

Evelyn said, 'Bugger that, Flora. He's one big bloke. And from what Caron says we don't want to make him angry. The next present's going to be dripping with poison.'

'Evelyn, did Bas know you got him on video?'

'How could he, Caron? When I didn't know myself? Until he'd gone and I unfolded from the floor. I didn't know until then whether he was worse than the mouse.'

'Then, Flora, maybe we shouldn't do anything yet. He would tell the cops he was getting his own things back. Well, we could prove the Picasso prints were theft as he didn't own those, but it might lead to the recipe, if you know what I mean.'

Evelyn said, 'Where's your brain, Caron? The frames of all the fake Picassos are worth more than one magazine page.'

'Never underestimate the value of a brownie recipe, Evelyn.'

'Well, whatever, don't you dare report the bugger. If the bloke got done for theft, they wouldn't keep him for life. Even murderers are getting off all the time. After prison, he'd have another forty years to find me.'

Flora said, 'She's right, Caron. A rich man would only

get ticked off for stealing copies. Maybe community service for a first offence. He could look for Evelyn while helping deliver meals on wheels.'

I personally thought Bas would prefer becoming a hit man rather than delivering meals to the old folk's home. 'Good point. So maybe it really is better to do nothing.'

Flora said, 'Why did you go to the dating agency anyway, Evelyn? What happened to your favourite gardener?'

Evelyn smiled. 'I fancy him like mad. And I've got his phone number. But I thought I'd play it cool. Wait for him to ring.'

Flora said, 'You mean wait at a nightclub with another man?'

'You are so dense, Flora. It wouldn't be very cool waiting here and answering the phone, would it? Men always ring and say what have you been doing. So I need to have been doing something, don't I?'

Flora said, 'I think you're supposed to say you've been washing your hair.'

'Or you could say come for coffee. He wouldn't ring if he didn't want to talk to you. That's the simple answer.'

'That's probably why I didn't think of it.'

Flora said, 'Aren't we forgetting something, Caron? I mean about Bas?'

'Trying to forget, do you mean? Like what he's going to do when he finds out he's stolen a bunch of fakes?'

'Fancy him really coming into the house.'

'He was probably sure he'd get the recipe, that possession being nine tenths of the law thing. And the man he sent didn't even get inside. If that's the one Henry stopped. But now Evelyn's a witness to his theft.'

'Oh, double bugger. He really is going to murder me.'

I said, 'Think, Evelyn. Did he touch anything else?'

'Not that I noticed. Look, you two. I need your help. Do you think he'll shoot me or what?'

'Flora, maybe I should frighten him by saying we've got the video. To protect Evelyn. I don't need to mention it's mostly of his left knee.'

'Well, in crime novels, that wouldn't work. I mean, right now he thinks Evelyn thinks he's a Frenchman signed up with the dating agency. So he'd feel safe. For a few more chapters.'

Evelyn shrieked, 'Don't tell him, Caron! Right now he's just after you. But when he's also after me, he'll know Flora knows too. That bloke will turn into a serial killer.'

'She's right, Caron. Three deaths does make a serial killer. Well, unless it was a bomb and we all died at the same time.'

'Please listen to Flora, Caron. I like you, I really do. But bugger it, one death is better than three.'

Things seemed to be getting out of hand. 'Look, I don't think Bas is a serial killer. I don't think he's going to kill anyone. I mean he wouldn't like the food in prison. So let's keep cool.'

Flora said, 'So what's our next step?'

'Shit, I don't know. I'm sorry I've got you both messed up in this. But don't tell anyone else, especially not Mervin, James, or gardener Henry. If the safest thing is for Bas to think he's put one over on Evelyn, it wouldn't help for some man to rush him shouting, Geronimo! And no matter what happens, don't open any more parcels.'

301

Flora said, 'But what do you really think Bas is doing this minute?'

'Working out a way to make me eat six copies of a Picasso that he's covered with horse shit.'

22

The day I was due to go away with James for the weekend was warmish and sunny. Flora had gone into work early, so I decided to walk across to Hampstead High Street and catch the tube at Belsize Park. The route went past Keats' House, and I always loved to see the tree under which he wrote poetry. Not that I was planning to begin writing poetry. The world would probably pay me extra not to. But I liked reminders that the really famous did ordinary things, lived in normal houses and had to go through doors instead of walls. Even Flora's house might look important in another couple of hundred years, or at least a little older.

Before I got to the tube station, James pulled up to the kerb. I hadn't seen or heard much from him recently. He was probably camping out on the top floor. Hostile takeovers and missing millions turn the most resistant VPs into workaholics. And reluctant, going by our friendship, James was not.

He stopped his car and said, 'I don't usually pick up hitchhikers.' He was grinning.

'As I wasn't hitching a ride, it should be all right.' After I got in and he re-entered the stream of traffic, I had a good look at him. He looked tired and seemed preoccupied, but then the traffic was heavy. It was very pleasant just to sit beside him, not feeling the need to make social chatter. Just to feel comfortable. He looked about as sexy as one could in profile while driving through London rush hour traffic. But real involvement still made me extremely nervous, if wanting to run away screaming was anything to go by. If I got together with James at this point in my life, it might not be fair to him. Fifty per cent of me would be right there with him. And the other half would be trying to reach the fire escape.

'I haven't had the chance to properly congratulate you, Caron. On the beautiful shop windows. Well, clever, anyway. Do you plan to begin wearing your own clothing that way?'

'You'll have to wait until the weekend starts to find out.'

'All right if I collect you about six this evening? Maybe tomorrow morning would be better?'

'Tonight.'

'We won't arrive until late. I've had to pull out all the stops to get away at all, there's so much going on.'

'If we arrive late, we might need to go straight to bed.' With an innocent voice, I added, 'You did book separate rooms?'

He looked at me and I thought he might crash the car. 'Joke. Joke, James. Where are we going?'

James also grinned. 'I was thinking you might like to stay at my place. I mean we wouldn't get lonely with Stoner there.'

We both laughed, and then he said, 'But you will need to wait until tonight for further information. Curiosity might have done in cats, but I should think you're immune. It might have been better had we gone earlier. The scenery and weather aren't very good this late in the year.'

'No need to be pessimistic, James. Remember that

beauty is the eye of the beholder and people see pretty much what they want to see.'

'Is that a promise?'

James let me off on the side street next to work and carried on to the underground parking area. As soon as I reached my desk, Flora rang, sounding unhappy. 'Caron, I ran into Mervin coming into work.'

'Well, that's good, isn't it? You two seem to be an item.'

'He's already got an interview set up. You know, with an ad agency?'

'Well, cheer up, Flora. That's even better, isn't it?'

'Not really. He just seems in such a hurry to leave. You know, leave Chambers'. I'd no idea that would be the result of the windows. You don't think, well, that he used us to further his career?'

'Men love women who do that, and I speak as the horse's mouth. Anyway, wouldn't that make your relationship easier? If you didn't both work for Chambers'?'

'Not if Mervin goes away and forgets me. Do you think that'll happen?'

'I doubt if the ad agency's in China. And he didn't have to tell us he wanted to be headhunted. Or to tell you he's got the interview. Look, Flora, don't panic and pressure him. Be supportive. This is definitely not the right time to become heavy. Nothing turns men's brains into chicken noodle soup faster than ultimatums.'

Greatly cheered, Flora rang off. She was always happier when she was given an exact action to carry through. She liked the assurance that at least someone knew where the path would lead. It didn't seem to matter that she had asked me, whose thoughts at the moment were competing with the North Circular.

Whether because I now had a higher profile and was in demand, or whether Mrs Brown was feeling sympathetic because of the overtime worked, she gave me a plum assignment. One of the VP secretaries had to go to the dentist. All I needed to do was answer the phone in her absence.

As I was clearing my desk, Melody said, 'My dear, I forgot to give you this earlier.' She handed over a small anonymous envelope. She was acting like it was an old magazine she'd already read and quickly returned to her shotgun typing.

Realising the envelope must have come from upstairs, I said, 'You know, Melody. It's sort of amazing.' I patted the envelope for emphasis. 'Well, certain people seem to trust me, but they don't even really know me.'

'That's as may be, dear, but certain people have known me forever.'

She reached a stopping point and looked up. 'And some good news. We are both due bonuses. Whenever things are sorted.' Then she typed so fast I expected the computer to flash a no-smoking sign on the screen.

Shirley, rushing to get away for her appointment, handed over a set of keys. 'I've left Mr Biggs' office door open, Caron, in case you need to check his appointment book, top drawer on the right. But if you go out, to the ladies', or for coffee, do remember to lock it. Even for five minutes.'

'Am I supposed to make appointments for Mr Biggs? Without checking with him?'

'He's away all week, and he's the one most likely to ring in and ask you to check his diary. He's got his good points, but memory, efficiency, and computer skills are not amongst them. Just take messages and I'll do whatever's needed later. And thanks loads, Caron. Just lock up and go to lunch at your usual time.'

Alone, sitting at a large mahogany desk, I opened the envelope. All it said was SGGIBSGGIB. I started laughing so hard I nearly choked on my coffee. When I'd been asked to choose my own lowly Chambers' password, I'd been severely warned against using birthday digits or house numbers and such. It was fairly standard procedure. If the security people found out about Biggs, it would be instant death by shredder.

Mr Chambers had probably thought, She can use Biggs' password, as he won't notice and whatever she does can only be traced back to him. Never mind that Mervin and Harvey at the very least had probably also used it. Whoever was attempting the hostile takeover probably toasted Biggs' good health daily. And Chambers' Emporium should be using Biggs' head for archery practice.

I only had a couple of hours, so I did the two most important things. First I needed the phone number which let one access one's work computer from outside. I got this from Biggs' diary. I'd half expected to find a section called secret information. I spent the rest of the time accessing the list of VP passwords. Security normally got hysterical at the thought of this but allowed it, because if one VP died suddenly another would need the data. It took longer than I'd expected because there was no way Chambers' had up-to-date computer programmes. It was like the difference between Frank Sinatra and the Beatles.

I returned to my desk after lunch and slogged away at routine stuff. And I watched the clock. However much an employee does that mid-week, on Fridays it's nearly a national pastime.

Flora had to finish a last-minute job so we were too late to leave by the main front entrance, which was by then locked. As we neared Chambers' rear door, we ran into Jack who was chatting with one of the lingerie sales assistants. He turned and asked if we'd like to go for a drink.

I said, 'Thanks, Jack, but we're in a bit of a rush. Another time?' He grinned and turned back to Miss Underwear.

On the way to the tube, we took a short cut across a pedestrian area past a large fruit trolley, a news-stand, and various market stalls. The crowds had thinned a bit, half the workers were rushing home to cook dinner for the other half, who were themselves dashing to the pub for a pre-dinner drink. Flora and I were zigzagging through the outdoor tables and chairs of a sandwich bar. Suddenly I felt a tug on my shoulder bag strap. I quickly turned as I clasped the bag to my chest. Flora turned at the same time, as my movement had been so abrupt.

A tall, spindly, moustached man, wearing sunglasses and a hat low over his brows, with his corn-coloured hair sticking out all around, shouted, 'Give me your bag!' He was trying to cut through my shoulder bag strap with a pair of blunt-ended children's scissors. Flora and I immediately backed up, at least as far as the strap was long, as I was still holding the bag. This trapped us with a trestle table each side and the shop wall to the rear. OK, we could have climbed over or under the tables. But then any assailant could be evaded if he were willing to cover his eyes and count to ten.

Flora whispered, 'We should give him our bags. Don't make a fuss. I've read that!'

'We need to scream and holler and kick, that's what I read!'

'Isn't that for rape?'

That conversation took only a second, by which time the man was brandishing the scissors and yanking like hell on the strap of my bag. 'Give me the fucking bag!' He added in a quieter voice, 'I don't want to hurt you.'

I said, 'We're agreed on that! Anyway, those scissors could hardly cut hot butter.' It was hard to take him seriously, what with those scissors, the moustache and fake hair. I half expected him to say, 'Musical Telegram,' and then start singing 'Happy Birthday'. Enough oddities and one gets distracted from danger. Also, in a fair fight, Flora and I probably could have clobbered him. And if you're not seriously afraid, I suppose it unnerves the villains. Because he then replied in a perfectly normal voice, 'I can't be caught carrying around an illegal weapon.'

Flora said, 'Here!' and tossed her handbag to him. He caught it, then hurled it to the pavement. Turning back to me, he again said, 'Let go of the fucking bag! Please!'

By that time Flora and I had backed up to the wall of the sandwich shop. I kicked a chair towards him, hitting him in the waist. Below the waist. It hurt and made him very angry. I started screaming, 'Police! Help, police!' And Flora yelled, 'Rape!'

By this time we'd got a chair between us and the man, who looked nervously around but stood his ground. He still had hold of his end of the strap and continued to tug like mad. Several people had stopped to look but were some distance away. We again shouted, 'Help, police!' and 'Rape!' Just as the man, who was by then looking desperate and frustrated, picked up the chair and hurled it aside, Jack Howard came running up. But before he reached us, he had begun shouting, 'Police, stop! Don't move!' With one last futile tug at the bag, the man turned and ran.

Another man joined us and said he'd rung the police on his mobile. And several women asked if we needed any help, if we were all right. The manager of the sandwich bar came out and said to sit down and he'd bring coffee. And soon after that a police constable arrived. We described the man, as did several witnesses, and soon it was just Flora, me and Jack drinking coffee at the outdoor table.

We both thanked Jack for his help, and he said, 'Are you two all right?'

Flora said, 'It all happened so fast there wasn't time to get too upset. I mean we were too busy.'

I was still trying to catch my breath. You wouldn't think you could get so out of breath when pretty much standing still. But fright provides a real adrenaline high. 'That was weird, Flora, that he didn't want your bag. I mean, you just handed it to him.'

'I found that pretty insulting, that even a mugger didn't like my bag.'

She seemed so dispirited that Jack said, 'I'm sure it wasn't personal, Flora. He was probably drugged out of his skull.'

'No, he wasn't. His eyes were clear and he didn't slur his words.' Turning to me, she said, 'I know yours is better, more stylish and expensive, but surely muggers are after what's in the bag and not just the bag?'

Jack turned to me. 'Have you got anything special in your bag, Caron?'

I looked at the bag. The way the strap was cut made the incident seem more real. 'Not really. Just the usual.'

As if something had crept inside while I wasn't looking, I opened the bag. 'Makeup. Tissues. Sunglasses. Money and a credit card and a bank card. Miscellaneous rubbish.'

Jack said, 'What about you Flora?'

'Pretty much the same. And a paperback called *My Hero Comes Home At Last.*' We all laughed, Jack probably thinking it was a joke.

Jack said his sports car was too small for three, but insisted we wait for him to get us a taxi. As soon as we were alone, Flora leaned across the table and said, 'Do you think it was Bas? Someone sent by Bas? I know that wouldn't be good, but I'd feel better about my handbag.'

'I think it's got to be connected to Bas. Or else we've just met the world's most dysfunctional mugger. But the Picasso wouldn't fit in a handbag. And who would carry a painting around, anyway?'

'Yes, but that mugger was definitely after your bag, not just any bag.'

'It doesn't seem Bas' style, to get us cut up. On the other hand, wouldn't a real mugger have a knife or a Stanley blade? It doesn't make sense. It sounds like someone told the mugger to get the bag but not to break the law, while any idiot knows that stealing handbags is itself illegal.'

'In books and films, he would have been slashing away, shredding our clothes, his eyeballs frozen by drugs. And all the onlookers would have run away and not offered help.'

'Fortunately life's sometimes better than books, Flora. It's even better than the tabloid newspapers.'

'I was quite proud of Jack. I mean he could have got scissored but he just charged in anyway.'

'I have to admit he's nicer than I've been giving him credit for.' We could see him standing at the edge of the pavement trying to flag down a taxi. Then he waved at us as a taxi drew to the kerb. Before we could argue, he gave the driver a twenty-pound note for the fare. 'Ring me if you get worried about anything or have delayed shock.' We thanked him again and waved as the taxi edged into the traffic.

As we neared the house, Flora said, 'Well, I don't know whether to feel terrified because it was a close call. Or if it was just one of Bas' tricks.'

'It's not very comforting if Bas is hiring muggers. The next one might not use kiddie scissors.'

23

Flora and I arrived home in reasonably good humour. Well, survival does make you feel good, especially compared to the alternative. Also, maybe survival includes convincing yourself your own personal mugging wasn't such a big deal. Flora started filling Evelyn in on the details of the attempted bag snatch, while I got out an overnight bag. It wouldn't be long before James arrived.

I wasn't sure what to pack, not knowing the weekend destination. I settled for jeans and thick sweaters and one dressy outfit. And I packed my new cashmere sweater set. And sturdy walking shoes and a pair of trainers. As James jogged, his idea of a holiday might be a mountain top in North Wales where the military trained. Love me or leap.

James arrived promptly at six to find me sitting on my luggage at the kerb. He screeched to a halt and ran around to take my bag. 'Caron, I would have come to the door.'

'I got tired of debating with Flora chapter two versus the last chapter. She's convinced weekends away are the finale.'

'The finale of what?'

'Friendships. Let's just get out of here. I need and deserve a bit of a holiday, and I'm sure you do as well.'

As he drove away from the kerb, I said, 'Aren't you forgetting something?' When he looked puzzled, I leaned over and whispered, 'To kiss me. We are sneaking away for an illicit weekend, aren't we?'

Leaning over, he grinned and asked, 'Do you want me to marry you first?'

'Who did you have in mind to be second?'

We kissed lightly but lengthily, enough to convince me the ghost of Bas wasn't travelling in the boot. I didn't want to spoil the weekend by discussing the mugger, but he was sure to hear about it from Jack. So I played it down a bit, just the usual big city mugging attempt.

'Caron, that's awful. Are you sure you're all right? And Flora?'

'Of course we're both all right. He didn't succeed, that's the main thing. So it's a happy tale.'

He laughed. 'You could get into the *Guinness Book of Records* for optimism, Caron.'

I laughed as well, then said, 'Wake me up when we arrive, James.'

'I thought the idea was that you would make scintillating conversation. Perhaps attempt to seduce me.'

'And would that be difficult?'

'Talking for a few hours might be.'

The rest of the journey, still a good few hours once we cleared the worst of the London traffic, went fairly smoothly. I got James to point to our destination on the map, and then proceeded to give instructions as to the various turnings on our way to Devon.

Finally James said, 'Caron, if you continue, we'll end up in Scotland. Besides, I know the route well.'

'So,' I teased, 'have you taken lots of girlfriends there before?'

'Never, in fact.'

When we arrived at the Devon coast, it was dark. I

looked about but could only see one tiny cottage. A darling precious cottage, maybe, but nothing else. I could hear the roar of the sea.

As we unloaded the car, I asked, 'James, where are we going to eat? I mean . . .'

He laughed as he unlocked the cottage door. 'Caron, in all the time I've known you, I haven't heard you mention so much as dunking a teabag. I've brought adequate provisions. And there's a decent restaurant along the coast road.'

'But I haven't brought much in the way of dress-up.'

'The clientele is mostly hikers and birdwatchers this time of year. It should be all right unless you wear feathers.'

'Can you cook, James?'

'Excellent scrambled eggs and toast. So we won't need to go out for breakfast.'

I could see most of the cottage interior from the door. One large room with an open fireplace, exposed beams and rough plastered walls. Two chintz-covered easy chairs flanking the hearth. A much used oak table and two wooden chairs. Kitchen appliances along one wall, the tops forming the only workspace. A wardrobe, ornately carved, stood to attention against another wall. Tiny deep-set windows with muslin curtains. A delightful smell of previously burned logs. Basic, really rather rustic. Like a Hollywood stage set, except behind it probably wouldn't be a health club, three cafés, a supermarket, a taxi rank, and other normal necessities.

'James, it's lovely.'

He smiled and stuck a match to the readied kindling for a fire. Logs were already in place on top and in good supply to the side, filling an enormous copper cauldron. Then he opened the only visible inside door.

'Have a look at the bedroom.' It was more a peep than a look, as it was a very, very small room. To the left, a double bed extended from wall to wall, one side abutting the tiny high window. A midget chest of drawers held a tall mirror. Another door led to an en suite bathroom, the actual tub had high sides but was so short in length that one would need to bathe sitting upright.

'James, in that bed, your head will touch one wall and your feet the other. You might get stuck and be unable to get back out.'

He grinned. 'Is that a problem?'

While James was unpacking, I opened the fridge. 'This is full of fresh food – milk, butter, bread, eggs, cheese, all sorts of stuff. Are you personal friends with a gang of elves?'

'My neighbour. You can see her cottage during the day. She looks after the place for me, and gets it ready and airs it before I come down.'

Soon the logs had caught, flames twisting between them and showering odd sparks onto the quarry-tiled floor. But the room was still not really warm, so we moved the wing chairs so that we could sit on a small rug on the floor and lean back against them. James poured some wine and opened the hamper.

'I'm starving, James. What's in it?'

'The usual. Sardines, baked beans.' He laughed then looked a bit sheepish. 'Our first picnic was so wonderful I thought we'd have an encore.'

Suddenly the hamper was shoved aside, as I reached my arms out to James. He held me close and very soon we were stretched out, touching from nose to knee. Between kisses, he ran his hands through my hair, just looking at me and smiling. It was the biggest turn-on

I'd ever known. Bas was very sexy, but he never travelled in the slow lane. With James, it was as though there had been months of foreplay since that first kiss. I smiled, thinking James was one crafty devil.

I pushed his mop of dark hair off his forehead and kissed him there and then on both cheeks, then on the tip of his nose. He was kissing the side of my neck and moving his hands along my ribcage, then up under my T-shirt. If we'd had soap on our lips, we could have made the bathtub redundant.

I'd never realised my ribcage was an erotic zone. I slid his hand back down so he could slowly move it up again. The fire was gaining strength relative to our progress. 'Maybe we should move back a bit, James.'

'Or we could remove some clothes.' Soon we were nude, the firelight playing off our bodies, giving them a golden aura. As James lay there stroking my breasts, he said, 'God, you're beautiful.'

'You too, but the best word to describe you, James, is sexy. Whoever would have thought, what with your being so shy.'

James said, 'I'm not normally shy. Just for the first few minutes each time I see you, then you seem to make it go away.'

Our lovemaking was skiing smoothly over the Alps when James said, 'Would you be more comfortable on the bed, Caron?'

'I'm fine.' And things just got finer and finer. It went on a long time and the climax left us both looking thunderstruck. After a long silence, holding each other tightly, I said, 'What happened? I feel shell-shocked.'

James leaned on his elbow and looked down at me. 'I suspect that when two ambitious, determined but cautious types let go, there is a lot to let go of.'

317

'I still feel like I'm floating.' Then my body twitched and shuddered. 'What's that, James?'

'It's just my power over women. Actually, it must be your taut muscles relaxing. I understand that sex is extremely healthy.'

After a moment I asked, 'What'll we do if it isn't this good in future?'

He laughed. 'Practise.'

We didn't bother with our clothes, but simply moved the wine and hamper to the bed. As we climbed in, I said, 'These sheets feel like ice.'

Then when James said, 'Ouch,' I kept my toes pressed into his side. 'But,' I added, 'you don't feel like ice.'

As I'd expected, it wasn't really sardines, and I tucked into the smoked salmon with relish. Shoving a grape into his mouth, I said, 'How did you ever find this place, James?'

'I was brought here for a holiday as a child. I'd been planning to buy a house in town, but then I inherited the place on Well Walk. So I used the money for this. Sort of a hideaway.'

'But if you don't bring women here, what do you use it for? To escape them?'

James laughed, 'Perhaps once or twice. But basically I like to keep it private, a place to come to think, to be alone, to get away from work. The sea air works wonders.'

'Then I'm quite honoured you brought me here.'

'And I'm honoured that you came.'

He lay back against the pillows, and we stretched body to body along our lengths. With his arms wrapped round me tightly he said, 'You absolutely fascinate me, Caron. Every time I decide what you're like you surprise me. For example, I'd heard you were good with numbers. Then you splash out with the artistic talent. Is there anything you can't do?'

I reached up and kissed him. 'I find it difficult to kiss my own cheek. And I need hugs and affection. There's been a serious shortage.'

'For a week or so, or longer?'

'That was definitely a question! But as you ask, not just for a week or so. After tonight, I wonder if there hasn't been a lifelong shortage.'

We made slow and quiet love then fell into a deep sleep. During the night I felt something and woke up. It was James turning on his side. I snuggled closer and smiled and drifted off again, thinking he made a very good substitute for a hot-water bottle.

The following morning, I opened my eyes to see James returning to bed with a breakfast tray. With a blanket wrapped around our shoulders and the covers pulled up to our chins, it was passably warm. 'I've got the fire started, Caron. Perhaps we should stay in bed until it warms up? Or we could get into the bath. Plenty of hot water.'

'That sounds like a plot to me. I bet you got up early and opened the door wide, to let the icicles in. Umm. These eggs are delicious.'

He mentioned jogging and I quickly decided to have a bath. He returned to find me leaning back in the tub in a cloud of bubbles. Because the bath was so short, my knees were sticking up. 'Come on in, James. The water's fine.' I blew some bubbles towards him. 'What's the matter? Don't you think we'll both fit in?'

As he removed his tracksuit with indecent haste, he said, 'I doubt it, but I'm willing to find out the hard way.'

Soon bubbles and water were covering the floor. The

language of romance may be poetic and flowery, but the vocabulary of sex is small. Um . . . Ah . . . Oh! Oh! Oh! Oh! Oh!

After we'd dried off, I began to put on my new cherry red cashmere sweater. As I was pulling it over my head, James reached over and unhooked my bra. 'James! What are you doing?'

He held the bra up. 'I thought you were going to demonstrate how it would look over the sweater?' We tried and ended up in a hilarious mood. 'You look, well, it looks interesting that way.'

'I can hardly breathe, James. Help me get it off.'

'With pleasure. Do you think I should swap you for a mannequin that doesn't need to breathe?'

'Definitely not! The thing is, we used bras two sizes larger for the window.' He was tickling me and I added, 'If you keep that up, the next window will feature men.'

As we stood there, arms around each other, gently swaying, I said, 'James, does all this frighten you a bit?'

'In what way?'

I ran my finger along his chin. 'All the sex, the passion. It feels so good. Well, does it feel too good? It sort of makes everything else lose its urgency. And where does that lead? I mean, mediocrity has got to be the worst thing.'

He tilted my face up and looked deep into my eyes. 'Why shouldn't great passion enrich one's life, Caron? Profound experience in one area should pervade other areas, if you're talking about careers, ambition, success, those sorts of things.'

'You don't think we each only have maybe a cupful and could use it all up?'

He laughed. 'I should have thought you of all people

would think in terms of at least a gallon. But no, I think the more you use the more you have.'

The day and the next night were like a dream. Walks on the beach, a very long stroll into the nearest village. Well, James called it a stroll. I called it a cross-country hike.

We stopped by James' neighbour's cottage so he could introduce me. We had a makeshift lunch from the remains of the hamper, and later a delicious dinner at the restaurant. We had walked both ways in the dark, quite some distance, with only the sound of the sea and slight rustlings in the hedgerows. Laughing and teasing, discussing whether we believed in ghosts. Like many educated people, he said he didn't but probably did. I took the position that I didn't believe in them, but would change my mind very quickly should one appear at the foot of my bed. And the nightly encore of sex was so great we decided we wouldn't need to practise but would do so anyway. I said, 'Forget cupfuls and gallons. We're talking about reservoirs, my friend.'

But on the Sunday morning clouds began to form, both in the sky and inside us. The horror that it couldn't last forever seemed far worse to me now that I knew what I'd be losing. And James had seemed distracted, maybe worried about work, he wouldn't say. He just claimed nothing was wrong. I thought it was probably work-induced, as I didn't like to think it could be because of me.

Then, with a flash of honesty, I realised the problem was too much being left unsaid. The unasked questions were forming fog, preventing commitment. It hadn't been a flighty weekend we could walk off and forget. I knew I was being selfish. Refusing to commit but also refusing to let him go. Well, the night before I would have needed to chase him away with a stick. But that would be better than hurting him later.

It wasn't fair to blame it on Bas, but he was my problem. I didn't know what he might do, but knew he was going to do something. And if I were committed to James, he would insist on handling Bas for me. It would just be me exchanging one trouser leg for another. Yet how could I end the relationship? It wouldn't be just a perfect memory, but rather a loss I would feel for the rest of my life.

We had planned to have a sandwich lunch followed by a beach walk, then head for home at about four o'clock, hoping to avoid at least some of the London-bound traffic. I'd managed to open a tin of tuna and splash some mayonnaise on bread. But even after adding lettuce and tomato slices, the result still looked a bit pitiful. All the ingredients kept sliding to one side of the bread. And when I pressed the slices together, all the fillings squashed out onto the counter.

Finally I slapped the plate of lopsided sandwiches on the table. 'I admit it, James. I cannot cook. I cannot clean very well or dust.'

His chin had been dejectedly resting on his hands with his elbows on the table. 'Forget it. We can stop at a pub on the way back.'

I sat down and took his hand. 'We have to talk, James. We can't just communicate with sex. Or we'll lose both the friendship and the step up.'

He poured us some coffee. He'd made it. Well, I make excellent coffee, but first you have to be able to find the coffee pot and he found it first. 'So we'll talk. You first, Caron?'

Shit. That was like being told you'd won a jackpot, followed by the news that it would all go to the taxman.

'OK. This weekend has been heaven, James. That must be obvious. But I've still got to sort myself out a bit more. And I don't want to lose you, but I'm not sure there's a road from the cottage bed back to being just buddies.'

He smiled. Faintly, but it definitely wasn't a frown. 'I understand that, Caron. And that's fine. I take it you mean about Horse or Ankle?'

'Horse's Ankle will do nicely. And I'll add that I don't want him back, would never return to him. You don't have competition in that way, not that you'd suffer with competition from anyone. Your turn.'

It was really a bit sad. We were only sitting across the table from each other. But with us not even touching hands after such a weekend, the distance soon resembled that between heaven and hell. I expected him to have to shout for me to hear.

'To be honest, Caron, I'm completely over Ice Queen. That's no problem. To give you an idea of that, even though I owned this cottage while we were living together, I never brought her here.'

He stirred his coffee and turned back into a clam. 'Honestly, James, if we just list what isn't a problem, St Peter might need to send a search party for us before we finish.'

'Well, to be even more honest, there is a problem but it wasn't a problem before. Before I knew you better. So in a way, I haven't been completely honest, but the difference has been so subtle I've only now realised the extent of the problem.'

'James, dammit. Einstein's theories would be easier to understand than that. Talk to me.'

'Well, the problem is in a way connected to Ice Cube. The thing is, she was a high-flying executive and got offered a job in Paris. So we either needed to split up or one of us move. She was so furious when I said all right, split, she was pretty insulting. About me, how I did things. Everything. Is that clearer?'

'Keep stirring and it'll get smooth.'

'Well, I sort of transferred my determination to my career. She was right in that I'd never had to work for everything as she had, I mean I hadn't begun at the bottom. So an ambitious streak that must have been dormant, well, I want the top job at Chambers' now.'

'But what has any of that got to do with the problem increasing because you know me better?'

'I feel like I've been fraudulent. When you seemed simply to be working in the accounts section, it didn't matter. But now it's obvious you have lots of other assets.'

'Are you saying I'm getting like Ice Cube? That I'll one day get a job in Paris? I mean, how could that make you feel fraudulent?' He sounded like a Russian-speaking politician who stuck in a few random words of English, and then wondered why the other country sent bombs. Threw bombs.

'My ambition could make a big difference. My need to prove myself. That's possibly not the way you've been seeing me. It's not the way I've been seeing me. But for even our old friendship to continue, I thought you should know about my ambition and how far I'd go to get the top job.'

I was going to throw bombs at that Russian myself. 'James, no one gets any top job without ambition. And what's wrong with ambition anyway?'

He laughed. Not the laugh depicting humour, but more the sort to crack eggshells. 'I wish we were merely talking about ambition, Caron.' He gave me a long appraising look, as if measuring me for a facelift. 'You know there's a lot going on at Chambers' at the moment. Someone seems to have the idea that they can make serious money and then be able to quit the rat race.'

'But what's that got to do with you, James?'

He grinned wryly. 'It's like a black cloud over Chambers'. And when the cloud's big enough, everyone gets caught under it. So everyone is under suspicion and gets checked out. It's not very pleasant, and that sort of situation is always dangerous.'

His words had travelled a million miles from mere ambition. Was James doing a Jim Chambers? Hinting strongly? Was James the one taking the millions, maybe assisting the hostile bid to ensure the top job? Or did he see the real top job as being so rich he didn't need a job at all? While no one liked being under suspicion, surely it shouldn't affect the honest so strongly. My brain felt like a steaming kettle with the spout blocked.

Very slowly and carefully, I said, 'If I should know how far you'd go to get the top job, then tell me. How far?'

He still had his elbows on the table and again he rested his head on his hands. I had to listen carefully to hear him say, 'I don't know, Caron.'

We sat in one of those battlefield silences when you know more bombs are coming but not where they're going to land.

Then he said in a different, more conversational voice, 'I guess what I'm saying is . . .' More silence. 'I can put it this way. No, I don't think I can.'

My suspicions of that 'how far' bit were alarming me, and the fear was making me angry. Hotly, I said, 'Are you saying that you'd never want me to go further than the accounts section? Bearing in mind that almost everyone there who wants to move up or out manages it. How would that have made things different?'

He smiled. 'In that case, you probably wouldn't be bothered about whether I got the job or not. And what I might need to do to get it.'

'That is a disgusting insult. I've heard, the whole damn company's heard, that you and Jack Howard are in the running. And except for wanting you as my friend to win, it's never crossed my mind to think what you're accusing me of.'

'Oh no, Caron. I'm not accusing you. It's me. Because I've always had it easy, and because of the taunts of Ice Cube, which, granted, it's my fault for paying attention to, it's me I have to prove myself to. The problem is not what you'd think if I didn't make it, but what I'd think.'

'That still sounds like you actually believe what Melody said as a joke, that I some day want your chair, that we're in competition.'

'I just wouldn't want to be in the situation where you ever thought I'd put the top job before you. When it's really a matter of proving myself.'

'Well in a way that's the same as my own position, in that I need to prove myself first. But with me it's a case of the timing being bad. At least I think I know how far I'd go, whatever.'

'In that case, Caron, I envy you. Sometimes doing the right thing can be the wrong thing.'

I wasn't sure if I was more worried than muddled. James came round the table and pulled a chair next to mine. He put his arm around me, and at first I resisted. But then I moved over to sit on his lap and we hugged for a long time.

Then he said, moving me back where he could see my face, 'I don't want to lose you, Caron.'

'But why should you worry about that? I mean if you're patient.' And not a crook, I thought to myself, reminding myself how that wasn't James at all. But then Bas hadn't been Bas at all, either.

'Please listen to me, Caron. I don't want you to worry.'

'But what, James? Worry about what?'

He ran his hand along the side of my face. 'I don't want you to worry about anything at all. I do trust you.'

'Oh, you mean about Jack Howard? Or about not being able to ask questions?' The thing anyone would have expected me to say would have been I trust you too. I wasn't sure I could get the words out.

He went on as if I hadn't spoken. 'Just remember, whatever happens, we can sort it out. We'll find a way. I don't want to lose you.'

I hugged his neck tightly and brushed tears from my eyes. 'Oh, James. Dear wonderful James. I've never met a more wonderful man. Whatever happens, don't go too far. Whatever you're talking about.'

He went outside and sat on a large boulder and stared at the sea. I watched from the window as the fresh pot of coffee percolated. Then I filled two mugs and took them to join him.

'Thanks, Caron. And it really will be all right.'

We both sat and drank in silence. I didn't know about James, but I hoped against all odds that the waves would somehow rise up and spell out letters telling me what was going on.

After that it was a race to return to London. Both of us seemed to want the weekend to end before the last remaining drop of the magic spell spilled. When we got to Flora's house, he set down my bag and took a small brass key from his pocket. 'I want you to keep this, Caron. A key to the cottage.' He seemed shy and hesitant again. 'So we'll have that in common. I haven't put that too well, but maybe you know what I mean.'

'I think so, James.' I took the key, thinking that understanding the key was simple. Freud, astrologers, dream interpreters, they would all understand the key. Unfortunately they probably wouldn't have had any doubt about the rest he'd said, either.

24

James didn't come in. Well, I didn't suggest it, but he seemed in a hurry anyway. It was a horrid irony that Bas could grease talk his way through any subject, but had lied. Whereas sometimes James would be better off communicating with a chimpanzee, but wanted to tell the truth. But didn't dare because he didn't think I'd like it. I've never been sure what the top line is, but hardly anyone shouts hallelujah when told the bottom line.

I tried to sneak past Evelyn and Flora who were watching television, but it was made difficult because they both were looking at me.

Evelyn said, 'Well, you little bugger, where did you and hunky James go?'

'Devon. To a lovely cottage.'

Flora said, 'Are you, like, near the end of the book?'

'I think the book's been remaindered.'

'But that means it got finished and published first.'

'True. I meant to say pulped.' That must have been a fate worse than death to a compulsive reader like Flora, because it certainly stopped the questions.

Before I could leave the room, Flora said, 'Oh, Caron, your mum rang. She said not to bother ringing back.'

'Was there a message?'

'Only that there's no new players, the same old game. And she said for you to wait for aces, that a pair of diamonds wouldn't cut it. Do you and your mum play a game through e-mail?'

'Not really. She's never quite come to terms with having given birth to a singleton instead of a pair. And she keeps hoping a nine of clubs will turn into a queen.'

Evelyn asked, 'What's your mum think of your dad?'

'She considers him the joker.'

'But they don't have a card like that in bridge, do they?'

'She calls him that because he doesn't play. I'd better ring Mum. She frowns at a pair of diamonds, so it might be important.'

Evelyn said, 'My mum talks straight out, always criticising. It'd be better if we could use a foreign language like bridge.'

'It's not real communication, Evelyn. Often Mum's the only one who knows what she means. Anyway, she e-mailed earlier that they were booking a Christmas cruise, and I need to let them know to count me out.'

Evelyn said, 'Tell your mum I'm your age and I'd behave myself if she wants a substitute. Porter, bodyguard, everything. Flora here will recommend me. I should have rich housemates. Then you two might pay to get me out of the house.'

I quickly rang my parents. After general chat, I said, 'Thanks, Mum, but I've got to work right up to the day.' When she suggested they come to the UK instead, I said I'd still be busy working right up to Christmas. Because they hadn't liked Bas, we'd all travelled in different directions over the holidays. So while it was nice of her to want to include me, I was sure she didn't really expect me.

'One more thing, Caron. That merger thing about Bas. They ended up partners.'

'Who'd he merge with, Mum?'

'I don't recall. He only had two pairs and the others

had four aces, but he still ended up where he plays the hand. But the game won't start for a month or so. After that he should be too busy to kibitz your game.'

When we rang off, I said, 'Well, Flora and Evelyn, if we can last out a month or so longer, we should be off the hook with Bas. His merger went through, I gather with a much larger firm, and he's going to be CEO. When he starts that job, he should be too busy even to think of us.'

Evelyn said, 'That doesn't sound like good news to me. He's still got time to try to kill us!'

I thought for a minute. 'Not to kill us. But to do something. But Bas in a hurry might make a mistake.'

Flora said, 'It's not really comforting, Caron, for him to be desperate. Is it?'

'Hell, maybe he's dropped us already. Who knows?'

'Double bugger. You don't really believe that. You're treating me like an idiot.'

I shook my head back and forth. 'OK. Then he's going to kill us, whatever. End of subject until provided with further data. Or constructive suggestions.'

Evelyn said, 'If you've ditched James, Caron, I wouldn't mind having a go. Backup for Henry.'

'Fine. He's not mine to give, but certainly you have a go.'

She stood up and hollered, 'I was only joking, you bugger! You looked sad and pitiful when you came home and I wanted to cheer you up. You look pale, your hair is limp, your shirttail is hanging out. I wouldn't be surprised if you threw up your dinner.'

'Honestly, Evelyn, what do you say when you want to make someone sad. Or suicidal?'

Flora said, 'Come back and have a glass of wine, Caron, and we won't ask anything.'

It was really too early to go to bed. Well, it would be too long a time to spend sulking. So I joined them. Friends, female friends, were becoming more precious by the minute.

'It was really a lovely weekend. And then at the end it fell apart. That's all. Don't let me spoil your programme.'

Evelyn said, 'It's just the news. People dying everywhere. That bugger James is still alive?'

We all laughed. 'Yes, he's still with us. More precisely, he's still with you and Stoner but not with me.'

Flora said with alarm, 'You broke up? You're not even friends?'

'I don't really know. One minute we were a hot Italian dinner. The next it was cold sticky spaghetti. And even you and Stoner couldn't turn cold pasta into smoked caviar. Never mind. I was off men when I met James. Now I'm off men again. I'm going to focus on my career. It's more reliable.'

Evelyn said, 'It's not as much fun as bed.'

'I don't mean forever, Evelyn! Don't be so literal. When I'm top of the heap, I'll meet more men.'

Evelyn said, 'They'll all be men like James, with your luck. Or there's gigolos.'

Flora said, 'Have you, er, tried gigolos, Evelyn?'

'I couldn't afford it after paying the dating agency. It'd be interesting, line them up, take your pick. I could hold auditions, like they do for modelling.'

Flora said, 'Are you serious, Evelyn?'

'Nah. I'll probably marry Henry, if he ever rings me.'

I said, 'But what about your modelling career?'

'Doctors and med students stay so busy he probably wouldn't notice if I was running a brothel.'

After we laughed, Flora said, 'Would you like being

married to a man who didn't have much time for you?'

'It'd be better than a bloke on the dole. Or a dead one. Or one who's ninety. Life's not perfect, Flora.'

I left them to work out life, the universe, and more particularly, men. They, even Evelyn, had cheered me in a way. They were friends and things seemed back to normal. Life might not be perfect, but baths very nearly were. So I soaked in the tub and then went to bed to make plans.

But it's hard to make plans when your life is like a circus, too much going on at once. It was Bas' turn to make a play in his game. I wasn't even sure what James' game was. So that left me with the Chambers' puzzle. I was definitely living in interesting times. Probably dangerous times.

With James, Bas, and Chambers' all vying for number one on my sort-out list, I couldn't seem to get any further. And while I knew James and Chambers' were connected, it would be helpful to establish if Bas might be an entirely separate issue. But he might not. I had a sudden, horrible thought. Mum had mentioned a Bas merger: could it be connected in some way with the rumoured hostile takeover of Chambers'? I mean a hostile takeover is just a very impolite merger. So I rang Mum.

It would be so neat and tidy, and would explain so much, if Bas was merging with someone who wanted to take over Chambers'. 'Mum, it's me again. About Bas' merger, can you try to think who it's with? Or look it up?'

'As I said before, I don't recall the name. And the newspaper's been taken to the recycling centre. It was a strange name, and made me think of duplicate bridge. It's called something like Smith Smith or Jones Jones.'

After we rang off, I decided the Bas merger couldn't have a connection to Chambers'. Any company trying to take over a London department store would need to be large enough for the name to be familiar, at least to someone like myself who'd worked with Bas buying and selling companies. But something was ringing a bell in my brain. And then I remembered Bank Bank.

I got out of bed and looked in my luggage underneath, and sure enough, one of the disks I'd brought over to use for a CV had the report I'd done on Bank Bank. It was a medium-size conglomerate, with companies dealing with almost everything except retail merchandising. Disappointed, I was tucking the disk back into the suitcase when a two hundred-watt light bulb went off in my head. Holding the disk, I stood up and shouted, 'Flora!'

She got there just as I was opening the bedroom door. And I heard Evelyn shout, 'I'm off to bed. Feel free to call me if Caron's dying or anything.'

'Flora, I know what Bas is after!' I danced around the room waving the disk. 'I need to talk to him right away.'

After I explained, she said, 'That's a relief. Well, in a way. He must be even more desperate than we thought. Are you going to ring him?'

'I'll probably need to see him. He wouldn't want to talk about it over the phone. I'll ring now to set up a meeting.'

Flora looked worried. 'But what if he's only around the corner? And barges in and steals it? And shoots all the witnesses?'

I laughed. 'He won't know it's not in a bank vault.'

Flora laughed. 'I like it. The Bank Bank in a bank.'

It took an hour to get through to him. He wasn't at the New York flat, and a professional answering service took the call and said they would contact him and give him my message. I gave her Flora's number so we could use the conference call thing. When she asked my name, I said, 'Just tell him it's Yankee Doodle Dandy.'

She said, 'Would that be Miss or Mrs?'

Flora sat looking at the phone as if to ensure it didn't grow wings and flutter out of the window. I went to the kitchen for a bottle of wine. Evelyn could hear a cork pop from a coffin six feet under. I mean if she were in it. As I poured her a glass, I said, 'I think Bas is going to be leaving us alone in future. He wants a disk that was under my bed.'

She said, 'You mean you've had it all the bloody time? With a man, the first thing I would have checked would've been the bed.'

When Bas rang, his first words were, 'Don't say a word, Caron.' When I didn't, he said, 'I'm in Vienna, but I can catch the first flight. Name the time and place and bring it with you.'

'And what are you bringing, Bas?'

He sounded like a chicken that had tried to cross the road at the wrong time. 'I thought that was obvious. I'll bring my chequebook.'

'Damn you, Bas, I'm so insulted I could spit. Not everyone's like you.'

'Sorry, honey. Remember not to say too much on the phone. The Picasso fakes and your music box are at the Ritz. Where they keep guests' valuables. And the Picasso papers. I knew you'd eventually see sense and want to deal. So we can meet there.'

Another insult. I said, 'Not there, Bas. We'll meet at

335

McBurgers.' I couldn't think of any place he would like less. Or anywhere he'd be more likely to have a kid smear ketchup on his suit. 'The one on Oxford Street nearest Marble Arch at one o'clock.'

'Damn it, Caron, be serious!'

'That's where I'm going to be. And that's where it's going to be.' I rang off and Flora and I started laughing.

'Are you free for lunch tomorrow, Flora?'

'Are you joking? I'd be free even if it meant turning down lunch with the Queen. But shouldn't you have gone for the twelve-course lunch at the Savoy?'

'Bas can take care of that for mentioning his cheque-book. And we'll have more fun eating without him. Anyway, with my plan you won't be exactly eating at McBurgers anyway.'

When I arrived at McBurgers the next day, Bas was already there. He stood while I sat at the red Formica-topped table by the window. The place was crowded, with people milling about looking for seats, and tired children crying. In that setting and in his three-piece bespoke suit, Bas looked like a sales rep who had hit hard times.

'I've tipped the bus boy, honey, so we can use the table without having to eat their crappy food.'

'Well, tip him again and have him get two orders of burgers, fries, and Cokes to go. I'm a working girl and this is my lunch hour.'

Bas looked as if I'd asked for fried doodle bugs and mud pie with horseradish soup. I realised that had I even once seen him so stressed and out of his element, it might have opened my eyes to everything else. But I'd probably wanted to preserve the fantasy just as much as he had. I was just so relieved that I could feel objective about him. The fact that my having the disk gave me some power in our relationship said everything about the original attraction. Grab a trouser leg and see the world. Grab two trouser legs and get a career.

He smiled, looking about nervously as if every burger were bugged. 'I've told the Ritz to hand over everything to you, Caron.'

Before he could say more, I punched Flora's mobile number on my phone. She said from the cruising taxi, 'Number double oh seven and three quarters here. Over and out.'

I said, 'Carry on to the Ritz, give them my name, and see what happens.'

Bas dropped all efforts at charm. 'I haven't got time for games, honey.'

'Really? I thought you said you liked them. And Bas, don't be thinking I'll pay for this later. I'll still know what's on the disk.'

He grinned. 'That's not the same as having it.' Then he frowned. 'You haven't made copies?'

'Bas, when I made up that report, it was in good faith. I didn't know it would have more dirt than a field of turnips. And I never dreamed you'd somehow use it to merge with them.'

'I didn't do that, honey. The merger idea was theirs, and then I remembered the report and the disk. Under the circumstances, it's dynamite.' Immediately he relaxed and was his old self. Even McBurgers couldn't keep him off form when it was business. 'You remember old Milton? The one we did the report for? Well, he got shafted and couldn't pay, so he never saw it. Then when I was approached for the merger and the CEO job . . .'

'You joined a load of crooks.'

He smiled. 'No, honey, they cleared the decks. I'm the new wave.'

'So they think.'

'I am, dammit! That's why I didn't want any miscellaneous rubbish like that disk floating around.'

'But why have you sent all that stuff? The rocking chair and chocolates, the knickers, the gardenias, everything? Why didn't you just ask about the disk?'

Bas, like many high-flyers, wasn't good at showing embarrassment. Not enough practice at that level. Rather than fluster, it tended to come across as subdued anger. Now his face turned slightly pink. 'I wasn't sure if you'd taken the disks on purpose, honey, to hold me to ransom. And if you hadn't, I didn't want to tip you off to their importance. So I was fishing, really. Trying to find out what you knew or planned to do.'

He stopped as the bus boy set the takeaway orders on the table. Then the teenager began to dab a damp rag at invisible spots on the table. Bas tipped him again, which apparently made the table clean.

'And what about the illegal stuff, Bas?' He looked blank and so innocent. I began to worry he hadn't been involved. 'I'm talking about the burglary attempt, the mugging.'

He grinned and said, 'Negative.'

I had to try again. If it hadn't been Bas, then who? Why? 'Come on, Bas! You want me to believe I'm personally accounting for half the crime statistics of a city the size of London?'

'Negative.'

I got up. 'Well, thank you for the lunch. The table.'

'Wait, Caron! Dammit, I thought we were supposed to be negotiating, not having confessions! When I was pretty sure you weren't going to deal, I hired the burglar. Now, don't be angry. You got a hell of a nice barbecue, and the asshole didn't succeed. After the Bank Bank Bas merger went through, I got someone to arrange for the handbag snatch. When the music box turned out to be empty, I decided you probably carried the disk around with you. I'm surprised the police don't catch all the crooks here. I've never hired such a bunch of morons in my life! Do your own dirty work, I say.'

'Well, you're one of the morons, Bas. Hiring crooks is not exactly legal.'

'I made it clear you weren't to be harmed, Caron. Snatch the bag, take only the disk, return the bag to Flora's house that night. Knock and run away. Her doorbell's broken.'

'A well-intentioned crook is still a crook. Well, that explains your letter, although I wasn't up to anything. And the cornflakes I guess were your way of saying that the kid gloves were off. And all that time you were really after the disk, and not the Picasso.'

He actually smiled like his old self. 'You're wrong there. I still want you back, Caron. I can't tell you how much I miss you.'

'Don't even try, Bas.'

'I thought a little pressure would make things tough, so I'd look a better prospect. It was insulting that I couldn't compete with your dinky job at Chambers'. And yeah, I wanted back the Picasso because it's a valuable asset.'

My mobile rang. Flora said, 'Just leaving the Ritz with the Picasso copies, the Picasso ownership papers, and Yankee Doodle Dandy. Do I come there and give Bas the disk next?'

'Yes, but hang on to the cab when you arrive. I'll keep an eye out.'

Bas said, 'You've got a great friend in that Flora. I thought she'd like the garden furniture. With that tumbling down house she sure needed something nice.'

'Flora is a wonderful friend, Bas. And before she arrives with the disk, I want your word that all these games will stop. I promise I haven't copied the disks, and you'll have to take my word for that.'

'Count all games stopped, here and now, Caron.' High-flyers don't do sheepish very well, either. Bas looked like he'd swallowed a fish bone, or half a whale, as he said, 'I've got off light, I can tell you that. I appreciate it.'

'How much cash have you got on you, Bas? Right now?'

Puzzled, he pulled out his wallet and started counting. When he got to three hundred, I said, 'Stop. That's enough. For expenses, Flora's taxi, and you owe her a nice dinner. She wasn't even involved with you.'

'I don't like for it, us, to end like this, Caron. We had so much for so long.'

Just then a toddler broke away from his mother and with unsure steps made it nearly as far as Bas' knee. No ketchup or dripping ice cream. Just as the kid was about to fall, Bas reached out and steadied him. The little boy giggled, and Bas' face showed pure pleasure, as he said, 'That's a good boy. Steady now.' He ran his fingers through the tot's blond curls.

It was as if a magic wand had been waved, turning Bas into a stranger, maybe one with green antennae sticking out of his head. It was his tricks and the disk that had made him nervous, not the venue. Suddenly I was seeing a family man who loved his children and was, except for the pricey suit, at home in a burger place. The really rich tend to complain louder, but even their children insist on fast food. I'd been a business partner who provided fun and sex on the side, not a true love who happened to be in business. We'd talked business in the bath because primarily that's what I'd been to him, business. I finally felt free of Bas. I realised I'd probably been feeling guilty because I should have known what was going on and had chosen to ignore it.

I looked at him and felt a wave of strong emotion. But it was the pity you feel for a stranger. 'I wish you well, Bas. But you really need to leave me alone. And you should think of your family. Stop your dirty tricks with thieves and muggers. And stop playing around on your wife.'

He said indignantly, 'Can I help it if I fell in love with you?'

'Married men can up the odds against that happening if they stop asking single women out on dates.'

Bas smiled, rather like a sick kitten, and quickly changed the subject. 'About the Picasso, honey. If you're planning to sell it, could you wait a couple of weeks? So I can sort out the company records first?'

I wondered if people who like numbers have to be dead to forget about them. 'Bas, can you make the Picasso as pay over four years to lessen my tax bill? Of course if you quickly died and it was an inheritance, there wouldn't be tax on the main bit.'

He really laughed then. 'I truly miss you, Caron honey. And I'm never going to find anyone else like you again. Whatever the hell happens in my life, I'm just going to have the memories of you to get me through.'

I smiled, too. There had to have been a reason why I connected with Bas in the first place. And it was so much better for it to end this way. It's the laughs that keep you going in life.

He said, 'There's a taxi out there, probably Flora. Will you keep in touch, let me know if you ever need anything, Caron?'

'Probably not, Bas. That's the whole point, that I want my own life. Friends, OK?'

I waved at Flora and she came in. After she handed him the disk, he shook her hand. Walking with us to the door, he said, 'And you're positive you haven't made any copies?'

Flora said, 'I can vouch for that.'

Just as we got outside and were in reach of the taxi, I thought how Bas would have preferred to lose his bank balance rather than his pride. I said, 'No copies, Bas. But if you cause any more mischief, you should know that we have a super video of you stealing the fake Picassos and the music box.'

25

In the taxi, Flora and I laughed all the way back to the office, while we gobbled up the takeaway burgers and fries. She was horrified at the idea of spending all that money on one meal, so we decided to hang on to the cash for meals at the Italian. For days when the sun didn't shine on us. But I was feeling so relieved and cocky with success that I thought I'd be able to see sunshine through the thickest clouds.

With Bas out of the equation, that left only James and Jack and the Chambers' puzzle. Hopefully, and I realised it was probably the same odds as winning the lottery, Jack would fade into the woodwork. And I couldn't fathom what James was up to. So I decided to focus on Chambers', a situation where I could take some direct action. I'd already been promised the window bonus plus the six-month incentive pay rise. And from what Melody had said, there was a bonus involved with whatever I was supposed to be doing to help Chambers'.

I was beginning to think of Melody as a fairy god-mother. Talk about patrons. Of course if I came to a bad end, she'd need to swap her wand for a broomstick.

The possibility of danger meant that I needed to work fast, because the bad guys wouldn't exactly be taking long coffee breaks. Any danger would only increase, as not all the Chambers VPs were like Biggs. James wasn't the least bit like him. The first thing they'd do would be to change all the company passwords. And if they weren't already in place, extra security programs would be put in the computer. Which meant the thief would be able to jump up and down and shout, That bloody woman in accounts is snooping. Well, the thief wouldn't do that. Not shout. Whisper. Take her out. And not for dinner.

Actually, if there was danger, maybe it had started when I did the first of Melody's confidential work. When I innocently found errors. So I had nothing to lose and perhaps much to gain from diving in headfirst. Well, you can crack your head doing that, but it might hurt less than a bullet.

My laptop was state of the art, as Bas hadn't believed in second class. And I could do what I needed to do anywhere there was a phone line. But of course I didn't want to use Flora's line in case the crook could trace my activities back to her. So I took the little laptop in to work with me the next day. It fitted very snugly into my shoulder bag.

The day after what Flora and I now called Bank Bank Bas Day, I asked Mrs Brown if I could leave for several hours, unpaid, as I had errands to run. She said I had time in hand anyway and not to worry. Outside Chambers', I hailed a taxi and went to a cyber café in Kensington.

I asked the cabby to make sure we weren't being followed and he almost died laughing. 'Best one I've heard today.' Well, it works in films.

I used Biggs' password and accessed Mr Chambers' computer, making sure I wasn't online more than half an hour. Basically, I was checking the suspicious transaction files to find out which passwords had been used to access them. Earlier, with Melody's work, I'd only had the files and disks Chambers sent. Now I had the entire database available. After pressing the right buttons, it was mostly waiting for my disks to fill up.

I constantly looked to see if anyone was watching me. On the whole, computer buffs tend to keep their eyes glued to the screen. But then someone tailing me wouldn't be stupid. Drooling over James had maybe softened my brain. I should have become more cautious earlier, especially after my first talk with Harvey in accounts. This wasn't a case of random muggers on the street. The bad guy was going to be someone I probably knew and who certainly knew me.

Then I took a taxi to another cyber café, then another. Transferring the data was slower than I'd have liked, but fast enough that there was no time to actually read what I was getting.

When I left the second café, I thought a man in a biker jacket was watching me. After the third one, I was pretty sure of it, although the man seemed to have changed from leather to an anorak. Or I could have been merely paranoid. When I left the last cyber café, in Soho, I was positive it was the same man. But as I stood in the queue for a taxi, he ran to a nearby car with a driver and jumped in. They drove off quickly without looking in my direction. I was nervous as hell as I got into the taxi and headed back to Chambers'. It was almost worse not to know either way if I'd been followed than if I'd been sure. Like in the situation with Bas, it was what I didn't know that magnified the fear.

That night Flora went out with Mervin. Flora said, 'Will you be all right on your own, Caron?'

'I'll be fine. And I'll have Super Karate here.'

'She's out with Henry.'

I could feel my palms getting sweaty. 'I'll be fine, Flora. No one will know I'm here alone except for you and Mervin. You have a lovely time. Remember, don't skip any chapters. It's no good reading the end before the middle.'

She smiled and hugged me before she left.

I opened a tin of Mexican chilli and put it in a dish and into the microwave. After closing the curtains, I set up my laptop on Flora's desk and began. I didn't even wait three minutes for the microwave to finish. Between bites of chilli and tapping in instructions, I peered out the front curtains. There was definitely a man sitting in a car a few doors down. But then there were probably millions of Londoners sitting in cars at that moment.

I'd already found that fifty million pounds had gone missing from Chambers' when I thought the list of accessing passwords was full enough to analyse. But the amount of the fraud was probably far more. And of course the money holidayed all over the world, ending up in Switzerland. Without having a team of detectives and my funds multiplied by a trillion, I couldn't check that out further. Even governments dealing with the Swiss often couldn't get much more out of them than a cuckoo clock.

About ten o'clock, someone knocked on the door. I was wondering if I should open it, when James called out, 'Come on Caron, we need to talk.'

I cautiously opened the door a few inches, and he was standing there in his jogging clothes. I could see over his shoulder that the man in the car was still there. Well, at least it proved James wasn't in the car.

I'd backed up and he'd come in when I remembered

all the computer printouts behind me on the desk. 'Why don't we go to the pub for a drink, James?'

After he agreed, I asked if he'd mind checking that I'd turned off the cooker in the kitchen. 'Heating up soup, that's about my limit.'

'It smells more like chilli,' he said, heading for the kitchen. I quickly slid the laptop into my shoulder bag.

As we walked towards South Hill Green, I noticed the car pull out and pass us and then turn the corner. When we reached the turning, it was nowhere in sight.

After some general chat, I set my G&T on the table and said, 'You remember, James, the weekend I worked as standby? Have you lot on the top floor sorted out whatever the problems were?'

He hesitated, then said, 'There are always problems in a company the size of Chambers'.'

'But Flora said it was unheard of, to have standby staff. So I thought, well, that the problems might be unusual.'

'Every problem is different, or it wouldn't be a problem, Caron. One could simply apply what was used in the first instance to solve it and that would make it routine.'

He leaned across the small round table and took my hand as he spoke earnestly, 'Look Caron, I don't want you even thinking about this. If I were able to talk about it, I wouldn't because it wouldn't do you any good. And . . .' He looked at me carefully, before continuing, 'This isn't personal or jealousy, but it would relieve my mind a great deal if you would keep clear of Jack Howard.'

We had been holding hands and I held his up and kissed it and grinned. 'I told you, James, you have

347

nothing to fear from Jack Howard. I do my best to steer clear of the man.'

'But I understand he's still sending flowers to you at work. Couldn't you somehow scotch that?'

'I was hoping he'd have gone bankrupt by now. Anyway, they've become a bit of a joke. And none of the flowers looks particularly poisonous. No hidden spiders.' I smiled and reached out so both my hands were holding his. It was very difficult to maintain my suspicions when I was actually with James. I quietly withdrew my hand as I remembered how, when I'd been with Bas, I'd avoided questioning Bas about anything unusual.

He reached out and took my hand again, and his grip tightened as he said, 'I wasn't thinking of spiders, but one never knows. I'm serious, Caron. No contact. Humour me.'

I grinned. 'That's so much easier to do in bed.' Oh, please, James, I kept thinking, just tell me you wouldn't do what I fear.

He smiled before resuming his stern look. 'Couldn't you ring the florist? Have the deliveries diverted to a local hospital?'

'Insult the man and get the sack? And what about poisoning all the patients?'

James smiled. 'Just an idea, Caron. I'm sure you can think of something better.' After a pause, he added, 'It's not just Jack himself, being such a swine. But it isn't a good idea at the moment to be drawing extra attention to yourself.'

It was all he would say, and I didn't think it made a great deal of sense. Unless he was projecting his own fears onto me. So, nibbling crisps from a shared packet, we took the long route back to Flora's house, window-shopping en route on the High Street. He kissed me goodnight at the door. 'Do you want me to stay? I mean do you feel safe here alone, Caron?'

'Of course I feel safe, James. I'm not a shrinking violet. Flora and Evelyn will return any minute. And I've got your mobile number.'

He said, 'I'll keep it with me at all times.'

What the hell was that all about, I wondered, as I got back to my laptop. Could it be so simple as a touching bit of jealousy? Bas had always had guile, quite apart from having a wife. Could someone like James possibly have a secret life? He'd had a flat to live in with Ice Cube while owning his current home. And now it turns out he has that cottage that no one knows about. Probably not even the vigilant Stoner. Why would a single guy need three separate homes?

I got back to work, to take my mind off things like treachery and men. People who don't know computers only see the results and think it takes genius. What it really takes is concentration and patience. Basically the programme is the horse and you're the rider. Bas had had a reason to worry about fraud, because he'd been buying up companies already on their knees. So the programme I was using was the best.

The dad of a university friend of mine owned a restaurant, and he took her and me to a fancy eatery about once a month. He used to glance at the menu, take one look at the diners, and then say what the evening takings would be. He was incredibly accurate because several times when he mentioned the figure to the owner he was accused of spying. So when I was designing the fraud detection program, which someone else would write, I went to see Mr Vitamin to discover his trick. That was our name for him as he maintained that cream and everything fattening was full of them.

'You kinda get a feel for it, Caron. Each person's an individual, but all together everybody's statistics.'

'But what if someone only had a drink?'

'It still works out. What you want to do, test for something different. Extra large amounts, extra small amounts. Except for seasonal differences, and occasional inflation changes, the basic data stays the same. A good crook needs to take action with great regularity, but that's too risky in most cases. And check for names. A different name, a supplier, anything. Just check for anything different.'

I didn't like the idea that whether I had a drink or seven courses wasn't shit to a tree regarding the universe. But he was very, very wealthy, and they always say if you want to get rich ask someone who is rich.

Remembering Mr Vitamin, there was another test I needed to run. I queried any names that hadn't been in the database prior to the last six months. In spite of the size of the English language, only a few hundred words are used often. And Chambers' had been supposedly going downhill, so there wouldn't be lots of new company and manufacturing contacts.

The computer coughed up a list of about fifty names. Some were just odd words, or misspellings of normal ones. But there were six companies that were new. Another search, and three of them had been mentioned only in e-mail. I was willing to bet that one of them had initiated the hostile takeover bid.

Soon Evelyn, then Flora, returned. I quickly put away the computer.

'Well,' I said, 'I hope no one else's book of life got pulped.'

Evelyn said, 'Well, bugger it, Henry hasn't proposed yet. It's a bit sick-making.'

'But Evelyn, you've only had a couple of dates with him.'

'I don't mean propose marriage, Flora. You're still living in the last millennium.'

Flora said, 'No, I'm not. I've, well, I've been on more dates than that with Mervin and he hasn't proposed anything either.'

'Count yourselves lucky, friends. Keep it cool, and keep it, if you take my meaning.'

'Oh, Caron, I'm sorry.'

'No need. The man came tonight and took me to the pub for a drink. It's back to Miss Carlisle and Mr Smith.'

'Well, bloody hell. Does that mean you're winning or losing?'

'Winning. Gin and crisps are predictable.'

'There's not much buzz in crisps, Caron. You're getting it wrong again.'

'No, I'm not, Evelyn. That's why I added the gin. There are lots of women who prefer gin to men.'

'Yeah. I've heard about them. Rather than that, I'd hitch up with that bloke who loved the crossword puzzles.'

It was really rewarding baiting Evelyn. She never came up with the same answer twice. Her logic was so unique it came in disposable tins. I gave her a hug.

'Did either of you by any chance see a man in a parked car out there when you came in?'

Flora quickly looked out of the window. 'He's gone. We missed him. Oh, sorry, Caron. I mean, did he do anything?'

'When he saw James, he left. I just wondered if he'd

returned. Don't worry. James must have scared him away.' Or told him they didn't both need to be watching at the same time.

The following morning, Jack rang me at my desk, something he'd never done before. I jumped when I heard his voice, thinking about what James had said. Was the phone bugged? Was someone listening in?

'Caron, I need to talk to you. How about lunch?' As fast as I could think up excuses, let alone voice them, he kept adding, 'Or dinner tonight? Perhaps just coffee?'

'Well, I don't know, Jack.' That was the most awful kind of man, who sort of asked if you were going to be free for even ten minutes during the rest of your natural life.

'It's important, Caron. Surely you can set aside ten minutes? We could meet at the corner café at the beginning of your lunch hour. Then you could be on your way to whatever.'

I agreed, to get it over with and because he had been so nice on attempted bag snatch day. And then I spent the remainder of the time before lunch wondering what he could possibly want. Well, I knew what he was after, but in ten minutes? In a coffee shop?

I rang Flora to say I wouldn't be able to go with her on her errands. Flora's opinions about chapters weren't going to be much help, unless she switched to crime novels. I wasn't feeling very encouraged when I set off to meet Jack.

All the tables were occupied and there was a crush at the take-out section. It meant a repeat of Mervin's show, ninety sardines in a tiny tin. Jack was standing in the middle of the café, balancing two cups of coffee, and trying to dodge hurried hungry people as they elbowed past.

I took the coffee and thanked him. 'Do you want to step outside, Jack? To talk? I mean it's so crowded.'

'Actually, Caron, this is better. The crowd. We're less likely to be overheard.'

'Overheard by whom?'

He smiled, trying to make light of it. 'By anyone.' I'd never imagined a man like Jack could look so nervous, so unpolished, so uncool. It was like thinking of Bas busking outside the tube station.

'I know, Caron, that we haven't exactly hit it off yet. After the pub, then after Mervin's show, and when we went for a walk. But I think we can. In time, when everything's sorted. The flowers, well, I just don't want you to forget me at the moment.'

This seemed the perfect time to dump on the flower deliveries. But he looked so upset and nervous, and more human than usual. And while I loved a challenge, I hated being blatantly unkind. 'Jack, I've only got a little time. Is that what you wanted to say?'

'No. But it's difficult, I mean I don't wish to be mis-understood. For you to think it's personal.'

I wondered, is this what it's like when your best friend tells you you've got bad breath? Jack was acting ridiculously. 'I'll do my best to understand, Jack. Just say it.'

'It's the company you've been keeping, Caron. Especially James Smith. You need to be really careful of the guy. He's a bit of a persona non grata at the moment. It won't do you much good to be seen with him.'

'Jack, it's nobody's business whom I see.'

'I don't mean dating, Caron. Not that. Just believe

me and stay away from him for the moment.' When I said nothing, he added, 'Just tell me you'll think about it?'

Realising this could go on forever, I said, 'Well, I consider anything anyone says to me. So don't worry. But what's this all about?'

'I really can't say. But you remember the weekend you and your friends worked? Because of problems? It's to do with that. And please believe me, I'm sticking my neck out by telling you that much. But I've been really worried about you.'

I was furious at his maligning James, even though I had my own doubts. And I wanted to put his comments down to jealousy. But he looked very sincere and very upset. Trying to think of an exit line so I could leave, I said, 'Are you all right? You don't look particularly well, Jack.'

'I'm fine. But thank you for thinking of me. I mean, for caring.'

I had one last go at cheering him up. And I didn't want to leave things on such a personal level. 'Lots of people care about you, Jack. Word is you're even tipped for the top job at Chambers'.'

Then he looked really angry. 'I'm in the running, Caron. But so is James. And bastards like him, born rich, always attract good fortune. Those who have seem to get more and more in life.'

'Jack, Mr Chambers is known for being a fair man. And he started at the bottom himself. I can't believe he won't choose on merit.'

Looking more depressed than ever he said, 'James has the merit of not having slept around in the company.' If it's possible to look both down and confident, Jack managed it as he added, 'But don't worry about me, Caron. I've made sure I've got some insurance.'

Shocked I said, 'Jack, you're not thinking of, well, of jumping off anything tall?'

He laughed. 'I'm not going to jump into the Thames, if that's what you mean, Caron. I meant that people like me have to walk the extra mile to get where they want to go.'

I patted his arm and smiled. 'That's not always a bad thing, Jack. Sometimes I seem to have to walk an extra million miles myself. Thanks for the coffee.' With a weak smile I handed him my empty cup and rushed out.

The assignation had taken more than ten minutes, and what with getting there and back, there wasn't really time to eat in the canteen. After getting a tuna sandwich to eat at my desk, I arrived back at work a few minutes early.

Melody was sitting at her desk, looking depressed. My chair was disconnected from its base and sitting on the floor. Beside it on the floor was my computer. Talk about a computer crashing. Some of the connections had come out of the back and were dangling. 'I think you'll need to help me, Caron . . .'

'Are you all right, Melody? What on earth has happened? Shall I call the doctor?'

'No, dear. It's my ankle.'

I looked down but couldn't tell if anything was wrong just by looking.

She said, 'I came back early and sat at your desk to sort out the new batch of work Mrs Brown had put there. But the chair gave way. I must have grabbed the computer for balance, although I don't remember doing that. And then it crashed on top of me.'

She was shaking all over and was very pale. 'Where exactly did the computer fall on you?'

'On my side.'

'We've got to get you to the emergency room to be checked out, Melody. Right now.'

'No, no, dear. We'll be playing into their hands. We must carry on.'

I wasn't sure what to do. I thought she was probably in shock and didn't know what actually hurt.

'Just help me get up, dear.'

I tried to help her, but her ankle gave way. As she settled back into her chair, something caught on my shoe. I turned and saw a spider-web-thin cord attached to both the computer and the chair. It definitely hadn't been an accident. And that reminded me of the bus she claimed someone had pushed her in front of.

'Don't argue, Melody. Let me at least get you to somewhere safe, somewhere private.' Mentioning private did it.

'Before everyone comes back, please.'

Mrs Brown had come in and I frantically motioned to her. When she joined us, I said, 'I think someone's played a trick, Mrs Brown. Booby-trapped the chair. Could you help me roll Melody and her chair to the ladies? A doctor needs to check her out.'

Mrs Brown was horrified. 'I'm ringing security this minute!'

Melody said, 'It's all just so embarrassing.' She looked close to tears.

We got Melody to the ladies' room just as a security man arrived. He put an out of action notice on the door and came inside with us. A few minutes later, the company nurse arrived. All I could think to do was stand with my arm around Melody. She was clutching my hand.

The nurse said, 'Her ankle may be broken. She needs to go immediately to casualty for X-rays.'

Two more security men joined us. And Mrs Brown got through to the top floor for instructions.

Melody pulled me close and whispered, 'Please go and get my handbag, dear.' I remembered my laptop in my own bag and rushed back to my desk.

When I returned, James was there taking charge. He was saying, 'For now, it would be better for no word of this to get out.' Two security guards were lifting Melody in a saddle grip, their arms forming a sort of seat.

'Use the back corridor,' James told them, then added, 'And I'd like Caron to accompany Melody.'

The nurse said, 'But I can go.'

He turned to her. 'The incident involved Caron's chair and I'd prefer for her to be safely out of the building until we've investigated further.' No hesitancy there. James was totally no nonsense when taking command.

I sat in the back of the ambulance holding Melody's hand. Melody was made to lie flat, and kept apologising about how embarrassing it all was.

'I'm so sorry, Melody. It was meant for me. And if you hadn't been helping me . . .'

'We switch seats all the time, dear. It could have been meant for either of us. Could it have been an accident?'

The hospital quickly found that Melody's ankle wasn't broken but was badly sprained. But she was upset, and there was also a slight chance that she had hit her head and had concussion. They decided to keep her in for observation overnight. Then they asked me to wait outside while they finished taping her up and sent her for precautionary X-rays of her ribs.

I got some hot mud from the coffee machine and

sat in the waiting room. The whole thing was bizarre. Why would someone go to all that trouble while obviously not intending any real harm? I mean what happened to Melody was probably the most that could have happened, and while it wasn't nice it definitely wasn't lethal. And with my being so much younger, it might merely have meant sitting about waiting for X-rays.

And then I realised what the perpetrator had probably had in mind. I dashed to the taxi rank and rushed home. While the taxi waited, I stashed all the disks and printouts in my travel bag along with my laptop. I ran back to the taxi and said, 'Euston Station.' After selecting a sheaf of papers and switching them into my shoulder bag, I went to the left luggage office where I stored everything else. Then back to the hospital. I was innocently sitting, waiting, sipping cocoa that also tasted like mud, when James arrived. After having a word with the doctors, he sat down beside me on the fake leather sofa amidst a quantity of litter from previous occupants.

'Caron, I want you to take paid leave for the remainder of this week. Go somewhere safe.'

'But James . . .'

'I'm not asking. As CFO of Chambers' Emporium, I'm telling you. Ordering, if you like.'

'But where would be safer than in a room full of people, like the accounts section?'

'It wasn't very safe today. Melody will be all right, but that's because what happened was only a warning.' He looked directly at me as he said this. 'And we don't know what might happen next.'

An icy fear crept through my veins. How could James be so sure that what happened was only a warning? Was he warning me off? Trying to isolate me so he could get rid of me permanently? I said with great innocence, 'But what's happening? Surely all that with Melody was an accident?'

He gave me his wry look. 'Do you really believe that, Caron?'

Of course I didn't, you bloody idiot. I said, 'Well, if it involves me, James, then perhaps you should explain what's going on?'

'I can't explain, Caron. The problem is you may know too much already.'

'They say a little learning is a dangerous thing, James. So make my learning a bit bigger.' When he said nothing, I added, 'And I thought your department was finance, not security.'

James ran his hand over his face wearily. 'Caron, why must you always argue? Flora's house is the last place I want you to go. And your parents live abroad. You could come and stay at my house.'

James was interrupted by bleeps from his mobile phone. He stood up and moved closer to the outside door, apparently to improve the reception.

When he returned, looking more worried than ever, I said, 'Speaking of phones, what's the story supposed to be about Melody? I mean what are we supposed to say?' One way or the other, he needed to unbutton his brain so I could see in it.

'That she's not well, for a start. If that doesn't do it, say it was an unusual accident that's being checked out.'

It sounded ridiculous, but I didn't bother to tell him. No one in accounts was dumb enough to accept a story like that. People wearing Sherlock Holmes hats were probably crawling around the department floor at that moment, peering through magnifying glasses.

I looked at James who had obviously been watching

me, seeming to ponder something. 'One more thing, Caron. If you're planning to remain here to support Melody when the doctors have finished . . .'

'She's going to try to talk them into letting her go home.'

'We've asked them to keep her at least overnight. She lives alone and until we know more, it's safer.'

'Well, I'll need to go to her place and get her things. And before you say anything, I won't go alone. I'll see if Flora can come with me.'

'Good. Now, would you mind giving me your house keys? I'd like to have it checked out.'

'For what? Dust? Woodworm?' And then I thought, bombs? Exceedingly relieved I'd already been there and removed all the computer evidence, I agreed. 'All right, if you must.' I got out the keys and handed them over, careful not to let him see the printouts taking up most of the space in my bag.

James got up and smiled broadly. 'Thanks,' he said, waving the keys. 'Now you'll have to wait for me to collect you here later.' He ruffled my hair and smiled again before going.

As he was leaving, my mobile pinged. 'Caron, it's Flora. What's going on? Are you all right?'

'It's Melody who's not well.' I asked Flora about going with me to collect stuff for Melody, and of course she readily agreed. 'We can talk later. When you get here. Take a taxi. We can charge it to Chambers'.'

After checking with the nurse and finding it would be another hour before Melody was available, I went to the waiting room attached to the children's ward. Quickly I got out the printouts and began to go through them.

Selecting one crucial file, I made a list of everyone

who had accessed it in the past six months. It didn't of course give actual names, but this time I also had printouts of company passwords and a list of whom each computer terminal was assigned to. The only people who had accessed the record were: Jim Chambers; James, the CFO; Jack Howard, VP of import/export; old Harvey of accounts.

Plus access had been made from one computer terminal in the accounts section. The latter was a block of numbers and not individually named. Mervin? Someone on the top floor using a more anonymous machine? More recently there was access by Biggs from an outside line, but that would be me. And in the past two weeks there were numerous accesses from a different outside line. Either a team of experts had been called in or I wasn't the only one poking my nose in. On the whole, I thought the team of experts more likely – though I did wonder who the outsiders might be.

I crossed Jim Chambers off the list, as he was hardly likely to be stealing his own money. And the theft had been going on before the recent, but nightly, access – that of the probable outside security team. So the most likely suspects were: James, Jack Howard, Harvey, and Mervin.

I broke into a cold sweat. I'd felt fairly safe because it would be nearly impossible for anyone to trace cyber café phone lines back to me. But whoever was accessing the system from an outside line every night . . .

I looked at the data in my lap. They would have this very same printout, with everything but my name on it. Everyone would know Biggs didn't know a computer from a bottle of stout. And I'd accessed the password list from his office. Suddenly, there was no doubt at all that someone had been following me around the cyber cafés. The man who had followed me had gone on ahead because he'd already found out all he needed to know.

My mobile began to bleep, and with shaking fingers I pressed the on button. 'Caron? James here. I want you to promise me you'll take extra care. When we got to your house, well ... It looks like a burglary.'

26

I was sitting with Melody when Flora arrived carrying a large bunch of flowers, sent by the accounts section via Mervin. After getting a vase from the nursing station, we placed the flowers next to the even larger bouquet that had been sent by Chambers' Emporium.

Melody was sleeping, but I'd already got a list of what was wanted from her flat. And I'd also questioned Melody again, who apparently hadn't seen anything or anyone suspicious when she returned from lunch. 'There was no one in accounts at all, Caron.'

In the corridor, Flora whispered, 'I'm near to, like, bursting with questions.' She indicated a man standing waiting for us. 'I was looking forward to using taxis, but they sent security. He's going to drive us.'

He also went in first at Melody's and refused to leave while we packed a bag. 'Goodness, Caron, Melody's flat is gorgeous. So old-worldly, faded florals and good antiques. I often wondered about her home life. Not once has she ever mentioned it.'

On our return, we found Melody still asleep, so we went to the hospital cafeteria. 'Get everything you want, Flora. It's all on Chambers'. We're official, looking after Melody.'

Flora said, 'We'd take care of her anyway, but good idea. I'm, like, trying to save my bonus. Now tell me all. And I want to know why James asked me to stay at my mother's tonight.'

'Did he?'

'Yes. And James asked me not to mention anything, but that couldn't include you. He must think you're going to stay all night at the hospital.'

That didn't make a lot of sense. I mean why did James want Flora out of the way all night? I could see his not wanting to alarm her by searching her house, but surely that would finish before we left the hospital? And she would need to know about the burglary sometime.

'The official story, Flora, is that Melody tripped and fell.'

Flora laughed. 'We're supposed to believe that? With security marching up and down the accounts aisles all afternoon?'

I laughed. 'That brings us to the second story. Melody's had a mysterious accident and they're checking it out.'

Flora laughed again. 'I'm surprised PR didn't, you know, say they were measuring for new carpets.'

'What actually happened is that someone had tampered with the chair.'

Flora said, 'That's drastic! You could have died!'

'Died? How died?'

Flora said, 'Well, I guess I mean that if the bad person could get to your chair, he could have done something worse.'

I took a deep breath and let it out slowly. 'Too true. What's the word in accounts? And why does anyone think it was meant for me, when, well it's poor Melody who's injured?'

'They all thought it was meant for Melody at first. But Mrs Brown, who can talk to Mervin without leaving her position, leaned over to Mervin. She said, 'Mervin, quietly go to the back and move Melody's chair to

Caron's position.' So then they all, like, noticed the missing chair was yours. Before they hadn't thought about chairs. I mean they thought Melody broke the chair when she fell.'

'And what did Mervin say about that? To you.'

'Mervin said shit.'

I said with astonishment, 'You mean Mervin had hoped it would have been me?'

Flora seemed affronted. 'I think he meant it was even worse for you to be the target. Mervin worries about you, Caron. He really likes you.'

'Sorry, Flora. It's just that it's all a bit scary. Melody is quite certain that someone is out to get her. To make her retire, which seems a bit far-fetched.' I didn't want to mention my work on the confidential Chambers' stuff, as it might put Flora in danger.

'But what could it be? Jealousy? Mervin says no one else knows it's Jack Howard sending those flowers. One of the girls suggested you were, well, sending them to yourself. Until Mervin just laughed and mentioned the accounts' pay scale.'

After we'd finished the main course, I said, 'I feel a bit guilty, our tucking in while Melody's not well.' After a minute's thought, I added, 'In for a penny, in for a pound. Chocolate cake?'

'We'd better have some. You especially, Caron. I'm surprised what with all's that been going on, first Bas, now this, that you haven't grown old before your time.' Laughing, she added, 'Surely chocolate cake will hide any white hairs?'

I didn't know about the white hairs, but at that moment I thought some cake might look good on the tip of Flora's nose. Later, when she mentioned leaving, James still hadn't yet returned with my keys. As I was walking her to the hospital's main entrance, she said, 'Do you think James meant not to go by my house at all tonight? I wanted to get . . .'

I imagined what her house probably looked like at the moment. All the furniture upside down and maybe even the mattresses ripped up. 'No, Flora, don't go there. If that's what he said.' Maybe I could put every-thing back in order before she saw it.

'But what about you, Caron, if it's, like, unsafe for us? Are you spending the night here watching Melody?'

'I won't know until James returns. And I must say, he's turned awfully bossy.'

'I'm sure he's only, you know, trying to help.'

When I returned to Melody, she was just waking up. She seemed enormously cheered. 'You know, dear, this isn't the way I would have chosen. But all the attention has been nice. And room service.'

'You are so wonderful, Melody. Always making the best of everything.' The nurse was shooing visitors off the ward, but Melody reached out for my hand. 'It's all right. You can stay, dear. Chambers' security has apparently told them you're a relative.'

It was getting late and still no James. Melody had long ago been given the statutory sleeping pill to make things easier for the night nurses. So I paced the dimly lit corridor. Walking seemed to help people to think, like with those puppets where you pull a leg string and the head bobs up.

This was my first chance to digest the information about the hostile takeover. Obviously the Chambers' crook was getting himself rich. But was the fraud also to ensure the takeover took place, that Chambers' wasn't so valuable? And if the fraud and takeover were connected, could more than one person be involved?

I found it hard to think that James would physically harm me. But then Jack seemed truly to fancy me, and certainly Mervin was my friend. And old Harvey would lose if we had a fair fight. Harvey would lose if he cheated. But it was naïve to think that with fifty or a hundred million pounds at stake, they'd all be thinking, Now don't hurt sweet little Caron.

Thinking over the list of suspects, I wondered if it could be the most obvious? I really didn't want it to be James or Mervin. Well, it was perfectly ridiculous even to consider such a thing. Now poor Jack Howard, if I really had to choose, why not him? But was he the most obvious, or was I prejudiced because I didn't much like him? And why, if Jack wanted me out of the picture, had he come to the rescue when that mugger tried to snatch my bag? He could have just cheered from the background. Poor Jack Howard, I thought, mentally marking him number one. But I wrote very slowly.

The Chief Financial Officer was always the main suspect. And James had been nearby when Melody had her battle with the bus. The thing I didn't like to consider was that Jack had been with me at the beginning of the lunch hour. So how could he have set the trap that caught Melody? And what about the earlier attacks on her? How could they be connected and what was their purpose?

Mervin? Well, he had definitely been accessing the files. And he jumped at the chance to do the window ruse. Now he seemed to be trying to leave Chambers' with unseemly haste. And his saying shit, about me not being hurt. He'd know the accounts routine better than the others would, too. Money might be the motive for them all, but Mervin certainly had the most opportunity regarding the chair.

Harvey Harris? The stereotypical bookkeeper stuck in a dusty back room. Risking all for the main chance? Well, do those types of people really take risks? He had definitely worked out some way to get past the limitation of his password, which led to the question of why. I smiled. Maybe the name should be changed to Chambers' Emporium Computer Hacking Agency.

James? I couldn't bear to think about it. I walked up and down the corridor a few times trying not to think of it. As Chief Financial Officer, the fraud would have been easier for him than for any of the others, maybe easier than all the others put together. The front pages of the newspapers seemed to be full of photos of CFOs smugly sunbathing in Brazil. Of all the VPs, James seemed to roam about Chambers' the most. If he'd been seen near accounts, his presence would have been taken for granted, probably forgotten.

An especially horrid thought hit me. As I'd given James my house keys, he could have searched the place himself, before ringing me. I was finding it more and more difficult to believe Jack was the most likely and James the least likely. Even I knew there had been one Agatha Christie book where the guilty person was actually the little old lady. The obvious little old lady that you thought trustworthy because surely Agatha Christie wouldn't do that. Just like surely I wouldn't point to James.

James had warned me off Jack. Jack had warned me off James. Mervin had warned me off Harvey. Harvey had warned me off all of accounting. What did that mean? Could they all be in it together? Scrap that. James and Jack singing a duet? But it certainly indicated each one knew something, and worse, that they all believed I knew something too. Probably believed I knew more than I actually did know. But at least one person knew who was guilty. And he could be working out how to get rid of me already.

James arrived a little after ten. I was anxious to get home to see the state of the house. But he hadn't eaten yet. 'And we need to talk, Caron.' In the hospital cafeteria, I drank more of the muddy coffee while watching him eat.

'For one thing, I didn't realise that Evelyn was away at the moment.'

'What's that got to do with anything, James? Surely you don't suspect Evelyn? She couldn't hide in the Sahara Desert, much less creep up behind my office desk.'

'It means there's one fewer person in Flora's house. I mean, she's big and strong, and it would have been safer with her there.'

'Well, if I'd known all this would happen, I'd have invited Manchester United to move in. Don't manufacture extra worries. Flora and I can manage.' That would have been the perfect time for him to mention that Flora wouldn't be there because he'd asked her to stay at her mum's. But he said nothing.

Then all the way to the house, James argued for me to go home with him. 'But I can't just run, James. From what? To where? Running could go on forever.'

The house had been tidied up a bit, and the brownie recipe was still hanging in the bathroom. I'm not one of those people who collect lots of stuff, so there hadn't been much for an intruder to look through or take. It was interesting that while the kitchen and living room had also been done over, the other bedrooms hadn't been touched. And there weren't many people who would know where I slept. James and Mervin had of course gone in to see the Picasso copies.

The mattress hadn't been ripped. That might mean it had definitely been someone I knew well. Someone who would realise that if I'd stuffed anything inside, I'd never have managed to sew the damn thing back together again.

James said, 'Look closely, Caron. Is anything missing besides all those Picasso copies?'

'They aren't missing, James. I gave them to Flora. She hasn't had time to hang them yet, so they're stacked under her bed.'

I looked carefully around. 'Nothing seems to have been taken. Pity the burglar didn't take away the stuff in the rubbish bin.'

James didn't laugh. 'Normally, Caron, a burglar would have taken the television. Jewellery? What do you think the intruder could have been after?'

'Obviously a lot of the sort of things I don't own.'

I was beginning to feel creepy about staying in the house alone, and I couldn't ask Flora to return if there was the slightest danger. But I didn't think I could go home with James while I had the least suspicion. It would be so horrid, wondering if everything he said really meant something else. Not that I had any serious doubts, I reminded myself.

Finally I won the argument by saying, 'Look, James. The place has already been turned over. This is the last place anybody'd return to.'

He gave me a neighbourly kiss goodbye before reluctantly leaving. I watched him get in his car and drive away before sinking onto the bed and stretching out. Alone at last, where I could think.

But my first thought had me immediately on my feet

in horror. My argument that the burglar wouldn't return had a gigantic flaw in it. That would only be true if he'd got what he came for.

I poured a glass of wine and turned on the television. When I still imagined I was hearing noises coming from other parts of the house, I turned the volume up further. I'd already decided to sleep in my clothes. Well, I'd probably ring James later. Enough later not to be embarrassing. He might just have relented, letting me stay alone, because he'd thought the burglar had got all he wanted. Or he was the burglar himself.

I kept peering through a gap in the curtains to the street. To see if anyone was watching. Tempted to take a taxi to a hotel, I realised that letting anyone see me do that would be like signing my own death warrant. A person who knew nothing about what was going on at Chambers' would believe the attack had been meant for Melody. An uninvolved person wouldn't realise she was in danger. I kept reminding myself that someone had stolen many millions and knew they were close to being caught. Whoever it was would be feeling far more desperate, if possible, than I was.

Steeling myself, I went all through the house, check-ing that all the windows and doors were locked. I didn't dare turn on a light. Occasionally I heard something in the attic and stifled a shriek, holding my breath. Probably a mouse or a squirrel. Back in my room, I closed the door and pushed a chair against it.

Maybe it would be better with the television off? Where I could hear if something happened. It had started to rain and the drops splashing on the window sounded unduly loud. Wind whipped an empty Coke can down the street, the rattling sound jangling my nerves.

Sitting upright in the chair that wasn't propped against the door, with my feet on the bed, I must have nodded off. Suddenly I was sitting bolt upright. A sound of glass breaking. Or had I been dreaming? I looked at the clock. Three a.m. It had been long enough now for me to ring James. Without the loss of face involved with my having changed my mind. Another crash. Definitely breaking glass. A window or the upper pane of the rear door? A neighbour chucking empties? Absolutely no way I was going out of my room to check. I was digging in my handbag for my mobile phone when I heard steps outside my window. That made my bedroom the unsafest place in the universe. I rushed to the front door thinking I could run out of the house while someone got in through my bedroom window. Then I stood frozen as the front door handle began to turn slowly. Punching in numbers, I was waiting when I realised I should have dialled the police. And what if I heard phone beeps from outside the door and then knew it was James out there?

When the phone was answered, even before anyone spoke, I whispered, 'James, help! Police! Help!' And then rang off. I quietly moved to the spot that would be behind the front door when it opened into the room. I'd already switched off the table lamp, and I stood there holding high a marble bookend.

It seemed like years passed as the door jiggled. Then I could hear keys being tried. Oh, don't let it be that James had had a copy made. I should have waited to make sure it was him answering his mobile. That I'd punched in the right number. Or he could have hired someone, what with millions at stake. Oh, please not James.

There was no other sound for a couple of minutes. Then the door splintered from its frame as it was forced open. Before I could wield my weapon, the door banged against me, knocking my breath away and causing the bookend to fall to the floor.

A tall man dressed all in black came in. He stood in the middle of the room, looking around, probably letting his eyes adjust to the dark. He had his back to me. Too tall for Mervin or Harvey. The physique could be that of Jack or James. I looked at the marble bookend near my feet. Dare I risk bending to get it?

The man turned around and I dived for the bookend at the same moment. He grabbed me as I was rising, and I only managed to bash it against his knee. He grabbed his knee and cursed aloud.

It was Jack Howard.

I rushed to the door, trying to shove him aside. But in the scuffle he managed to get hold of my arms and twist them behind me. Holding me flat and tight against him with one arm, he used the other to extract some tape from his pocket and taped my wrists together. This meant he had both arms around me. He kicked behind him and the door slammed shut.

Trying to think what to do next, I relaxed for a moment and he kissed me full on the mouth. I kicked out at him and he shoved me away, where I fell against the sofa and then onto the floor.

Is that what this is all about? The bloody man's so frustrated he's come to rape me? But while I really knew better, I realised I could use it. 'Jack Howard, don't tell me James was right? About your not being a gentleman?'

He none too gently lifted me up and sat me on the sofa. Then he moved a straight chair so that its back was to the door and sat down. I thought that would make it easier for James to sneak up behind him. Where the hell was James? Then my spirits sank even lower. It would take him a good ten minutes to get there, and probably take the police an hour.

Jack leaned towards me and spoke softly. 'I'm so sorry, Caron. I didn't want it to be like this. Where have you put the tapes or disks?'

'What tapes and disks? I don't even have a computer.'

'There was a laptop on the desk the night James and I were here.' He opened my handbag and extracted the printouts. Shoving them into his parka pocket, he smiled sadly. 'I really fell for you, you know? Hook, line and sinker. Especially, as it turns out, sinker.'

Wishing James would hurry up, I said, smiling brilliantly, 'Maybe it's not too late, Jack? We would make a splendid team.'

He just laughed. 'You're right about our making a good team. That's what I was hoping all along. But fairly early on I worked out who you really are.'

I was horrified and imagined everybody at Chambers' really knowing about my living with Bas and laughing at my fall from grace to the lowest position in accounts. Fortunately before I said anything, Jack spoke again.

'It was a clever ploy Chambers' having someone work undercover in the accounts section. At first it was too ridiculous to believe. But when you started supposedly being called to work in other offices, it became pretty obvious. And then of course when information started flowing from accounts to Jim Chambers personally, I knew for sure. It was clever of you to try to put some blame on Melody and Mervin.'

Stalling, I said, 'But why, Jack? You're already a VP. You make very good money.'

He smiled. 'That was enough for a while. But even if I'd beaten James to the top job, I still wouldn't be as rich as him. I hate that bastard. All that old money, and he doesn't even seem to use much of it. I was in a win-win situation until you came along. Fiddle Chambers' for a nest egg, then if I got the top job no one would ever know. I'd be in charge of the investigation, and of course then the fraud would stop. If I didn't get the top job, I would be out of there fast.'

'And that's what you meant by insurance? Ripping off Chambers'?'

He laughed. 'Well, I wouldn't want the kind of insurance I'd need to die to collect.'

Unable to stop myself I said, 'Ha! Caught you! You were never in love with me!'

He looked very sad. 'You're wrong, Caron. I even considered calling the whole thing off. I wouldn't have returned the money, but in any event they'd never have been able to trace it. The banks that hide money are known for being obstructive. But you see, Harvey had somehow worked it out. What I was doing.'

I was amazed. 'Harvey was blackmailing you? He'd worked out the fraud?'

'Not the money part. My second insurance policy had to do with the hostile takeover bid. Obviously the loss of money was making Chambers' balance sheets wobble. So I leaked this to another company, Acquisitions Unlimited, and suggested the hostile takeover possibility. Even if James got the top job, they'd throw him out and put me in. But of course old Harvey can't say anything without giving himself away as well. So the only real problem is you, Caron.'

Stalling for time, I said, 'I didn't really know anything until you came just now. What made you believe I did know something?'

He laughed. 'Don't forget I saw you on the top floor

on the day of your interview. And then I discovered you secretly meeting with James, under the pretence of walking on the Heath. For a while, I actually thought there was romance involved. I wasn't entirely sure about you, I suppose I was hoping you were really on the level.' He laughed again. 'After all, I'd been suspicious of everyone. But then I saw that Biggs had been accessing the files. And Biggs can't even retrieve his own e-mail. So I knew it had to be you temping in his office.'

'What about Melody? How did you manage that while being at the café with me?'

'It was done by a messenger. No one pays attention to delivery persons these days. I knew Jim Chambers was sending his confidential work to her, so at first I arranged pranks to try to scare her off.' He laughed again. 'I had you followed your first week at Chambers', but all it seemed to prove was that you are one hell of a busy woman.'

He wiped his hand across his forehead and all his seeming benevolence evaporated on the spot. He held me down, and as I tried to break free I said, 'But why did you come to the rescue when that mugger was after my handbag?'

He laughed his acid laugh again. 'Once I realised it was your bag he was after, I wanted to find out what was so important in your bag.' He then taped my mouth.

'Sorry about this,' he said. 'But I need some time to get out of the country. I can't risk leaving you here where someone could find you and alert the police.'

Then he began to lead me towards the door. Realising that if he got me out before help arrived I was dead meat, I began to fight. At the same time I tried to protect my head so he couldn't knock me out.

He stopped at the front door. 'We've got twenty feet to go to get to my car, Caron. As I can't trust you to keep still . . .' and he doubled his fist and punched me in the face. I was stunned, but went limp so he would think I was unconscious. It would be better to be outside in full view of anyone passing before trying to get away. But I was so exhausted and aching that I wasn't sure I could do much.

Outside, there was absolutely no one in sight. Imagining myself with my legs also taped and me stuck in the boot of his car, I made one final effort. Hooking with my leg the railing in front of the house, I managed to trip him and we both toppled to the ground. He put his hands around my throat and began to squeeze. No sound of approaching cars, no police sirens, nothing. Slowly I began to see stars and then everything went black.

27

I was sort of drifting in and out of consciousness, vaguely aware of pain. Jack Howard. He was dragging me along the ground. James. Had I spoken too fast, had he not understood the message? Was he still in New York? No. That was last week. Last month.

I managed to open my eyes and could only see metal. A car. Then Jack was picking me up. Fucking shit. I'm going to die in a boot of a car!

Suddenly he dropped me. As I fell, I thought with horror, he can't fit me in. He's going to chop part of me off. I tried to scream but no sound came out.

Then I heard Jack shout, 'Fuck you!' Doubling up against further blows, I heard him yell in pain. He seemed to be falling, a thudding weight against my legs.

I couldn't see much in the dark, but could hear punching and running footsteps. And then sirens. Hearing sirens was the most beautiful music I'd heard in ages. Then I seemed to drift away.

As though from afar, I heard my name being called. 'Caron, Caron, can you hear me?'

Slowly opening my eyes, I said, 'James?'

I blinked and tried to focus on his face. A black eye and a bleeding lip. Him, but probably also me. In a weak, barely managed voice I said, 'What the bloody hell took you so long?'

James smiled. 'You must be feeling better than you look. Don't try to get up.'

He took his coat off and stretched it over me. 'Don't try to talk, Caron.'

I felt that surge of adrenaline that comes when you realise the lights haven't been turned off forever. 'Of course I'm going to bloody talk. First, thanks for saving my life.' My voice was gaining strength. Probably I'm more shocked than injured, I thought. Hoped. 'I want to know if you caught him?'

'Absolutely. Now, is there anything I can get you?'

'Please. There's a half-full bottle of wine in the kitchen.'

James laughed. 'More likely porridge and hot milk. But I promise you, Caron, as soon as the hospital checks you out, I'll crack open the champagne.'

'Hospital? Soon the whole accounts section's going to be there.'

'Not any more. Nothing more should happen. Well, not if I can keep your imagination tamed for a few days.'

'Don't insult my imagination when you took twenty years to get here.' I tried to grin and it felt like my face was in a meat grinder. I was thinking of asking the judge, when Jack went to trial, if I could send Evelyn in to beat him up.

'I came as fast as I could, Caron. I got a phone call on my mobile an hour before you rang. I was parked at Heathrow, as there had been word that Jack had purchased airline tickets for a late flight. The detective who was following Jack said he'd lost him, that they'd been sure he was still in his house but later noticed his car was gone.

'I asked how the bloody hell he could not notice a car driving away. He said it had been parked around the corner. Then he had the gall to ask me for further instructions.

'The thing is, Caron, I knew exactly where Jack was likely to be. When I asked how long it was since Jack left, the detective said no more than an hour. I was already driving here like a maniac when I got your call. I shouted for you to hang on, not ring off, but . . .'

'Take it from me, James, I was too busy to talk.'

He laughed and shifted his jacket under my head so a different part would ache. 'Anyway, I punched nine, nine, nine. And then I got the bureaucrats. All that shit. Repeat everything. Different extensions. I was driving faster and faster. I knew I'd probably be caught by police cameras, and then I realised that might be a good thing. So I drove even faster. And faster, as I imagined the sneaky bastard creeping about your place in the dark like a fucking creature of the night.'

He stopped for breath, and it gave me time to realise James had a decided poetic streak, at least in his description of Jack.

'Once I saw blue lights flashing behind my car, I put my foot to the floor. Sirens began to sound, and a few minutes later I saw flashing lights in the distance in front of me. Wiping sweat from my eyes so I could see, I took my foot off the accelerator and began to coast to a halt, steering the car towards the verge.'

'Shit, James. I'm surprised you're not bleeding in a jail cell.' I looked around nervously. 'Have they taken Jack away?'

'Absolutely. Two cop cars with six cops. But tell me, Caron, how did you get on to Jack?'

'For some reason Jack seemed to have got the idea that I was a spy put in accounts to trap him.' When James didn't appear very convinced, I added, 'But I managed to get him to talk just now, so I know lots more.' Still flat on my back and terrified even to try to move, such did I ache, I smiled weakly. 'Did you know Harvey was blackmailing him?'

James looked surprised. 'Jack told you that?'

I'm not dead yet, I thought. Such fun getting one up on James. 'I'm feeling a wee bit better. Could you help me try to get up? Just sit up. There's a stone under me.'

James rubbed my hand. 'We'll wait for the ambulance medics, Caron.' He looked about to ensure no one was within hearing distance. 'A funny thing, your not having worked the whole thing out yourself.' He smiled. 'That you only know what Jack told you.' He took the print-outs from his pocket and showed them to me, then quickly replaced them. 'Jack had these on him. Strange thing for him to have been carrying about, don't you think? And there was this key.' He held up the key to the left luggage at Euston.

'Actually, James, I'm too tired to talk at the moment.' I raised one arm, then the other. Well, that meant two parts were still working. Three counting my mouth. 'You know, James, if you leaned closer I could whisper something.' He leaned very close and waited. 'You clod, James. I mean for you to kiss me. Gently.'

He did, then brushed my hair back from my forehead. 'I've been so worried, Caron. Promise me you haven't got any more tricks up your sleeve?'

'Nothing dangerous. But James, surely you want me to be at least a little mysterious, surprise you?'

James smiled. 'Absolutely. But three or four times a day is a bit much. Anyway, you can slow down a bit now. We of course were on to Jack, but it's been a devil of a job getting any proof.'

I said, astonished, 'You mean I'm lying here half dead for nothing?'

James smiled and held my hand a bit tighter. 'If you

hadn't brought Jack into the open, we might never have nailed him.'

Whether I passed out, or more likely went to sleep from exhaustion, I was barely aware of ensuing events. A faint memory of James riding in the ambulance with me. His fishing my driver's licence out of my handbag to give to the ambulance person. Odd flashes of memory of the emergency room, mostly my answering if I hurt here or there or where as nurses stabbed at the most painful parts. Wonderful James seemed to be sorting everything, making phone calls, and explaining things to the hospital registrar. And I distinctly remembered the doctor saying, 'A cracked rib, bruises, perhaps slight concussion. Nothing much wrong with her.'

I remembered that because I remembered thinking how disappointed doctors seemed to be if you were simply healthy and going to live.

I woke up in the hospital room alone. I could feel a bandage on my forehead. I could hardly move my mouth for the cut on the edge, but the nurse had probably wiped away any blood. Black and blue splotches were likely decorating my face. And my hair probably looked like Dracula's on a bad hair day. I couldn't isolate exactly what hurt most, feeling just a general overall ache. But I was alive. Very happily alive. And there's something about cheating death that makes little aches and pains resemble salted peanuts in a bar. Small, perhaps not terribly healthy, but not really very serious in the scheme of things.

A nurse rushed in and took my blood pressure. Evelyn would have loved it, just like being on television. Except Evelyn would have preferred a male nurse.

I felt much better, could even move my arms and legs without too much agony. With effort I sat up. Resting back, I decided that except for my rib making it difficult to take deep breaths and shift too quickly, I was all right. I'd be out of there soon.

Opening the drawer of my side cabinet, I found my wristwatch. Six a.m. I might even be able to leave before lunch.

I heard clanking from the corridor. Probably the morning tea trolleys. And breakfast. I was absolutely starving. My hospital room light was switched on. It was my mother. My first feeling was alarm. Wasn't she supposed to be in another country? Almost another life? Was there an angel behind her with fluffy white wings about to say, 'My dear, are you ready for your next journey? Do come with me, it'll be fun.'

Before I could say anything, Mum took my hand and leaned down to kiss my cheek. Immediately everything seemed normal again. I asked, 'How did you hear what happened so quickly?'

'Flora rang me. Shortly after that a New York reporter came to the house asking for a photo of you. He wanted to send it by computer to London. A bridge game was in progress. It was the first time we ever allowed anything to stop a bridge game.'

I was greatly honoured. On one occasion, Dad had set some fat alight in the kitchen and the bridge continued while the firemen put out the fire. After we spent a few more minutes catching up on news, she said Dad was fine and I was famous.

'What? Famous how, Mum? Don't you mean notorious?'

'You were in the newspapers I read on the way here from the airport. And you're sure to be on television. Your next hand is sure to have lots and lots of lovely aces.'

Before I could take this all in, she added, 'Now, if you're sure you're all right, I'll just go and check into the hotel and return after a bath and breakfast.'

Breakfast was then served. Well, maybe that's stretching it, I mean there was no butler carrying kippers, more's the pity. Instead there was a tiny glass of skimmed milk, not nearly enough to drown the few flakes from the matchbox of cereal. A lonely piece of cold toast. A pitiful little egg that looked as if it wanted to go back home to the hen.

I was practically licking the dishes when James and Jim Chambers arrived. They brought flowers and a bottle of Bollinger in ice, the bucket being a bag labelled 'Laundry'.

Jim Chambers took my hand and said, 'I've come to thank you, Caron, but first I owe you an apology. I had no idea you and Melody would be in danger. I talked to no one besides Melody and Betty, to protect you and Melody. And my confidant told me that you and James, because of – well – all the flowers you were receiving . . . So I thought that he would be able to protect you even if he didn't know he needed to.' His face held a combination of worry and relief, with the relief winning hands down.

I smiled. 'Well, James did protect me, in the sense of a great rescue.'

James said, 'I owe you an apology as well, Caron. Because Jim hadn't told anyone about your helping him, I didn't know what the hell you were up to. When it became obvious you'd accessed the confidential files . . .'

I laughed, greatly relieved myself. 'You didn't know whether your ambition to get selected for the top job included turning in suspicious women and saving the company?'

'Something like that. And when I told you that the top floor had worked it all out, I didn't realise it was because of data you were feeding Jim. If you've got any leftover crow from breakfast, I'll be happy to eat it.'

Jim said, "He won't have time to eat more than a bite or two, Caron. As you already know, I'm retiring. And I've asked James to take on the CEO position.' He coughed slightly and said, 'Is there any particular job you'd like, Caron? We could create one for you at Chambers'?'

I smiled. 'Thank you so much. But I finally got some redundancy pay from my last job.' I couldn't help thinking about my Picasso as I added, 'And I'm thinking of starting up my own business.'

'Oh dear,' teased Jim. 'You're in for it with Caron for competition, lad.'

We were all laughing when Melody arrived in a wheelchair. I felt really guilty because I'd been too busy to give her a thought. 'I didn't realise you were still here, Melody.'

She grinned. 'I told them I still couldn't think straight and that I lived alone. And they weren't in a hurry for my bed. It isn't the Ritz, dear, but room service is room service.'

As the nurse wheeled her closer, Melody said, 'I hope you gentlemen have finished talking. I came to watch Caron and James on television.'

The nurse turned on the TV and before she left, smiled and said, 'We don't often have a celebrity on the ward. Well done!'

Melody noticed the laundry bag and peeped inside. 'James, be a dear and do the honours.'

'What's everyone talking about? I mean I never thought you could get famous just for staying alive.'

Jim Chambers said, 'Photographers were at the hospital entrance last night when you were brought in. The press was probably monitoring the call James made to the police. And you've already been on the earlier news. Certainly combined with Jack Howard's arrest, you'll make the front pages. If you want a PR job, you've got it. Chambers' hadn't made the front page in over twenty years, and now this is the second time because of you.'

I thought of replying with something humble like Aw, shucks, but my ribs were still aching. I didn't do humble very well, and everyone might laugh.

James had just passed around champagne in paper cups when the news began.

'London has a new heroine! Caron Carlisle, working undercover as a clerk in the Chambers' Emporium accounts section, faced danger today as she saved the company and managed to survive an attack on her life. There have been suggestions, although none have yet been confirmed, that Miss Carlisle has extensive training in karate, and it is possible she trained with the SAS.'

This was so over the top we all started laughing. So we missed a bit and then heard:

'Asked about the hostile takeover rumours, Jim Chambers said the rumours were false.' The camera switched from the announcer to footage of Jim Chambers standing in front of the store.

Next there was an unposed still of James. After saying, 'Miss Carlisle risked her life today to expose wide-ranging fraud she discovered through using her computer skills,' the cameras quickly switched back to a picture of me outside casualty lying flat out on a stretcher. It could have been anyone, thank goodness.

Back to the picture of James with a bruised face and

wearing dishevelled and ripped clothing. 'Miss Carlisle was rescued at the eleventh hour by James Smith, the Chambers Emporium Chief Financial Officer . . .'

The only photo of me besides the one on the stretcher was the studio portrait my parents had in a frame on their piano. I looked about sixteen. Well, I was sixteen.

Then the news turned to the story of second importance, twenty people killed by a bomb in a suburb of Moscow. Well, a local mosquito bite wins over remote disaster every time. When I was in high school, the local paper reported a football game loss by saying our team had played against a strong wind.

I said, 'Well, Melody, you should have been given some credit.'

'Oh, no, dear. You might have been working as an undercover agent, but I work under deeper cover. You see, now your cover's blown, while I intend to keep on until I'm ninety.'

Chambers laughed and said, 'I think Melody means she's my eyes and ears in the company. She picks up on things no one wants to tell the boss. I don't know what we'd do without her.'

Melody smiled. 'This isn't generally known, Caron, but I worked for Chambers' from the start. The pay was low but Jim was generous with company shares. So I own a tiny, precious bit of the business. It's my life, really, and the Chambers are like my family.'

I said, 'I should have taken your saying someone was out to get you more seriously, Melody.'

'No, no, dear. At first it was just the usual, others wishing I'd retire and provide a job vacancy. It surprised me when so much else began to happen.'

'Jack Howard was responsible for the bus incident

and the other things. He paid people to do the dirty work.'

Melody sniffed. 'Jack Howard is a great disappointment. I've never really liked the man. Far too flash in his manner. And it was all so complex, dear. I was happy for whoever it was to think it was me, and not you. Jim had no one else he could trust, but I couldn't really cope with all those numbers. Then when that incident happened while I was using your desk and chair, I was horrified that I'd put you in danger.'

'It's all worked out fine, Melody. But maybe now's the time to extract a no-numbers promise for the future?'

Jim laughed. 'She's already done that, Caron, believe me!'

'Good for you, Melody! And what about the hostile takeover bid?'

Jim said, 'The CEO of Acquisitions Unlimited rang me and dropped the bid the minute it became public that Jack was involved in fraud. He said Jack had approached him at a conference and told him Chambers' was going downhill and would be a cheap buy. He maintains he didn't know it was Jack himself making the value drop. And now, Caron, without the fraudulent drain on company funds, Chambers' will be all right. Of course, I'm counting on James here to work wonders as well.'

James said, 'It's Caron who's worked the wonder. Because the police have Jack in custody, he's probably already working out plans to do a deal. And we should get much of the money back.'

Melody said she had better get back to her bed before they gave it away to another patient, and Jim waved goodbye to me as he wheeled her out.

James grinned. 'You're so popular that I'd better speak quickly. Will you spend Christmas with me? At the house, as Stoner wants to play nurse.'

'Lovely, James. As long as you don't plan to play doctor.'

'I thought, on the whole, that we might just play. I'll pop down to the nurses' station to find out what time they plan to release you.'

I had a few minutes on my own to realise that I felt better than ever. Praise and glory are terrific painkillers. My rib had even stopped acting like it should give up and get spread with barbecue sauce.

And then Flora came rushing into the room. After giving me a big hug during which I yelled 'My ribs, my side, my arm' she said, 'Oh, Caron, I'm so glad you're still alive!'

'Yeah, me too. Not that there was any serious danger, anything I couldn't handle.'

She laughed. 'A huge bouquet of flowers was delivered for you this morning. The hospital said you'd probably be coming home today, so I didn't bring them. But here's the card.'

The envelope had the International Petals logo, and the card said, 'Congratulations, honey. I've been stupid to lose a treasure like you, but just remember, if you change your mind, the door's always open.'

Flora read it and laughed. 'Goodness, Bas doesn't give up easily, does he?'

Before I could reply, the morning cup of tea arrived and Flora was given a cup as well. I could tell I was getting better because the brew tasted like they'd inserted a syringe and extracted all the flavour.

Flora said, 'I could hardly believe it when the news said you were an undercover agent, Caron. That you'd even trained with the SAS. Even I was surprised. I mean it's so wonderful.'

'Honestly, Flora, you can't believe everything you read or hear. Melody hated numbers and I hated doing letters, so we kept switching work. And I found a few errors. That's all.'

She laughed. 'You may think it's all, but even my house has been photographed and reporters came. I didn't say anything, but Evelyn said you were a delightful bugger. That she taught you all you know.'

'Evelyn taught me karate?'

'More than that. She's quoted in the papers as saying she turned you into the Mata Hari of the modern world. And that it hadn't been easy, what with her needing to take time out to demonstrate forty-two kinds of cheese in supermarkets.'

We both laughed. I thought about me as Mata Hari, I must admit with some pleasure. Well I could pull off a retired version. 'What are they saying in the accounts section?'

Flora laughed. 'Practically everyone but Mrs Brown hinted that they'd worked it out but kept it quiet to help you.' She added hesitantly, 'It makes a super story, Caron. I hope you aren't going to disappoint everyone. I mean by, you know, explaining.'

'Maybe you're right, Flora. Maybe I'd better take to heart what they say in the States, that you can't fight City Hall.'

I pointed to the champagne and insisted Flora have some. 'And you'd better refill my glass, as well. I'm treating the stuff as medicine.' As I watched her fill the glasses, I felt so happy. And I felt like somebody. As I watched her pour, I thought of my friends, and yeah, I included Evelyn. Then I understood that everybody was somebody if you really looked at them, and cared enough.

Before Flora left she said, 'Is this it, then? Where James takes you away and we hear wedding bells? The, you know, end of the book?'

'Flora, don't look so sad.'

She smiled. 'It's like, I'm sometimes sad when a really good book ends.'

I laughed. 'You're living your own book with Mervin. And mine isn't over yet. First I would want to try living with a man who isn't already married. I've agreed to spend the Christmas holidays at James' house. Just a few days.'

'A few days isn't really very long. I mean for interesting things to happen.'

I laughed. 'It's been my experience in the past that lots can happen. Actually, I'm hoping for a quiet time.'

James returned in time to hear my last comment, and said, 'I'm glad to hear that.'

After Flora left, James kissed me very gently. 'But of course I realise that with you recuperating, Caron, we can't do more than drink and eat and hold hands and reminisce about our weekend at the cottage.'

My eyes widened. 'But James, don't you remember that I love a challenge?'

He grinned sheepishly. 'Actually I did remember.'